Copyright © 2006 by Michael Thompson
Cover illustration by Linda Sholberg (and Breece!)
All rights reserved.
ISBN 1-4196-3308-2

To order additional copies, please contact us.
Booksurge, LLC
www.booksurge.com
1-866-308-6235
orders@booksurge.com

Acknowledgements

To Brian Greene of Columbia University,
whose brilliant book on string theory,
The Elegant Universe, was the prime inspiraton
behind my story. I read his book until it
was dog-eared, used everything I could understand,
and shamelessly made up the rest.

To Linda Sholberg, whose talent and
hard work allowed my dream to come true.

And last but certainly not least, to Dorothy,
who somehow retains her patience and
good nature after 27 years with me.

Pay attention to the dominoes........

Bad Vibes

An Apocalyptic Tale of
Jealousy, Music,
Organizational Behavior,
and Theoretical Physics

MAIN CHARACTERS

<u>The City:</u>

Dunstan	-	*Incidental Minister of Music*
Michael	-	*Omniscience Council Chairman*
Peter	-	*Omniscience Council Sub-Chairman*
Thomas	-	*Omniscience Council Member*
Gabriel	-	*Omniscience Council Honorary Member*
Timothy	-	*Festival Preparation Committee Chairman*
Matthew	-	*Festival Preparation Committee - Working Level Staff Member*
Joel	-	*Efficiency Committee Chairman*
Deborah	-	*Efficiency Committee Senior Member*
Bartholomew	-	*Underling Oversight Committee Chairman*
Esther	-	*Lead Technician, Underling World Observation Center, Quality Assurance dept.*
The "Architect"	-	*Designer of the Underling World*

MAIN CHARACTERS (cont'd.)

The Underling World:

The String Theory Team -
- Jason Poe
- Max Cherry
- Melina Valin
- Zena Dunn
- Darryl Johnson
- Sean Masterson
- Rose Pupa
- Glenn Glass
- Bryce Thomas
- Serena Madison
- Courtney Ellis
- Grant Zenkman

Kathy Leigh	-	*Journalist*
Elmer Schmidlapp	-	*National Research Council Director*
Adam Parson	-	*Theoretical physicist, specializing in String Theory (Eve's husband)*
Eve Parson	-	*Theoretical physicist, also specializing in String Theory (Adam's wife)*
Christopher Parson	-	*Son of Adam and Eve Parson*

"Say not so," replied the count, "or I shall launch upon a great sea of praise for music, reminding you how greatly music was always celebrated by the ancients and held to be a sacred thing; and how it was the opinion of very wise philosophers that *the world is made of music*, that the heavens in their motion make harmony, and that every human soul was formed on the same principle, and is therefore awakened and has its virtues brought to life, as it were, through music."

From "The Book of the Courtier"
Baldassare Castiglione
1528

Monday, 12:00:01 a.m.:

Dunstan was upset. He alone had declined to join the all-City celebration in the Main Square, choosing instead to stay in his tiny bungalow until these damnable festivities were complete. Still, he could not resist looking out his window. "*I* am the music guy," he fumed to no one in particular. "*I* am the Minister of Incidental Music. That should be *me* out there."

Dunstan allowed himself to dream of it for the millionth time. Dunstan, wearing the ethereal white robe. Dunstan, standing before the entire City. Dunstan, raising the golden

Trumpet to his lips and blowing for all he was worth. The sounding of the Consolidating Tone, the awesome grandeur of the Great Unfurling. And finally, the whole of the City clapping and cheering in the long-overdue display of recognition, as Dunstan graciously bowed and accepted the accolades.

But no. It was Gabriel, that untalented hack, who now held the Trumpet before the entire City and played the Consolidating Tone, initiating the first dimension of the Unfurling. *Sounds a little flat to me*, thought Dunstan. A bone-rattling shudder rumbled through the City. Gabriel followed with three more Tones in rapid succession to release the second, third, and fourth dimensions, and the citizens gaped in amazement as the full majesty of the Great Unfurling burst forth into the vastness above them. Finally a great roar arose from the Main Square. *A bunch of yahoos who wouldn't know a major seventh from a scherzo*, Dunstan said dismissively.

The chaos slowly began to sort itself into order, the beauty of the structure evident even at this early stage, and a feeling of great pride swept over everyone. It was their baby now. The Architect had moved on to the next project in another city, and the final six levels of permeation would be their responsibility. The system was designed to run by itself and would follow its inevitable course, but still, it was theirs to oversee and manage. The citizens stood together in the Square, arm in arm, as they shared this magnificent moment.

Dunstan kicked at a deceptively hard and heavy table leg and yelped, hopping on one foot while he grabbed the other, trying in vain to stifle the pain and the feeling of stupidity sweeping over him. On his sixth hop, he landed awkwardly on a piccolo he'd left out the day before. The piccolo rolled sideways, out from under his only operational foot, rendering Dunstan horizontal and two feet above the floor, at least momentarily. Unfortunately, as is usually the case in such situations, graviton particle flow commenced forthwith, the result being a significant impact between Dunstan and the floor, and even more damage to both his body and his psyche. Injured but undeterred, Dunstan muttered to himself, *They should a let me blow the Trumpet, they really shoulda.*

Wednesday, 6:59 p.m.:

The droning buzz of hundreds of voices filled the immaculately detailed conference room. For most of the City residents in attendance, this was the first time they had been invited to the Omniscience Council meeting chamber, and conversation among the impressed gathering was non-stop. Only an announcement of surpassing importance would justify the unprecedented invitation of working-level staff members to an Omniscience Council meeting, and the sense of anticipation was palpable. Everyone in the City had felt the by-now familiar shudder a few minutes before, so the announcement could mean only one thing.

Although certainly not the largest conference room in the City, its only purpose being to hold the meetings of the 12-member Council, the chamber's opulence certainly matched all expectations. Its dimensions measured 75 feet on a side, and lighting was supplied by four magnificent chandeliers that hung from the vaulted ceiling high above. At the front of the room was a stage, elevated three feet above the main floor, with a massive mahogany podium facing the audience. The first two rows of seats in front of the stage were wide, high-backed, generously cushioned chairs with enormous armrests, reserved for the Omniscience Council and the Senior Members of the three main Committees, and upholstered in a purple crushed velvet. Behind the Council and Committee seats, taking up most of the room's floor space, were 500 tightly packed inexpensive folding chairs for the Committees' working staff members, which had been brought in for this meeting. The huge ornately carved marble table normally used by the Council during its meetings had been moved to the back of the stage to create space for the folding chairs. The near-gleaming silver-gray walls matched the intensity of the plush gold carpet, the two precious metal colors combining to imply the exalted status of the Omniscience Council. All around the room, spaced at perfectly even intervals, were enormous gilt-framed, glass-enclosed documents - each one a concise exhortation to the leadership, wisdom, and achievement that was the hallmark of the Council. "Leaders lead, they do not act," said one. "The best solution is always a simple solution," said another. "Leave the small details to the small-minded," said a third. Dozens of similar framed aphorisms filled the walls of the grand room.

"They need one more," said Matthew, a tall, lean young man on the staff of the Festival Preparation Committee, sitting in a folding chair in the third row with his friend Esther. "How about, 'Idiotic platitudes are the exclusive province of management'?"

He said it a bit too loudly, and a mortified Esther told him to shush.

At precisely 7:00 p.m., a low rumble of stringed instruments began to emanate from the giant speakers in each corner of the conference hall. As the higher-pitched instruments

4

began to join in, the conversation through the audience began to subside. An exquisitely controlled swelling of sound gradually filled the room, hundreds of instruments joining in the musical celebration of the event. For ten minutes the hall was filled with a symphony of unimaginable beauty and power, melodies and harmonies soaring over and under each other in perfect pitch and rhythm, creating an effect that was nothing less than divine.

"This will get me noticed for sure," chortled Dunstan to himself as he puffed with pride in his seat at the back of the room. He had conceived the symphony, written the entire score, and played every instrument. Surely the City leaders would be calling to congratulate him on his magnificent achievement, and would elevate him to a much-deserved position of status.

A moment after Dunstan's masterpiece came to its stunning conclusion, a man of ponderous girth slowly entered the stage from the wings. Brother Michael, Chairman of the Omniscience Council and the most powerful person in the City, was known to all City residents. His size, along with his hard eyes, ruddy face, and bushel of white hair, lent a certain ferocity to his presence, even on a happy occasion such as this.

Michael cleared his throat and spoke in the familiar voice that boomed with authority. "Ladies and gentlemen, the Consolidating Tone has sounded once again, to indicate the completion of the 7th level of Underling World development. Before we announce the special significance of the 7th level, I wish to inform you that our progress to this point has been flawless, a testament to the leadership of the Omniscience Council and its subordinate committees. The policies of these teams have been sound, their plans have been properly

5

executed, and all procedures have been followed to the letter. It is only through the City's wise and forward-thinking leadership that we have come to this point, and I believe the entire staff should be acknowledged accordingly."

A giant banner unfurled down the wall on one side of the Omniscience Council conference hall, honoring the chairmen and senior members of the Omniscience Council and the three most important City Committees:

OUR LEADERS - THE CITY THANKS YOU!!!

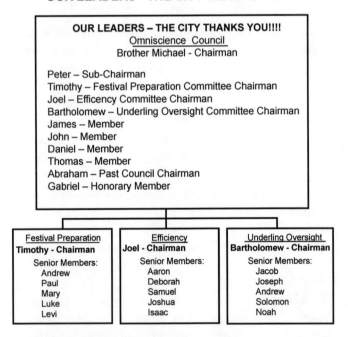

OUR LEADERS – THE CITY THANKS YOU!!!!
<u>Omniscience Council</u>
Brother Michael - Chairman

Peter – Sub-Chairman
Timothy – Festival Preparation Committee Chairman
Joel – Efficency Committee Chairman
Bartholomew – Underling Oversight Committee Chairman
James – Member
John – Member
Daniel – Member
Thomas – Member
Abraham – Past Council Chairman
Gabriel – Honorary Member

<u>Festival Preparation</u>	<u>Efficiency</u>	<u>Underling Oversight</u>
Timothy - Chairman	**Joel - Chairman**	**Bartholomew - Chairman**
Senior Members:	Senior Members:	Senior Members:
Andrew	Aaron	Jacob
Paul	Deborah	Joseph
Mary	Samuel	Andrew
Luke	Joshua	Solomon
Levi	Isaac	Noah

Brother Michael stepped back from the podium and applauded, more for himself than anything.

The Committee chairmen and senior members in the first three rows of the hall also clapped vigorously, while only a mild ripple of accompanying applause came from the staff behind them. It was no surprise that Michael had not even mentioned the working level staff members, who carried out all the actual work.

Michael shot an irritated glance to his left, where Peter waited in the wings. Peter had promised an overwhelming show of admiration from the rank and file; indeed, this was the only reason Michael had agreed to allow their attendance. Michael was no fool, and this response was not the standing ovation he had anticipated. He had better things to do than spend time with subordinates, if there was nothing in it for him. Michael turned again to the microphone. "For the details of this evening's announcement, I will turn the proceedings over to your Omniscience Council Sub-Chairman, Brother Peter." Michael strode off the stage, and most of the senior Committee members followed him, satisfied to have heard their own praise, but not interested in the mundane details of the project status, which they considered to be minutiae.

As Michael walked out through the exit at the back of the room, he happened to pass within a few feet of Dunstan. Dunstan eagerly jumped to his feet and held the door open for Michael and Brother Joel, chairman of the Efficiency Committee, who was leaving with him.

"If I had known how long that, that *music* was going to drone on, I would have put a stop to it," said Michael. "Imagine - me having to wait like that. Besides, it was too loud, and too complicated. Far too complicated. I should never have allowed Peter to make the arrangements. We won't be repeating that mistake again." Joel nodded gravely.

Michael pushed past Dunstan, casting only a glance of irritation in his direction.

Dunstan, realizing that Michael had no idea who he was, felt any sense of his own significance evaporate completely.

Back at the front of the room, a tall, thin man with straight dark hair strode confidently to the microphone. Brother Peter possessed an engaging smile that crossed his face easily and often, and eyes alight with his positive attitude. His sincere interest in even the lowliest City resident aroused a certain distrust among the other Omniscience Council members, but security in his position as Council Sub-Chairman was ensured by the fact that when an actual task needed to be accomplished, Peter was always willing and often the only one capable of carrying it out. Although not an ideal leader in the eyes of the Council, Peter was definitely useful, and so the remaining Council members put up with his deficiencies.

Reaching the microphone, Peter looked out to the crowd. He spoke in a high voice, but one filled with strength and purpose. "As you all recall, the entire City congregated in the main square for the Great Unfurling when the strings began to vibrate in the first four dimensions early Monday morning. You may be wondering why we have invited you to a special ceremony to celebrate the completion of 7th-dimension permeation, when similar ceremonies were not held at the conclusion of permeation through the 5th and 6th dimensions."

There can only be one reason, thought Esther, brimming with anticipation. The tiny young woman squirmed in her seat, lifting herself as high as possible, first putting one leg under her, then the other, in an effort to find a vantage point where she could see over the ornate high-backed chairs of the Committee members seated immediately in front of her. It had been Matthew's idea to sit in the third row and be as close to the stage as possible, and Esther had not realized she would not be able to see the stage until the crowd had filled in all the seats behind them.

Esther was pleased that Peter seemed to understand at least a little bit about vibrational permeation. From what she'd seen of other City leaders, they didn't even seem interested in the string system. They discussed progress through the ten dimensions in terms of "levels," as though it was like walking up ten flights of stairs. To Esther's reckoning, even her own understanding was inadequate. She certainly did not comprehend the science behind it - nobody did - but she burned with curiosity regarding the concepts of strings and tension and frequencies and wavelengths and harmonics and intensities, and the physical phenomena of the progressive permeation of the string vibrations through each of the Underling World's ten dimensions. In her position as Lead Technician of the Underling World Observation Center in the Quality Assurance department, she watched its development with great interest and curiosity, and even in her lack of true understanding, she probably knew that strange other world better than anyone else in the City. The entire system had been so perfectly designed by the Architect that no interference was needed, or even possible, for that matter. Esther had a dream job: the joy of watching the Underling events unfold, with no deadlines to meet or pressure to correct anything. She assumed she would learn how it all worked when the project was complete. Esther looked down at her Liquid Time Correlation chronometer. Almost three full days of City Time had passed since the Great Unfurling. Although remaining diligent in her work, she had to admit to a certain boredom - not much had happened since the Great Unfurling of the first four dimensions early Monday morning. The completion of vibrational permeation through the 5th and 6th dimensions had passed uneventfully with little fanfare. All the interesting visuals had come with the first four dimensions, and the only evidence of the 5th and 6th were slightly modified readings on the Underling World monitors. She fervently hoped the 7th dimension would bring something new - and based on Peter's hints so far, she was pretty sure she knew what that something was.

Esther pushed the button on her Liquid Time chronometer to switch to Underling World Time. She was continually amazed at the varying relative rates of time passage between the City and the Underling World. The normal pattern was that a few minutes or even seconds of City Time corresponded to eons in the Underling World, but in certain critical moments the relative rates of time could vary enormously. Esther wondered how much Underling Time would pass in the three days remaining before 10th-dimension permeation would come to pass. She turned her attention back to Peter.

Peter looked at the chronometer on his own left wrist. He knew the effect his words would have. "Seventeen minutes ago," he said, pausing for dramatic effect, "full permeation was established for the 7th string dimension. The Consolidating Tone has cemented the process, *replication has begun*, and vibrational permeation has now begun into the 8th dimension."

A huge roar arose the moment the much-anticipated word "replication" came out of Peter's mouth, and everything after that was drowned out by clapping and cheering. Esther stood with the rest of the audience and applauded loudly, her hopes fulfilled, and she wondered about the future significance of these events. Michael, still in the next room, heard the roar and fumed at the notion that any announcement of Peter's could draw more response than his own tribute to himself and the other City leaders a few moments earlier.

Peter continued. "Completion of the 7th dimension is a milestone quite unlike those previous, and we felt that this event was worthy of our acknowledgement of your efforts to date. We are very pleased to have you in attendance, and the City leadership extends its heartiest appreciation to all of you." Peter was well aware that none of the other Council or Committee members shared his desire to recognize the staff members, but there was certainly no need to mention that. "There are only three dimensions left to be permeated, and with replication finally underway, we anticipate an acceleration of significant events in the Underling World, and, correspondingly, more activity for us here in the City. We must redouble our efforts to prepare for the Eternal Festival, which will commence at the completion of permeation in the 10th dimension. As you know, our six-day schedule means we must be ready by Saturday at midnight - that leaves us slightly more than three days to complete everything."

Pausing and smiling broadly, Peter concluded, "And then we will have all day Sunday to rest." A wave of cheers and laughter flowed across the room.

Peter concluded, "Thank you all for coming here today, and let's continue the great work!" Another round of applause followed, and the staff members slowly began to file out of the room. The celebratory parties ran well into the night.

Dunstan, still sitting alone in the back of the room, silently seethed. *Hope that idiot puts the damn Trumpet away this time.* As the ultimate insult, not only had Dunstan not been recognized for his musical genius, he had been ordered shortly before the meeting to find the Trumpet. The talentless hack had forgotten where he left it! Dunstan, like some lackey, had searched half the City Headquarters before finding the Trumpet and getting it back to Gabriel's chief assistant only moments before it was needed for the Consolidating Tone - with no thanks offered, of course. He'd also been told in no uncertain terms not to open the case, so he hadn't even gotten to see what this oh-so-mystical Trumpet looked like.

Besides all that, Dunstan was quite unimpressed by everyone's excitement at completing the seventh dimension. The big hubbub was over an event - a "replication," whatever that was - that had taken place in a space less than a billionth of an inch across, and he really couldn't see what all the fuss was about.

As Peter descended from the stage amid handshakes and claps on the back, Brother Thomas pulled him aside with urgency and implored him, "You make it sound like we deserve the credit for all this. Despite what Michael said, it is *not* through any great leadership on our part that we have come this far. Wake up, Peter, we don't even understand how the process works. Somebody in Quality Assurance measures the degree of vibrational permeation using ancient equipment that we don't know how to repair, Gabriel plays the Consolidating Tone when vibrational permeation is complete in each dimension, the next level starts, and we tell ourselves how wonderful we are until the next time. We are responsible for the Underling World all the way to the end of this project, and I for one would feel much more comfortable if we had some control and actually knew what we were doing."

Peter replied, "Tom, my old friend, you add a whole new

meaning to the word 'doubt.' Don't worry so much. The first prokaryotic cell just divided. Enjoy the moment."

February 21, 1902:

The young Patent Clerk Second Class yawned and stretched, tired after his long day reviewing dull-witted "inventions" by would-be millionaires not half as bright as himself. At last he could devote himself to his beloved theories and equations, pondering the imponderable, as he did every evening until sleep overtook him. "Elsa, coffee please, and make it a tall one," he called out to the poor woman who served the seven clerks in the Bern patent office. The clerk wanted his attention revived for his true love, that elusive truth he knew filled the universe, yet also lay undiscovered inside his own brain. He leaned back, letting his mind drift to where he left off the night before, trying to restore the flow of thought. He was happy in this process, but also unsatisfied, feeling that the key to his theories was right in front of him, but yet his fingers could not grasp it.

"Elsa, where is the damn coffee!" he exclaimed. It had been ages since his simple request. Here he was pondering the mysteries of the universe, and this daft woman could not even provide a simple cup of coffee in a reasonable time. The irony of the situation brought a smirk to his face. *Ah, the arrogance of Man,* he thought. *On the one hand I propose to unlock the mind of God, and on the other I cannot even get this miserable woman to bring me a cup of coffee!*

Just then Elsa arrived, not a little piqued. "Here you are, oh Mr. Genius," she spat out in a mockingly submissive voice. "How delinquent I am. *Seven minutes* to provide a cup of coffee to His Majesty. And with the wildly extravagant wages I am paid, how ungrateful I must be to fail you so badly. I should be thanking *you* for the two extra hours I stay every night for no pay, while you indulge your big ideas." She fell to the ground, clutching his ankles and kissing his feet, mocking him. "Oh, how can you put up with me, I am not worthy of you, I am not worthy of one such as Your Magnificence!"

The clerk turned to check the clock, and sure enough, a mere seven minutes had passed since he had requested the coffee. He had lost himself in thought, and merely perceived that significant time had passed. He tried to sputter an apology, but Elsa, with justifiable anger, cut him off.

"Don't bother yourself. You are just like every other 'master.' You place yourself above those who serve you. You think big ideas but your soul is small. It is always the same. I may bring the coffee in ten minutes, or five minutes, or one minute, but no matter how fast I go, to you it is just one speed. *Too Slow*. To you, no matter how hard I work or how long something takes, you say the servant is *Too Slow*. It is the only way to make yourself feel like a big man. The time may vary, but the speed is always the same. *Too Slow*. You are a pathetic little man." Elsa paused, looked the clerk in the eye, and calmly lofted a hefty wad of weirdly greenish spit directly onto his nose. "I shall find other employment," she said, and turned to leave.

The clerk, quite taken aback by Elsa's outburst of emotion, sat motionless for some time. His mind was quite empty, oblivious even to Elsa's saliva slowly dripping off his nose, his usual flurry of conflicting thoughts stilled by Elsa's outburst. As he tried to consider his behavior and just where he had gone wrong, however, his attention was distracted more and more by that phrase Elsa had uttered. "The time

14

may vary, but the speed is always the same." He rolled this phrase over and over in his mind, turning the words upside down and backwards. *Speed. Velocity. Distance divided by time. It is always constant. Time, time itself, the universal, constant, inexorable march forward, can vary." What? This made no sense. How could time's rate of passage vary? How could velocity always be the same to any observer? What would the consequences be if time itself could vary? What if..........?*

The young patent clerk leaned back and stared into space, consumed in wondrous thought, sensing a new picture being revealed to him, Elsa's outburst of a moment ago completely forgotten. After a moment he heard a slight buzzing. Albert shook his head to clear it, but the sound, most unnervingly, seemed to seep into his very being.

Thursday 6:55 a.m.:

To:	All Festival Preparation Committee Senior Members
cc:	All Festival Preparation Committee working staff
From:	Brother Timothy <fest_prep_chairman@omni.com>
Sent:	Thursday, 6:55 a.m. City Time
Subject.	Festival Planning Status - Gravitational Light Deflection Verified

I have new information to report regarding the vibrational permeation, which as you know is currently progressing through the 10th and final dimension in the Underling World. My analysis shows that the Underlings have experimentally verified the deflection of starlight by their Sun's gravitational field during a solar eclipse, as predicted by the recently discovered relativity theory equations. The significance of this event to our Festival planning activities cannot be underestimated, in terms of its hastening of full permeation throughout the 10th dimension. This knowledge opens the door to thought patterns previously unknown to the Underlings, and while we share your excitement at this event, we cannot state strongly enough that planning efforts must be redoubled. The Underling year is A.D. 1919, and time is running short. Please make whatever efforts are necessary to ensure that all preparations are completed on schedule. This is extremely important to all of us. The Omniscience Council expects the Festival to come off on time and under budget.

Please also make sure that all employees have watched today's safety video and signed the appropriate roster form.

Brother Timothy
Festival Preparation Committee Chairman

Brother Timothy leaned back and nodded with self-satisfaction. The memo was clean, concise, and compelling. "A perfect example of the three C's of writing," he said to himself. Straight out of the Management Handbook. His well-written e-mail conveyed just the right balance of command authority and technical understanding, and he hoped his subordinates would learn from him.

The majority of the memo was a copy and paste from a technical update sent out by Sister Esther in Quality Assurance, but Timothy had drafted the critical information about adhering to schedule and watching the safety video. Timothy also thought it was a nice touch to rewrite Esther's third sentence to indicate that it was his own analysis that showed the Underlings had verified starlight deflection. Esther had actually performed the analysis, but the impact of the entire memo was so much stronger if Timothy was perceived to have done it himself.

Timothy had no idea what Esther's description of "starlight deflection" was all about, or just what a gravitational field, a solar eclipse, or a relativity theory equation might be. But that was of no consequence. After all, "Leave the small details to the small-minded."

October 5, 1957:

Everything in Mikhail's upbringing told him to believe the words written on the page before him. In the past he had experienced occasional pangs of doubt, but always been able to put them aside. He had been personally summoned from Stavropol after only two years in the Party, to speak before the Assembly on the occasion of this glorious victory over the West. His youthful face was no accident in this setting, as the Inner Council wished to send a none-too-subtle message to the world, proclaiming that today's accomplishment was only the start of a glorious future for his homeland. "We stand before the world as its leader - not only in space exploration as we proved today, but in all branches of science, in politics, in equality, and most of all, in human spirit," he heard himself saying. Only twenty-six, he well understood his position as the Party's brightest young star, and his value as its symbol of future world primacy. He knew his face and words would be shown the world over, that his dynamic performance was intended to inspire his countrymen and demoralize his country's foes. "Here the lowest laborer is the equal to the Party Chairman....."

Suddenly the high-pitched squeal of feedback pierced at his ears and he flinched, taking several seconds to let the intense vibration subside; indeed, it seemed to literally seep into his very being as it faded away.

"What is wrong with you?" shouted his mentor Leonid from the wings.

"The feedback, what do you think?" mouthed Mikhail, still trying to gather himself, as he returned to the microphone, noting the quizzical faces in the audience.

"What feedback?" muttered Leonid, hoping this slip from his protégé had not tarnished his own image.

Returning to his message, Mikhail tried once again to whip himself into a messianic fury, as he had so many times before. Much to his embarrassment, however, a grin slowly creased his face, and from deep within him, laughter tried to erupt. Each sentence came with greater difficulty, his voice halting, each slogan suddenly ringing empty, silly in fact, distracting him from the simple truths of the Party's message. He paused to wipe his brow, then to take a sip of water, completing only a sentence or two at a time, trying to finish without collapsing completely in laughter. "The dominance of the people is our global destiny. The western powers will drown in their own obesity and sloth." He practically doubled over in laughter, putting his hand over the microphone. Leonid was beside himself with anger, that odd vein on his forehead standing out as it did when his wrath boiled over. Fortunately for both of them, Mikhail's audience only heard the platitudes they wished to hear, and his poor presentation in no way diminished the impact of his words.

The final few minutes of his speech were a nightmare of barely uttered slogans and frequent pauses to regain his composure. "The elitists have had their day, now the worker will have his."

How can anyone utter this poppycock with a straight face? wondered Mikhail. At one point he even pointed toward Leonid and grinned like an idiot schoolboy, a move sure to have personal repercussions, but he simply didn't care anymore. He actually spit on a woman in the front row as one of the guffaws at last managed to escape his control, and her baffled reaction just made him laugh all the more. The crowd, however, its collective mind in a lockstep of Party dogma, merely took his laughter to be a mocking of the western powers and cheered all the more.

Summoning his last ounce of resolve, Mikhail looked straight into the television camera, pointed a finger, and managed to stammer, "It is simple human destiny that all those who oppose the people's movement will be crushed." The camera still on him, he lowered his eyes and admitted to himself, *No - no, it's not, is it?*

The audience, so caught up in its emotion that it was totally unaware of the conflicts within the speaker, rose as one, and erupted into a deafening roar. Leonid breathed a sigh of relief. Still feeling the din of the feedback whine, Mikhail realized the slogans were dead words that would never come to pass. The Assembly still applauding, he let himself dream of the new world he suddenly envisioned, saying under his breath, "Someday, someday." He later went out for a night of vodka, smiling oddly as he pondered previously unimagined destinies.

Thursday, 7:57 a.m.:

Matthew found Esther in the City Headquarters cafeteria,

just sitting down to munch on a bagel prior to work. He grabbed a bagel himself, along with an orange juice, and joined her at her table.

Esther looked up from her reading and smiled, pleased to see a friendly face. Her smile was bright and sincere, but somehow restrained, not from lack of emotion but rather from the distraction of the multitude of other thoughts that constantly flowed through her curious mind. Her short, functional blond hair framed a pale face that to others usually appeared weak until her imagination was engaged. She held up a tiny index finger, requesting Matthew to wait a moment before speaking, and her eyes returned to the book to make a mental note of the page she was on. She had found another old operations manual and was trying to decipher it. Assured that she would remember the page number, Esther fixed her intense green eyes on Matthew, knowing he would initiate the conversation. Although not really shy, Esther found it much easier to converse in response to someone else, rather than instigating the conversation herself.

"Did Timothy screw anything up with his email?" Matthew asked.

"Fortunately, no," Esther replied with a smile. "But he made it sound like he's the one that performed all the observations."

"Yeah, well, that's what he does. His only job is to yell at everyone about the schedule, so he just used your report as a reason to do it again. So how is it all going? What are you seeing?"

Esther loved it when people asked about her Underling World observations. She found them fascinating, and she was delighted on the rare occasions when other people expressed interest as well.

"Oh, there's so much activity. They have so many inventions and incredible ideas happening now. It's all coming together, just like it's supposed to. They are becoming what they were meant to be. It's incredible to watch."

"What exactly do you see?"

"It's not like we know every single thing that's happening. The monitors don't work that way. Most of the useful information comes from general overviews, the statistical compilations of overall trends throughout their world and new thought patterns developing. We can't see the whole picture at once, but we can use the Isolation Monitor to zoom in on a single location as closely as we want to. It doesn't have a very precise control system, but we can lock onto a single object and track it as it moves. That's mostly just something we do for fun, however, there's no real information we gain from that."

Esther changed the subject. "You know what else is interesting? The Liquid Time Correlation. It's changed since Monday morning."

"I know that," replied Matthew. "They already explained it to us. Their time slows down in relation to ours when there are significant events on the Underling world. It's like the two rates of time passage can slip over each other, and that's why they call it the Liquid Time Correlation."

"But there's more to it than that. There's a definite pattern."

"What do you mean?"

"Until about Tuesday morning, for maybe the first 30 hours of City Time, the Underling World time just flew by, except for those certain key events like you mentioned. Since then, however, their rate of time passage has slowed tremendously in comparison to ours, by a factor of tens of thousands. It's not just for special significant events, it's a general slowdown. I first noticed it during 8th dimensional permeation, but it's really changed dramatically here in the 10th."

Matthew, impressed, said, "Interesting. I wonder why the Architect set it up that way. How does all this affect you personally?"

Esther laughed. "You know how I was complaining Tuesday and Wednesday about how boring my job was, with nothing worth observing during the 5th and 6th dimensions? Well, there's times now that I wish for those days to come back. There is so much Underling World activity to monitor. This final portion of the 10th dimension is so hectic it's driving me nuts."

"Yeah, well, Timothy is driving *me* nuts," said Matthew. "You're not the only one who has to deal with all this activity. Every day he's got a new idea about how he wants the schedules to match up our Festival Preparation activities with all your Underling World reports, to guarantee no schedule slides."

"How can you do that? You can't predict Underling World activities. I can't either, and I watch them all day long."

"I know. But Timothy doesn't want to hear that. So we make up a new way to status our progress at almost every meeting, and it's just crazy. Then we don't have time to do any of the actual work. Speaking of meetings, I have another one now, and I'm sure several more today. It never stops."

"Well, good luck."

Bad Vibes

<u>July 20, 1969:</u>

Eve Parson took a deep breath and exhaled slowly, closing her eyes. Watching the lunar landing on television had been an incredible experience, and this was the only appropriate way to celebrate the event. She thought about her life. She so appreciated her husband Adam. Of course, ever since their first date everyone had teased them about the "Adam and Eve" thing. They would offer her apples, question whether she had spoken to any serpents lately, or ask Adam if she "ribbed" him too much. Eve had to stifle a giggle as she adjusted her position to get more comfortable. Their friends were never being malicious, since it was apparent from the beginning that Adam and Eve truly belonged together. In the first place, as the two most brilliant physics students at Oxford, no one else could converse on their level. And in a very real way, they completed each other. The teasing had, in fact, undoubtedly been beneficial to Adam, establishing him as one of the group. The joke at Oxford was that any offspring of theirs would certainly be the one to finally find the key to the conflicting theories of the universe and solve the mystery once and for all.

Eve stretched and inhaled, this time letting herself smile contentedly with closed eyes. At their first meeting Adam had certainly been nice enough, but he struggled to find words in this social setting which was so unnatural for him. Their instant rapport on the subject of particle physics, however, led him out of his shell, and as her natural grace and charm allowed him to expound on his feelings about his work, she saw his passion, his tenderness, his desire to find the truth, and his selflessness. As she allowed him to warm up to her, he began to share his feelings about himself, and finally his feelings about her, and the transformation

23

from shy, withdrawn academic to warm, caring lover was complete.

She sensed Adam's breathing was becoming more intense, and realized he was almost done. He was a tender and attentive husband and lover, but tonight her thoughts were elsewhere. Of course, the great secret to their relationship was that she was every bit Adam's scientific equal, and what won her heart was his enthusiastic embrace of that fact. For as socially accomplished as she was, it frustrated her that theoretical physics represented an entire aspect of her life that she could not share, for no one else she knew could comprehend her ideas - no one until Adam, that is. Only he could see the art, the poetry, the music behind the equations, how every new concept brought us one step closer to the completion of the great universal symphony. Adam gratefully ceded her a great deal of the attention that had been his, and the two developed a symbiotic relationship - each becoming more, both professionally and personally, than either would have been alone.

At his climax, Adam snorted slightly, and Eve had to bite her lip to keep from giggling. Her mind drifted to the record playing in the background, letting Sinatra's music seep into her very being, as though it was a part of her. Adam slumped against her, and after a moment he softly asked, "Is everything all right, honey?"

"Oh yes, everything is fine. I love you so much."

She lay back, letting her body relax, blissfully unaware that she was now pregnant.

<u>April 30, 1973:</u>

Doctor Robinson hated this conversation. He'd been through it a hundred times before, but that never made it any better. The parents were waiting, he was late, and all he could think about was that he just wanted another five minutes. *Just like a criminal on death row,* he thought. *I'm willing to go through with it, but does it have to be right now?* He smiled ruefully, knowing that it wouldn't be any easier in five minutes, five days, or five years. He took a deep breath and exhaled, set his jaw, stood up, and walked into his office, where the Parsons were waiting.

"Mr. and Mrs. Parson, there is no easy way to tell you this, so I'll just come straight out with it. We have examined Christopher extremely thoroughly, and we have triple-checked all our results...."

Hearing this and knowing there was only bad news to come, Eve inhaled sharply, and then, trembling uncontrollably, collapsed against Adam's shoulder. For his part, Adam wanted to be strong for Eve, but tears flowed freely from his own eyes, as deep down he had already known what the doctor would say.

Doctor Robinson had not wanted to stop. The emotions were much easier to keep in check when he could make the entire statement in one go. Once he paused, his grief usually matched that of the parents, and sometimes he was forced to request a nurse to complete the talk, which was most unprofessional but unavoidable when he was in such a state. This particular boy's glowing sweetness gripped the doctor with even more futility and sadness than usual, and he considered calling the nurse, but felt himself duty-bound. These fine parents deserved his best. "We have triple-checked our results," he continued, "and the disability is permanent and irreversible. Christopher will be physically healthy and live a long life, his speech will continue to improve, and he will be able to speak well enough to make himself understood. But he will be unable to read or write, except for individual words he memorizes, and he will be unable to grasp complex concepts. With your intellectual background, I understand that this must be a tremendous blow for you."

Doctor Robinson took another deep breath and gathered himself. He had to be strong for this part of the discussion, it was vitally important both for Christopher and for the strength of the Parsons. "Now, listen to me very carefully," he said. "I have seen dozens of children like this. Yes, it tears at your heart, but he is fully human, and just as deserving of love and happiness as anyone else. I have seen many cases where something miraculous happens in such a child's soul, where the dark side of humanity is simply not present, where love rules the heart, unimpaired by the jealousies and frustrations that afflict the rest of us. I have worked with Christopher for many hours, and I believe he might be one of those children. He hardly made a sound, but I could see so much goodness in him. I'm sorry, I just can't be very clinical right now, because what Christopher will need isn't anything clinical. He can be special like no one you've ever met, if you will just help him. He can't be special in the ways the world measures, but sometimes you have to ignore the standards the world sets. He can still make a difference, more than you can imagine. You will have to change your lives to raise this child, but he will in turn share blessings of his own. God be with you."

Adam and Eve were escorted into the waiting area where Christopher sat silently, looking at the mobile hanging from the ceiling. Eve was still trembling and ran to Christopher, hugging him tightly to her chest. Adam put his arms around both of them until Eve's sobbing subsided a bit, then gently pulled Christopher into his own arms. The three-year-old's eyes aimlessly wandered the room until they settled on Eve's puffy face, and a slight open smile came to his face, his wide eyes saying something inexpressible. Adam and Eve briefly looked at each other, hearts dropping, tears welling in their eyes. Although neither had ever admitted it, they had anticipated the possibility of their two sets of "genius genes" combining to create someone very special indeed. That dream dashed, they could only hold each other and cry. Adam slowly led Eve out to their car, one arm holding Christopher, the other draped around Eve, who continued to stare into Christopher's eyes, until his gaze again drifted. Adam and Eve silently opened the car doors on opposite sides as they had so many times before, and reached across to the middle of the back seat to place Christopher into his car seat. Adam whispered, "We'll still be the best parents ever. You wait and see. It'll be OK." There were no more words between them for three days.

October 7, 1976:

Bus 37 rounded the corner at the top of the hill and began to slow. The driver disliked this stop in particular; cars coming from behind were unprepared for the presence of the bus and frequently had to brake hard, as deceleration was difficult on the steep downgrade past the peak of the hill. For this reason, the bus driver always went a bit past the intended bus stop, and then tried to rush the boy off the bus as quickly as possible, to minimize the time spent in this

27

vulnerable position.

Since the driver chose not to reveal his motives to the only boy who got off at this stop, young Grant Zenkman was continually puzzled at the driver's constant impatience with him. Assuming him to be merely another dolt of the adult persuasion, Grant made a point of taking his time getting off the bus, intentionally goading the driver into an apoplectic fit. Once finally off the bus, Grant turned to the right, and headed back up the steep hill toward his house.

3706 Starlight Lane was a small three-bedroom ranch style house at the end of the street. Grant stepped past the broken gate and proceeded to the front door, lifting the mat to retrieve the key. Not that he really needed it; because his older siblings occasionally forgot to return the key to its proper place, Grant was in the habit of leaving his bedroom window cracked slightly open when he left for school, allowing him to reach up and push it open, then grab the windowsill and pull himself in, which he was just tall enough to do. His father did not know of Grant's habit and continually complained about the electricity bill. Grant, of course, did not tell his father about the window, but was confident in his calculations, which indicated that having the window slightly open during the day added only a dollar or two to the bi-monthly electricity bill. Grant felt this small fee was more than fair in comparison to the potential risk of a first-grader being trapped outside on a cold day - after all, the police would never understand and would certainly hold his father accountable, so in Grant's mind, he was doing his father a favor.

Upon entering the house, Grant was happily surprised to see his sixteen-year-old brother Kurt in the living room, watching TV. Since their mother's death when Grant was two, Kurt had seldom come directly home after school, preferring instead to hang out with his friends, where the absence of his mother was not so palpable. Mary and Jane, the twins who were high school seniors and the oldest Zenkman siblings, were gifted at the social games played by that age group, and as such were almost never home. Grant's father, who had found after his wife's death that the combination of a limited income and a considerable drinking habit were not conducive to attracting and retaining a new mate, typically stopped at his favorite tavern after work in an effort to blot out the reality of his new existence, usually not returning home until Grant had gone to bed.

Such an environment would have quite possibly spelled developmental disaster for another child, but all of this was rather to Grant Zenkman's liking. He had never really known his mother, and so did not miss her like the others. In addition, the age gap between himself and his older brother made it apparent that his very existence had been a mistake, so it was quite possible his mother would not have been all that enamored with him anyway. Perhaps it is more accurate to say not that Grant actually preferred the lack of familial support, but that he adapted his personality and desires to suit the reality of his existence. On most days he was able to complete his homework in school while the teacher droned on in the afternoon about vowels and consonants and counting to a hundred and the number of legs on spiders versus the number on insects. Once home, Grant could freely read or go fishing at the stream behind the house, or take apart and reassemble all his toys. He also did the dishes, took out the trash, picked up the house, and performed many of the other tasks necessary to maintain a household, none of which seemed important to the other family members, who had never yet come to terms with the death of Grant's mother. Her strong, nurturing presence had held the family together, and her absence made painfully obvious the cracks in the remaining family structure. In the evenings it was Grant's habit to read about optics or astronomy or chemistry, sometimes conducting experiments of various sorts in his backyard, where messes could be easily concealed. In contrast to the stereotypical image of children with a scientific bent, Grant was extraordinarily popular. His gifts as a storyteller, even at the age of six, ensured that he was constantly surrounded by listeners eager to hear of the latest exploits of this boy who lived in a fantasy world of minimal parental supervision. Furthermore, he regularly invited the other boys over to his house when he had a particularly interesting experiment planned, usually involving a small explosion, which Grant always pretended was accidental, to add to the dramatic effect. Perhaps the best part of his odd existence was preparing Kraft Macaroni and Cheese for himself for dinner every night; such a culinary lifestyle made him the envy of all his classmates, chained as they were to the lima beans and beets forced upon them by their totalitarian mothers.

April 9, 1978:

Jason Poe went through everything for the eighth time, making sure the rubber bands were still holding the proper tension, pulling back and forth as they should, and that the tiny motor moved the table properly. The All-City Science Fair was about to open, and he was beside himself with worry that something would go wrong with his three-body gravitational simulation. His display provided a rough simulation of the gravitational effects of three stars of varying masses interacting with each other. Jason was a bit embarrassed that his equations were only approximate and that he hadn't even considered relativistic effects, and he dreaded having to explain the various shortcomings to the many observers who would momentarily be examining his work. The science fair evaluators had apparently been suitably impressed, however, and made him one of the two entries on the fourth-grade level, in fact, setting those two exhibits in an open area in the center of the auditorium, a rather uncomfortably conspicuous location, thought Jason. The stars moved very slowly and he could verbally describe the gravitational interrelationships as they occurred, illustrating the inverse-square proportionality of gravity as described by Newton's theories of motion. It wasn't a comprehensive mathematical description of the phenomena, but it was the best Jason could do. Adults seemed to be appreciative despite the flaws of his exhibit, and Jason told himself he would have to be happy with that.

The other fourth-grade exhibit next to Jason was still open, the other student not having arrived yet, and with the fair starting in thirty minutes, Jason assumed the other student was not coming. There would be no time to prepare properly. As he turned back to his exhibit to rehearse his discussion one last time, however, another boy strode toward him, breezing confidently toward the exhibit next to him. "Hey, you the other fourth-grader? Hi. I'm Max Cherry." Jason tentatively introduced himself, watching Max take his display from a box carried by his mother and furiously assemble it. Jason quickly recognized it as an illustration of the photoelectric effect, which had earned Einstein a Nobel Prize. In Max's display, glass marbles of various size swung down on a simple pendulum and hit a small ball bearing. The ball bearing would be knocked backward, and if knocked far enough, graze an electrical contact, turning on a small light. Jason was amazed at how quickly Max was putting the equipment together, just slapping it up. It would have taken Jason five times as long with his methodical approach to things, but Max just flashed through everything. If the marble was of sufficient size, the ball bearing would be knocked back farther, setting off a second or even a third light of different color. The arrangement was set up geometrically to approximate a central atomic nucleus, with the ball bearing outside the nucleus, representing an electron. The intent was obviously to show that atomic energy emissions were quantized, that if each individual marble, representing an incoming photon of light, was of insufficient energy to drive the electron to the next energy level, then no matter how many photons hit an atom, the electron could not jump to the next higher energy level and create its own photon emission and give off light. But even a single incoming photon, if it carried the proper energy, could create an energy level jump, as simulated by the turning on of the lights.

Max glanced up at Jason's exhibit and said, "Oh, cool. Three-body gravitational interactions? You must be smart too. Did you actually work out the equations?"

Jason looked down and admitted, "Well, they're only approximate. I couldn't resolve it for an indefinite future. I wish it was better."

Max looked at Jason quizzically. "Are you crazy? Look around. Over there - that *eighth grader* has a project where he tests bleaches by seeing which one washes out colors faster. He got his mom to buy three kinds of bleach, then he took some old fabrics and bleached them, and then he made up a display that tells you which one changed the color the most. Whoop-de-do. That's what other kids think is a science project. I guarantee that every kid here will look at your three stars and think that gravity will just make them slam together. They won't even understand when you explain F=ma and how the gravitational force relates to the two masses and the inverse square of the distance."

Jason started to object again, still protesting that his exhibit was inadequate, but Max reached over and put him into a fierce headlock.

"Shut up, you idiot. I have wanted a friend who's as smart as I am since I was in first grade. Well - you're it. So quit being a baby and let's talk about science. Okay?"

Max released the astonished Jason, who was quite taken aback, yet thrilled, at Max's unconventional but nevertheless sincere compliment. He was also relieved that Max could relate to the difficulty of explaining concepts to the other kids. It was a problem Jason dealt with every day. Here was someone who understood. He looked at Max's display again and ventured an unsolicited opinion, a bold move for the usually withdrawn Jason. "It's kind of cool that my display shows Newtonian gravitational forces, you know, like on a macro scale, and yours shows a quantum effect of what happens on a microscopic scale."

Max enthusiastically agreed, saying, "That's better. Yeah, I think me and you make a good team."

During the Science Fair, the two boys talked to each other much more than the lumbering parents milling about the displays. The parents wouldn't have understood the explanations anyway.

October 17, 1979:

Christopher Parson ran into the living room crying. "What's wrong, Chris?" his father asked, who had been watching the Angels game on television.

"They don't fall when I want," sobbed Chris.

"The dominoes?" asked Adam.

Chris nodded through his tears, grasped his father's hand, and pulled him into the den. Adam stopped short at the doorway, amazed at the sight before him. He and Eve had long ago accepted Christopher's mental limitations, and instead fed him great helpings of emotional support and love. It was not possible, of course, to converse with him at any depth, but he instinctively understood how to act toward other people, and was quite a charmer in his own way. But what Adam saw before him was something new. Chris hadn't adopted any hobbies to this point; he filled his days with coloring and watching children's TV shows and had shown no particular intellectual curiosity. But last week he had seen a dominoes demonstration on television, and had been fascinated as thousands of dominoes fell in perfect order, forming a beautiful geometric pattern. After his 400th demand for a set of dominoes, Adam and Eve had taken him out and bought a few sets, enough to spread a few feet across the flat tiled floor of their den. The parents were quite curious themselves to see if Christopher would have the discipline to make the dominoes work.

The source of Adam's amazement was in one corner of the den, which was covered with black dominoes in a lovely double spiral pattern, rather reminiscent of the spiral arms of the Milky Way Galaxy, Adam thought to himself. Adam was frankly amazed that Chris's limited mind could conceive of an esthetically pleasing design like this; it was wonderful to find out such a thing about his son. Caught up in this thought, he hardly noticed Christopher pulling at his arm, still crying. As he looked again, Adam saw the problem. In numerous places, Christopher had been unable to place the dominoes with sufficient accuracy and had inadvertently knocked many of them over, so that he couldn't get the entire pattern set up.

"Show me how you place them, Chris," said Adam, and watched as Chris picked up a domino in his fist and attempted to set it in place behind another, knocking over two other dominoes, causing another sobbing outburst. Adam hugged Chris close, then said, "Here, Chris, give me your hand." Christopher's small hand extended toward him. "Now, Chris, just go like this," said Adam, extending his thumb and forefinger and holding them about an inch apart. As he lifted a domino from the floor between his own fingers, Adam said, "Pick them up like this." Christopher slowly lowered his own hand toward a domino and slowly closed his thumb and forefinger around one end, just as his father had. He lifted slowly, and the domino cleanly came up. His eyes brightened through the tears. "Now Chris, when you place one behind the other, you have to come straight down, like this. Even I have to be very careful to make it work. You have to go very slowly," Adam said as he demonstrated. Chris found a single domino already standing, and with the care of a brain surgeon placed the domino he was holding right behind it. He slowly pulled his fingers straight apart just as his father had, releasing the domino, and beamed as it remained perfectly in place. Adam repeated the lesson until Chris had lined up about fifteen dominoes. Not a single one had fallen. Adam also noticed that Christopher's row of dominoes was straighter than his own.

"Now, Chris, let's have some fun and knock 'em over." With that, Chris drew back his fist and took a great whack at the first domino in the row he had created. It shot halfway across the room, but at an oblique angle. It did collide with the second domino, but the angle was wrong and it deflected sideways, missing the third domino. The rest of the dominoes stubbornly remained standing. For a moment Christopher's face began to dissolve into tears once again. "Chris, Chris, it's okay," said Adam, "You can do it. But when you want to start the dominoes falling, it's not a big bang. It's a perfect tiny little touch. Just a perfect tiny little touch, that's all it takes, and all of them will tip right over." Adam extended his forefinger and gently touched the first domino in the row he had laid out, and the dominoes obediently fell in perfect order. Christopher clapped his hands and giggled with delight. He laid down on the floor and put his face to within about six inches of the first domino still standing in the row he had created. He extended his forefinger, just as his father had, and moved it to within about half an inch of the first domino. A big smile radiated from his face.

"A perfect tiny little touch, that's all it takes, and all of them will tip right over," Chris repeated in his barely formed voice. His finger touched the first domino, and sure enough, all the dominoes fell in perfect sequence, just like on the television show that had so fascinated him. Christopher jumped up and crowed, unfortunately scattering most of the dominoes he had laid out across the floor, but this did not concern him as he reveled in his feeling of accomplishment. Seconds later he was back on the floor, recreating the spiral pattern even more beautifully than before.

"I'm going to have to buy some more dominoes," thought Adam.

<u>November 12, 1980:</u>

Sean Masterson's eyes opened and he turned to look at the alarm clock. 5:43 a.m., he noted with satisfaction. He reached over and flipped off the alarm button, which was set for 5:45. It was a Thursday, and for the third morning out of four this week, Sean had managed to wake up on his own within five minutes of the alarm's set time. He felt this mental discipline exercise would help him deal with the rest of his daily morning routine.

Having awakened two minutes early, Sean had no problems making his bed to military standards by 5:53, as his eight-minute allotment for this activity was based on the 5:45 wake-up time. He brushed his teeth quickly, but was not careful about his time in the shower, weakly allowing his mind to be seduced by the soothing warmth of the hot water, and despite all haste to dry himself, he did not emerge from the washroom until 6:10, four minutes late.

Alas, Sean's father was standing by the breakfast table, in full dress uniform, arms crossed, feet wide apart, when Sean finally scrambled into the kitchen at 6:16 a.m., where a steaming plate of bacon and eggs prepared by his mother awaited him. In his haste Sean sat down directly, rather than waiting to receive permission. This was a big mistake.

Albert Masterson's appearance totally belied the force of personality he projected. Five feet seven inches tall but weighing only 122 pounds dripping wet, with a face oddly canted to one side, large open eyes, and gangly arms with long, delicate fingers, an initial sighting of him conveyed the impression of an older version of the eighth grade boy in every school who was beaten up every day. But when Albert's jaw set and his eyes narrowed, the raw force of this man could be palpably felt. His climb to the rank of major was rapid and inevitable; his lack of further promotion to this point in his career had nothing to do with lack of talent and everything to do with keeping him in a position where the actual ability to get things done was what mattered.

Sean stood before his father, determined not to lose his composure - ramrod straight, raising himself to his full height of four feet seven inches, his eyes straight ahead and focused at infinity. The dressing-down was quick and merciless.

"Shirt?"

Sean ran his hands around his waist, finding the spot where his shirt was not tightly tucked in, and quickly corrected the discrepant condition.

"Shirt again?"

Sean closed his eyes in frustration. Two errors with the shirt were unforgivable.

"Permission to look, sir?"

"Granted."

Sean ran his hands and eyes over the front of his shirt momentarily, then grimaced in recognition as he noticed the five baseball cards he had left in his pocket the night before.

Albert extended a sinewy arm, palm held flat.

As he handed over the offending cards, Sean pleaded, "Sir, one of them is my favorite, it's my Hank Aaron rookie card -"

The cards were ripped in half before the statement was out of Sean's mouth. He clenched his teeth, his eyes boring a hole in the wall in front of him.

"Shoes?"

Sean blinked. "The shoes are perfect, sir." He had polished them to a high gloss the night before.

"I know. Polish them again."

Forty-three seconds later, Sean Masterson was back in his bedroom, repolishing his shoes, which already glinted in the sunlight. As his father had taught him, each shoe was divided into seven zones, and each zone received fifty rapid strokes, the first twenty-five with heavy pressure, and the second twenty-five with very light pressure. In the public school he attended this year, the other fifth-graders had mercilessly teased him about his gleaming black shoes.

Until he beat them. At everything.

As Sean started on the second shoe, his father stepped inside the bedroom door. Sean began to struggle to his feet, but his father held up a hand, indicating that this was not required. Sean knelt again, picking up the second shoe, but not polishing until his father spoke.

"It is now 0624 hours. You still have six minutes to get ready, although of course you will have no time to eat the breakfast your mother prepared for you. If you follow your morning procedures correctly, I have allotted you twelve spare minutes as an allowance for the fact that you are ten years old. You do understand that when you are a military officer, there will be no such allowances. That is why I attempt to convey to you the importance of correctly following procedure, to benefit you in your future life." With that, Albert turned and left Sean to his shoes.

Sean Masterson had no intention of becoming a military officer, but those thoughts could not be spoken until he was much older. He was insightful enough, however, to realize that his upbringing would surely not leave him unaffected.

<u>August 16, 1982:</u>

Kathy Leigh stretched out on the cool grass, looking up at the star-filled Arizona sky with her father, the crickets chirping their summer song in the distance. "OK, sweetheart, what's that one up there that looks like a W?" Kathy rolled her eyes. Her dad was always into this star stuff.

"It's Cassiopeia, daddy, you've told me that one 20 times, OK?"

Her father pointed to another constellation and said, "Well, what about that one?"

"Orion," she sighed. "And the big bright star down to the left is Sirius, the Dog Star. The big reddish star that represents Orion's left shoulder is Betelgeuse, and billions of years from now it will turn into a supernova. The second star in Orion's belt is actually not a star at all, but the Great Orion Nebula, a giant gas cloud where new stars are forming. These objects are all inside the Milky Way, which is just one of billions of galaxies, all flying apart at unimaginable speeds, as discovered by the great astronomer Edwin Hubble, who also demonstrated that the most distant galaxies are moving away from us the fastest, thus originating the Big Bang theory-"

"Okay, okay. You proved your point. Geez."

"Daddy, I know about astronomy, and I love you. But can we *please* talk about my newspaper articles?"

"Sure, honey," whispered her father, sadly realizing his endless fascination with the stars would never be shared by his daughter.

"I want to start up a real school paper. There's never been

an official newspaper for our elementary school. I could be the first. And I'm going to write all kinds of controversial articles. I'll write how the cafeteria uses the cheapest food they can, and how teachers are always trying to show they have power over the students, and how students need to get together themselves to stop bullies, and ooh, I'll tell the *inside story* about what the girls say in the bathroom, and, and, (her words running faster and faster), and I will find out how much money the school board gets and what they spend it on and how much really goes to kids and I'll write how nice teachers should get paid more than mean ones and especially the old grouchy ones and I'll do a study of rich kids and poor kids and find out who is more popular and who is really nicer and ......"

Kathy's father sighed and closed his eyes, realizing there was no stopping her now, and he'd have to wait till tomorrow to get back to his beloved quiet contemplation of the wonderment of the universe. Oh well, maybe she'd write a story about astronomy one day.

Thursday, 8:03 a.m.:

"I hereby declare this meeting of the Festival Preparation Committee officially open. The first item on the agenda is a review of the Project Schedule. Brother Andrew, would you put up the schedule chart?"

The committee members stared dull-eyed at the item-by-item schedule before them. "Tut, tut, this will never do," said Brother Timothy. "Look at all those items behind schedule, and some items are still open! Our superiors will not be happy with this." Timothy sighed condescendingly. "I suppose we need yet another working meeting, since

41

some people apparently cannot be counted on to be properly prepared, eh? We can take the opportunity to upgrade the schedule format as well."

Having heard similar diatribes at every recent meeting, and his patience exhausted, Brother Matthew unwisely erupted. "Brother Timothy, it's all so very nice that you and the senior Committee members can make orders for a perfect schedule that all goes off on time, but the fact is a lot of these events are out of our control. We don't know when 10th-level permeation will conclude, and neither do you or anyone on your committee -"

"What are you talking about?" inquired Timothy harshly. "Of course we know when it will conclude. It will conclude at midnight on Saturday, per the Master Schedule."

Matthew stood up, unconsciously trying to assert himself before the Committee chairman. His tall, rangy body and erect posture gave him a certain presence in public situations that served him well, and for this reason his co-workers usually chose him as the spokesman when the situation called for it. He looked to the back of the room, trying to find his friend Esther and get some moral support. Matthew took a moment to gather his thoughts, running his long, almost delicate fingers through the waves of his light brown hair. Good-looking in a genial way, Matthew tried to use this quality to ingratiate himself to the Committee with a forced smile, but the consternation he felt transmitted itself directly through his pale blue eyes, and was evident to all.

After a few seconds, Matthew continued. "That's not what I meant. I know the project ends Saturday night. Your schedule format requires that for every Tier I activity on our schedule, we show a corresponding major activity for the Underling World. There is no way to do that for future activities. We have no way to show what Underling date or events will be occurring Saturday at midnight. No one has explained how we on the working level staff are supposed to deal with the Liquid Time Correlations. How can we make a schedule and coordinate to events we can't control? If you'd get out here with us, you'd understand what's going on. We've got too many ivory-tower types making decisions, just like always. Even Sister Esther of the Underling World Observation Center says -"

"Matthew, Matthew - now don't go blaming this 'Sister Estelle' for your problems," said Timothy with a smile. This time it was Timothy's turn to pause for a moment - not to collect his thoughts, but to quite intentionally cause this Matthew fellow a bit of discomfort and reassert control of the proceedings. Timothy was a member of the Omniscience Council, and his primary responsibility was to serve as chairman of the Festival Preparation Committee. He thoroughly enjoyed the give-and-take with the committee staff, although it baffled him that they showed so little appreciation for his leadership. Timothy was not alarmed at Matthew's outburst. He had heard this sort of tirade before, and was expert at defusing such situations. He remained seated, realizing that a seated dignitary projected much more power than one who had to resort to standing and physical gestures. Besides, Timothy was short, clumsy, and unattractive, and remaining seated was the best way to de-emphasize those traits.

"I want to assure you first of all - you have no idea how much we appreciate your enthusiasm," Timothy began. "That sort of fighting spirit is what makes us a world-class organization - or should I say, a *universe-class* organization, that would be more correct, wouldn't it?" He chortled, and the other senior Committee members laughed along with him. "Matthew, I understand the difficulties you face, and to resolve those issues, the Festival Preparation Committee wants you to consider yourself empowered to use all resources at your disposal. We're behind you a hundred percent, and have complete faith in your abilities. Now - moving on….."

Matthew interrupted again, startling the assemblage, which was unaccustomed to such audacity. "You didn't answer the question - how are we supposed to coordinate our schedules to Permeation events we don't understand and can't control? Please answer the question."

Timothy, still unflustered, said, "You do raise a good question. I think it's appropriate to have the Detail Planning Subcommittee take it up, so we can move forward." Matthew interrupted one last time, pushing as far as he dared.

"But we *are* the Detail Planning Subcommittee! When the Subcommittee meets, it's all the same people we have here!"

Now Timothy crossed his arms and gave his most patronizing look. He knew he had the situation well in hand.

"Now Matthew - as you know, we have agreed-upon procedures, correct?"

"Yes, but -" Matthew began.

Timothy continued uninterrupted. "Do you suppose there might be a *reason* we have these procedures?" Matthew just sighed, defeated. "If we don't have everyone following our standard procedures, we'll just have everyone running off in every direction, and we wouldn't want that, now would we? Would we, Matthew?"

Matthew rolled his eyes and gave in, muttering, "No, we wouldn't want that."

Esther, watching Matthew's humiliation from the back of the room, simultaneously felt shame at not having enough courage to stand up for him, and great relief that she was spared such an experience.

"Well, good, I'm glad we agree," concluded Timothy. "Anything else?"

Matthew rubbed his forehead in exasperation. He did have one more item to address, and he may as well do it now, despite his crushed ego.

"I do have a recommendation for the Festival Progress Report Forms."

"And what might that be?" asked Timothy with his most gratingly condescending smile.

"There are several improvements that could be made to the current form to increase our productivity. Do you want to hear about them?"

"No, I do not," said Timothy with a brusque satisfaction.

"Uh - excuse me?" said Matthew, trying to remain polite.

"Were you not listening before?"

"I assure you that I have been listening to every word you say, Brother Timothy."

"Did you not hear me say that we have agreed-upon procedures, and that there might be a reason we have these procedures?"

"I am not trying to violate procedures, I promise you. It's just that there are some simple changes that could be made to the Progress Report Form that would be extremely helpful.

"Oh - then you want to *change* the procedures, is that it?"

"Yes, that's right."

"Well, you appear to be misinformed about what Committee meeting you are presently attending. We are the Festival Preparation Committee. We are not responsible for changing procedures."

"But it's such a minor change."

Timothy now spoke slowly through clenched teeth, but still in total control. "We are not responsible for changing procedures."

"May I ask who is?"

"The Efficiency Committee is responsible for changing procedures. That information is in your Committee Staff Procedures Guide. Have you not read it?"

Matthew decided not to debate that particular issue. "May I speak to the Efficiency Committee about changing the Festival Progress Report Form?"

"Certainly. Be my guest," Timothy concluded dismissively.

Matthew could only grind his teeth in frustration. He again looked for Esther, resentful that there was no one to defend him.

Timothy, realizing the best course of action at this point was to conclude the meeting as quickly as possible before further unrest could occur, summarized quickly. "I understand the Main Hall is already reserved. I trust that chairs and tables have also been ordered. We will require seating for twelve billion. Not nine, not ten, not eleven, but twelve billion souls. Make sure that happens. It is very important that no one feels left out. We also must make sure plenty of food is available. We prefer something light, as the Festival is expected to last quite a long time, and we don't want any stomach upset, now do we? Dunstan, of course, will handle the music, I'm sure he will find something peppy to lift everyone's spirits in preparation for the Consolidating Trumpet Call. Well, I think that's all for tonight. You can all see the missing items on the schedule chart, I trust you will correct them by next meeting."

Dunstan, sitting in the back of the room, continued to seethe, and couldn't stop thinking about the Trumpet. Something peppy indeed.

August 1, 1985:

Having given this speech for the past four years, Elmer Schmidlapp understood that its most important quality was brevity. Before him sat one hundred fifteen-year-olds in varying stages of adolescent distress, and no amount of genius and scientific curiosity could make them want to listen to an adult wax poetic about the scientific vistas opening up before humankind. In addition, Elmer questioned the value of this whole affair anyway. This was the twentieth year of the Future Scientists of America convention. Each state nominated two ninth-grade candidates, who were flown at federal government expense to Washington, D.C. for a whirlwind tour of the Smithsonian Institution, ostensibly to inspire the students, followed by three days of presentations and discussion, all intended to pique the career interest of these gifted young people, and enhance the next generation of American science.

As director of the National Research Council, however, Elmer could not help but think there might be better things to do with his time, especially considering that not one attendee from previous Future Scientist conventions had gone on to become a researcher of any note. Not that new talents were lacking, it was just that holding this convention every year did not seem to further the cause in any noticeable way.

As Director Schmidlapp concluded his introduction to the discussion portion of the week's activities, Zena Dunn fidgeted in her chair. She was one of the few attempting to pay attention to Mr. Schmidlapp's speech, but the constant whispering and giggles by those around her made it difficult to follow. She hesitated to say anything to the people around her, particularly the loquacious boy behind her who had not stopped talking the entire time, partly because she knew it would not be received well, but also because Zena was still quite self-conscious about her rapidly changing body, especially the rampant acne ravaging her face. Her mother continually told her she would be a very pretty young woman in a couple of years, but that seemed an eternity to Zena.

At the end of Director Schmidlapp's speech, a number of large adults in boring suits herded the young people into groups of ten and directed them to a room with a number of large round tables, indicating that each group was to sit together at its own table. All the students sat down and waited for whatever was scheduled next.

A small fortyish woman, the least oppressive-looking among the adults, went to the front of the room and stood before the blackboard.

"Hello, everyone, my name is Eve Parson and I am a theoretical physicist at the University of Princeton, and this is the first year I have participated in the Future Scientists of America. They requested me to introduce a one-hour discussion on any topic of my choosing, and instead of naming a particular field, I wrote up three simple, open-ended questions to frame your discussion, but not to limit it.

The intent is to allow you as much freedom as possible and encourage your creativity."

Eve Parson wrote the following three questions on the blackboard, in perfectly lettered printing:

1) What is the most important scientific objective for the twenty-first century?
2) Is this objective achievable?
3) How can America best sponsor scientific research to achieve this objective?

Mrs. Parson concluded simply, "All right, we'll see you in an hour."

Although wildly interested in hearing the undoubtedly passionate views held by other scientifically gifted young people, Zena Dunn had dreaded this moment all week, when face-to-face confrontation was inevitable. Her mother had told her that these people would be different, that they would judge on the basis of intellect and content rather than appearance and fashion, but the foregoing inane chattering during Director Schmidlapp's speech had made it abundantly clear that scientific aptitude did not exempt young people from being shallow. Zena silently cursed her parents for urging her to apply for the convention, and she desperately hoped that her bangs, her shoulder-length hair, and her silence would keep attention off her acne-ridden face.

The ten ninth-graders at Zena's table stared at each other, all but one unwilling to be the first to risk speaking. After a few uncomfortable seconds which seemed an eternity, the boy who had been sitting behind Zena broke the ice.

"Can you believe that hotel? That is a four-star hotel. I've never been in one before. Oh man, I was ordering room service all night long."

A tall thin girl with dark-rimmed glasses responded for the group. "Your - your parents let you do that?"

"What parents? My dad's not here, he just had my sister drop me off at the airport. I'm in my room by myself." He saw blank stares from the others. "Are *all* of you staying with your parents?"

The lack of response indicated that his situation was unique.

"Oh, too bad. How can you have any fun? I ordered a banana split and a chocolate cake, you wouldn't believe how fancy they are. I ordered a couple of beers too just for fun, and told them my parents were out of the room, but they needed a signature from an adult. Maybe tonight."

Nine faces of puzzled amazement, including Zena's, greeted the boy. Completely oblivious to the confusion around him, he went right on talking. Zena leaned over to get a look at his name tag. It read, "Grant Zenkman."

"So nobody's been out at night? A couple of blocks from the hotel is a whole strip of restaurants and bars and music clubs. Out on the street, you wouldn't believe the people you see. There are punk rockers with blue spiked hair, black guys who are from the jazz clubs, and rich old white men sipping cognac at the outdoor French restaurant. They are really interesting people to talk to. There was this one guy I ran into -"

"Shouldn't we be answering the questions?" interrupted the tall girl with glasses, arching her eyebrows. "I think the most important objective for the twenty-first century is eradicating world hunger, and to accomplish that, I think we need to emphasize agricultural technology over profit-centric efforts." She crossed her arms with a look of self-satisfaction at having retrieved control of the discussion from this anarchic young man.

Seven heads nodded in eager agreement, uncomfortable with Grant's blithe departure from the scripted questions. Zena stared at Grant, wondering what he would do next.

"Come on," replied Grant, "we can do better than world hunger, can't we? That is so Miss America."

The tall girl, visibly affronted, huffed in disgust, then replied, "So, Mister Does-Whatever-He-Wants, why don't you tell us the most important scientific objective of the twenty-first century?"

Zena's eagerness for a real scientific discussion finally got the best of her, and she blurted out, "Grant is right. World hunger is certainly important, but it's mundane. The scientific minds of the twenty-first century should dedicate themselves to finding the Grand Unified Theory of the universe, to explain all physics from the atom to the galaxy, from the Big Bang to the end of time."

Zena's intensity was quite involuntary, and she quickly retreated back into her withdrawn posture, her face flushing.

As the others quietly snickered at Zena for her loss of composure, Grant laughed and responded, "Wow. Looks like somebody's got a real live opinion."

Zena tried to gather herself, realizing that further silence was no longer an option. "I just think that cosmology is the most important thing. All of human history is the story of learning about the world around us."

"I disagree," said the other girl firmly. "It's only important from an academic standpoint, it doesn't help disadvantaged people, and I think scientists need to have a conscience."

"But - but…" stammered Zena, who was most definitely not a good debater.

Grant sighed audibly. "Guys, we're only here for three more days. We can be good little boys and girls and make up answers that sound big and important, or we can do something different, something we'll remember. You think ten years from now you'll remember how we answered these questions? You think it will matter? What we'll remember is whether we had a good time or not. None of us has ever had a week like this - let's enjoy it, have some fun, talk about things we actually care about. Tell you what. I'll be the one to report on our discussion at the end of the hour. If anyone thinks my answers aren't good enough, you can come to my room tonight and I'll order you a room service dinner, anything you want. I mean, I'm not paying, so why not? Okay?"

Grant's insouciant challenge was irresistible to the other nine students. They allowed the next forty-five minutes of discussion to range from fashion to hair to cars to parents to public schools to bullies to boy/girl relationships to opinions on which speaker was the dorkiest, all the while being exceedingly curious about Grant's ability to improvise a report at the end of the hour, Zena most of all. While the other tables were embroiled in conversations of Deep and Significant Things in hushed tones, Zena's and Grant's table rocked with laughter at the stories, jokes, and shocking opinions offered on dozens of subjects, with every student speaking up enthusiastically. After a while even Zena joined in the fun, forgetting her embarrassment over her appearance. Truth be told, she would have preferred a heated exchange of opinions on various cosmological theories, but it was apparent that these students were adolescents first and scientific minds a distant second. Zena wondered where she would ever find a place to share the ideas that burned within her.

At last Eve Parson returned to the blackboard and asked for a volunteer table to report first on its discussion. Grant's hand shot straight up. Mrs. Parson motioned to him, and he slowly rose to his feet, at first turning, leaning over to get a look at Zena's name tag.

Grant strolled to the blackboard, taking his time, just as he had getting off the school bus back in first grade. He turned toward the entire group. He motioned toward Zena.

"My friend Zena is the one who suggested cosmology as the most important field of scientific endeavor, and she got all of us to agree with her." Zena cringed at Grant's public mention of her, but couldn't resist a tiny smile. Grant winked at Zena and went on. "Cosmology is rooted in the most fundamental of all human desires, the desire to understand the world around us. From the cave man inventing the wheel to Neil Armstrong walking on the moon, human history can be basically defined as our quest to comprehend the nature of the universe, the mind of God, if you will. We are a part of something bigger than ourselves, and our lives lack significance if we do not understand what that bigger something might be. There are a thousand objectives that can be pursued, but there is only one that is literally a biological need, and we must pursue it. A hundred years ago we literally had no understanding of the nature of the atom or the large scale universe. The twentieth century saw the conception, development, and verification of general relativity and quantum mechanics, marvelously verifiable visions of the universe on the largest and smallest of scales. Humankind, does not yet, however, have a single Grand

Unified Theory to combine these large-scale and small-scale visions, and that simply must be the primary goal of twenty-first century technology. Is it achievable? Of course. It is not only achievable, it is inevitable. We can no more stop this pursuit than we can stop breathing, it is what makes us human. What will it take? Certainly a larger-scale commitment than what we have seen to this point, but there is nothing mysterious about that. Just as the Manhattan project brought the finest scientific minds together for a specific goal, so could a long-term dedicated team of top-flight researchers find these final answers to the question that has been asked since the beginning of time. It is only a matter of time; these answers *will* be found, perhaps by some of the people sitting in this room today."

The other nine adolescents at the table gaped in amazement.

At nine o'clock that evening, Zena Dunn, accompanied by her parents, knocked on Grant Zenkman's hotel door. He had not yet left for his nocturnal tour of the more interesting parts of the City. Grant stood just in front of her, nearly the same height as Zena, a slightly stocky boy, with eyes alert and penetrating, but an easy smile. Zena took a deep breath and spoke. "I told my mom and dad about you, and I told them I wanted to talk with you. They said it's okay if I go with you when you go for your walk tonight, they will follow behind us. They said it would be fine for me to talk to you, and it would be safer for you to have some adult supervision anyway."

Grant took all this in for a moment, then reached back and grabbed his jacket, and said, "Great! Let's go!"

Minutes later, Zena and Grant were strolling the streets of what appeared to be an entirely different planet than the buttoned-down atmosphere surrounding the hotel. The hotel district was populated by the Washington insiders to whom appearances meant everything, and conformity to the values of that world, including certain fashion boundaries, was mandatory. The world into which Grant escorted Zena that evening consisted of people who pursued a lifestyle because they loved inhabiting it, not because it was a contest to be won or lost.

Zena and Grant walked about ten feet in front of her parents, who could not help smiling at the sight of their brilliant but conflicted daughter chatting with this young man who fascinated her so. This attention was quite unlike Zena; this boy must have made quite an impression. Normally boys interested her much less than the surplus table-top size cyclotron she had received from Stanford University that spring. She was already capable of generating and identifying elementary subatomic particles formed in the miniature particle accelerator, and was audacious enough to be writing her first research paper, in hopes of becoming a published research scientist before the age of sixteen.

As the walk began, Zena tried not to appear overanxious, pointing out people and sights she found mildly amusing. Not being entirely capable of containing her emotions, she kept walking ahead of Grant, and having to wait for him. For his part, Grant made no effort to keep up; indeed, he seemed quite oblivious to Zena's direction and pace, taking off in whatever direction he preferred as the spirit moved him, with no apparent thought that Zena might have her own preference, or that she was even present. Once aware of this pattern, Zena began to feel irritated, but Grant's obvious enjoyment of his conversation with her quickly demonstrated that there was no malice or intended selfishness, merely a benign ignorance of the desires of others. Within a few minutes Zena had put aside any personal hurt from Grant's neglect, and made up her mind to simply enjoy this personality so diametrically opposed to her own. Finally she decided to get to the point.

"Can I ask you a question?"

"Sure," said Grant, in a blithely carefree tone of voice.

"How did you do that today?"

"Do what?"

"You know, how you answered the questions for our table."

"I still don't get what you mean."

"Did you have your answer planned out ahead of time?"

"No," Grant said tentatively, clearly thrown for a loop. "I just made it up. When would I have had time to plan out an answer?"

"That was Eve Parson leading the discussion. She is one of the top physicists in the world. Are you telling me you just 'made it up' in front of someone like that?"

"Ohhhh," said Grant, the implications of Zena's quizzing now becoming slightly less opaque. "Did you think I gave a bad answer?"

"No, that's just it, you gave a wonderful answer. You sounded like you've been giving that speech all your life. You're only fifteen years old. How can you do that in front of someone like Eve Parson?"

"Well, first of all, thank you," replied Grant. "But no, you don't get it. That answer didn't come from some great deep fountain of passion pouring forth from within me," he said, overly dramatizing his words for effect. "What difference does it make who they are? It was just an answer to a question, that's all."

"But - but, it was a *perfect* answer."

"Thanks again, but come on. We're a bunch of fifteen-year-olds. You don't think they actually care what we think, do you? There's no right or wrong answer anyway, it's just a game they play. So to make an interesting answer, something the adults will like, you act like you're putting some *deep feeling* into it, and they'll eat it up." His eyes widened to mock the adults who invariably bought into his charade. "And as far as improvising in front of Eve Parson, well, she's just a person like anybody else. I really don't think about other people all that much. I just don't see the value in it."

Zena, disillusionment sweeping over her, continued. "You mean you didn't believe what you said? But it was beautiful."

"It's not that I don't believe it. I agree with you about studying physics, but I don't get bent out of shape over it."

"But isn't that what you're studying?"

"Yeah, mostly, but some other things too."

"How can you work in a field and not get emotionally wrapped up in it? How can you excel without that feeling like your work is the most important thing in the world? I can't imagine working on something I didn't care deeply about."

"What does that have to do with whether you excel? I think I could argue the opposite, that to excel, you *must* be detached. If you are emotionally involved with your work, you'll be more likely to make bad decisions, right? You think surgeons are all fired up every time they operate? Or pilots, or police, or teachers?"

"But science is different. How can you pour yourself into something if it doesn't mean anything to you? How do you achieve your goals without a burning intensity to succeed? How do you satisfy the people who need to approve of you?

Grant was quite unable to restrain the smirk that now crossed his face. This Zena Dunn was a piece of work, all right, a twitching bundle of nerves, emotion, and self-doubt. He wondered how she survived such an existence. But he couldn't help liking her.

"Why do you need anyone else to approve of you? Look, Zena, nothing against other people, but I never put too much attention into what they think. I do a good job, I do what I have to do, I'm responsible. I think the way I am actually helps with that. You can't help anyone when you're all upset and everything. But it's my life, so nobody else has the right to tell me whether or not I'm good enough. I do what I think is good enough, and that's all that matters. So there's no reason why I should be nervous about what Eve Parson or anybody else thinks."

Though Zena's bubble of optimism about this boy was now thoroughly deflated, she realized that, ironically, Grant's attitude probably made it easier for him to impress people, as he had done with her today. She softly stammered, "I don't think I could live like you. I don't feel alive unless I totally embrace whatever I'm doing. I want everything so badly, and I can't stand it when I don't succeed. That may sound like I'm nuts, but I need that emotion as much as I need oxygen. You must think I'm pathetic."

"If I thought you were pathetic, I wouldn't be here talking with you."

Zena brightened noticeably at the affirmation.

Grant went on. "Maybe you need all that motivation to do good work, but I don't. Heck, I don't know. I suppose sometimes my way is better, and sometimes yours is." He shrugged, pausing to stare at a huge man with pink hair strolling by.

Zena started to walk forward again, her head down, puzzling over whether Grant had just proven her entire approach to life was completely backwards.

"Why are you in science anyway?" Zena asked.

For the first time, Grant reflected for a moment. "It's just, well, compared to everything else in life, science is just, um, more.. it's more *real*, you know?"

Zena nodded knowingly, having finally found a point of commonality with Grant.

Grant asked, "You know why I used cosmology as my answer today?"

Zena stopped and looked at Grant.

"I could have said world hunger like Little Miss Tight-Ass wanted, or medicine, or transportation, or computer technology or a dozen other things, and I could have made them sound good. I used cosmology because of you. You were the only person who had anything interesting to say. Those guys - they don't really care about that stuff, they just take quotes out of fancy books. Sure, all those kids have 160 IQ's, and they're all going to get 1550's on their SAT's, and someday they'll get Ph.D's from Ivy League Universities, but they're *boring*. You're not."

Zena's face flushed and she felt a silly grin burst across her face. She impulsively lurched forward and kissed Grant Zenkman on the cheek, then shrunk back in embarrassment.

Zena's parents looked at each other in surprise and delight.

At the next corner, something caught Grant's eye, and he turned right with no warning whatsoever, forcing Zena to retrace several steps and run to catch up with him.

April 14, 1987:

"Where is that boy?" muttered Adam Parson. "I told him five minutes ago the cake was just about ready, and off he goes again."

"I'll get him," said Eve. "He's probably outside staring at the stars again."

Eve Parson opened the sliding glass door and looked out into the blackness of the vast back yard. An obvious perk of two world-renowned physicists living under the same roof was that money was most definitely not a problem. Although not enormously wealthy by any means, the Parsons were more than comfortable, a much appreciated fact that had allowed them to provide Christopher with a wonderful environment in which to grow up, despite his mental limitations. Considering their life's work, it was only natural that Adam and Eve had a great fondness for the twinkling gems of the night sky. Several years before, they had located a lovely four-bedroom house on four acres at the end of a secluded lane, several miles from any bright city lights. The Parsons' back yard provided a wide open look at the entire sky, and the tall trees surrounding the property wonderfully blocked any remaining ambient light, making for a near-perfect stargazing environment. Inside the house, the largest room had been set aside as a dedicated playroom for Christopher, where he spent most of his days still happily playing children's games, including the ever-evolving complexity and beauty of his domino arrangements.

"Chris! Chris!" called his mother into the darkness. His days spent in the playroom, Christopher's nights were more and more frequently spent in the solitude of the back yard, silently gazing up at the night sky. Although his mental capabilities remained resolutely in the realm of childhood, Eve took satisfaction in a certain maturity which continued to grow within Christopher. He certainly loved his parents as much as ever, but he had grown out of much of his emotional neediness, and was happy to spend much of his time alone.

"I'm here," said Chris blankly, barely loud enough for Eve to hear. She tried to follow his voice, having to call out two more times to properly get her bearings. The stars were particularly bright tonight, as a rainstorm had washed through the area earlier in the day and cleared away any remaining impurities from the air. Finally Eve came upon Christopher, who sat cross-legged on the cool grass, his face lifted upward toward the Milky Way. Eve sat down next to him in the darkness.

"Chris, your father baked you a wonderful birthday cake, and it's ready."

"What kind?"

Eve smiled. "Chocolate with chocolate frosting."

Chris softly clapped his hands, his face smiling broadly, but still pointed up toward the heavens. Christopher's birthday cakes were always chocolate with chocolate frosting, and his pleasure at hearing the same news every year never diminished.

"Chris, do you think you could come in now?"

Christopher Parson slowly leaned backward, letting his legs extend, and reclining to the point where he lay flat on his back, face to the sky. His mother reached out her left hand and lovingly stroked his forehead, brushing his hair back, away from his face. She looked down at her beloved son, his ever-present beatific child's smile beaming.

She looked at him again. His eyes were closed.

She softly repeated herself, "Chris, do you think you could come in now?"

"The stars need me a little bit more."

"Umm - excuse me? What do you mean, sweetie?"

Christopher remained silent, eyes closed, face to the sky.

"Honey, your eyes are closed." Eve laughed affectionately. "You can't see the stars that way."

"I don't need to see them. I can hear them."

"How can you hear them?" Eve looked up at the sky, then back at Christopher. "The stars don't make any sounds."

"Yes they do. They play music." He paused for a moment. "Can't you hear it?"

Eve smiled bemusedly and sat with her son for another minute or two, pretending to listen to the "music," and then rose and went back into the house. A few minutes later Christopher returned, and thoroughly enjoyed his chocolate birthday cake with chocolate frosting.

November 9, 1989:

Mr. Leland hung up the phone without any closing pleasantries, inadvertently offending the regional network news director in the Portland office, who had called with the urgent news. KMAX, the CBS affiliate in Bend, Oregon, had to get on the air. Now.

George, the only other supervisor in the studio as yet, brought to Mr. Leland's attention the fact that the station did not normally go on the air until 6:00 a.m.

"I don't care, I don't care. That's what Portland wants, that's what I do. Besides, this is big stuff." Mr. Leland looked around the office, realizing that the normal on-camera prima donnas would certainly arrive late due to last night's two-foot snowfall, and wondered who in the world to put on the air.

Five minutes later, Kathy Leigh felt herself near to hyperventilation. She looked at herself in the mirror, eyes wide, cheeks flushed, adrenaline pumping. A pair of unfamiliar hands came up from behind and gently turned her head, and Kathy found herself staring into the face of Martha, the make-up artist. "Now look, honey, you're gonna be fine. I've been through this a hundred times with all the new ones, and I can tell ya, you're gonna be a good one." Martha grabbed both of Kathy's cheeks and squeezed them. "I'm tellin' ya, I've never been wrong yet," said the plump, middle-aged woman, her eyes alight, a contented smile dancing at the corners of her lips, her fingers and brushes flying over Kathy's face as she performed the quick transformation. Since Kathy had been unprepared for any of this, Martha had to do a rush job on both the face and hair, and she found the challenge energizing. Martha enjoyed coming in for an hour each morning to make up the passably attractive newscasters, even if she wasn't paid. It was a reason to wake up, a refreshing way to greet the morning, before beginning the 12-hour days in her beauty shop making up the daily parade of housewives whom God had forgotten in the looks department. The studio gig was especially fun when there was another new girl, all agog with breathless excitement, as they always were. And this one seemed special - young, pretty and perky, yes, but with an underlying sense of intelligence and gravity the new girls usually did not possess.

"You don't think you're ready, do ya?" remarked Martha. She knew the look in Kathy's eyes. "Listen to me. What you're gonna do is you're gonna look in that camera, you're gonna take a deep breath, and that camera is gonna fall in love with ya. And sweetie - there's no reason to be nervous - for God's sake, this is Bend, Oregon, it's 5:15 in the morning, and we're not even s'posed to be on the air - there's nobody watching anyway."

Kathy couldn't help smiling at that one.

"Now shut up and quit fidgeting and let me put on the make-up, will ya? Just look in the mirror and think about how you're gonna tell your grandchildren about this someday." Martha then turned Kathy back to the mirror, quickly and expertly adding just the right dabs of color, smoothing out the variations in Kathy's face, adding an unearned maturity, all the while humming aimlessly. Slowly letting herself be absorbed in Martha's art, Kathy watched in fascination as her face became nearly perfect, amazed at what could be done in scant minutes. A pretty girl, yes, but not any sort of remarkable beauty, Kathy's self-confidence involuntarily rose, looking at the now flawless woman reflected before her.

Five minutes before, Mr. Leland, the morning show producer, had told Kathy that she was anchoring the news, and they were getting on the air as quickly as possible due to the breaking story. She had been interning at the station since June, and had observed all aspects of the production, but no way was she ready for this.

"You're it, Kathy," said Mr. Leland, telling her she'd be fine, but not believing it for a second. Kathy always arrived an hour and a half before air time, and today that made her the only choice he had. "None of the other newscasters will be here anytime soon, and the rest of the crew is butt-ugly guys who'd frighten the little old ladies to death. You know the story, I know you follow world news real closely. All you gotta do is introduce it, and we'll cut to the network feed. No pressure."

Yes, Kathy thought, that's what Mr. Leland had said, but he was plainly sweating bullets at the thought of the disaster that was likely to ensue. *He* was feeling pressure, for sure. The story had come in from Berlin just seventeen minutes ago, relayed through New York to the major affiliates, including the one in Portland, and finally on to the fringe markets like Bend, Oregon. The CBS correspondent in Berlin wasn't even ready yet; there was only raw video footage being transmitted at this point by a single cameraman. There had not been time to write any copy, and this untested little girl would have to wing it. On any other day, if the regular staff was not present, he would have just waited until CBS was ready and let them run the story. But he had no choice other than to put Kathy Leigh on the air right now. This was legitimate world news, and the station had to report it, no matter how ill-prepared they were.

Kathy's head once again turned in a sudden movement, and Martha's face was no more that two inches from Kathy's. "When you look in that camera, focus completely on the words. Got that?"

Kathy, confronted in such a fashion, silently nodded her head.

"Okay, you're on. Go kick their ass," Martha whispered, winking. She had made up Kathy Leigh's face and hair from start to finish in less than seven minutes.

Kathy rose from the make-up chair, her eyes narrowing. She slowed herself down, let her mind take in everything around her, and slowly walked to the anchor chair. "Okay," she thought to herself. "This is what you worked for your whole life. That perfectly awful grade school newspaper, the junior high annual, editing the high school paper, graduating two years early to get a head start on your career, straight A's at the community college so far and next year off to the University to get that journalism degree. Little sweetie-pie Kathy's gonna do it."

"OK, Kathy, thirty seconds," called Mr. Leland. "You ready?"

Kathy nodded slightly, barely acknowledging him.

"Five, four, three," Kathy heard, followed by Mr. Leland holding up two fingers, then one, and then pointing at her. Kathy looked deep into the camera.

"This is Kathy Leigh for the KMAX morning news, with a major breaking story. Approximately twenty minutes ago, CBS News was alerted to extraordinary events occurring in Berlin, Germany."

At that moment, the feed from Germany went down, leaving no options for Mr. Leland other than to have Kathy Leigh fill the time. He gestured frantically to her, bringing his hands together, touching the fingertips together, and then drawing them apart again, as though pulling taffy.

"The country of Germany was divided in half after World War II," Kathy began, picking up Mr. Leland's cue, "the eastern half falling under Soviet domination, while West Germany became a democracy. The ancient capital city of Berlin, in East Germany, was itself cleft in two. West Berlin remained democratic and free, but isolated from East Berlin, the infamous Berlin Wall separating the two halves of the once-great city. For more than forty years, within a single city, two diametrically opposed world views have coexisted in a constant state of fear and antagonism."

Just then, an underpaid technician in the CBS affiliate

office in London completed the re-routing of the television signal through a different satellite, and the feed from Berlin was restored. At Mr. Leland's signal, George hit three switches on the control board, and the KMAX broadcast now showed a split screen, with Kathy Leigh on the left half of the image, and the Berlin footage on the right. Mr. Leland waved unnecessarily at Kathy, who had already seen the revised image on the monitor to her left.

"I see we now have our image from Berlin," Kathy continued. The Berlin image seemed to be nothing more than a ragtag collection of misfit vandals, beating away at a large concrete structure, and not very successfully, with the crudest of implements. Kathy still needed to fill time until the image conveyed the true impact of the event.

"Watch carefully. There, to the left. Those three young men are participating in perhaps the greatest single act of defiance in human history."

The Berlin camera zoomed out far enough to show dozens of people bashing away at a giant wall. At last the picture was telling the true story.

"These people are ordinary citizens of East Berlin - bakers, shoemakers, shop owners, manual laborers - ordinary citizens who now stand together, demanding the rights they believe are due every ordinary citizen in every country: the rights of free speech, equality, and self-determination."

The camera was now pulled back far enough that the full height of the Berlin Wall could be seen. Hundreds, perhaps, thousands, of East Berliners beat at the wall, evidently with any sort of tool they could find. Several ladders scaled dangerously high up on the Wall, so that the climbers could strike near the top, where they hoped to break through more easily.

"The Berlin Wall symbolizes far more than the separation between two halves of a city, even more than the struggle between Communism and Western democracy. It symbolizes what humanity perceives itself to be. Berlin serves as a microcosm of the destiny of humanity - which will prevail, liberty and the spirit of the individual, or obedience to the seemingly omnipotent will of governmental authority?"

The camera now closed in again, focusing on two men forty feet in the air, perched precariously on ladders not more than four feet apart. One man was clearly in his fifties, perhaps even older, short, squat, his balding head rimmed with white hair, his fingers short, stubby and well-worn, his boots, trousers, flannel shirt, and suspenders those of a man who has worked long and hard every day of his life. His fellow climber could not have been more of a polar opposite - perhaps seventeen years old, with no apparent need to shave, wearing sneakers, blue jeans, a white Bruce Springsteen T-shirt, and a headband inadequately restraining his shoulder-length hair. And yet these two men, who obviously shared nothing personal, strained together as one, united in a statement of defiance, simultaneously drawing back their heavy sledgehammers and crashing them together against the Wall only inches apart, to apply double the force.

By now, Kathy felt a strange symbiosis with the unknown cameraman ten thousand miles away, his pictures and her words flowing together seamlessly. The next blow formed a visible crack in the Wall.

"There appears to be a breach in the Wall. Yes, yes, there it is! The Berlin Wall is breaking open for the first time in over forty years. The Wall is now starting to crumble, that first breakthrough apparently weakening it, and these two men are now opening a large hole. They are working their way back down the ladders, opening the Wall as they go."

The camera again pulled back to show multiple breaks now being made in the Wall, and large crowds jumping up and down in celebration. The camera then swept up the Wall again, settling on the East German guard outpost at the top of the Wall. The guard stood rock-still, his gun at the ready, awaiting an order that would never come. To his right stood a Soviet official, regal in his Communist uniform, but as the camera zoomed in, it was plain that there was no light in his eyes, that they reflected the broken will of the great Soviet empire.

The CBS news force in Berlin was nearly assembled, and Mr. Leland motioned to Kathy to wrap it up.

"Ladies and gentlemen, today we are privileged to witness history. For seventy years Soviet Russia has believed that global domination was its inevitable destiny. Today that destiny is literally crashing down in the streets of Berlin, brought down not by a great superpower armed with nuclear weapons, but by an ill-equipped gang of ruffians armed with shovels, pickaxes, sledgehammers - and an unquenchable desire to be free."

"One can only imagine the criticism of Soviet Premier Mikhail Gorbachev that will come from the hard-line Communists."

"I understand our CBS correspondent is now ready in Berlin. We are now cutting to the CBS feed. This is Kathy Leigh, reporting for KMAX News."

Kathy exhaled as the broadcast cut to the network video signal from Germany. Mr. Leland stood with his arms folded, beaming with pride. A total of thirty-seven residents of Bend, Oregon, had witnessed Kathy Leigh's first on-air appearance.

Nine thousand miles away, Mikhail Gorbachev, watching a Soviet evening news report on the same story, wistfully remembered that laughter-infused speech from so many years ago, where the seeds of today's events were first planted in his mind. He smiled softly to himself and hit the remote, turning off the television, and slept a deep and satisfying sleep.

Thursday, 12:21 p.m.:

Matthew took a deep breath and addressed Brother Joel, Chairman of the Efficiency Committee. "Thank you for putting me on the agenda, Brother Joel."

Joel nodded graciously.

After the embarrassment of his appearance before Brother Timothy and the Festival Preparation Committee, Matthew was much more careful about preparing this presentation to the Efficiency Committee. Timothy's out-of-hand dismissal of his complaints about the Festival planning schedule left a few bruises on Matthew's pride, but he decided to focus on the positive. Matthew had succeeded in obtaining Timothy's permission to address the Efficiency Committee regarding the Festival Preparation Report forms. An improved form would provide significant benefit to his beleaguered co-workers. A positive reception here would redeem his efforts, no matter the battering his ego had experienced at the earlier meeting. He would be positive and upbeat today, with a clear and concise message to convey regarding the action requested of the Committee.

Esther, regretting her lack of support for Matthew at the previous meeting, helped him considerably with the presentation. She was careful, however, to avoid saying anything to indicate that she would stand with him before the Committee. Despite her feelings of guilt, that sort of courage was simply beyond her.

"I represent the Festival Preparation Committee workgroup members, and I requested to speak to the Efficiency Committee on the issue of the format required by our progress report forms," Matthew began. "I understand that the Efficiency Committee has authority over the approval of new or revised report forms. As Festival Preparation staff members, we are required to prepare regular progress reports to document the Festival preparations, but the current report format only allows a few types of activities to be reported. As it turns out, our preparations require several more kinds of activities that are not on the form, from seating to food to transportation to arranging speakers to entertainment and on and on."

Matthew noted hopefully that the committee members were watching him intently and sympathetically, many nodding their heads.

He continued, "Furthermore, the current report format only allows a ten-word description of each activity, and that just isn't sufficient. There is also a lot of extraneous information which must be included on the form, making it a three-page document which requires most of an afternoon to complete. So we have taken the liberty of drafting a revised Festival Progress Report form with all the options we have identified as being necessary. It also has the advantage of being a one-page form, which only takes a few minutes to complete, and we are submitting it for your approval."

Matthew sat down, thinking his short proposal might be painless enough that the Committee would look upon it favorably. Esther, again far in the back of the room, smiled hopefully. Matthew and his co-workers struggled endlessly with the report forms and all sorts of other issues. The progress reports were particularly egregious because the format did not allow adequate explanation of the activities, and coordination with different groups had become quite unwieldy. In light of his public squabbles with Timothy at the Festival Preparation Committee meeting, Matthew had begged his friend and fellow staff member David to be the one to address the Efficiency Committee, but David had no appetite for public speaking. Matthew considered asking Esther, but knew that this burden would be overwhelming to her. Hopefully the dealings with this committee would be different. Having stated his position well, he thought, an unexpected feeling of optimism coming over him. In a few minutes he would be out of this room, and the staff workers would be much better able to make preparations for the Eternal Festival.

Brother Aaron, one of the younger committee members, spoke up immediately. "I think the initiative shown by this young man is entirely commendable," he began. He turned toward Matthew. "We on the Efficiency Committee appreciate your frustration, and it is our intention to provide you with coaching on resolving your problem. It seems to me that we need to brainstorm all the potential options available to us."

"Excuse me, Aaron," interrupted Sister Deborah. "We mustn't get ahead of ourselves. In this circumstance, we are required to follow Protocol 17B, of which the first step is, of course, Problem Identification. Now, young man, have you filled out a Problem Identification form?" Matthew stood up again, uncertainly, and cleared his throat.

"Well, ma'am, the problem is very simple. The current

form doesn't include all the information we need, and it takes too long to fill out. We know what we need on the form, so we drafted up a much simpler version, and all we need is your approval and we'll be out of here and not take up any more of your valuable time."

Deborah replied, "So, I take it that is a no? You haven't filled out the Problem Identification form?"

"Umm, no, I didn't think -" began Matthew.

"So that *is* a no," said Deborah dismissively. "Young man, I assure you that the Committee is firmly on your side on this issue. We greatly appreciate your efforts to become a more productive City employee, but we do have to follow procedure. I believe if you look up Protocol 17B you will find all the steps you need to follow in order to successfully accomplish your objectives. Which were, umm, what exactly were your objectives?"

"To stop wasting time filling out forms and get more work done," said Matthew with a puzzled look.

"Oh yes. Commendable, most commendable," said Deborah. "Out of respect for your proactive efforts, we will reserve a spot on the agenda at our next meeting, and you can present everything at once. Thank you so much. " She nodded to Brother Joel, indicating that the matter was resolved for now.

Joel returned an acknowledgement and brusquely continued, "Now - moving on....."

June 26, 1991:

"Rat - tat. Rat-tat ----Tat-TAT----tat-tat-tat."

Bryce Thomas sighed and hung his head, instantly recognizing the familiar rhythm of the knock on his door.

"Come in, Glenn." Glenn Glass came through the door and bounced into the room, and plopping down on the new sofa. Bryce winced.

"Gently, gently. I'm trying to keep this place nice."

Glenn looked around the room, feigning interest in the décor which was quite stylish for a campus apartment. Not being able to think of any particular words, the looking around was Glenn's strange way of making small talk.

Bryce broke the ice. "What can I do for you, Glenn?"

It was the most uneasy of partnerships. Both twenty-one years old, both post-doctoral researchers with full faculty credentials, they shared the title of youngest and smartest Ph.D at Cal Tech University. They also shared the practice of staying up till 4:00 a.m., a habit which Bryce reconsidered every time Glenn dropped in unannounced like this.

Aside from brilliance, they shared nothing. Bryce, in fact, found little practical value in his own intelligence, more frequently finding it a detriment to his social life, for the types of girls he favored tended to be put off by the occasional inadvertent observation regarding the unlikelihood of diagrammatic perturbation theory solving the renormalization problems with quantum electrodynamics. It wasn't that Bryce liked dumb women, particularly, just that the smart ones took everything so seriously.

His cool good looks, sense of style, quick-witted confidence, and smooth dance moves were all he needed to impress women, and he kept his academic talents a well-guarded secret. For male companionship, Bryce gravitated to the undergraduates in the mechanical engineering department, which for some reason attracted young men with an adequate level of intelligence, but blessedly lacking in that most nauseating infatuation with homework problems that was prevalent in most other technical disciplines.

Despite this aversion to his own gifts, Bryce Thomas needed an ally of equal intelligence, and Glenn Glass was the only real candidate. In a world where the gifted were expected to fulfill the desires of the powerful, Bryce found himself in endless conflicts with the dim-witted senior faculty, whose only mission in life seemed to be to restrict his options in life, and who could not understand his lack of desire to commit to a single field of study, and in particular to support their own pet research projects. Bryce's struggles to maintain his independence were infinitely easier with a partner at his side, and since Glenn was willing to provide whatever support he could, Bryce reluctantly accepted Glenn as his academic colleague and friend, after a fashion. By aligning himself with Glenn's cutting-edge theoretical developments, Bryce had a ready excuse for avoiding participation in the plodding banalities that most professors passed off as research.

And although he would deny it vociferously, even to himself, Bryce's intellect possessed a will of its own and did crave a relationship of equals, which only Glenn Glass could provide. Oddly, despite his outward social cluelessness, Glenn himself was well aware of this characteristic within Bryce, and obtained no small amount of satisfaction from knowing that Bryce needed him.

Glenn's eyes finally stopped wandering the room and settled on Bryce. He studied Bryce's wide-set brown eyes, the sandy hair held in place with exactly the right amount of gel, and the perfectly fitting shirt that accented Bryce's strong shoulders. Glenn self-consciously ran a hand down his own slightly pudgy cheek, and tried to tuck his shirt in without Bryce noticing.

For Glenn, this collaboration was pure necessity. He did not fit anywhere in the graduate school social scene. Anyone close to his academic equal was at least ten years older and worlds away from the immaturity and social gracelessness of the still-awkward Glenn Glass, whose parents' love of poetry had inspired Glenn's alliterative name, now a constant source of embarrassment. Furthermore, he did not possess Bryce's knack for dialing back his apparent intelligence in order to relate to students his own age.

Glenn's real need for Bryce, however, had nothing to do with social interaction. In total contrast to his friend, Glenn's entire identity was wrapped up in his intelligence, his ability to conceive thoughts and ideas on the extreme edge of scientific knowledge. Glenn's intelligence was literally who he was, and his only real home was inside the dazzling thoughts which danced around inside his brain.

As repellent as Bryce found the idea of a single academic focus, Glenn found it just as strongly to be absolutely compelling, due to his need to find significance and relevance in this world in which he did not fit. Even as a young boy, Glenn's attention had naturally gravitated to that unseen realm beneath the microscopic, in the zoo of particles and forces that exist within the atom. Only when you understand what happens on the smallest of subatomic scales, he would say to himself, can you comprehend what is happening on the largest of universal scales.

But even the greatest mind must have a partner, a reflection, so the thinker can see his ideas from an outside perspective, and that was Bryce's essential role. As such, Bryce was stunningly brilliant. By himself, Bryce would never have the discipline to work through these labyrinthine lines of thought. But even when Glenn spent weeks laying a theoretical foundation for some particular concept, he would still be amazed at Bryce's ability to immediately grasp the entire vision and provide cutting insights into its strengths and weaknesses. This was Bryce's true gift, and only Glenn Glass understood what a waste it would be to chain Bryce to a single field of study.

Finally Glenn asked the question that Bryce knew was coming. Despite his sincere wishes to be socially correct, Glenn always had a question to ask when he made these visits. He was so damn predictable.

"I came up with a concept for excluding certain of the Calabi-Yau shapes as possibilities for the six extra dimensions," said Glenn. "Would you take a look at it?" He pulled out some papers.

Bryce glanced over the scribbled pencil marks for a minute or two. "This is that ten-dimensional mumbo-jumbo again, right? With the particles bouncing around in ten directions at once?"

"They're not particles, they're strings. And they don't bounce around, they vibrate in ten dimensions."

"Yeah, right." Bryce softly hummed the Twilight Zone theme, mocking Glenn.

"I know you read this stuff."

"Not by choice."

"Whatever. You know very well what I'm talking about. I agree that there are some mathematical problems with the various forms of string theory, but we might not be all that far away from proving that the theory is correct. It's not all that complicated, really. String theory starts with the idea that the smallest, most fundamental building blocks of the universe are tiny vibrating strings."

"Which you say vibrate in ten dimensions," Bryce said

dismissively.

"Well, not just me. But yes, the mathematics doesn't work if the strings only vibrate in the time dimension and the three familiar space dimensions. All the difficulties, however, disappear if we modify the equations so that the strings are vibrating in ten dimensions instead of four. It can't be pure coincidence that it works out so perfectly -"

"And just what are those six extra dimensions supposed to represent in the real world?"

Well, we don't know."

"Yeah."

"I know, I know. Hear me out. And don't play dumb." Glenn looked Bryce straight in the eye. In these moments, they were true equals, with all differences in looks, social skills, and temperament stripped away. "Just because we don't understand it doesn't mean we never will - and you know that. The hypothesis is that at every point in three-dimensional space there are six tiny dimensions, curled up into a complicated geometrical shape, within which each string vibrates. The structure of this six-dimensional shape determines the vibrational properties of each string, and hence the physical properties of each associated subatomic particle - and the effects of all of them collectively on the large-scale universe.

"So what we need to do," Glenn continued, "is to isolate the exact shape of these six tiny dimensions, because that shape will have a profound impact on the vibrational properties of the strings. The good news is that string theorists have already identified one particular class of six-dimensional geometry, called Calabi-Yau structures, that provides the correct geometry to make all the equations work."

"Calabi-Yau?"

"Named for a couple of mathematicians who developed much of the understanding of these geometries."

Bryce nodded, now recalling that article he'd read a few months ago mentioning it.

"The bad news is that there are tens of thousands of possible Calabi-Yau structures, and only one of them can be the correct one. The problem is figuring out how to isolate the one exact shape that matches the real structure in which the universe's strings vibrate."

"So the strings vibrate in all ten of these dimensions, right?"

"Yes," said Glenn, having not anticipated the question.

"All at once?"

"Yes."

"How do you know that?"

"How do I know what?"

"How do you know the strings are actually vibrating in all ten of the dimensions?"

"Well, it's obvious," said Glenn uncomfortably. "They always have, since the Big Bang. For the universe to be fully formed, they have to vibrate in all ten. I mean, you can just look at the world, and the sky, and space, and see that the universe is fully formed. It is complete as a structure. So the strings must be vibrating in all ten dimensions."

"You don't know that," countered Bryce. "You only know about the dimensions you can see - time and the three large space dimensions. I suppose you can assume that those four dimensions are fully vibrating, but the six Calabi-Yau dimensions are too small for us to observe, right? So you have no idea what is happening with the vibrations in those dimensions. Do you?"

"Well, umm - that's not what I came up here for, Bryce , I

wanted to -"

"I'm just asking a question. How do you know that the strings aren't vibrating in five dimensions or eight dimensions or some other number? How do you know that they have vibrated in all ten dimensions since the beginning of the universe? How do you know the vibrations aren't progressing through the dimensions or evolving along with the universe?"

This inquisition was more that Glenn Glass could handle. He had spent five weeks preparing for this visit. "Look, Bryce. I came up here to talk about my concept for eliminating some of the potential Calabi-Yau shapes, not to brainstorm some crazy idea that you came up with off the top of your head."

"Okay, okay. Don't get mad. It just seemed like a sensible question."

Glenn rolled his eyes. His concentration completely thrown off, he returned to his own small, unkempt apartment just as the sun was coming up, to review his proposal for eliminating the Calabi-Yau shapes by himself. He found an error in his mathematical derivation later that morning, unfortunately, and had to discard his entire hypothesis.

Thursday, 4:37 p.m.:

Matthew once again stood before the Efficiency Committee, a large sheaf of papers in hand. "Thank you for allowing us to appear before the Committee again," he began. "We have made copies of all the forms for each of the senior Committee members, and I believe you will find everything to be in order." He said nothing else, but he and the rest of the working staff of the Festival Preparation Committee had found that the Festival Progress Report form was a model of elegance and simplicity compared to the other required forms. They had gone through several drafts each of the Problem Identification form, the Solution Brainstorm form, the Solution Downselect form, the Benefits Analysis form, the Ergonomic Checksheet, and the Environmental Impact Statement. There had been many questions regarding exactly what information was being requested, and they had called a couple of Committee members with questions, but the replies had always been that a subcommittee would have to be formed to resolve that issue, so they just muddled through, filling out the forms in the clearest language they could employ.

After a few moments reviewing the documents, Aaron began once again. "Well, I must say, this is most impressive. I have not seen Protocol 17B followed in such detail in quite some time. Please allow us a moment to formulate our questions, and you will be given the opportunity to defend your position." Matthew felt a drop of sweat begin to form on his brow.

This time Brother Samuel was the first to address Matthew's proposal. "I noticed on the Solution Downselect form, your final selection was 'revise Festival Progress Report form as shown.' Can you provide us three reasons why that was your selection?" He smiled encouragingly at Matthew, and Matthew thought for a moment.

"Well, sir, our problem was that we needed a modified form. And we thought the best solution was to modify the form the way we did. That's about all there was to it."

"And?" replied Samuel.

"And, uh, what?" asked Matthew.

"What are two other reasons?"

Matthew gulped and looked back toward Esther and David, both of whom were slumped in the back row, so as not to be seen. Each wanted someone to speak up, but each wanted the other to actually do it, and Matthew was once again left alone before the Committee.

Matthew's face flushed red, and he regretted ever thinking that he could act as group spokesman. "Well, um, the second reason is, uh, we wanted to, ah, save paper, right, yes. And the third reason, the third reason, was, umm, that, that a newer form would instill a sense of newness and adventure and reinvigorate the entire group's morale and productivity."

"Good, very good," said Samuel, apparently satisfied at having heard three reasons, whatever they were. Matthew breathed a sigh.

Brother Joel spoke up. "I see that in your proposed form, for each activity category, you have the phrase, 'Preferred Committee Choice'. I find the word 'choice' to be rather weak. I believe 'selection' would be better, don't you?" The rest of the Efficiency Committee members furrowed their brows thoughtfully.

"I rather prefer 'preference,'" said Samuel. Brother Joshua recommended "alternative," and others favored "option." The discussion went on for quite some time until Deborah recommended that the issue be tabled for later discussion.

Matthew helpfully suggested, "Well, sirs and madams, I'll change it to 'selection' or anything else if you want. "I can do that right now. I can run in the other room and change it and bring it right back for you."

"Oh no, that wouldn't be following standard procedure," said Samuel. Each change request must be evaluated in completed form. Didn't you read paragraph 17.2.5.c?"

"I assure you," replied Matthew, trying not to let his tone of voice betray his exasperation, "I read every word of that document, sir, but it's just a simple word change and I thought we could just be done with it and move on." The Committee members chuckled among themselves at Matthew's naiveté.

"I have a comment," said Isaac, one of the other Committee members. "I've just pulled out my calipers, and it appears the new form they are requesting uses font size eleven type instead of font size twelve, as per requirements. Obviously this will have to be changed." The entire Committee nodded gravely.

Matthew uttered, "We had to go to a font size of eleven because with twelve, you just can't fit everything onto one page. It seemed silly to have an entire second page just for a couple of lines. It was a simple thing to reduce the font size, and it won't affect anyone's ability to do their job."

Isaac responded, "I suppose we can consider it, but the issue will have to be referred to the Uniformity Subcommittee, and they're already embroiled in a controversy over whether italics or underlining should be the standard format for emphasized text, so we can't say when they would be able to take up this new issue."

Matthew had one more thrust. He stood up a bit straighter and spoke in a more dignified tone. "Sirs and Madams, I understand there are still format issues, and we will work to resolve them. May I ask, can you take a look at the actual content of the revised Festival Progress Report form and advise us on whether it is acceptable? Our team is very anxious to write productive reports which materially advance the Festival preparations, and once we have resolved these format issues, we hope to avoid further delays in obtaining approval from your august Committee."

Deborah asked, "Content? Content? We are the Efficiency Committee. We don't address content. I don't understand what you are asking." Matthew took a deep breath and replied very slowly.

"Well, ma'am, our team is one of many whose task it is to make the Festival preparations."

"Yes, I understand that," responded Deborah in a patronizing manner.

"Well, to help plan the Festival," said Matthew, "we do need to communicate our decisions to the other Project Teams."

"Young man, are you attempting to insult the intelligence of this Committee?" asked Deborah.

"No, ma'am," said a now exasperated Matthew. "We just need a report format that allows us to communicate our decisions clearly and simply. And we would like your Committee to, um, coach us on proper substantive content, to best accomplish our objective."

"Um, Matthias, that is your name, isn't it?"

Matthew opened his mouth momentarily, then thought better of it while Deborah went on. "The Efficiency Committee finds that smooth corporate operation is optimized by standardization via the three P's -- Proven Practices and Procedures. Actual content is merely a technical issue, not significant enough to spend Committee time on."

"But you have to approve the technical content!" stammered Matthew, in a last gasp of effort.

"Actually, we don't do that," said Deborah. "An interesting idea, to improve the performance of the work tasks themselves. I'm not even sure we have a Committee that addresses anything like that." She shrugged at the realization that Matthew's idea was nothing more than an academic exercise, not worthy of the Committee's attention.

"Excuse me, I have a point of order," called Brother Joshua. "I notice that you have merely submitted a modified report format. You do realize, of course, that you are skipping over another essential step, that all form revisions must be proposed via the Report Format Change Request, Form A-192. Submit that form and we will of course consider it. Until that is accomplished, our hands are tied and we really should not even be helping you as we have."

"Well, sir," began a defeated Matthew. "We tried to use that form, but the Report Format Change Request Form doesn't allow us to modify the form the way we need to. The Report Format Change Request Form only allows you to modify the selections that are already on any given form, it doesn't allow you to add new inputs. So you can't really modify the Festival Progress Report form, or any other report form, with the Report Format Change Request Form. So we just changed the Festival Progress Report Form to be what we needed." Matthew now looked forlornly at the Committee members, waiting for their final dagger.

Joshua chuckled and said, "So, tried to shortcut the system, did we? Well, obviously we can't have that, although I do appreciate your moxie. Now don't be discouraged. Don't think of this as a problem, think of it as an opportunity to think outside the box. And we on the Committee are here as your mentors to help you become the kind of team player we know you want to be. Our door is always open." He leaned back in his chair and folded his arms, proud of his ability to pass on his experience and wisdom.

Deborah concluded the proceedings. "It is obvious that you are well-intentioned, but that you do not grasp the larger picture. I commend your team's fine efforts here, and you should certainly continue them. Perhaps we can have you back in another four or five meetings to address these significant issues once more. A word of advice: If you want to be a productive Festival Preparation Committee member, you need to use the Proven Practices and Procedures. Ooh, I rather like that, if you want to be on the FPC, you have to use the PPP's." Deborah smiled in a self-satisfied way at her own clever use of the acronyms and looked around the table at the other Committee members, who laughed and began talking among themselves. Deborah continued, "Now - moving on...."

Matthew slunk from the room and never returned. Esther cried herself to sleep that night, ashamed and not feeling worthy of calling herself Matthew's friend.

<u>April 14, 1995:</u>

"Happy birthday. I love you, sweetie!" said Eve Parson to her beloved son Christopher. "You're 25 years old, and I love you more every single day." Christopher's innocent eyes glowed. Adam put a final tug on his bowtie and turned to wrap his arms around his wife and son.

He whispered into Christopher's ear, "You watch. Your mom and dad are going to knock 'em dead tonight." Christopher hugged both parents a little too eagerly as usual, and Eve softly squealed and pulled herself free, causing them all to laugh.

"OK, Christopher, we have to go out there now. You stay here and we'll be back soon."

"OK, Mommy," said Christopher. He didn't understand all the things his parents talked about, but he glowed with pride at the opportunities to be with his Mom and Dad when they spoke to all these important people.

Adam and Eve Parson waited backstage together in the moments before their appearance at the annual String Theory conference at the University of Southern California. Their academic path had led them to the Institute for Advanced Study at Princeton University, where they continued their string theory research, and this trip had been very welcome. They had enjoyed the southern California weather in April, certainly in comparison to the still frigid temperatures on the east coast, and Christopher had of course been delighted at the California beaches and amusement parks. They each took a deep breath and exhaled simultaneously, then looked at each other and laughed at the realization of the other's similar nervousness. Tonight was a big night. Despite their mutual cases of nerves, the Parsons knew that their presentation tonight would rekindle the fires of interest in string theory. Adam kissed Eve, winked at her, and marched to the podium.

Adam paused for a moment and looked out over the audience. So many faces, so many names he knew. Most he respected; a few he did not, but Adam was too well brought up to ever admit to that. He raised himself to his full height of six feet four inches, towering over the podium, which had to be especially low to accommodate the five foot one Eve, who would follow him and was far too proud to stand on a footstool. As always, Adam wore a tan coat, white shirt, and red tie, a curious mix of the formal and informal. It was his standard wardrobe for presentations, and had served him well since high school. Eve, as the guardian of his sartorial standards, always made sure Adam was dressed with a certain degree of style, but she recognized his emotional need for a consistent outfit, his "battle gear," for the big presentations, which to a scientist are his proving grounds.

Adam reset his gold-rimmed glasses with the large lenses and swept a hand across the dark hair now flecked with gray throughout. He had waited long enough.

"Once upon a time," he began in an airy sing-song voice quite unlike his normal speech, "no one knew how the universe worked, including all of us who fancied ourselves to be scientists. No one knew how to predict the motions of the stars, the planets, the sun, the moon, the tides, the birds in flight, baseballs, or anything else in our familiar but incomprehensible world. It was all a mystery. And we who fancy ourselves to be scientists were very very unhappy with ourselves."

Elmer Schmidlapp watched from the wings and furrowed his brow in puzzlement. He had witnessed numerous presentations by the brilliant but normally reserved Adam Parson, and he had never seen anything like this. "I hope he doesn't lose them with this act," he thought to himself.

Kathy Leigh, a newly hired employee in the newsroom at KIRO-TV, the CBS network's affiliate station in Seattle, stood next to Dr. Schmidlapp, amazed at what she had been able to pull off. Despite a career in "show business," such as it was, she had never quite lost the bug for science that her father had planted so many years ago, looking up at the stars in Flagstaff, Arizona. She had read enough to understand that string theory was the newest potential breakthrough in the world of theoretical physics, and wondered if her position in a "real" newsroom would allow her access to the annual conference. Instead of writing and asking for permission to attend, as any other neophyte reporter would have done, she tracked down the home phone number of Elmer Schmidlapp, Director of the federal government's National Research Council, and personally pleaded her case. Elmer's intention was to severely restrict media access to this event, and to allow the scientists to address each other with complete candor, because he knew that the string theory movement had lost momentum in recent years and needed a shot of adrenaline, not a meeting dominated by political correctness. Despite Kathy's enthusiasm, string theory had in recent years fallen out of favor as having the potential to be the ultimate theory of the universe so long sought by cosmologists. As it became apparent that the many deep and subtle aspects of string theory would take prolonged effort to unravel, the enthusiasm of the 1970's and 1980's had understandably waned. His initial reaction, therefore, had been a quick rejection of this relatively ignorant young lady's request, but as with many older gentlemen, he quite involuntarily allowed himself to be swayed by the persistence and energy of an attentive young woman. After a number of contacts, Elmer was won over to such an extent that he invited Ms. Leigh to be his personal escort backstage during the presentations.

For her part, Kathy had to plead with her new boss at KIRO to be allowed to attend, and even then, she had to take unpaid leave and pay her own way. Standing now in the wings with Elmer Schmidlapp, however, Kathy had no regrets whatsoever about the wisdom of attending.

Adam continued with his story about the unhappy scientists. "But then along came a very silly man named Isaac. Isaac sat down and thought. Isaac thought and thought and thought some more, about silly things like force and mass and acceleration and gravity. And Isaac said to himself, 'If I were sitting on the planet Jupiter, and observing how consistent my pathway through the heavens is from year to year, I would believe that there must be a set of rules that determine my motion through space.' And then one day, Isaac had an idea. He said to himself, 'What if there are ordinary mathematical equations that describe everything we see in the universe?'

"Well, this idea was *crazy*. We who fancy ourselves to be scientists had tried to make sense of the motions of heavenly bodies since the time of Aristotle. Why, if Isaac's 'laws of motion' were correct, it led to an *insane* perception of the universe, where the motion of *everything* could be summed up in a handful of simple equations! Our unimaginably vast and forbidding universe could not *possibly* behave that rationally.

"Well, this was all obviously very silly, and we all laughed and said that old Isaac must be a foolish man indeed. But then we saw his equations, and since we fancy ourselves to be scientists, we realized that it was very easy to perform some experiments and test Isaac's crazy ideas.

"And lo and behold, Isaac was *exactly correct!* We measured the motions of the stars and planets and baseballs and such, and everything exactly matched Isaac's equations.

"Well, not wishing to look *too* silly ourselves, we who fancy ourselves to be scientists all suddenly changed our minds and accepted all of Isaac's crazy ideas, and Isaac became a very famous man.

"And so we all rejoiced and said, 'Yes, indeed, *now* we know how the universe works for everything we can see.'

"And best of all, we knew that these rules would hold for

any location and any time since the dawn of the universe. You could run a test and get the same result every time. We knew that time and space and matter and energy were eternal and unchanging, and that once set in motion, every object in the universe would obediently fulfill its inescapable and unique destiny.

"And we who fancy ourselves to be scientists were very very happy with ourselves."

After sitting through numerous interminably boring lectures in the previous two days that were invariably dominated by differential equations and other esoteric mathematical concepts, Kathy Leigh found Mr. Parson's little story to be quite a delight. She fully understood the references to Isaac Newton - her father many times had explained to the young Kathy Leigh how Newton's revolutionary laws of motion in the 1700's had, for the first time, made the universe comprehensible to the average person.

Elmer Schmidlapp was no less puzzled than he had been at the start, but he was willing to give his friend Adam the benefit of the doubt and allow him a little more leeway before passing judgment on this strange presentation.

"But alas," continued Adam, "Isaac's happy universe was not to last, for along came another very silly man, this time named Albert. Albert sat down and thought. Albert thought and thought and thought some more, about silly things like time and matter and energy and how fast light travels. And Albert said to himself, 'Isaac's rules work for everything that travels at a normal speed. What about Very Very Fast Things? If I were sitting on a beam of light, I don't think that Isaac's rules would be correct anymore.' And one day Albert had an idea. He said to himself, 'What if Isaac was wrong? What if time and space and matter and energy are *not* eternal and unchanging? What if time and space are inextricably intertwined, and matter and energy are interchangeable? What if time itself can speed up and slow down? What if you tried to go faster than speed of light?'"

Adam paused for a moment, losing his train of thought, and he stepped back from the podium. Adam Parson would have gladly given his right arm to be a fly on the wall on that magical day in February 1902 when Albert Einstein hit upon the divinely inspired notion that the *speed of light* is the defining constant of the universe, and that time, time itself, the universal, constant, inexorable march forward, could vary from one observer to another, depending on the velocity through space of the observed and the observer. Numerous apocryphal stories regarding Einstein's epiphany had sprung up over the years. For his part, Einstein never revealed the truth to his dying day, making only cryptic, seemingly sheepish references to asking for a simple cup of coffee and getting Relativity instead.

Adam refocused his thoughts and continued his discussion. "Yes - yes. What if time and space and matter and energy are not eternal and unchanging?

"Well, this idea was *crazy*. We who fancy ourselves to be scientists completely understood the universe already, thanks to Isaac. Why, if Albert's 'Theory of Relativity' was correct, it led to an *insane* perception of the universe, where matter can be turned into energy and back again, and time slows down and speeds up, and things become shorter and heavier the faster you go, and a straight line isn't always a straight line, and the circumference of a circle does not necessarily equal pi times the diameter. Isaac's well-ordered universe could not *possibly* behave so strangely.

"Well, all this was obviously very silly, and we all laughed and said that old Albert must be a foolish man indeed. But then we saw his equations, and since we fancy ourselves to be scientists, we decided to perform some experiments to test Albert's crazy ideas. But this time it wasn't so easy. How do you perform a test for something that only happens near the speed of light? But Albert himself was happy to suggest one. His theory predicted that light itself would be deflected by gravity. Therefore, if a star went behind the Sun during a solar eclipse (when the Sun is darkened enough that starlight would be visible), we would see the light from the star just *before* it emerged from behind the sun, because the Sun's gravity would slightly bend the light from the star."

The following image flashed on the screen just behind Adam:

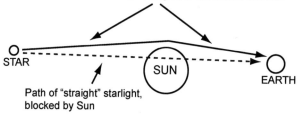

Path of starlight as deflected by Sun's gravity.
Star is visible from earth, although it is still behind the sun.

STAR   SUN   EARTH

Path of "straight" starlight, blocked by Sun

Adam paused for a moment to allow everyone to see the diagram. "And, as everyone in this room knows, just such a test was performed during the solar eclipse of 1919." He added farcically, "Can you imagine the interoffice emails that were passed around heaven on that remarkable day? The angels must have been awfully proud of us."

Tentative laughter came from the audience, still uncomfortable with what Adam Parson's intentions might be with this strange presentation.

"And lo and behold, Albert was *exactly correct!* We did see the star's light while it was still behind the Sun.

"Well, not wishing too look *too* silly ourselves, we who fancy ourselves to be scientists all suddenly changed our minds and accepted all of Albert's crazy ideas, and Albert became a very famous man."

"And so we all rejoiced and said, "Yes, indeed, *now* we know how the universe works for everything we can see.

"And best of all, we knew that these rules were eternal and unchanging for any location and any time since the dawn of the universe. You could run a test and get the same result every time. Even though things were a bit more complicated than Isaac's universe, we knew that once set in motion, every object in the universe would obediently fulfill its inescapable and unique destiny.

"And those of us who fancy ourselves to be scientists were very very happy with ourselves.

"But alas, Isaac's and Albert's happy universe would not last, for along came another very silly man, this time named Werner. Werner sat down and thought. Werner thought and thought and thought some more, about silly things like electrons and protons and the locations and velocities and momentum of all these particles inside the atom. And Werner said, 'Isaac's and Albert's rules work for everything we can see. What about everything we *can't* see? If I were sitting on an electron, I don't think that Isaac's *or* Albert's rules would be correct any more.' And one day Werner had an idea. He said to himself, 'What if Isaac and Albert were wrong? What if an electron or some other Very Very

Small Thing does *not* have to be in one specific place at one specific time? What if the only correct description is a *probability* of where a particle is and how fast it is moving - that the particle would be in one location 75 percent of the time, and another location 15 percent of the time, and a third location the remaining 10 percent of the time, but we could never know for sure which location it was in *this* time?

"Well, this idea was *really crazy*. We who fancy ourselves to be scientists completely understood the universe already, thanks to Isaac and Albert. Why, if Werner's 'Uncertainty Principle' was correct, it led to a *completely insane* perception of the universe, where particles can appear out of empty space and then disappear again, where objects are both particles and waves, and where you can simultaneously travel from Point A to Point B by an infinite number of pathways. Werner's Universe of the Very Very Small was not only insane, it was *incomprehensible*. Worst of all, we couldn't predict a definite future, as we could with Isaac's and Albert's equations. You couldn't run a test and get the same result every time. We could only calculate the probabilities of various future possible futures occurring. Our well-understood universe could not *possibly* behave so strangely.

"All of this was obviously very silly, and we all laughed and said that old Werner must be a foolish man indeed. But then we saw his equations, and since we fancy ourselves to be scientists, we decided to perform some experiments to test Werner's crazy ideas. It took some doing, but we developed some experiments to evaluate these strange notions of probabilities and multiple pathways and particles appearing out of nowhere.

"And lo and behold, Werner was *exactly correct!* We did

see that Very Very Small Things behave in the exact strange ways that Werner predicted.

"Well, not wishing to look *too* silly ourselves, we who fancy ourselves to be scientists all suddenly changed our minds and accepted all of Werner's crazy ideas, and Werner became a very famous man.

"And so we all rejoiced and said, 'Yes, indeed, now we know how the universe works for everything we can see, *and* for everything we *can't* see.'

"And although we frankly were still rather uncomfortable with Werner's concept that there are many possible futures and you don't always get the same result when you repeat an experiment, we knew that the rules themselves were unchanging and eternal for any location and any time since the dawn of the universe.

"And we who fancy ourselves to be scientists were very very happy with ourselves."

Kathy had understood everything in the Isaac Newton story, and a good deal of the Albert Einstein story, but although she had heard of Werner Heisenberg and the Uncertainty Principle that had made him famous (within the confines of the world of quantum mechanics, at least), she was certainly not especially knowledgeable about the inner workings of the particles which inhabit the atom. She hoped Mr. Parson's story would not get any *more* obscure.

Elmer was frankly getting tired of Adam's little stunt. Every scientist in the room was intimately familiar with Isaac Newton and Albert Einstein and Werner Heisenberg, and Adam's presentation was geared more toward an audience of high school science students than the world's leading theoretical physicists. He looked out into the crowd and saw a number of yawns and pencils tapping in boredom.

Elmer hoped for Adam's sake that there was a point to all this.

Adam went on, seemingly oblivious to the fact that he was losing the crowd. "And so it was, that for one brief shining moment, we did not need any more silly men. We understood both Albert's Large Universe and Werner's Small Universe. Our knowledge swept from one end of the universe to the other, and from the beginning of time in our far distant past to the end of time in our far distant future.

"But alas, Isaac's and Albert's and Werner's happy universe would not last either. But this time, the reason was different. For there were no silly men to disrupt our happy state, just a few of us who fancy ourselves to be scientists. We said to ourselves, "If Albert's Theory of Relativity tells us about the Large Universe and Werner's Uncertainty Principle tells us about the Small Universe, perhaps we can put them together and obtain a Theory of *Everything!*

"Well, this idea was not crazy at all. We who fancy ourselves to be scientists were convinced that the universe must have a single set of rules that applied to everything, not one rule for Large Things and another for Small Things.

"And so we put Albert's and Werner's ideas together. The equations of Albert's Theory of Relativity were bent and twisted and modified and made to fit inside the equations of Werner's Uncertainty Principle.

"And the result of this marriage of concepts? Absolute *nonsense!* Why, if you tried to fit Albert's Large Universe into Werner's Small Universe, you obtained Albert and Werner's *Ridiculous* Universe, where everything is everywhere all the time, and the microwave oven in your kitchen generates enough heat to melt the entire universe."

Kathy laughed out loud - loudly enough for Adam to hear

out on stage, and he turned toward her, acknowledging her with a wink.

Turning back to the audience, he said, "Well, even if you find the silliest man alive, you can't get him to believe *that*, now can you?"

Turning back to Kathy, he asked, "Can you?"

She shook her head and smiled in agreement with his point. She didn't understand all of this, but it didn't take a Ph.D physicist to figure out that there was something wrong with a theory that predicted a single microwave oven would melt the entire universe.

Elmer Schmidlapp just rolled his eyes.

"Well, this was all quite embarrassing for those of us who fancy ourselves to be scientists," continued Adam. Here we were, strutting about like peacocks, telling all who would listen about our understanding of the universe from the smallest subatomic particle to the largest galactic structure, but it was obvious that both of our theoretical universes were fatally flawed in some way, and the great truth of a single unified theory remained an unattained Holy Grail.

"And we who fancy ourselves to be scientists were very very unhappy with ourselves.

"As you have probably guessed by now, however, along came another silly man to rescue us from our dire situation. This time, actually, it was a whole series of silly men, with a whole series of silly ideas.

"The first silly idea, proposed by a man named Gabriele Veneziano in 1967, was really just an accidental discovery. He found that a dusty old mathematical formula from the 1700's called Euler's Beta Function provided a remarkably exact description of the experimentally proven properties and behavior of some types of subatomic particles. This was all very nice, but it had no physical significance, and nobody paid attention.

"The second silly idea was to change our perception of the fundamental building blocks of the universe. This is one of the most basic questions of science, and has probably been asked since the dawn of man: What is the smallest thing there is? Smaller than the molecule, smaller than the atom, smaller than the proton - how far does it go? Traditional quantum mechanics held that the smallest things are tiny little solid *particles*, and over the decades our atom-smashing particle collider experiments identified quite a number of these little creatures - some with familiar names like electrons, and other more exotic particles like quarks and neutrinos and muons and many more - each with its own mass and energy and charge and other unique properties. We always assumed these subatomic bits of matter to be individual particles, like infinitesimally small grains of sand, and since this concept worked marvelously well for all the calculations we needed to prove Werner's predictions for his Universe of the Very Very Small, we never questioned it. The absurdities of combining Albert's and Werner's theories, however, forced us to think in different directions. One idea was that instead of thinking of each member of the subatomic particle zoo as a tiny solid "point," this fanciful notion was to picture them as tiny circular vibrating *strings*. We found that if you started with the equations for ordinary vibrating strings in our everyday world, such as violin or guitar or piano strings, and applied them on the scale of the subatomic world with the appropriate string tensions, a very bizarre consequence occurred - the resulting frequencies and harmonies and energies *exactly* described the particle properties and behavior as predicted by Euler's function, which had been shown to match so many of the experimental values. All the subatomic particles were really strings - and the tension and vibrating frequency of any particular string determined whether it was an electron or a quark or any of the others. Suddenly we had a physical model to explain why Euler's Function described the actual particles.

"Mr. Euler, wherever he is, must have been very gratified at this new application of his Theorem.

"Well, this 'string theory' was all very nice, but there were many inconsistencies in the mathematics, and besides, we who fancy ourselves to be scientists were much more comfortable with the idea that subatomic particles were just that - *particles*. The idea of the universe as a huge collection of tightly stretched rubber bands just did not seem scientific enough. So nobody paid attention.

"But we were not done yet. The third silly idea, a *really* silly idea, was to conceive of the strings as vibrating in *ten dimensions*, not just the three space dimensions with which we are all familiar, plus the time dimension. Nobody knew what the six extra dimensions could mean physically, but if you used ten dimensions in the mathematical equations instead of four, all of the inconsistencies completely disappeared."

"And here is where it becomes interesting - if I were sitting on one of these tiny strings that was vibrating in ten dimensions, the rules we have about Werner's Small Universe inside the atom would still hold true. Better yet, according to the string theory equations, the rules in Albert's Large Universe outside the atom would *also* still hold true. We would have one theory that worked in both Werner's and Albert's universes.

"Well, this time *everybody* paid attention.

"And we who fancy ourselves to be scientists were once again very very happy with ourselves."

Adam momentarily dropped his storyteller persona, and felt a wave of sincere emotion sweep over him.

"And thus we have String Theory. From one simple elegant concept comes the most complete theory of the universe yet discovered. String theory says that at the most fundamental level, the universe is filled with an unimaginable number of tiny vibrating strings. In this infinitesimally small world so incomprehensible to our own, we find that what we have learned about violins and guitars and pianos turns out to explain the entire history of our universe. The properties of each subatomic 'particle' are determined by the precise resonant pattern - the frequencies and wavelengths and intensities - of the vibrations of its corresponding string. If this theory is correct, then when we consider all the universe's strings together, the interacting vibrational patterns and harmonies between the strings - their *music* - explains the universe from the beginning to the end of time, from the smallest neutrino to the largest galactic structure. Think of it. The mathematics of music in our everyday world is, in essence, the same as the mathematics of the universe.

Adam stopped for a moment and looked out over the conference hall wistfully. "Albert Einstein spent the last three decades of his life in a futile chase for a Grand Unified Theory to explain the entire universe. He never achieved this goal and he felt he had failed. We know now that he simply didn't have the mathematical tools to achieve his dream. But I recall that he once pondered his life and said, 'If I were not a physicist, I would probably be a musician. I often think in music. I live my daydreams in music. I see my life in terms of music." Well, Albert, wherever you are, string theory tells us that *the universe is literally made of music*. So perhaps you were closer to that ultimate truth than you ever realized. Here's to you." Adam smiled, looked to the sky, and raised his arm in a mock toast to his hero.

Adam then closed his eyes, inhaled deeply, and then exhaled, letting his shoulders slump in defeat.

"But alas, our happy ending was not to be." Adam glanced up very slightly. He realized no one had figured out his act yet. He stifled a smirk, then resumed his defeated demeanor.

"For as soon as the general mathematical framework was completed, we who fancy ourselves to be scientists all came rushing in to develop a full-fledged String Theory. The theoretical physicists happily whizzed through calculations of string energy, mass, electromotive force, and all manner of properties, including how the strings interacted with one another based on the their musical harmonies.

"These calculations were extremely successful - *too* successful - and string theorists developed not one but *five* separate and mathematically valid explanations of a universe composed of tiny vibrating strings."

Another image came up on the giant screen behind Adam, showing the names of the five string theories, and illustrating his point regarding the lack of connection between them:

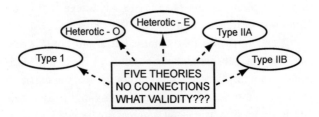

Elmer Schmidlapp and the rest of the audience were well aware of the difficulties in string theory caused by the dilemma of the multiple theories. Elmer saw the deer-in-the headlights look in Kathy Leigh's eyes, and quietly explained.

"Don't worry about the names, Kathy, they are just references to the mathematical techniques used to develop each version of string theory. The Type I Theory was the first one developed, seven years ago, and as the first coherent model of string theory, it was greeted with great acclaim. The Heterotic-O and Heterotic-E versions both came along about six months later, and the Type IIA and Type IIB theories, based on modifications to the Type I model, followed shortly after that. Our initial excitement slowly evaporated as each succeeding version appeared, because there was no way to know which of them, if any, was actually correct. And since then, we've run into one wall after another trying to solve this problem."

"This has become the great conundrum of string theory," Adam continued. "As a description of the universe, there obviously cannot be five correct theories. We must admit to ourselves that we have failed - that the inability of the academic community to identify a single theory lends doubt to the actual validity of any of the five, indeed of the entire string theory concept.

"And we who fancy ourselves to be scientists should be very very unhappy with ourselves."

At that, Adam turned on his heels and walked quickly away from the podium, leaving behind a stunned, silent audience. What was the point? There was no new information here. Had the purpose of this spectacle merely been to insult everyone in the room and label them failures?

A smattering of boos coursed across the auditorium. The scene was quite surreal. Until tonight, the reputation of Adam Parson, along with his wife Eve, stood head and shoulders above that of anyone else in the world of theoretical physics. To hear boos for Adam Parson in this room was to imagine all the U.S. Presidents brought together, booing Abraham Lincoln.

The emotion in the room was so distracting that no one noticed tiny Eve Parson making her way to the podium.

To Elmer Schmidlapp, his jaw hanging open at what he had just heard, the boos were bitterly painful. For so many years he had struggled to foster a national sense of direction among the scientific community, and Adam's dressing-down of his own compatriots would undoubtedly sow disarray in the entire world of theoretical physics. Elmer suspected that tonight's shameful exhibition would cost Adam Parson dearly.

The room snapped back to attention at the insistent rapping coming from the podium. Eve stood there, only her head and shoulders visible, smacking at the podium with a conductor's baton, which she often used as a pointer. A large whiteboard had been brought out just to the left of the podium, obviously for her use in making notes for the audience.

Eve wasted no time. She turned and looked back at the screen, which still showed the image of the five circles illustrating the five separate perceptions of string theory.

"As he so often is, I am afraid my husband is quite incorrect," she said. "The five string theories are not different. They are just different ways of describing the same underlying physics. It is *one coherent theory.*"

The audience sat up in unison. Eve paused, her timing

honed to perfection from years of making these kinds of presentations, then repeated her words exactly. "The five string theories are not different. They are just different ways of describing the same underlying physics. It is one coherent theory."

They were listening now, that's for sure, their animosity of a moment ago toward Adam a forgotten memory already. Eve continued, "The diagram behind me only reflects the five theories as evaluated for strings in the weakly coupled state. Without consideration of the coupling constant, it is true that no connections can be seen between them. But that's not the whole story."

"What's a coupling constant?" whispered Kathy Leigh to Elmer Schmidlapp.

"It's a number that refers to the tendency of any given string to momentarily break into two separate strings," he replied. "It's important because strings with large coupling constants, what we call *strongly coupled,* that are constantly breaking apart and re-forming, will have entirely different vibrational patterns and harmonics, and hence entirely different physical properties, than more stable strings with lower coupling constants, and these variations would fundamentally affect the nature of the large-scale universe.

"Then what's it mean if they're weakly coupled?"

A new pair of diagrams appeared high on the screen behind Eve:

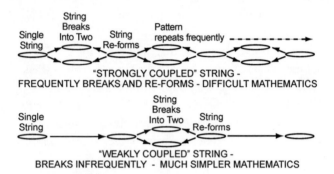

"STRONGLY COUPLED" STRING -
FREQUENTLY BREAKS AND RE-FORMS - DIFFICULT MATHEMATICS

"WEAKLY COUPLED" STRING -
BREAKS INFREQUENTLY - MUCH SIMPLER MATHEMATICS

Oh - well, how obliging of Eve," said Elmer with a smile. "There's your answer, Kathy. Do you see how the diagram of the strongly coupled string shows it breaking and re-forming and breaking and reforming, over and over? That means it has a large coupling constant, 'large' meaning greater than one, and the mathematics is very difficult. For the string in the lower diagram that breaks much less frequently, its coupling constant will be less than one, which makes the mathematics *much* simpler. All of the five theories were developed using the simple mathematics of the weakly coupled systems. But I have to admit I don't know what she's driving at with all this."

The diagram behind Eve was now updated to make the point that the separateness of the theories was based on an analysis of the weakly coupled state only:

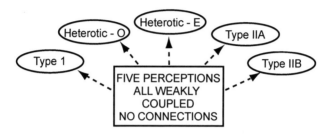

Elmer Schmidlapp took note of the change in this last slide. It did not say "Five Theories," as Adam's version had. It said "Five *Perceptions*." Interesting.

Eve continued. "The five theories only appear to be distinct because they were all developed assuming a weakly coupled state. Until very recently, the state of mathematical development did not allow analysis when a strong coupling constant was considered. Recent advances in mathematical techniques, however, include Boolean vector analysis and Sang geometries. Our thanks go out to Dr. Bradley Hermiston of Stanford and Dr. James Sang of MIT for these developments. These techniques, when applied to string theory, allow the calculation of certain string characteristics in the strongly coupled state that were formerly beyond our analytical capability. Although the current limited understanding of these and other yet-to-be-discovered techniques prevents us from understanding all properties of strongly coupled strings, there are certain properties that can be calculated."

Elmer Schmidlapp knew of the rudimentary analyses of strongly coupled systems which were now possible, but had not connected these analyses to the issue of the five separate theories. No one had. No one other than Adam and Eve Parson, that is.

Eve now began writing on the whiteboard. She wrote out a heading, "Weakly Coupled Type I Theory," and underneath she wrote out the familiar equations describing the string properties predicted by that theory. Then she wrote out the heading, "Strongly Coupled Heterotic-O Theory," and wrote out a series of more involved equations in her neatly lettered script, each line in perfect order and each letter exactly matching the size of all the others. The equations utilized the new mathematical techniques of Doctors Hermiston and Sang, and described a number of the properties that the Heterotic-O theory would predict for strongly coupled strings. There was no need for her to say a word. As she closed in on the resolution, an audible murmur arose from the audience as her conclusion became apparent. Before she even finished the final equation, the murmuring broke out into a frenzied discussion in the audience.

"What is it? What is it?" practically screamed Kathy Leigh, not understanding the significance of the equations, as she pulled so hard on Elmer Schmidlapp's sleeve that she tore his shirt. He did not even notice.

"She's shown that when you compare the Type I version of string theory in the weakly coupled state, and the Heterotic-O version in the strongly coupled state, you get *exact agreement* in the predictions of the known physical properties. Looked at this way, the two theories give identical results. They are not two separate theories.

"This is wonderful," Elmer whispered, beginning to realize where Eve was headed. "If she can tie all of them together......" His voice trailed off, leaving Kathy hanging in frustration.

Eve finally spoke. "The reverse of this conclusion is also true. It is possible to show that the properties predicted by the strongly coupled Type I theory agree with those of the weakly coupled Heterotic-O theory. The theories appear different when both are analyzed in the same coupled state, but when opposite states are employed, the theories are revealed to be identical."

The by-now familiar image of the circles behind Eve was updated again, to illustrate the newly realized equivalence of the Type I and the Heterotic-O versions of string theory.

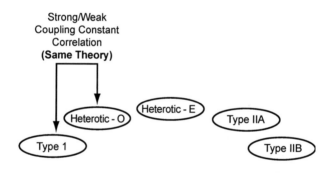

Seeing the visual representation of the significance of the incomprehensible equations, Kathy began to grasp the significance of Eve's discussion.

Stopping to think for a minute, Elmer felt a bit chagrined at his previous feelings of hostility toward Adam during his presentation. Adam's fanciful tale of the failures of string theory had obviously been nothing more than a setup, to maximize the impact of Eve's stunning revelations. Elmer looked over at Adam, who was watching his wife from the wings with a huge grin on his face.

Eve silently went on, writing more quickly now, her equations describing the same type of symmetry between the weakly coupled version of the Heterotic-E theory and the strongly coupled version of the Type IIA theory. The bubble diagram was updated once more:

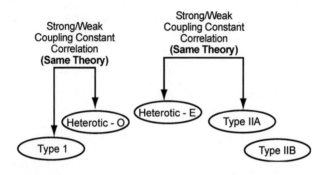

Eve Parson had shown that the Type I and the Heterotic-O theories were equivalent, and done the same for the Heterotic-E and the Type IIA theories. Elmer Schmidlapp and everyone else in this audience waited for whatever was coming next with rapt fascination.

Eve's shoulders, however, slumped a bit. "I wish there was more we could do with comparisons of strongly and weakly coupled states, but that's as far as that line of thought will take us," said Eve, and many in the audience let out a disappointed sigh.

Elmer turned to Kathy and whispered, "Well, at least it's a start. Before tonight we had five independent theories. Now essentially we have three. Maybe in the next several years we can figure out which one is correct."

Kathy Leigh was no expert in theoretical physics, but she was becoming a talented news reporter and could read body language better than most, and sometimes that was more important than all the schooling in the world. "Look - look at her eyes," Kathy said. "She's not done yet. There's more to come."

Elmer looked back at Eve, then at Kathy. Maybe she was on to something.

Eve stepped back, shook her arms a bit to loosen them, and comfortably leaned on the podium, taking a more relaxed stance. "My husband got to tell a story earlier. If you don't mind, I have one of my own that I would like to tell you."

A loud groan came from the audience, not really wishing to hear any more stories.

Nevertheless, Eve cheerily began.

"Several centuries ago, in a small country town, there lived a great artist. Unfortunately, the town had fallen upon hard times financially, and was in danger of bankruptcy. And so the artist, an aging man, decided to create one final masterpiece that would be so grand as to draw great fame and fortune and save his beloved town. For five long years he poured every ounce of himself into his great creation. At last, his painting finished, he applied the final perfect brush stroke, and promptly fell down dead.

"Upon hearing this tragic news, and knowing the peerless reputation of the artist, all the townspeople came out to the enormous barn the artist had built, in which he did all of his painting, to see the results of the effort for which the artist had given his life. The barn was in an isolated spot over a hill slightly outside the town, so that he would not be bothered in his important work.

"The massive doors were pulled open, and all the

townspeople gasped in amazement at what they saw. The painting was colossal - fifty feet high and fifty feet wide. Almost as impressive was the enormous table upon which the canvas was mounted. To avoid having to climb a fifty foot ladder to work on the upper sections of the painting, the table was set horizontally during his work sessions, and the artist hung in a harness supported by cables suspended from the ceiling. However, in order to look at the painting in the normal vertical state, the artist had attached a myriad of cables and winches to the table, so that it (and the painting) could be lifted into the normal vertical position for viewing. The apparatus for moving the table also included a geared wheel underneath so that the painting could be rotated if necessary.

"Having taken in the entire scene, the townspeople refocused their attention on the painting itself. It was not what they expected, not a portrait or a still life or a landscape, but a wildly energetic, imaginative, and totally incomprehensible abstract jumble, every inch a kaleidoscope of color, line, and imagery.

"What were the townspeople to make of this? Without the artist to explain his work of genius, the town's residents, who knew little about art, realized they were entirely unequipped to proclaim the greatness of this work to the outside world and bring honor and fame to the artist and their town. How could they carry this message when no two of them could agree on what the painting represented, what it meant, or even if it was very good?

"There was only one thing to do. The mayor called a town meeting, and decreed that he would venture forth into the outside world and identify the two most well-respected art critics in the distant capital city, and hire them to come and analyze the painting. Surely they would agree that the painting was beyond compare, and their message would be sent throughout the country. Upon hearing of the great painting, people would come from all the surrounding countryside and beyond, and the influx of tourists (and their money) would revitalize the local economy and save the town.

"'Wait!' exclaimed one. 'We are already poor. If we pay these art critics to come here, we will spend what little money we have left!'

"'And why do we have to pay for two of them?' called out another.

"'I understand your concerns,' said the mayor. 'But we have no choice. If we don't bring the art critics, our town will fail sooner or later anyway. And if we only bring one, people will say his opinion might be wrong, or biased. But if two critics both proclaim the greatness of this painting, as they surely will, then their reviews will have credibility and will be believed, and we will save the town.'

"And so it was that the two well-respected art critics came to the town to analyze the great painting. Being diligent and honest men, they decided to review the painting independently, so that the judgment of one would not affect that of the other. The first critic would study the painting during the day, and the second critic would come in the evenings. They insisted that no one else be present, and that they and the painting be undisturbed.

"For four long weeks the two art critics studied and analyzed and reviewed and pondered and considered the great painting. At last they spoke to one another and agreed that they were ready to present their conclusions to the town.

"'This is undoubtedly the greatest painting I have ever seen!' began the first art critic enthusiastically, eliciting clapping and shouts of joy from the mayor and the townspeople, thrilled at the vindication of the great artist who had lived among them for so many years. 'The painting is an expression of the overflowing potential for good within humanity, the unquenchable desire for truth and beauty that lies within each of us. Starting from a small, still, quiet region in the bottom center of the massive canvas, the Master Artist has shown light and power and hope and goodness erupting upward and outward across the painting, with great streaks of color symbolizing the vibrant spiritual growth of humanity as it reaches up into the great expanse of heaven.'

"'My opinion exactly!' exclaimed the mayor in a moment of overexuberance which fooled no one.

"The critic, caught up in his own enthusiasm, continued. 'Now, if I may begin my analysis of the individual sections and features within the work -'

"'No, no, that's quite all right,' said the beaming mayor. 'That was wonderful, and I'm sure the rest is even more so. But we must hear from your compatriot.'

"The townspeople leaned forward in anticipation at the words of equally enthusiastic praise for the painting that were sure to come.

"The second critic, however, was visibly apprehensive, and could not take his eyes off the first critic. Wishing to provide reassurance, the mayor stepped forward and patted him on the back, saying, 'There, there, we're all friends here. No need to be nervous.'

"But that was not the problem. The second art critic turned back to the mayor.

"'I do agree. This is undoubtedly the greatest painting I

have ever seen -' he began.

"'I knew it!' cried the mayor, and wild cheers and applause burst forth from the townspeople at this final affirmation of the painting's stature, and the good fortune for the town that was sure to follow.

"'No - wait - please - stop,' the critic pleaded. 'There is more I need to tell you.'

"'It is a great painting, no doubt. But I am afraid that I am in complete disagreement with my esteemed colleague regarding its meaning and significance. I do not see the painting as symbolic of man's potential for good or any of the other things my compatriot stated. I see the painting as a great and terrible representation of God's wrath being poured forth upon the wicked and unrepentant inhabitants of earth, a deserving punishment for an evil people who have turned their backs on faith and righteousness. From a dark, cold, and forbidding region in the top center of the massive canvas, the Master Artist has shown hellfire and brimstone and anger and power pouring downward and outward across the painting, with great streaks of color symbolizing the destruction of all wickedness which will surely come to the land of a people which denies their God.'

"He looked at his colleague, then at the mayor, and then at the assembled people from the village. There was total silence. No one understood how this could be, but everyone understood what it meant. With two such opposite descriptions of the painting, even if both proclaimed the painting to be the greatest they had ever seen, it would be impossible to spread their message and draw tourists from the entire countryside and beyond. What would they say? How could they say it was the greatest painting ever seen, when they had no idea if it was a message of shining hope or terrifying horror? Why, the town would be a laughingstock with such a conflicted message.

"The gravity of the situation slowly became apparent to everyone. There would be no great exhibition of the painting. There would be no influx of tourists and their money.

"The town would not be saved.

"A long painful silence followed. After several minutes, however, the silence was broken by a tiny twitter of laughter and a loud 'Shhhh!!!'

"More laughter followed, despite obvious efforts to restrain it. A quick search showed the commotion to come from a small group of teenage boys who were known to be troublemakers. They were quickly brought before the mayor.

"'What are you laughing about?' he inquired with all the forcefulness he could muster. There was no reply.

"The mayor had a thought. 'I think we should all go look at the painting.'

"With that, the entire town, along with the two critics and the trouble making boys, marched over the hill to the giant barn which housed the great painting. The doors were flung open, and everyone gasped once again at the magnificent piece of art before them.

"Despite the town's crisis, the first art critic could not resist the warm feeling of admiration for this spectacular achievement, and he smiled involuntarily as he looked at it once more. He also could not resist the urge to feel superior to the second critic, because he felt it was obvious that his own interpretation of the painting was superior to that of his colleague.

"A look of total puzzlement, however, came across the face of the second art critic. He looked questioningly at the painting for several moments, occasionally tipping his head from side to side. 'This - this is not the painting I studied,' he finally said, eliciting an even louder burst of laughter from the boys. Finally it dawned on him. 'The painting is - it's - it's *upside down.*'

"With that, the boys lost their last bit of composure and collapsed in waves of laughter, their prank finally exposed. The tallest boy then explained the story to one and all.

"'In the weeks before the art critics arrived, we would often sneak into the barn to look at the painting. We studied the table it was mounted on, and learned how to operate it. When the critics arrived, their schedule was that the daytime critic would study, and then leave the barn every day at exactly four o'clock. The evening critic did not arrive until six o'clock. So we had two hours to go in there without being caught, and since the critics had forbidden anyone else from going in the barn, we were never disturbed. The critics always wanted the painting to be vertical when they studied it. As soon as the daytime critic left, we would go into the barn and turn the crank to get the table horizontal, then rotate the painting halfway around, and turn the table up so it was vertical again. So when the evening critic came in, he would see the painting upside down. Then we would change it back again late at night after he was done, so it would be right side up again for the daytime critic the next morning.'

"The two art critics looked at each other. The mayor looked at both of the art critics. The boys looked at the mayor and the two art critics. The townspeople looked at all of them. 'What now?' asked the mayor finally.

"The second art critic was now completely absorbed in studying the painting from this new perspective. After a few minutes of deep thought, he proclaimed, 'I agree with my esteemed colleague. Viewed from this perspective, the painting is a brilliant expression of the overflowing potential for good within humanity, and I am certain that my detailed comments will closely match his observations.'

"The first art critic, now curious, requested that the painting be turned 180 degrees, so he could see the same perspective that the second critic had seen for the past four weeks. Since the boys were certainly more experienced than anyone else in the town at operating the giant table, they performed this operation, finally putting their expertise to good use.

"The first critic also found himself completely absorbed in the painting from the new perspective, and like his colleague, finally concluded, 'Yes, when turned upside down, the painting is a great and terrifying expression of God's wrath poured forth upon a wicked and unrepentant humankind.'

"The two critics again looked at each other. Both had the same thought. Which viewpoint was correct? Which orientation was right side up, and which was upside down? And suddenly the same perfect resolution occurred to both of them simultaneously. *Both* were correct. As magnificent as each considered the painting to be when viewed from only one perspective, they now realized the true brilliance of the great artist. For he had the vision to create a painting that was both an unsurpassed vision of the potential good within humankind, *and* of the wrath of a righteous and vengeful God. In one painting were two original, compelling, and spectacularly executed themes, making this painting truly the greatest work of art.

"And so the painting's greatness was proclaimed

throughout the country and beyond, and the resulting influx of tourists (and their money) saved the town, just as the artist had envisioned."

Eve now stopped and just stood, silent.

"What in the world was *that* all about?" wondered Elmer, echoing the thoughts of everyone in the hall.

Finally she spoke. "You may be familiar with the work done last year by Professor Brian Greene of Columbia University, showing that a reversal of string energy modes within reciprocal-sized universes can result in two seemingly different universes having the same physical properties. Now - a strange thing happens when we look at the five theories in the light of Professor Green's provocative insight." She began writing more equations on the whiteboard.

Kathy at least knew what a reciprocal was from junior high math. It was when the numerator and denominator of a fraction are reversed, like 3/4 versus 4/3, or 1/10th versus 10, or 1/100th versus 100. She had no idea what Eve meant by reversing string energy modes.

Eve continued speaking as she wrote the equations. "According to our theory, the energy of a string comes in two forms or "modes" - the winding mode and the vibration mode. There are physical significances to these, but in terms of mathematical calculations, the assignment of the modes is arbitrary. But when you are working within one particular model, you have to be consistent about it, or your results will appear to change if you switch your designations."

"Now - hold that thought for a moment, and let us switch to the concept of reciprocal sized universes," Eve continued, as she wrote out her fourteenth equation with perfect neatness. "In the world of mathematics, we can assign any size we want to a theoretical universe. We can conceive of a universe that is one million "units" across, such as one million feet or one million miles or one million light-years. We can also conceive of a companion universe of the reciprocal size, where the "reciprocal universe" would be one millionth of one unit across, such as a millionth of a foot or a millionth of a mile or a millionth of a light-year."

Elmer Schmidlapp, ever the rigorously disciplined scientist, cringed at this gross oversimplification of the highly complex concept of reciprocal sized universes. Seeing that Kathy appeared to be following the discussion, however, he realized that it did portray the basic idea.

"What Dr. Greene found is that when we are working with our mathematical models, we don't really know if we are looking at a standard size universe or its reciprocal. In the equations, it doesn't matter. What he further found - and this is the interesting part - is that if you and I switched our designations of the winding and vibrational modes, and the universe you were modeling was the reciprocal size of the one I was modeling, our calculations would indicate absolutely no differences between 'my universe' and 'your universe.' In terms of physical behavior, however, the two universes would be identical.

"It would, in fact, be quite like -"

"Like looking at the same painting but upside down!" shouted Kathy inadvertently, loudly enough to be heard throughout the hall. Elmer couldn't help staring at Kathy Leigh, a bit sheepish at the realization that she had picked up on the significance of Eve's previous story before he did - indeed, before almost all of the brilliant but hopelessly literal-minded scientists in attendance, who now looked at each other with surprise.

"Exactly right!" said Eve with a satisfied smile, as she

wrote out the next-to-last equation and her conclusions became evident. Dr. Greene, sitting in the audience, was justly proud of himself for his technical insights, but had never considered that the 'reversed mode/reciprocal universe' concept might apply to a comparison of the five competing string theories. He realized that if he'd thought of it, *he* could have been the one behind the podium revolutionizing string theory tonight. A sour look crossed his face.

At last, Eve completed the final equation. It demonstrated beyond question that the "universe" described in the Heterotic-O model of string theory used a reversed string energy mode designation from that of the Heterotic-E theory, and that the two were modeled on reciprocal-sized universes. In other words, using Dr. Greene's concepts, the two theories were identical. Another connection had been made.

"The same connection can be made between the universe models used in the Type IIA and the Type IIB theories," Eve continued. Instead of writing out the equations this time, she simply had them projected onto the screen behind her, and the audience could easily see that the thought process was the same. Following this, the final version of the bubble chart of the five theories was shown, this time showing that all five theories could be interrelated into a single unified framework of one overarching string theory.

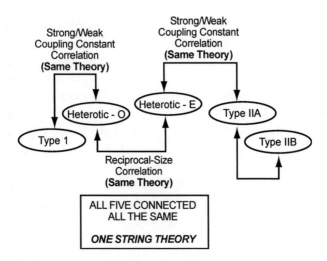

Eve ended her presentation. "There are not five separate string theories. There never were. There were only five different perceptions of the same reality."

There was only one string theory, and Adam and Eve Parson had proven it once and for all.

Everyone in the audience now understood what had transpired in the last hour. String theory, nearly given up for dead because the mathematics apparently showed that five unrelated theories gave the "right" answers, was suddenly resurrected, as in one fell swoop Adam and Eve Parson had shown the five theories to be in fact one beautiful vision of a unified, elegant universe.

As the entire hall buzzed, Eve crowed, "Let the games continue!" as Adam walked out to join her. She and Adam stood together at the podium, hand in hand, while applause rained over them.

"Isn't your mom the greatest?" Adam said to Christopher as they reached the backstage area. "Yep," crowed Christopher, hugging both his parents even more vociferously than he had before the presentation. He hadn't minded waiting backstage for the hour-long presentation; he could watch his parents in their element all night long. Eve looked up and smiled into her son's sweet eyes, softly whispering to him, "You're the best."

Just then Maxwell Cherry, a recent Ph.D recipient and something of a protégé to the Parsons, arrived backstage, bouncing up to Adam and Eve, patting them on the back, shouting, "Pretty damn incredible for a couple of old geezers." Christopher playfully punched at Max's shoulder, getting back at him for the mock insult of his parents. "Hey, Mrs. P, how about Chris spends the night at my place tonight? You guys have about two thousand hands to shake and some, uh, 'private celebrating' to do, if you know what I mean." Eve blushed a bit, as only Maxwell would have the audacity to make such comments to her.

"Can I, Can I?" uttered Christopher, tugging at Eve's and Adam's arms simultaneously. He considered Max his best friend. Although probably equal to Adam and Eve in brilliance, considering his age, Max was insufferably impish, and he loved Chris like a little brother, although they were almost exactly the same age. Adam and Eve nodded yes, and even before the nods were complete, Max and Chris were off for a night of who knows what. Although certain there was a bit of trouble making in store, they knew Maxwell would take good care of Chris, and they were ever so grateful for him.

As they expected (and feared), the glad-handing and

small talk went deep into the night. It seemed that every audience member believed his comment to be the one the Parsons needed to hear more than any other, and both were exhausted by the time they were able to escape. When they reached their car, Adam opened Eve's door as he always did, after all these years the quaint gesture still telling Eve how much he loved her. As he drove out of the parking lot, Adam leaned over and said, "Hey baby, when we get home, you want a little action? I know you're tired, you can just lay back and let me do all the work, I think we both deserve to have a good time after tonight." Eve just smiled, saying nothing, but she agreed that a love session would indeed be just perfect. She slowly closed her eyes.

Adam pulled out onto the main road, saw the green light at the first intersection, and headed through. In the dark of night he never saw the large pickup truck coming from the right at high speed with its lights off, four high school kids looking for some excitement on a Saturday night. The truck blasted into Eve's side of the car, crushing the door against her. The Parsons' small Toyota was driven straight across the intersection into another parked truck, the second impact collapsing the driver's side door against Adam. The tiny car was crushed to less than half its width, Adam and Eve being smashed together in what had been the front seat, remaining entangled that way for several hours until the paramedics were able to pull the car apart and separate their lifeless bodies.

June 6, 1996, 6:30 pm:

The letter had come two weeks before, inviting him, Jason Poe, flunky physics researcher, to the White House.

Jason entered the conference room, stomach churning with worry over the meaning of today's meeting. He pulled at his tie, hoping it was tied correctly. The *White House*? What was he doing here? Jason was one of a large number of physicists trying to make a bit of sense out of string theory, and living off an inadequate university grant to do it. He looked around the room, seeing a handful of other young physicists with whom he was familiar and breathed a sigh of relief. At least he wasn't being singled out for anything. He knew this wasn't any kind of award ceremony. So far string theory had created far more questions than answers, and there certainly wasn't anything tangible to show for the research efforts. Jason was motioned to sit at the larger table which occupied most of the dark room, and indeed there was nowhere else to sit. He took his place next to another of the younger people, with whom he was not familiar.

Jason took one more look around, trying to make sense of the situation. The room clearly divided into three factions - a number of old farts, who were obviously non-technical types, a handful of studious older men who just might have a clue, and twelve other younger people, seven men and five women, most of whom appeared to be quite out of place being dressed formally. Jason knew a few of the others as fellow string theorists, and assumed the others must be in the field as well. Max Cherry was his oldest friend, a certifiable genius and nutcase who could conceive of equations in his sleep but was unable to remain serious for five minutes consecutively. Seeing Jason, Max furiously scribbled a note on a scrap piece of paper, folded it, and slid it across the table. Jason picked it up.

The note read, "It's okay. You deserve to be here. You do better work than any of these losers." Jason couldn't help laughing. Max knew him far too well.

As Jason looked around the room again, Max was already pulling rubber bands out of his pocket and lobbing them at one of the old farts who wasn't paying attention across the table, trying to get the old guy to wonder where they were coming from without getting caught. Jason just shook his head at the audacity. *That's why he's the right guy for string theory*, thought Jason. *Max has enough disrespect for authority that he wouldn't have any problem stepping up to the task of figuring out God himself.* Jason recognized Darryl Johnson at the far end of the table from a picture in one of the technical journals. Darryl had critiqued one of Jason's papers in grad school, and Jason had been incredibly impressed that another student half a continent away had been that interested in his work. Lastly, Jason's eyes settled on a slender young woman, squirming uncomfortably in her chair near the head of the table.

Zena Dunn tapped her pencil nervously as was her habit. *I'm good, I know I'm good,* she told herself over and over. She too had worried about this White House meeting. Zena was a self-described lab rat, there was nothing she loved better that running the state-of-the-art NASA particle accelerator. Her most prized possession, in fact, was the working desktop-model cyclotron she had been given as part of a Stanford University research grant while she was still in high school, which could be powered by ordinary household electric current run through her specially modified generator. Although obviously not powerful, the little accelerator was capable of creating and identifying a few subatomic particles as a by-product of proton and electron collisions, and Zena zealously kept it as a beloved reminder of her youth and her love of science. Despite having a level of self-esteem more aptly described as self-flagellation, she knew she possessed a gift for understanding the nuances revealed in the test results from the subatomic particle collisions she directed, and in the work environment she relentlessly pushed her colleagues to strive for excellence. Unknown to herself, in fact, Zena was the most well-known of the young physicists present, her accomplishments almost better known to the outside world than to herself, such was her single-minded forward pursuit of knowledge. She only knew one other person there, the young man straight across from her, Grant Zenkman. Grant was her polar opposite in temperament, confident, outgoing. She tried to catch his eye, but he was already chatting up several of the older bureaucrat types, entertaining them with some undoubtedly fictional tale of his exploits. *Hasn't changed a bit since ninth grade,* thought Zena with a smile, and more than a touch of envy.

Glenn Glass arrived early, punctuality being one of his virtues, and waited impatiently for the festivities to start, being just as confused as Jason about the reason for his invitation. Glenn's eyes lit up when his old friend Bryce Thomas entered the room. Bryce's initial impulse was to sit with whoever appeared to be the most important political figure present and be closest to whatever excitement would transpire, but finally sidled over to Glenn, knowing how it would delight him. Despite their diametrically opposed personality types, Bryce fondly remembered the many raging late-night debates in which he and Glenn had engaged in his room at Cal Tech. Besides, something of a debt was owed. Bryce Thomas had found considerable success as a consultant within the theoretical community, despite work habits that were generously described as "emphasizing flexibility." Bryce had gotten a foot in the door only because

Glenn had sent glowing letters of recommendation to every major university's physics department head in the country.

Only one of the young people appeared to be comfortable in the presence of these dignitaries. Sean Masterson had grown up in the strictest of military families, and had been taught early on how to be cordial yet maintain formality in such situations, and learned not to be intimidated by any of this.

Silence came over the room, and the young people looked around, eyes comically wide except for Max, who had finally gotten the Very Serious Old Fart hilariously confused about all these rubber bands in front of him, and finally enraged when one seemingly dropped from nowhere onto the combover which pathetically attempted to cover his far-too-large bald spot. As he angrily swiped at the offending bit of elastomer, his combover flopped off the side of his head, and Max had to clasp both hands over his mouth to hold the explosion of laughter. Restraining himself was actually painful, and Max paused to collect himself and watch what was happening, for he was curious too, despite his irreverence.

President Bill Clinton opened the far door and took a step into the room, eliciting an instant hush from all present. He paused for a moment and turned back to wave goodbye to a heavy-set young woman who had been with him in the hallway. She was wearing a blue dress, and looked down thoughtfully at a spot on it, waving back absentmindedly. The President then closed the door and continued toward the front of the room, fixing his shirt, which was not properly tucked in. The old farts, knowing the protocol, stood and began to applaud with properly controlled enthusiasm, as did Sean Masterson. The studious men closely followed suit, but rest of the young people were momentarily taken aback, then leapt to their feet and applauded nervously with far too much volume to be appropriate. Except for Max, of course, who fired one more rubber band, this time a direct hit on the befuddled bureaucrat's forehead.

The President strode to the head of the table as Zena Dunn slumped in her chair, trying to make herself somehow be farther than four feet away from him. "Ladies and gentlemen," began the President, looking a bit flushed, but exuding confidence as always. "First I would like to introduce National Research Council Director Elmer Schmidlapp, without whose efforts, and those of his staff, this announcement would not be possible." The most elderly of the studious types smiled slightly and nodded at the assembled group. "I am certainly a scientific neophyte compared to all you fine young people here today," continued the President, making eye contact one by one with each young physicist. "Although strictly an amateur in the field of science, however, I am as interested in the origins and destiny of the universe as anyone you are likely to meet. The implications of understanding the universe have impacts on our philosophy, our science, our very relationships with one another. In the past few months, Director Schmidlapp has attempted to convey to me the concepts and the possibilities for 'string theory' to resolve the greatest mysteries of the universe, to resolve the contradictions of general relativity and quantum mechanics. He urged me to create a permanently funded core group of young physicists who would not have to worry about annual funding, who would not have to be concerned over petty details of bureaucracy, and who could spend the next several decades working unencumbered to learn the final truths about the universe.

Let me tell you," he chuckled, "there were many nights I forced him to teach some of the concepts to this tired old politically minded brain, and I think that was more difficult for him than all of his scientific work combined." A polite wave of laughter bounced around the room. "Some of you may have heard that I am not above bending a few rules and flaunting a few conventions to get what I want. Well, that is absolutely true. This will not be announced publicly, but I have authorized exactly the commission that Elmer has requested. What Elmer has done is assemble the twelve most brilliant young minds in the realm of particle physics, and here you are today. We have created an eternally funded program whose budget can be increased annually as you require, and we have divided the budget sources in so many ways and buried them so far into the substructure of the government's finances that no one will ever figure it out. We have established an entire wing of the National Science Institute right here in Washington which will be solely dedicated to your project. You are chartered today to find the mind of God, nothing less than that. You will be free to accomplish this as you see fit. You will not be interfered with in any way. The universe is yours. Thank you." He hesitated a moment. "Oh yeah, I almost forgot - we're gonna build the SSC too."

As the President strode out of the room, everyone stood and applauded once more. This time the young people followed suit with their elders much more closely. Director Schmidlapp stepped to the head of the table. "I have only a few words to say. Just for clarification, the President was quite intent about personally kicking off this effort, and meeting here at the White House was the only way to fit into his schedule. So enjoy the privilege and, uh, don't expect any more White House meetings." The young physicists only allowed themselves laughter when that of the older attendees told them it was acceptable.

"As you are all aware, the entire scientific community and string theory in particular suffered a terrible loss last year when Adam and Eve Parson were killed in an automobile accident. They were personal friends of mine and the two most brilliant people I've ever met, and I miss them every day. Had the accident not occurred, we would undoubtedly have put them in charge of this project. In their honor, we have invited their son Christopher to attend today's presentation."

All the young physicists knew of the Parsons, of course, and most had heard the touching story of Christopher, their mentally impaired son. Christopher, who had been shyly standing behind the dignitaries, smiled uncomfortably as everyone's eyes fell upon him. Then, spotting Max Cherry, his face brightened. He waved and called out, "Hi Max!" Max Cherry gave him a grin and a thumbs up.

Director Schmidlapp went on. "In the Parsons' final research paper, presented just before their tragic accident, they made a number of breakthroughs, the most significant of which showed that string theory is a single unified concept which has the potential of explaining all the fundamental forces and particles of the universe. Even in the short time since the Parsons' breakthrough, numerous other mathematical concepts useful to string theory have also been developed, and although we have a very long way to go, string theory has established itself as the most likely candidate for a unified fundamental explanation of the physical properties of the universe.

"It is clear that final string theory development will take

several decades, because there are numerous mathematical and theoretical tools we will need that are not available as yet. In addressing this issue and attempting to select the members of this team, we found that the people who were recommended to us as the most brilliant theoretical minds in the field are all quite young. This is fortuitous, of course, because younger people are needed, since the project is expected to take 30 years or more. Some of you are not as well known as others in your field with more experience or public exposure, but you are considered to be the best and brightest. In addition, your areas of expertise complement each other exceedingly well. Between the twelve of you we have specialists in all areas expected to be vital to development of the theory. In reality, the selection was easy. You twelve clearly stood head and shoulders above all the other potential candidates. It almost seemed like each of you was divinely handpicked for this project before we even started our evaluations."

Director Schmidlapp then projected a slide onto the screen at the front of the room. "We are aware that a number of you are not acquainted with each other as yet. Here are the names of your fellow compatriots, although believe me, you will have plenty of time to get to know each other in the future."

The simple projected text appeared as follows:

NATIONAL STRING THEORY PROJECT TEAM MEMBERS

Maxwell Cherry	Sean Masterson
Zena Dunn	Rose Pupa
Courtney Ellis	Bryce Thomas
Jason Poe	Melina Valin
Darryl Johnson	Glenn Glass
Serena Madison	Grant Zenkman

Elmer Schmidlapp believed in saying what one had to say and moving on. "So - to use the President's words - as of today, you all are permanently employed in a research effort to discover the mind of God. You will be working at the National Institute of Science, as the President mentioned, which is only about two miles from here. I will leave you to begin getting to know each other. Anything you need will be given to you. I wish you well."

The Director and all the older men walked toward the door. Christopher Parson moved with them, but Max Cherry stopped him, calling out, "Hey, Chris, stay here. You're one of us, buddy." Christopher beamed, and skipped back to the main table, sitting down next to Max. The young physicists, left alone together, stared at each other in silence.

Thursday, 6:66 p.m.:

The door was stuck. Just plain stuck. Brother Dunstan put his shoulder against it and pushed with all his might, but it wouldn't budge. After several tries which resulted in nothing but an aching shoulder, he slumped to the floor, exhausted. That Trumpet had to be in one of these rooms. Damn that Gabriel. It was bad enough that he got to play the Consolidating Tone at the completion of full permeation for each dimension, but he didn't even respect the Trumpet enough to take care of it properly, and this Dunstan could not abide. Dunstan had been frustrated seemingly forever that he had not been allowed to play the famous Trumpet. After all, he was the Minister of Incidental Music, he should be able to play any instrument he wanted. Even the title, "Incidental Music," rankled. *He plays one stinking note at the end of each permeation stage, and my music, which goes on all the time, is 'incidental.' We'll see who's the incidental one.* Finally Dunstan muttered to himself, *The heck with it, nobody comes back here anyway,* and found a stone tablet lying on the floor with some writing inscribed on it. He slowly turned and faced the hated door. He raised the tablet and brought it crashing against the door, punching a large hole. A few more prodigious blows and the old wood paneling in the door gave way, allowing entrance to Dunstan. The closet was dimly lit, dank, and altogether morbid. He stumbled about in the darkness, running into cobwebs, tripping over objects, lifting things out of the way and discarding them. By now he was a disgusting mess, and was perturbed by the thought that he might have to explain himself to one of his superiors. But he had waited too long for this moment, and he couldn't turn back now. Finally, in the back of the room, under a set of wings, was a small white case with the outline of a dove embossed on the surface. Dunstan instinctively knew he had finally found his quarry. He stepped forward excitedly, stepped on a scroll which was almost invisible in the darkness, and suddenly found himself flipping backwards, landing ignominiously on his large, soft posterior. It was all Dunstan could do to stifle the cry of agony and embarrassment that wanted to escape from his mouth. After shaking his head clear, he looked down. There, not a foot away, was the trumpet case, in reality quite unimposing, but in Dunstan's mind, bigger than life. He slowly picked it up, flinching at the thick layer of dust covering it. It had obviously not been touched since the Consolidating Tone at the conclusion of 9th dimensional permeation just over sixteen hours ago, coinciding with the awakening of Conscience in the Underlings. He opened the three latches, overcome with anticipation. All his life he had heard about the Trumpet. He had never understood why it wasn't kept in public and played regularly. The Trumpet became an obsession to him, especially with the city's acknowledgement of his position as Minister of Incidental Music. But yet he had never been allowed to play the Trumpet, indeed he had not even been told where it was. And now to find this supposedly special Trumpet stowed away with all the other refuse, seemingly forgotten by that undeserving poseur Gabriel, was more than he could bear.

Dunstan slowly opened the case and remarkably, the Trumpet itself was without any dust at all. He picked it up lovingly, and let his long fingers caress it with a true musician's love. He slowly fingered the valves, and much to his surprise their up and down action was smooth and fluid. All in all, the Trumpet was in remarkable shape, considering its abysmal surroundings. He lifted it, wiped the mouthpiece with a clean cloth, and silently blew air through it to warm the brass. His disgust at the resting place of the Trumpet now gone from his mind, he raised the beautiful instrument to his lips.

Dunstan inhaled deeply and blew a long, soft, supple tone through the Trumpet. Within the single note, Dunstan ranged from pianissimo to forte and drifted back to near silence, ending with a lightly fluttering vibrato. As Dunstan was not exactly in prime shape for playing the trumpet, being more into the harp these days, the tone was a bit weak, but this marvelous old Trumpet obviously was something very special. Dunstan held it lovingly and just looked at it.

After a moment, an ominous shudder filled the room and ran down the hallway from which Dunstan had come. Dunstan felt it to his bones, and it frightened him. This was not like the rumble of thunder or an earthquake, there was something that went deeper than the five senses. The experience quite unnerved Dunstan. He hurriedly put the Trumpet back in its case and scurried out of the room.

June 6, 1996, 7:00 pm:

The silence lasted for eight minutes and fifty-three seconds. In this room were the twelve most brilliant young minds in the scientific world, but not one of them could find words appropriate to the situation. That is not to say, however, that their mental activity had slowed down in the slightest.

Jason Poe's thoughts were no more settled than they had been before the presentation began, when he had no idea why he had been summoned. His thoughts ran to the literary, with a dash of the absurd thrown into the mix. *Ha ha ha - Mr. Poe, say hello to Mr. Dickens. It's the best of times and the worst of times. The highest echelon of science in the federal government considers me, Jason Poe, one of the* twelve best and brightest. *God, I should be bursting with pride. But look at the competition. Well, not competition, right, they're my teammates, I guess, but the comparisons will be inevitable. What if I don't stack up? What if I can't hold my own? I'd rather be in a lab somewhere than be elevated to this status and then brought crashing down. My God, there isn't anywhere to go but down. This could be the worst thing that ever happened to me. But what if it's not? What if I can be a solid team member? That would be the greatest compliment ever. Man, I think too much. Just do your job and you'll be fine. Maybe. OK. At least Max is here, he'll hold me together. I hope.*

Sean Masterson's reaction to the events of the past few minutes had no such ambiguities. *What is this? No introductions? No team organization? No statement of goals and expectations? Those bureaucrats have no idea of what's involved, either from a technical standpoint or in terms of project management. I suppose it will be up to me to ride herd on this ragtag collection. Bright, yes. Disciplined, no. Recipe for disaster. There's a right way and a wrong way to do things, and as usual, we're off on the wrong foot. We need a work statement, we need deliverables, we need a reporting structure. Surely the research council would have conducted psychological profiles on each person to help establish team member roles. Where is that information? Amateurs. Nothing but amateurs.*

Oh, my, my, my. The negatives of this new and unexpected situation weighed heavily on the mind of Serena Madison. Asking her to add the string theory team to her current life was like tossing an elephant onto the back of an already overburdened mule. It all seemed quite impossible. *I volunteer two nights a week. I'm helping organize the Broward County Folk Festival. I've got my garden, my painting, my correspondence. I consult for three astrophysics firms. Visits to mom and dad on Sundays. That doesn't include my regular job at NASA -*

Serena stopped herself. NASA's chief engineer had stood just to the left of Elmer Schmidlapp, and obviously had no qualms about giving up his brightest star to this string theory effort.

Perhaps he didn't see Serena Madison as his brightest star after all.....

Serena quickly dismissed that last thought as ridiculous.

Glenn Glass had questions of a legal nature. *Whatever happened to life, liberty, and the pursuit of happiness? Who restored indentured servitude? Where is Thomas Jefferson when I need him?*

Born into a poor family and uninterested in schoolwork as a boy, Glenn's interest in quantum mechanics remained his own private obsession until his freshman year at tiny Pacific Lutheran University in Tacoma, Washington. He happened to sit in on a lecture for postgraduate physics students one day, and by the end of the class period found himself in front of the room alongside the professor, sharing his own views on interrelationships between the various subatomic particles. Within a year he found himself at Cal Tech, where he was provided the freedom and isolation to explore the strange microscopic world he so adored. Given his Ph.D after only a year, he was blessedly left in anonymity, and might well have remained there forever, had he not become frustrated with his own superiors. Glenn Glass's membership on

Ba d V ♪ ♪

the string theory team was solely due to the brilliance of a lengthy paper written after the death of Adam and Eve Parson, commenting on their work and suggesting further avenues for research. The paper was so far advanced that his own university advisors had not understood it, and recommended against its publication. Incensed, he sent it to several journals on his own, and it eventually came to the attention of the string theory selection committee. Sitting here, realizing that his previous freedom was a lost commodity forever, Glenn questioned the biological value of an independent streak.

After a minute or two of such cogitation on the legalities of his present situation, Glenn tried to quiet his inner voices. Like most of the others, he explored the faces around him. He did not know any of them, and, as he had for most of his life, felt himself to be an outsider, looking in.

Okay, okay, slow down. When you think fast, you think very very badly, Mr. Glass. Inhale, exhale. Inhale, exhale. Now - what have you been looking for your entire life? Family. Stability. Financial security. Home. Maybe this is that chance. If they throw you into prison, but prison turns out to be everything you've dreamed of, you don't call the ACLU, now do you? Glenn Glass would wait to see what this new world held for him.

Grant Zenkman leaned back his chair, let his legs splay out in front of him, and interlaced his fingers behind his head, unabashedly reveling in this feeling of self-satisfaction. Too bad he didn't have a cigar with him. *Grant, old buddy, you've come a long way from Starlight Lane.* He smiled, the uncertainty of most of the others completely foreign to his own outlook on life. Taking a quick count, he said to himself, *Seven guys, five girls. Not the best ratio you could imagine, but better than usual for a bunch of egghead physicists. The girls are cute, too.*

Gotta play my cards right. Being the leader of this team could be one sweet deal. Yeah.

Grant's only regret was that he had not found a way to talk to Clinton. He felt sure the President could have benefited from his advice.

There's certainly no point in worrying about the long term, thought Rose Pupa. *Those decisions seem to have been made for us.* Rose pulled out her appointment book, pragmatically realizing that the most pressing short term activities would involve extricating herself from her current activities. She mentally listed a handful of appointments to cancel and friends and relatives to call, but found her thoughts drifting back to the present situation. This surprised her. Although it was certainly understandable that one would be preoccupied with this sudden turn of events, Rose considered her ability to stay on topic to be one of her strengths.

Hmm, interesting, she thought. *They've just thrown together the brightest minds in the field and will let us work it out - no introductions, no preconceptions. I wonder if that was intentional or an oversight. Not the way I would have done it, but I can see this coming from Clinton.*

Rose knew almost all of the other young physicists in the room. She mentally reviewed what she knew of each of them. This would be a team of remarkable creativity, but decidedly lacking in calm, reasoned analysis. Even Sean Masterson, whose strong personality and organizational skills would undoubtedly make him team leader, was not necessarily the voice of rationality. The challenge would be intriguing.

Melina Valin definitely fit into the nervous camp. *Oh, I don't like this at all. Who is in charge? Twelve of us, we mostly don't know each other, how will I get everyone on track? They must all be very bright, I hope I can stand up to them. I really hate this part of it when we all have to stake out our turf, I am so bad at that, why can't I just do my part of it? I'm sure I'll put together my usual organization tools but no one will want to follow them, and the project will get off track and they will say it's my fault because I've got the tracking tools when the problem is really that the others won't follow the tracking tools and I will talk to them about it and they will amusedly laugh at the silliness of my project management spreadsheets and they will be way off track (oh, I already said that, didn't I?) and not even realize it and it will all be so frustrating.*

I really don't understand what I'm doing here. These were the honest thoughts of Courtney Ellis, a plainspoken young woman from Grants Pass, Oregon, as the string theory team sat together for the first time. *I've heard of most of these people, and they're completely out of my league.* Courtney had arrived early and been the only young physicist to make small talk with the bureaucrats prior to the presentation. They had been cordial enough, happy to talk about the history and wonders of the White House, but quite closed-lipped regarding the day's true purpose. Nonetheless, she had charmed them as she always did. Courtney looked at the faces of her new teammates, and realized that they were just as anxious as she. *Well, look on the bright side. I won't have to worry about asking for budget. Every other team I've ever been on has worked together very well, and there's no reason this one should be any different. I'm not sure what I will be able to contribute, though.*

Darryl Johnson hardly noticed the silence, just as he seldom noticed what anyone else was doing. *So who are these people? Look at them. I can tell just by looking that they're bright. I wonder how this project will work. Oh darn, I dropped my quarter. Oh, there it is. Why are coins always round anyway? Who decided that? Some of the foreign coins are octagonal, but always the same basic shape. Why can't we have square coins? That would be cool. I wonder if there is any shape to strings in a real physical sense? Would it affect the vibrations? Maybe you could do a thought experiment with real musical strings - no, making them square would just result in an effectively shortened length at each of the corners, like four strings, not one. How could I make a four-sided string with a constant tension and one characteristic frequency? Would macro-scale strings represent anything happening on a quantum scale? Changing shape might affect resonances and overtones even if the basic frequency is unchanged. I'll have to think about that. Oh, I dropped my quarter again.*

Oh god no. I'm stuck here for the rest of my life? A feeling of dread consumed Bryce Thomas. *What sin did I commit? Why am I being punished? I have a life! Look at these guys. Pocket-Protectors-R-Us. Hey, I did my time already.* He was referring to his three years at Cal Tech as the friend and colleague of Glenn Glass. Yes, he had survived, and yes, he had come to respect and even like Glenn in an odd way. He had made a go of it with *one* Glenn Glass. Looking around the room, it seemed that in his new life, he was surrounded by *eleven* clones of Glenn Glass. He would blow his brains out in a month, he knew it.

Besides, he still thought the idea of a universe made of stretched rubber bands was quite far-fetched.

This is gonna play hell with my social life, he realized. *You don't clip an eagle's wings, that's unconscionable. I can't be restricted to this one little group, that's not how I operate, I do solo work, and I do it better than anyone else. I will not be some anonymous drone researcher stifled by a group, a bunch of nerds staring at each other when we're 70 years old.*

Zena Dunn's unbridled excitement far exceeded that of anyone else in the room, and for one specific reason: *They're going to build the SSC! They're going to build the Superconducting Supercollider! This is going to be great! Finally - somebody stepped up and authorized the funding and now we can just do the work. I can finally do the accelerator trials I want, and not be hung up by some utopian theorist techie with his own agenda, or worse, some clueless bureaucrat trying to make his budget work out by the end of the year. God, those morons were always making me run tests that were meaningless, while not allowing us to run the tests that would give us the information we needed. Free at last, free at last - thank you Mr. Lincoln - er, Clinton. We'll get the experimental verification and see which of these glorified algebra equation guys actually knows what he's talking about. Oh god, I can't wait. Superpartners, thresholds of particle breakdown, fundamental causes for the three families of particles, proving the graviton exists, and the holy grail - isolating the effects of an individual string. No more 'Hi-I'm-Zena-Dunn-and-I-have-three-Ph.D's-and-could-I-please-run-a-test-that-makes-some-sense.'*

Oh - oh - better calm down, they're probably all looking at my goofy grin and wondering what's wrong with me. Well, who cares, I'm going to get the SSC!

Chris Parson could not be happier. *These guys can all be my friends and I can be with them all the time? This will be fun. I hope they let me play dominoes. Oh yeah, I have to be careful not to bother them either.*

Thursday, 6:66:01 p.m.:

Brother Amos, sound asleep at the Sonic Frequency Monitor control board in the Underling World Observation Center, snorted at the sound of the alarm buzzer which was quite insistent but not particularly loud, certainly not loud enough to completely rouse him from his deep slumber. Opening one groggy eye, he reached up and hit a few switches until the nagging sound ceased. "I gotta remind myself to check that later," he mumbled to himself, trying to complete a thought about how much he disliked his job, but he was already halfway back into his slumber.

June 6, 1996, 7:10 pm:

Max Cherry looked around the room for the moment, chuckled to himself at how everyone else was obviously in such oh-so-deep thought, then slowly rose from his chair and walked to the opposite side of the room to the drinking fountain. He was not the least bit thirsty and only faked taking a gulp of water, then casually returned to the large table, subtly reaching for the rubber band which had bounced off the Very Serious Old Fart's forehead. As Max guessed, no one's attention was focused quite yet, and none of them observed his surreptitious act. Max sat down gingerly. He placed his left thumb inside the band and pulled it taut with his right thumb and forefinger, keeping his hands low and out of sight. A moment later, a loud smack reverberated off Darryl's cheek and snapped him out of his trancelike state, and he yelped in pain. Everyone looked at Darryl, and then at the broadly grinning Max.

"Is this great or what?" said Max. "The *President* walks in here and says we can have all the budget we want and work the greatest project in history any way we want. Well, I will humbly take it upon myself to make the obvious proposal, which is that we start with a week of deep conceptual thought on the beach at Maui. All those in favor say Aye."

Max's right hand shot straight up, and a huge grin crossed his face. Eleven brilliant 26-year-olds gaped at him in silence, while Christopher Parson clapped his hands in glee. Everyone else was dumbfounded, as Max knew they would be - what they needed was a little shaking up. He maintained his hand in the air, proud of himself for his audacity.

"Well, wasn't that entertaining," said Sean Masterson snippily. "Wake up and look at reality, boys and girls." His words came out rapidly, in clipped, short, precise phrasing, and he saw no point in waiting for a consensus to magically form from this disparate group. "Thirty or forty years might seem like an eternity, but it's not. I take my work seriously, and I expect everyone else to do the same. We have an assignment, a very large and difficult project to manage. We need to immediately address a number of items - objectives, current status, what we know, what we don't know, what we think, and start putting together a list of short-term and long-term tasks and objectives. We will need a Work Breakdown Structure, a milestone chart, and resources required - we will definitely need to coordinate lots of outside support." Max Cherry slowly reached out and picked up another rubber band and aimed it at Sean, then thought better of it.

Grant Zenkman interrupted, wishing to establish his own presence. Grant was used to doing whatever he wished, and realized that within this team, his best hope of continuing that trend was to become the leader. "No, no, no, those aren't the right project management tools, first you need to look at the scope, the strategic objectives, and the tactical approach before we can put anything down on paper." Grant saw the team members' eyes look back to Sean for guidance, and realized his bid for leadership had not succeeded.

Melina Valin was already thinking about how to develop an online interactive action item list, with hyperlinks from each action item to related project reports and associated overall group goals, but she didn't want to get between the two arguing men.

Zena Dunn's heart sank. She had several tests she was prepared to conduct, and the group was already getting mired in bureaucracy and they hadn't done anything yet. Several discussions broke out at once, each member trying to push his own view of how to initiate the work. Bryce Thomas anguished in torment over the party he was missing.

Rose Pupa sat watching everyone, her soft brown eyes quietly absorbing the room. In her distinctively warm yet placid manner, she said, "It's apparent we are a group of talented, opinionated, and independent-minded people.

That is to be expected, considering who we are. With no preparation, we're not going to reach consensus today on how to structure the project. I think we should all go home and put our thoughts together, not to mention make arrangements for our personal lives, and come back a week from now and hear everyone out. I think when we see all the ideas together, a project plan and team member roles will fall out naturally."

Grant began to object, but saw that the rest of the group was in agreement with Rose.

June 7, 1996:

Nina Owenby ran down the straightaway to complete lap number 9, glancing at her watch and seeing that she was two seconds ahead of yesterday's pace. One lap to go. It was impossible to define just what it was that drew Nina to the track every day to test herself, but each time out was an opportunity to push herself to her absolute limits and find out what she could do, what she was made of. It didn't really mean anything, and yet it meant everything, and she loved how it made her feel more alive than anything else. Today she had somehow forgotten her Walkman and had to run without music, but as she finished the ninth lap, she suddenly found she didn't miss it as much as she expected she would. As she crossed the start/finish line, it suddenly occurred to her that nine laps was quite a good workout all by itself, and the completion of ten full laps suddenly seemed quite unimportant. For the first time in four years, she slowed to a walk, giving up on the tenth lap, telling herself maybe she would do eleven laps tomorrow.

She didn't.

June 13, 1996:

Sean Masterson stood up and called out, "Can we get going please, we're already 20 minutes late."

Grant Zenkman replied, "Did we elect you pope already without knowing it?"

Sean's eyes narrowed. "At this point I seem to be the only one with the desire to make sure we get something done. We're wasting time, and I don't like my time wasted."

Max Cherry, Bryce Thomas, and Grant looked at each other, sharing the impression that Mr. Masterson was one snooty fellow indeed.

Sean said, "If the group elects another leader, that is fine with me," knowing already that this would never happen. "In the meantime, can we get started? Would that be acceptable to Huey, Louie, and Dewey?"

Everyone nodded, and the three would-be conspirators did not protest. Max and Bryce assumed that any objection would surely result in the ascension to a position of responsibility which they did not covet in the least, while Grant's silence reflected the realization that his insubordinate outburst had already cost him the opportunity to be team leader.

"Very well," said Sean. "I do have a great deal of experience chairing team projects, and I assure you I am well-qualified to act as team leader, just as all of you are well-qualified in your specialty areas. I've reviewed everyone's biographies, I hope you all have done the same. It was quite illuminating. We have an extremely talented and diverse group."

Glenn Glass, who had reviewed every piece of information relevant to the creation of the string theory team that he could get his hands on, concurred. "I agree. We're all qualified as theoretical physicists, and we have specialists in mathematics, quantum physics, astronomy, computer modeling, chemistry, data analysis, experimental methods, and even organizational functioning. I don't see any areas of expertise in which we're lacking."

"Except maybe in people who know how to have fun," sniped Max with a smirk.

Rose calmly replied, "On the contrary - from the looks of you, Bryce, and Grant, we seem to have that field covered quite thoroughly." An uneasy wave of laughter crossed the room.

"All right, all right," continued Sean. "Let's talk status. Where are we with theoretical, and where are we going?"

Various team members launched into animated supplications to the group regarding the merits of their various endeavors. Max, Bryce, and Grant sat back with their arms folded, not wishing to be forced into this team exercise, but after a time the ideas being discussed were so compelling and of such deep abiding interest to the three, no matter their feigned disinterest, that they found themselves participating as passionately as any of the group. Bryce found himself shocked to hear concepts entirely beyond his own previous thinking, and realized that his preconceived notions of a stultifying team atmosphere were entirely misplaced.

Sean noted with mixed feelings that Melina Valin was frantically taking notes on her laptop computer, even though the session was being audiotaped, as would be all future sessions. Melina's notes would undoubtedly fill in some blanks, but she herself was not participating in the meeting. The discussion coursed through topics ranging from the identification of the unique Calabi-Yau shape which defines the six microscopic curled-up dimensions, to the new forms of mathematics which would be required for complete string theory equations, to the many elegant simplifications that would be provided by a supersymmetrical universe.

Zena Dunn sat for an hour listening to the theoreticians rhapsodize about the beauty of their mathematical constructions, slowly grinding her teeth with increasing intensity. Finally she could stand it no longer.

"Wait, wait, wait. Just hold on. You number crunchers are going to declare string theory complete with no idea whether it's true or not. Don't run off and hide from us experimental types. You don't have a miracle theory until we perform the miracle of proving it for you. We need experimental data to prove out all your beauteous equations, some of which I guarantee will be 100 percent wrong. Anybody can make equations look elegant. That doesn't make them valid."

Zena's passion was clearly evident. In reaction, Max Cherry stood up and faced the entire group, lower lip quivering. "I take offense at that remark, Miss Dunn. I am *not* a 'number cruncher.' I am a 'mathematical manipulation facilitator'. You have hurt my delicate feelings. I think I'm going to cry." He then sat down with a petulant huff.

A few of the young physicists laughed, while Zena just rolled her eyes, acknowledging Max's point that not everything need be life and death. Furthermore, Courtney Ellis and Jason Poe nodded to indicate their concurrence with Zena's position, and she breathed a sigh of relief that she did not stand alone against the group. The experimentalists would have a voice after all.

Rose commented. "I agree we need to keep experiment up with theory as much as possible. But we have to realize that we are at a stage of development in scientific history where the traditional pattern of advancement has reversed itself. For thousands of years we had empirical evidence, observational data, experiments if you will, all around us, but no explanations. Theory always followed experiment. We could watch the planets move against the background of the stars, providing a wealth of experimental data from which we determined that they, and we, revolved around the sun. We could drop two objects of different weights and see that they fell with the same acceleration, and deduce some of the truths about gravity. We could study birds and learn about the principles needed for flight. But we are past that point. In regard to string theory, there are no simple everyday observations to provide an empirical data base. Zena, you know quite well that even the Large Hadron Collider will not provide all the particle collision data we will need, and God knows if the Superconducting Supercollider will do the trick. I remember reading that to focus enough energy to actually see a single string, we would need a collider the size of the galaxy."

"The universe, actually," replied Zena, very quietly, in assent. She could not argue Rose's point. The Large Hadron Collider, the next state-of-the-art particle accelerator which would hopefully prove the existence of the mathematically predicted superpartner particles, was on the drawing boards in Switzerland, but would not be completed for fifteen to twenty years. But even the Hadron Collider would not be sufficient. Only the SSC, the colossal Superconducting Supercollider whose construction Bill Clinton had pledged one week ago, held the promise of experimentally answering all the significant questions about string theory, and its construction would probably require thirty years to complete. So Rose was correct - the string theory world would belong to the theoreticians for the time being.

"But there's no reason why any of that needs to slow us down," continued Rose. "All I'm saying is that at this stage, we have to expect the theoreticians to lead the way, with experiments to follow only when suitable test equipment can be built. And in the case of string theory, that might be decades, unfortunately."

"Oh, not that long," said Serena. "The theory already has identified some experiments that might be done relatively soon that will begin to verify elements of string theory, and prove that point-particle theory cannot explain what we see in the experiments. We just don't know."

Zena began to speak, but Jason broke in first. He prided himself on being fluent in both the theoretical and experimental worlds, and knew the gap between them needed to be bridged.

"I think we're all saying the same thing," said Jason. "But I do think we should discuss theory with experiment, not separately. We need to identify the expected theoretical issues and the experiments that might provide the data to verify them. That's where the gold mine is. Why, thirty years from now -"

"You all are getting way ahead of yourselves," interjected the still-skeptical Bryce, who had uncharacteristically held his tongue for an hour. "We don't even know if string theory is true or not. We better start with that."

"You don't accept string theory?" asked Jason. "With all the questions it already answers?"

"Well, it's not like anyone has proven it yet...."

Bryce's comment set off a firestorm. He was obviously right, the top priority had to be establishing the truth of string theory beyond any doubt, but others were not happy that the concept itself was still being questioned. The debate quickly turned to how the validity of string theory might be verified in short order.

Zena tried to establish a strong position. "When the Large Hadron Collider comes on line, it will identify at least some of the superpartner particles, and that will answer all these questions," she said, trying to portray herself as calmly and coolly as possible.

"That might not be for twenty years yet," said Glenn. "I'm not waiting till I'm middle-aged and fat to find out whether my life's work is worthless or not."

"You're already fat, Glenn."

The comment came from Bryce, getting a huge laugh, from Glenn as much as anyone. Only his old friend could have gotten away with a dig like that, and Glenn had to laugh, because in truth, he *was* on the chunky side.

Glenn collected himself and continued. "A better bet is pushing to isolate the structure of the six microscopic Calabi-Yau dimensions. That will provide us so much theoretical information that it will be easy to find some string theory predictions that match up with experimental data we already have."

"And *that* might not happen for *thirty* years!" retorted Zena.

"I think proton disintegration experiments might be fruitful," suggested Jason Poe. It was Jason's pet concept, a minor offshoot prediction of string theory. Certain equations of the theory predicted that over billions of years, protons would slowly degrade and eventually disintegrate many tens of billions of years into the future. It was certainly not part of classical quantum mechanics theory. Some degradation might be provable utilizing present-day technology, and a gigantic particle collider might not be required for these experiments. The debate was now so intense, however, that he never could get the subject up for consideration from the entire group.

Sean Masterson, against his better judgment, decided to let the discussion follow its own course. He much preferred a tightly followed agenda to assure productive discussion, but realized that in these early sessions it was necessary to let all the ideas come out and the personalities express themselves. He worried, however, that too many ideas would be lost in such an unstructured discussion, and doubted his father would approve of this light-handed approach.

After several proposals regarding the possible proof of string theory, Sean gently turned the discussion into a brainstorming session regarding the milestones that would need to be achieved in the next several years. This was crystal ball gazing at best, and the conversation swayed drunkenly from one subject to another in five hours of heated argument. Each team member pushed for his or her own idea of what was most important, and the most likely avenue of research that would be fruitful. Only Darryl and Melina kept to themselves - Darryl in blank contemplation, Melina typing furiously on her computer.

Rose watched the discussion, and Sean's reaction, with detached curiosity. It was always amazing to see supposedly scientific minds in this sort of discussion, because the comments made were anything but rational. Scientists, even the least assertive of them, invariably have enormous egos, and cannot stand to "lose" in the determination of the technical direction that should be pursued. Rose also noticed that the ones who were most shy in social situations, notably

Zena, Jason, and Glenn, were invariably the most passionate in their arguments, while the gregarious Bryce and Grant were much less emotional, much less gripped by the theories and concepts that were their lives' work. Beyond all this, however, Rose understood team dynamics well enough to know that the true long-term importance of this meeting lay in the unconscious sensation of intimate bonding that was beginning to develop between the members of the group, as inevitably happens when a group of human beings struggles together toward a common goal. This was going to be fun, they all realized, and something very special, both professionally and personally.

Sean Masterson, despite his dour demeanor, likewise acknowledged a satisfaction within himself at the coming together of the group. The notion of putting together the final explanation of the universe was a powerful lure to any scientist, and to this collection of certified geniuses in the field of theoretical physics, it was positively irresistible.

When exhaustion at last overtook the team, Sean took charge once again to wrap up the meeting. He wanted to make it a point to have participation from everyone.

"Darryl, you said very little today. Do you have any comments as we close?"

"No."

"Do you have any thoughts on what was discussed today?"

"No."

"Well, umm, what do you think about string theory?"

"I don't know."

"You don't know?"

"No. I can't see it yet."

"What do you mean, you can't see it?"

155

"I have to see it. It - it's like a painting. You have to see the picture in your mind before you can paint it. I don't see string theory yet."

"Excuse me?"

Darryl sat silent.

Max could not help interjecting.

"Hey - Darryl - when do think you'll see it?"

"I don't know. Maybe - maybe…. twenty years? Maybe more."

Darryl Johnson was an odd duck.

Sean turned to Melina. "Melina, you've been typing all day. Anything you want to share?

"Umm - yes - I can show you a summary of what I put together - if you want."

Sean nodded that yes, he did want to see Melina's notes, and glanced around to assure her that everyone else did too, although he didn't expect anything coherent, he merely wanted to elicit Melina's active participation.

"Just a second - let me put a heading on it first," she said. "Can you turn down the lights and help me hook up my laptop to the projector?"

The lights went dark and an image appeared on the screen at the front of the room.

THE DOMINOES OF STRING THEORY

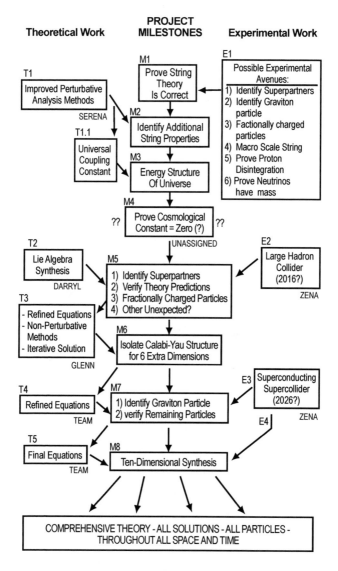

As the team members absorbed the information on the chart, two long minutes passed, making Melina Valin extremely nervous.

"Now *that* is impressive," said an awed Bryce Thomas at last, amazed that Melina had not only captured all the main concepts brought out in the free-for-all discussion, but condensed them into a literal roadmap to the future as she went. This woman could compartmentalize a hurricane. "How did you put that together so fast?"

Melina, much relieved, smiled slyly. "Practice."

In addition to making a excellent first impression in general, Melina Valin had, instantly and quite unknowingly, become one of Jason Poe's favorite people. In the six hours of discussion, he had only squeezed in one mention of proton degradation, and no one else had exhibited the slightest interest in the subject. But there it was, captured as Sub-Item 5 in Block E1 of Melina's diagram. She had incorporated it into the team's plan as one potential avenue for proving string theory to be correct. Tracking the entire project would obviously be Melina's responsibility from this point on. Jason took great comfort in the realization that if he coordinated his work with her, his pet projects would not get lost in the shuffle, as so often happened in the all-too-bureaucratic world of scientific research.

"Please go through your chart, Melina. It will be a good summary for all of us," said an equally impressed Sean, realizing that he would have a much-needed ally in keeping this monumental project focused.

"All right," responded Melina tentatively. She stood up a bit straighter, feeling a boost in confidence upon seeing the support of the others. Melina did not doubt her own abilities, but she knew she lacked that certain something in her personality in terms of convincing others to take her position in debates. Melina was five feet eight inches tall, thin, almost gangly, with a smooth, pale complexion. In terms of pure physical appearance, she carried a somewhat regal demeanor as a result of her height, her long white neck that was entirely visible due to her very short, almost boyish hairstyle, and the amusedly detached look in her eyes that hinted at a sly humor within. Her aversion to any sort of interpersonal conflict, however, revealed itself as a girlish tentativeness in confrontational situations, and she assiduously avoided them, aware that she would never be a "mover and a shaker," and with no desire to be so.

Melina consciously lowered her voice and spoke more slowly. For the next thirty minutes she succinctly summarized each project milestone and the tasks required to accomplish each one, as well as the multitude of interrelationships between them. As she became immersed in the details, she forgot her shyness and transformed into an animated, passionate speaker, convincingly articulating her own vision of the entire project. "I think we all see string theory development as an ongoing feedback cycle between theory, experiment, and the project milestones," she concluded. "Our current understanding of the theory suggests certain experiments. As we move forward, in particular when the Large Hadron Collider and then the Superconducting Supercollider come on line, the results of these experiments will undoubtedly validate some concepts while refuting others, and will point toward refinements in the theoretical equations. These new equations will then suggest additional experiments, and the developmental pattern will repeat itself until we finally see the total picture at the end."

Melina looked at Sean. "Oh - I apologize for not including

administrative aspects of the project in the diagram."

Sean resisted the urge to roll his eyes. Bryce and Grant decided that Melina was something of a head case.

Rose said what everyone was thinking. "This is a great overview of where we need to go. The big question is, 'Will we reach the end in twenty years or in two hundred years?'"

The significance of their entire lives depended on the answer, and it was an answer that none of them possessed.

As Melina concluded her summary of the project flow diagram, Grant said, "I don't get your title. 'The dominoes of string theory?' What's that about?"

"Oh," she said, bashfully. "Visually the chart reminded me of a branched pattern of dominoes, lined up and ready to be pushed over so they all fall in sequence. And I thought that was appropriate, because we can't succeed until we can get every piece of the theory to come together as one. Someday, when we finally see the ten-dimensional synthesis of the entire theory, I think it will be just like dominoes, as all the conclusions fall out at once. I hope we all live to see that day."

At the mention of dominoes, Christopher Parson, who had sat silent for the entire meeting, smiled brightly and clapped several times. "Yep - dominoes. It will be just like dominoes!" Everyone laughed, and agreed that Chris should be given the honor of making the restaurant choice that night, asking him to do it quickly because they were all starved.

Bad Vibes

<u>July 20, 1996, 12:05 am:</u>

It was obvious from the start that Max Cherry, Bryce Thomas, and Grant Zenkman were going to be fast friends. They shared an attitude of disrespect toward any authority figure, and considered the greatest waste in life to be a single moment without fun. Their overall intensity toward life carried over to their fascination with the nature of reality at the Planck scale, that most microscopic of worlds deep within the subatomic realm. Theirs was not a poet's rapture of the meaning and beauty behind it all, but rather a little boy's curiosity at what life was like for bugs. For "little boys" of their intellect, however, the bugs were not tiny crawly creatures, but were instead the electrons and quarks and muons and photons and neutrinos that populate the universe. After only a few weeks with the team, they would frequently arrive at the study center in the late morning, drawing rolled eyes from their far more buttoned-down teammates. Long after everyone else had gone home at night, however, Max, Bryce, and Grant hotly debated the correctness of their latest mathematical model (while simultaneously shooting each other with Silly String).

On this, their latest night staying up together, Bryce suddenly paused and looked at the clock. It was just passing midnight.

"Hey, today is the day," said Bryce. "July 20. Conception day."

"What are you talking about?" asked Max quizzically. "You mean the moon walk - right?" (It was, of course, the anniversary of Neil Armstrong's walk on the moon in 1969.)

"Oh, for me, it's a lot more than that. My parents told me that when they finally turned off the TV that night, they were

161

so moved by the whole experience that there was nothing for them to do but make love. And that's when I was conceived. So whenever I see those old films showing "One small step for a man," all I can think of is my parents going at it. Kinda weirds me out, you know?"

Grant asked, "Hey, when is your birthday?"

"April 22nd."

"1970, right?"

"Yeah."

"Hey, mine is the 16th."

"And mine is the 23rd," said Max with fascination.

Max put an arm around each of his new friends. "We're practically triplets. Let me buy you guys a beer and we'll call it a night, okay?"

July 20, 1996, 7:00 am:

As happened more often than not on their forays to the local bars, Max Cherry, Bryce Thomas, and Grant Zenkman never did call it a night, and stumbled into the 7:00 a.m. meeting the next morning without having gotten any sleep. As he sat in his chair waiting for the progress meeting to start, Max decided the only way to snap himself out of his funk was to have a little fun with the juicy tidbit of gossip he'd been told only hours before.

As Sean stood up before the group to kick off the meeting, Max interrupted. "Hey, what image do we all think of when we think of July 20th?" he asked brightly.

Bryce dropped his head in his hands and smiled ruefully, knowing what was coming. *I knew I should have kept that to myself,* he thought.

Darryl answered warily, "The moon landing -- right?"

Max slowly stood, spread his arms, and began to speak with great élan. "Wrong, way wrong, my befuddled friend. I just found out about this last night, and I feel compelled to share it. The answer is - drum roll - Bryce Thomas's parents humping away, really going at it. Yes, my friends, 27 years ago today there was an exchange of bodily fluids that resulted in our friend Bryce's presence with us today. Let's hear it for Mr. and Mrs. Thomas!"

Most of the group howled with laughter. Serena Madison and Jason Poe, however, felt their jaws drop. After the laughter died down, Serena gathered herself and said, "Uh, you won't believe this, but that's what my parents told me too. They said they made love after the moon walk, and that's when I was conceived."

Jason now felt his face flush, as the group stared at Serena. Before anyone could speak, Jason quietly said, "Me too, guys. My dad went out of town for an extended business trip the next day, so that's how my parents are sure that's when it happened."

The entire room sat silent. The odds were astronomical. How could three of this elite group of twelve have been conceived on the same day - in fact, within an hour or two of each other? Grant looked around, his brilliant though sophomorically inclined mind picturing all these couples simultaneously conjoined in all manner of erotic positions. His eyes met those of each of the other team members. He had thought it odd from the start that all of them were so close in age. He knew they did not share the same birthday, but they were all within a few weeks of each other in age. The lascivious images receded momentarily from the forefront of his consciousness, and he considered the remote likelihood of such a narrow age range occurring by random chance.

"That's what my mom and dad said too," remembered Christopher Parson suddenly. "They said that's when my dad's seed went into my mom's egg."

By that afternoon, every team member had called their parents or closest living relative, quizzing in a most pointed way about their own conception. When the team met again, nine of the twelve were able to confirm at least a strong likelihood that their conception had occurred within hours of the first moon landing, and none was able to rule it out.

Grant's imagination reeled at the imagery.

<u>January 12, 1997:</u>

The red light on Camera 2 came on, and Kathy Leigh turned toward it and smiled the personable yet professional smile she had perfected in the last eight years. She was tired, ready for the weekend, and glad to be finishing up the evening newscast. Had she realized her dreams? Not exactly. Not as the cute and perky "Entertainment Girl," getting forty-five seconds of airtime at the end of the Friday late-night news, plus a whopping ninety seconds each morning at 6:18 a.m. A serious journalist she definitely was not. Yep, she was eye candy, all right, but that was the reality of the business. Oh well, she had made it out of Bend, Oregon, and was on the air. A lot of other girls couldn't say that. She was still only 25, and there still might be a good break someday, hopefully before she lost her looks anyway. "Our closing story this evening just might signal the end of the universe," Kathy said, laughing gently. "I'm not sure what this says about American society, but the latest Nielsen ratings were released today, and the Jerry Springer show, whose ratings were spiraling downward only 18 months ago, this week officially beat out Oprah Winfrey as the number one daytime TV talk show." The camera left Kathy as the producer cut to a quick couple of shots from the Springer show, one with an anatomically impossible woman ripping off her blouse, another with two men punching each other who appeared to be closer to Neanderthal than human. The camera switched back to Kathy and she shook her head with a smile, and said, "Oh my. Edward R. Murrow must be rolling over in his grave." She had ad-libbed that last line, and she cringed a bit as she remembered how her producer hated that, especially when she invoked a name not likely to be found in the National Enquirer. "Industry experts have no reason for the sudden turnaround of the Springer show and other 'trash talk' shows, as this reverses a trend toward more sophisticated programming that had been occurring in recent years. I guess the days of good taste are gone forever. What could be next in television entertainment? Scary to think about, isn't it? This is Kathy Leigh with the KIRO Late Night News in Seattle, good night." She involuntarily let out a sigh.

April 17, 1997:

Christopher Parson clapped his hands.

Courtney Ellis uttered, "Oh my, how pretty!"

Serena Madison gushed, "Oh my heavens. This is the most beautiful, glorious, enchanting sight there has ever been!" With that, she twirled around and around the intersection of two walkways, her full skirt billowing outward as onlookers gawked at the free-spirited young woman.

It was springtime in Washington, D.C., and the three young people were enjoying a long walk through one of the beautiful parks of the city on a cloudless, windy day, as Washington's renowned cherry blossoms filled the air, floating on the breezes, seeming to settle as much on the hair of the passers-by as on the ground. The delicate, weightless white blossoms, set against the deep blue sky, were enough to melt the heart of even the most jaded resident of the Washington political scene.

Serena, instantly recognizing that she was in her usual position as the center of attention, took to flight. Five feet eight inches tall, with strong features and a large mane of dark cascading hair curling to her shoulders, she took on the air of a carefree gypsy woman, spinning up to an elderly gentleman and his wife. With a wordless gesture she conveyed her message of harmless fun to the wife, who graciously allowed her husband a momentary dance with the effervescent young woman. As the dapper and surprisingly nimble gentleman stepped lightly around the red brick walkway, gently directing Serena but never restricting her flowing motion, she made it a point to surreptitiously sweep up close to him, brushing her curvaceous form against him, providing him a sweetly naughty moment, of which she was sure he would never speak but always remember.

After returning the lucky gentleman to his sporting wife, Serena motioned to Courtney to join her. Courtney, however, frantically shook her head and gestured no, more than happy to project herself vicariously onto the outsize personality of Serena Madison.

Serena then flashed an imploring look at Christopher, not really expecting him to respond, but he picked up the signal and surprised everyone by gallantly stepping up to a young mother and her daughter, bowing deeply before them, receiving permission from the mother, and then sweetly bending down to lead the little girl in a waltz. Even Serena stopped at the precious sight of Christopher motioning the girl to stand on his feet, and laughed as she literally floated across the bricks, carried by his hands and feet. An appreciative wave of laughter wafted through the now-substantial crowd as Christopher lightly lifted the girl high into the air and gently deposited her back into the arms of her mother, leaving the blushing girl with a kiss on the cheek.

Christopher, Courtney, and Serena resumed their walk, seeking the densest concentration of cherry blossoms they could find.

"That was wonderful," exclaimed Courtney, not sure whether she was more impressed by Serena or Chris.

"Oh, Courtney, how can you not dance?" asked Serena, still out of breath. "It's so freeing."

"Yes - a little *too* freeing, at least in public like that," laughed Courtney. "I'm more than happy watching you."

With Christopher seemingly not paying attention as he repeatedly paused to look at leaves or insects on the ground, Serena sidled up next to Courtney.

"Did you see my, umm, my little gift for that nice old gentleman?" she whispered softly. "He was so sweet, I thought he deserved a little fun." She grinned wickedly.

"Oh, yes, I noticed," said Courtney, who never missed a thing. "He'll go to bed with a smile on his face tonight."

"Yeah, big smile," said Christopher absently from at least ten feet away, and the two women looked first at him, then at each other, eyes wide in amazement.

A minute or so later the conversation resumed, Serena

asking, "How do you like the project so far, Courtney?"

"Well, it was a little hard at first. I'm not intense like most of the rest of you. None of this is life and death for me, like it is for Jason and Zena. I could never be like that."

Serena grimaced and touched Courtney's arm. "I agree - I think the two of them are quite enough. Can I ask you something? I know I'm way over the top with all my histrionics. I hope I don't make you uncomfortable."

"Oh no, you're wonderful, you're probably my best friend, Serena. You do all the things I wish I could do."

"Then why don't you just do them?"

"Oh, that just wouldn't be me. I wouldn't want to be out there like that."

Serena, having walked all morning with Courtney and Christopher, and kept up her "diva" persona all that time, finally began to tire of being the center of attention, something that only happened in moments of extreme fatigue.

"You know, Courtney, you and I have never really talked much, and you don't say a lot in the meetings. I don't know anything about your background. I'm not even sure what you're working on."

Serena, in fact, wondered what Courtney contributed, if anything. Courtney was obviously not the team's specialist in any technical field, and appeared not to make any visible contribution, as far as Serena could see.

Courtney already knew what Serena was thinking.

"I'm not sure myself," Courtney replied, still formulating her thoughts in an effort to both defend herself and be diplomatic. "I got my Ph.D in applied physics, but my research was sort of a mishmash of math concepts, theoretical applications, and experimental work. I did a lot of work on several intercollegiate technical development teams, so much of my university experience was team-oriented, rather than solo research. Through all that I picked up a fairly broad range of experience, and because of that, if anyone on the team discusses their work, I can follow it, but everyone else knows their field better than I do."

Unknown to Courtney, her selection to the string theory team had been based entirely on her contribution to the interdisciplinary teams from various universities, rather than remarkable capability in any specific technical field. Elmer Schmidlapp, in his role as National Research Council director, had closely followed the progress of these teams, and personally insisted that the young Courtney Ellis's subtle but strongly positive contributions to team-building be a part of the string theory team.

"Oh - oh - look. Aren't those great shoes?" Courtney pointed at a pair of red open-toed sandals, with interlaced spaghetti straps swirling up to the mid-calf of a passing teenage girl, who was desperately trying to break into the most desirable social circles at her school. For seven minutes the conversation diverted to an exploration of fashion, body types, and personality.

Finally, Serena returned to her original train of thought. "So what *are* you working on?"

Courtney would have preferred that the subject of conversation not be herself, but it seemed unavoidable.

"A lot of little jobs supporting the others, mostly."

"Like what?"

"Oh, let's see. You know how Melina is constantly updating and revising her tracking system and results database. She is really paranoid about releasing something that might be difficult for all of you to input your results into."

"Really? Why? She's set up a great system. I don't have

any problems using it, and the data retrieval capability is unbelievable. She's got it so I can tap into the databanks of every major university in the world."

"I know, I know. I just act as her test subject and sounding board. I try out all the features, and sometimes I make a suggestion or two. She's a little, well, fragile, and wants somebody to lean on a little bit. I guess I'm non-threatening because I'm not as much of a genius as the rest of you."

"What else?"

"Well, let me think. A lot of the time what I'm doing is almost more social work than technical, really. I mean, you've got the three nutcase types to start with - Jason, Zena, and Melina."

Serena nodded her head and laughed in recognition.

"They are so brilliant. And none of them thinks they are good enough. I guess that's common, but they torture themselves. It's kind of sad. I don't see how you have that much emotional commitment and not burn out. This is a great job, but in the end it's just a job."

Serena nodded again, seeing Courtney's point, but was not quite willing to admit to herself that solving the ultimate mystery of the universe was "just a job."

"I spend a lot of time with the three of them, trying to provide a counterbalance to their anxiety levels with a more stable presence. Then on the opposite extreme are the three jokers - Bryce, Grant, and Max. They are such a kick to hang out with. We go out a lot together at night, especially Bryce and Grant."

"So basically it's just party time?" asked Serena tentatively.

"You have to understand. They see Sean as the mean old Catholic school headmaster, always wanting to rap their knuckles with a ruler, and Melina as the police officer with a speed gun, tracking everything they do and constantly assigning action items. That's not how Melina intends it, but that's their perception, although they'd never say so. So to them, it's like Big Brother is watching all the time. They feel really isolated, like nobody else understands how they feel. So I'm somebody who's sort of outside their little gang that they can talk to and not feel like they're being graded. And a lot of the time some of the technical stuff comes into play too. Those three, especially Bryce and Grant, can't talk to Sean and Melina at all, and sometimes have a hard time carrying on a discussion with Jason and Zena because they're wound up so tight. And forget about Darryl. So when we get together, I can act as sort of a bridge between the joker group and the others and help ideas get shared.

"You said 'especially Bryce and Grant' twice. What about Max?"

"Max is a little different. Max may enjoy the role of the court jester, but deep down he is madly in love with string theory. When you get him alone, he's a lot more like Jason than he would ever admit. He'll talk about the equations like they are the different features of the most beautiful woman in the world. He and Jason may seem like opposites, but they share that love, and that's why they've been friends since childhood. Max might not show it, but he is terribly ambitious about succeeding, maybe even more than Sean. It will kill him if this project fails.

"Bryce is a trip. He thinks he's God's gift to the world of physics, and he may be right. It all comes so much easier to him than anyone else. He doesn't work half as hard as most of the others, but you know what? He probably doesn't have to."

Serena stiffened slightly at the mention of Bryce's prodigious talent. Courtney noticed, aware that Bryce's singular brilliance threatened the primacy of the attention-craving Serena, who preferred not to share the limelight.

"Grant is an odd character. He is brilliant and he has a heart of gold, but he has no clue what other people are thinking. He would give you the shirt off his back if you asked, but if you didn't say anything, he probably wouldn't notice if you were standing next to him stark naked."

Seeing Serena's reaction, Courtney amended her statement. "Well, he'd probably notice *you*, Serena," Courtney said, laughing, referring to Serena's voluptuous figure as well as to Grant's well-documented puerile instincts, his outlook on matters of sex apparently never having evolved beyond that of a thirteen-year-old boy.

"Do you talk to Darryl at all?" asked Serena. "I wouldn't have the slightest idea what to say to him."

"Oh sure, all the time. But it's kind of a one-way conversation. I talk, he listens. Usually while he's writing out equations."

"Doesn't he mind? Oh, probably not, he's off in his own little Zen world. In the meetings, he's not ever aware of what's being said."

"Don't be so sure," replied Courtney. "He's aware of more than you think." Courtney looked at Christopher, thinking the same thing about him. "Darryl doesn't talk much, but sometimes he needs someone there."

"I guess it's good to have Sean as the leader. With all these personality cases, we need somebody who's got their act together."

"Don't be too sure about that either. Sean's got his demons. Oh, let's see, who's left? Rose and Glenn are probably the most like me, but they're both better at the technical side of things. Glenn likes to help like I do, but although it doesn't show, he puts a lot more emotion into it. And Rose? Rose just puts ideas together like no one else."

Serena cast a sideways glance at Courtney. By now they had completed the return trip back to the National Science Institute, and stood just outside the main entrance. "So, Courtney. You certainly have everyone else figured out - what about *me*?"

Serena, three inches taller than Courtney, stood up to her full height, put her hands on her hips, and stared into Courtney's eyes with a look of pointed inquisition.

"You?" Courtney hesitated a moment. "Underneath that big dramatic public personality, you might be the most instinctively gifted technical mind we have, other than perhaps Bryce. You just get things more quickly than anyone else."

This was true enough, but what Courtney did not say was that Serena's need to be the "star" was not necessarily a strength, and that Courtney willingly propped up Serena's ego by playing the role of adoring audience. If that was what Serena needed, she would do it, and there was no need to talk about that.

Fatigued from the day's walk, Serena, Courtney, and Christopher eschewed the stairs and took the elevator to the team's offices on the sixth floor. Hearing the voices of the other team members as the elevator doors opened, Serena found herself instantly re-energized. She launched into the chorus of "I Could Have Danced All Night" from *My Fair Lady* and waltzed herself around the room, instantly putting an end to all conversation.

<u>June 9, 1997:</u>

The twenty-seven year old Max Cherry, accompanied by his close friend Grant Zenkman, exited the American Airlines Boeing 757 and quickly walked up the exit ramp from the airplane. Before Max even had a chance to search out the faces in the terminal, an eager young hand thrust toward him.

"Welcome to Seattle!" said Kathy Leigh excitedly. She had obtained a photograph of Max and recognized him instantly.

Max gave her his warmest smile, shook her hand, and said, "Great to meet you. I'd also like you to meet Grant Zenkman, one of my esteemed colleagues on the string theory project."

Grant shook Kathy's hand, and smirked at Max. What was this "esteemed colleague" crap? Max would *never* speak like that in a real conversation. He stepped back to let Max do his thing. Which was fine - this Kathy girl was kinda hot, something he could appreciate better from a distance.

This was Kathy's first "real" interview. She'd read about the formation of the string theory team in a science journal, and badgered the KIRO station news manager into letting her do the interview.

"Hey, my dad talked about astronomy every night when I was a kid," she'd told Mr. Pelton, "so I know the issues. Who else on your staff has the interest and the background to interview this guy? It'll be interesting, I promise."

"Typical Kathy," thought Mr. Pelton, and he let her do the interview more out of weariness than any real interest. And he had to admit that even though KIRO had not aired it, the report she had provided on that string theory conference a couple of years ago had been pretty damn good.

"This will only take a few minutes, I promise," assured Kathy, as she ushered Max and Grant into a small airport conference room she had reserved. The cameraman was already set up.

Easily the most gregarious of the string theory team members, and with a real knack for explaining the concepts in layman's terms, Max Cherry was the natural choice for these sorts of interviews, which occasionally came from journalists who happened to hear about the fledgling string theory team. Most frequently, these were independent requests from reporters with a science background, often from school newspapers. The granting of this interview request, however, coming as it did from faraway Seattle, was completely fortuitous, since Max had already planned the trip to visit his grandmother. When Kathy requested an interview to mark the first anniversary of the team's formation, and said it could be held right in the airport, Max had no choice but to say yes. And, seeing this lovely young woman, Max decided this was one of his cushier assignments.

Kathy took a moment to look Max over, trying to ascertain how best to conduct herself. Every interview subject was unique, and the right approach was essential. Assertive or passive? Argumentative or agreeable? Funny or serious? Pushing the subject with direct questions or quietly eliciting extended replies? These choices had to be made very early in the interview, and the subject's visual clues and body language were the only basis for an assessment. Max was five feet nine inches tall and a hundred ninety pounds, not really heavy but not particularly fit either. His small hands and stubby fingers moved in quick, choppy motions, expressive but definitely unathletic. His blond hair, gently enhanced with artificial streaks, added a definite sparkle to his well-tanned face. Max Cherry, thought Kathy, was obviously concerned with how he looked and the impression he made on others. His narrow, bright eyes constantly danced around the room; he wanted to be aware of everything happening around him. She noticed his slightly chubby cheeks and large nose. Although not bad-looking, Max Cherry wished himself to be tall and sleek, so that his appearance would match his mercurial wit and gregarious manner. He had not let his personal insecurities, however, prevent him from being the center of attention wherever he went.

"Let's get right to it," began Kathy Leigh. She knew that her ten-minute interview with a world-class physicist would be edited down to a snippet or two if it made the air at all, but she believed the raw footage of a good interview would show that she could do real news. She spent a couple of minutes showing a bemused Max Cherry where to sit, how to answer questions briefly, brushing his hair away from his forehead, and even dabbing on a bit of makeup, which greatly amused Grant. Finally she sat down with him, and the camera began rolling.

"In a couple of sentences, can you describe how the most basic particles that make up the universe might actually be tiny circular strings which vibrate, and that the equations for the combinations of these vibrating strings appear to match up remarkably well with the experimentally measured energy patterns we already have for the known subatomic particles? It's very exciting."

"Very good, I'm impressed," said Max grandly. He said nothing more, apparently satisfied with Kathy's description.

Grant smiled bemusedly as Max let Kathy squirm in the uncomfortable silence. Well, at least she was trying. Grant had only accompanied Max to Seattle because Max had badgered him for two weeks and simply wouldn't take no for an answer. Max had promised to show Grant the sights of the beautiful Pacific Northwest, and told him how much fun this interview would be, but Grant suspected Max's real motivation was that he didn't want to be stuck alone with his grandmother for a week.

Kathy winced, realizing her gaffe. The cameraman rolled his eyes. She decided to come clean. I'm sorry, Mr. Cherry, I wasn't supposed to -"

"Max, Max - *please* - call me Max. Well, OK, maybe Maxwell, since I'm such a bigshot scientist." He turned and flashed a grin at Grant.

"Okay. Thank you - Max. I'm sorry. Umm, I just goofed up. You're the one who's supposed to describe the theory, not me. Could you briefly describe what string theory is all about?

Max smiled at Kathy and said, "Certainly. Theorists have proposed that the most basic particles that make up the universe might actually be tiny circular strings which vibrate, and that the equations for combinations of those vibrating strings appear to match up remarkably well with the experimentally measured energy patterns we already have for the known subatomic particles."

Max smiled and slipped Kathy a wink. Kathy, for her part, blushed slightly, flattered at the compliment inherent in Max's verbatim repetition of her own explanation of string theory.

Gathering herself after a brief pause, and thankful for the miracle of video editing, Kathy continued. "What progress have you made in the first year of the team's existence?"

Max laughed. "Well, we're still trying to agree on how many meetings to have each week, to tell you the truth." He paused a moment, collecting his thoughts, and said, "Mostly we have worked at breaking the whole effort down into several smaller subprojects, defining the mathematical fields we will have to develop, and the future experiments to verify the validity of the theories. We're sort of visualizing what the final solutions will look like, so that we have a target to aim at."

"And what will your personal contribution be?"

"Aside from keeping everybody laughing? Some of those guys are way too serious." Max smiled at Kathy. "I'm one of the math guys. Right now I'm trying to solve some of the riddles we have concerning structural geometry of the string combinations, but we have lots of problems to solve, so I'll be working in several new mathematical fields."

Grant considered jumping into describe his responsibilities, but fortunately realized this was a dumb idea.

"Isn't one of the problems that five separate theories seem to work, so you don't actually know which one is correct?"

Max stared at Kathy and tried to suppress a knowing grin. This young lady had done her homework, and was feeding him a softball question to which she already knew the answer.

"Yes, that was one of the issues that convinced many scientists that string theory wasn't valid. But two years ago, Adam and Eve Parson, who were the world's leading theoretical physicists, proved that the five theories could be combined into one. And suddenly string theory made a lot of sense."

A sympathetic look came over the face of Kathy Leigh.

"The Parsons were tragically killed in a car accident two years ago, right?"

The usually irrepressible Max Cherry felt a lump in his throat. "Yes. That really hurt. They were brilliant. Great people, too. They were close friends -."

Kathy had hoped for some emotion, it would be a nice touch to this supposedly pure-science discussion, but she didn't want the interview to turn maudlin. "How much does their loss affect the progress on string theory?"

"Oh, it was a big blow to the effort. Our team was specifically put together to maintain the momentum that the Parsons had created."

"Do you think that's happening?"

"Not yet, we still have a long way to go to catch up with their understanding." Max laughed uncertainly. "I think the most productive work we've done so far is just reviewing their notes."

"How long do you expect the string theory project to take to complete?"

"Decades. Maybe our entire lives."

"Is that how you want to spend your entire life?"

Max's face brightened. "Let's put it this way. Someday I might be able to say, 'I helped figure out how God put the universe together.' You tell me - would that be cool or what?"

Kathy smiled and nodded. "That would be cool."

She reached down and picked up a large sheaf of notes. Max Cherry seemed happy to talk to her, and she was enjoying the role of interviewer.

"What can you tell me about Calabi-Yau structures?"

Max leaned forward, eyes lighting up. This girl wanted to play ball.

The cameraman rolled his eyes again, knowing he would be here all afternoon, a victim of Kathy Leigh's blazing intellectual curiosity once more.

Grant leaned back against a wall and tried to make himself comfortable. As Kathy began firing questions, two conflicting emotions welled up within him. The first was fascination with this young woman. Her interest was so genuine, so deep-rooted, so obviously part and parcel of what she was as a human being. She had nothing more than a decent layman's understanding of cosmology, but she burned with the desire to understand the universe she lived in. And yet, and yet... why should she be interested? What difference did it make? She would never be the one to figure out these great mysteries. For Grant and Phil, it was their job, their mission, and they had the intellect and background for this monumental task, but why should a lay person have such a need to understand, to feel like this was her quest too? What was it about the human spirit that created this hunger? Was it a vital aspect to human nature, or just an unnecessary defect?

Grant looked on throughout the interview, making a mental imprint of the face of Kathy Leigh. He hoped he would meet her again someday, and perhaps come to understand this mystery.

The "ten minute interview" ended three hours later. What made it on the air was a brief introduction by Kathy, and a four-second clip of Max Cherry saying, "the most basic particles that make up the universe might actually be tiny circular strings which vibrate." From that point on, however, Kathy Leigh was usually offered the assignments requiring in-depth interviews on complicated subjects.

<u>March 26, 2002:</u>

Federal Way, Washington (as reported in the Tacoma Morning News Tribune):

Goodbye "Glory." So long "Schindler's List."

Those are just two of the films no longer allowed in Federal Way classrooms after the school board voted 3-1 Monday to ban R-rated films and to strongly discourage all other movies from being shown. The vote prompted a chorus of cheers from a crowd of about 200 parents, students, and teachers who packed into the board's meeting room. The move represents a growing trend among districts to avoid using films in the classroom.

A few in the Federal Way audience spoke in support of movies as educational tools, but many others told the school board that parents should decide what movies their children can watch. "It's an issue of morality," said parent Scott Foster. "I tell you these movies undo what I am trying to do. They do not support me in the tone that I am trying to set as a parent."

Very few spoke in support of keeping films in school, while many students agreed with their parents that many of the films they see in class are inappropriate. "We all feel like we can learn without Hollywood in our classroom," said Alyssa Rivers, a sophomore at James Madison High School.

<u>November 2, 2004:</u>

Kathy Leigh looked at the giant map on the wall in the KIRO newsroom. *Nobody's reporting it*, she thought to herself. *It's so obvious.* She waited for Tom Brokaw or

Dan Rather or Peter Jennings. Although now an established reporter, Kathy still did not feel she possessed enough of a reputation to start making proclamations about the significance of national electoral trends. But she couldn't get it out of her mind. *Florida fell to Bush. Ohio is falling to Bush. It's close, but there isn't one single blue state anywhere in middle America, and they are the ones who should be voting for Kerry. The economy has been in the toilet for four years, jobs are disappearing, Iraq is a quagmire, and we've got a huge voter turnout. This ought to be a landslide for Kerry, but the country is right on the edge of sweeping the Democrats right off the map. Everyone is saying the country is so polarized, as though this is a hopeless deadlock with no end in sight, but the trend is all Republican. Without California and New York, this would be nearly a clean sweep. And Schwarzegger's the Republican governor of California now. In another ten years there might not BE a Democratic Party. Today's Republican Party represents conformity and a single mindset, and that spirit that is slowly sweeping the country. It seems to be what the people really want. Not saying it's necessarily bad, but this is exactly the opposite of what America was built on, the establishment of a nation with minority rights and freedom to express even the most unpopular ideas. This could be the last competitive election for decades, maybe forever. Doesn't anyone see that?*

Kathy wanted to say something once she got on camera, but she demurred, thinking it might be better not to rock the boat. Surely someone else would.

January 19, 2009:

Jason Poe and Courtney Ellis sat in seats 44F and 44G,

Courtney reading a romance novel, while Jason impatiently tapped his foot. Without looking up, Courtney said with slight annoyance, "There's no point getting worked up. We're not going anywhere for fifteen minutes at least." She wanted to finish the chapter before disembarking, and Jason's agitation wasn't helping. Jason's eyes strained to see through the hundreds of passengers between himself and the exit door at the front of the plane. He knew Courtney was right, but also realized that he was constitutionally incapable of turning off his emotions. He wished he could attribute his anxiousness to having been wedged into an economy class seat for the past eleven hours, but knew full well he would be experiencing the same unpleasantness had it been a walk across the street. He had spent three years working toward the moment that would come tomorrow, and he could no more be calm about it than he could stop the earth from spinning. Ever a font of conflicted feelings, he rationalized that his constant state of near-paranoia over failure was the same force that supplied his desire for excellence. Whatever he was doing, he wanted - no, he *needed -* to make sure that every detail was right. And the only way to ensure that every detail was right, to Jason's way of thinking, was to obsessively worry about every minute aspect of his work, indeed of his life. All the time. It was that simple. In truth, he didn't understand how other people could be any different, at least if they cared about what they did. The same characteristic that was his great strength was also his great weakness. It was not possible to have one without the other. Too bad not everyone saw it that way.

Jason Poe's physical appearance was a direct outgrowth of his overly intense personality. Blessed with the metabolism of a hummingbird, the five foot eleven Jason was rail-thin at only 140 pounds. He possessed long, expressive fingers and virtually no musculature. His fine, straight brown hair, parted on one side, was invariably blown into disarray by the slightest breeze, a fact which continually irked him. Although not imposing physically, he was quite gifted as an athlete, having played a number of sports growing up, all of them well. Sports, in fact, had been almost his only bridge to other children, and he was entirely unhappy with the reality that most adults ceased their participation in sports the moment they completed high school. Jason's thin lips, pale complexion, and high voice combined with his overanxious demeanor to significantly detract from any sense of authority in his personality, and he seldom carried the day in disputes. He was well aware that every emotion he felt revealed itself in his facial expressions, and he futilely wished he could disguise his feelings as others could. One-on-one, however, this trait became an asset, and Jason was an excellent communicator, intuitively able to sense the needs and desires of the other person, and to articulate proposed courses of action that were invariably highly satisfactory. His pale blue eyes, which so irritatingly betrayed his negative emotions, also conveyed the strong sense of sincere empathy which Jason possessed. After meetings with him, people were invariably confident not only of Jason's technical capabilities, but also that he understood their viewpoint and had their best interests at heart.

Jason's maelstroms of emotion were completely foreign to Courtney Ellis. *Just let me finish my book,* was her only thought at the moment. Life was good for today, and that was all that mattered. She'd gotten a free trip to Naples, tonight she'd be eating authentic Italian lasagna in a restaurant featuring a man strolling about playing the mandolin, and the experiment wasn't until tomorrow. There was no sense losing today's enjoyment over something that wouldn't happen until then.

Courtney and Jason each thought the other completely insane. Courtney, however, had been the obvious choice to accompany Jason. Her matter-of-fact approach to life would serve as a good counterbalance to the life-and-death turmoil Jason would undoubtedly be experiencing.

Later that evening, filled with risotto and red wine, Jason was in a much more convivial state. Truth be told, Courtney liked him better this way. Jason was still excited about tomorrow, but the wine had tempered his anxiety into an appreciation of the good things about his life. Just think - he, Jason Poe from Beaverton, Oregon, had been flown to Italy and been personally greeted at the airport by Luigi Franconi, a world-renowned innovator in the field of microscopy, and tomorrow Luigi would conduct an experiment, conceived and designed by Jason, which could provide the first solid proof of the validity of string theory. *I bet Zena's jealous as hell*, he said to himself with a smile. His fragile ego boosted by such thoughts, not to mention the wine, Jason allowed his fun side to come out, and this is what appealed to Courtney. Luigi was a genial host, escorting Courtney and Jason to a quaint little bistro which, as Courtney had requested, employed a mandolin player. Luigi enjoyed the dinner and the conversation, but was oddly disinterested on the subject of tomorrow's experiment. He seemed to regard it as an assignment, a duty to be carried out, nothing more. Seeing Luigi's disinterest, Courtney and Jason directed the conversation to other subjects.

As the dinner went on and the wine provided the welcome chemical alteration to his demeanor, Jason became quite the raconteur, regaling Courtney and Luigi with stories of Max Cherry's antics in their earlier years at the private high school for science prodigies which they had attended. "And so it's about 2:00 a.m., and I'm at my desk, notes scattered everywhere, trying to get my brain around a complete conceptualization of special versus general relativity. At that point, I've got about a hundred concepts in my head, but they're all independent and unrelated, and I'm trying to see it all as one big picture, that's the only way I really learn things. Anyway, I'm in this total Zen state of concentration, and suddenly there's a bustle from the hallway. Without changing a single thought, I glance up, and there's Max, naked as a jaybird in the doorway, jumping up and down, and there's his penis - which is nothing remarkable, by the way - bouncing up and down like a twig in a hurricane." He paused for a moment to take another sip of wine while Courtney laughed out loud. "So I look up, see Max exposing his inadequacies, and quite naturally I return to my contemplation of relativity, a far more interesting mental pursuit than staring at Max's equipment, to my way of thinking. Max, of course, is incensed at his inability to disturb my concentration, so he goes into a slow bump and grind, doing his best Chippendale's imitation, and I'm just oblivious, and he slinks back to his room a broken man. I don't think he's ever gotten over it." Courtney had to stop herself from spitting out her wine as she envisioned a 16-year-old Max Cherry gyrating naked in the hallway in front of the unimpressed Jason. "And the great thing is I did figure out relativity that night." Jason paused for another moment and thought some more. "Of course, had it been a naked girl in the hallway, I wouldn't have been able to think about science for a month. Hey, I was sixteen."

After dinner, strolling down the Neapolitan avenue on the way back to the hotel, Courtney took Jason's arm and they walked silently together. Their minds were in completely different places, however - Jason was sobering up and obsessing about tomorrow's experiment again, while Courtney couldn't help thinking that Naples was a better place than the National Science Institute.

January 20, 2009:

At 9:00 a.m., Jason's mind unfortunately no longer clouded by wine, he and Courtney greeted Luigi once again in the entrance lobby of the Italian Institute of Technology with a handshake of formality. His excitement and nervousness once again getting the better of him, Jason had to force himself to be cordial, and to slow his walk to match the pace of the rest of the party. Courtney just shook her head and smiled, having known Jason for twelve years now. Despite his lunatic intensity, she knew him to be sweet and kind and always supportive, and when caught at the right moment (or imbued with wine like last night), he could be charming and hysterically funny and even sexy in his own way.

Luigi Franconi, along with a cadre of Italian research scientists and a handful of bureaucrats, whose job it was to question budget expenditures, escorted Courtney and Jason through a maze of corridors, finally entering a key-coded but otherwise non-descript door.

This is our Enhanced Electron Microscope Laboratory," spoke Luigi Franconi, his English accented but so formally impeccable as to be an obvious product of training, not upbringing. Luigi systematically described each equipment item in the laboratory, all of it being as specified by Jason

Poe, much to his satisfaction. There was a custom high-precision power generator, photo-receptor cells sensitive only to specific frequencies, a temperature/humidity control apparatus for the room, various pieces of recording equipment, and others. The centerpiece was the gleaming electron microscope itself, a twelve-foot tower of titanium focused on a specimen insertion location less than a square centimeter. It looked like a missile trained on an ant.

Luigi continued in an informative but curiously robotic tone, describing the laboratory for the benefit of the non-technical observers present. Pointing toward the top of the microscope, which could only be accessed via the attached ladder, he said, "Although equipped with an eyepiece for standard visual observation, the true functionality of the microscope, in the realm of fundamental particles, lies in the frequency receptors installed inside, which relay their signals to the photo-receptor cells. Actual observation of proton breakdown, of degradation at the quark level, is far beyond our standard observational techniques. Under stimulation from electron bombardment, however, according to the predictions of our American colleague Mr. Poe, quarks should emit a characteristic frequency signal. If proton decay is a reality as predicted by string theory, the measured emission frequencies will reflect the transmutation and decay of a certain percentage of the protons and component quarks." Seeing the puzzled looks on the bureaucrats' faces, Luigi clarified. "The conventional theories of matter describe the fundamental particles as each being a single point, having zero size. This 'point-particle theory' does not predict proton decay. If decay is evident and the emissions come at the frequencies predicted by Mr. Poe's equations, it will prove that the fundamental particles which make up the universe are not point-particles at all, but rather tiny circular vibrating strings. Personally I am more impressed by the vibrating strings on a mandolin in Vienna, but that is only a personal observation, and I am doing the task I was assigned to perform." The bureaucrats nodded, hoping the test would be conclusive, so they could put an end to these budgetary expenditures which did nothing more than answer questions of academic curiosity.

"Please to wait. I have question," said a well-dressed gentleman at the back of the crowded laboratory. "You say proton breakdown. This is bad thing, correct?"

Courtney and Jason smirked at the lack of understanding from this non-techie, obviously a government official.

Luigi spoke several sentences in Italian, then reverted to English. "I express my apologies to those present who are not scientists by profession. I explained to the gentleman that proton breakdown is a phenomenon predicted by string theory. Although the gentleman is correct in his statement that the universe's existence does depend on the integrity of the proton, its decay is not an immediate threat to our well-being, because it will take several billion years to reach appreciable levels. It is hoped by the Americans, however, that our detectors will be able to identify even the slightest variation from the standard proton signature. This would be a very strong indicator of the validity of string theory."

An aide carried out the final test setup, inserting a concentrated sample of hydrogen gas into the tiny observation chamber. The hydrogen atom nucleus, consisting solely of a single proton, would provide the clearest emission signal.

The aide switched on each piece of equipment, and a low hum filled the room. Jason was beside himself with anticipation, and even the ever-placid Courtney found her heartbeat racing a bit.

Jason's eyes locked on the digital readout. A pure proton signal would read 74.257985, and the detector could read any variation down to one part per hundred billion. Any random scatter would be filtered out by the system computer. String theory predicted that the proton, composed of two up-quarks and one down-quark, its fundamental constituents, could decay in one of three ways. If decayed protons were present at a measurable concentration, the readout would indicate a frequency of 53.219653, 57.112947, or 68.777431, along with the percent composition of each. This could be history, right here, right now, thought Jason.

After a few moments, the characteristic proton emission signal showed on the readout:

Signal Type	Frequency	Fraction of Signal (Parts Per 100 Billion)
Degraded Signal 1	53.219653	0
Degraded Signal 2	57.112947	0
Degraded Signal 3	68.777431	0
Total Degraded Signal		**0**
Standard Proton	74.257985	100,000,000,000

No other frequencies appeared on the readout.

The assemblage waited for any change. None came. Jason felt the eyes of the group increasingly trained on him to see his reaction, a certain satisfaction in some that the young hotshot American physicist had failed. After 20 minutes, several observers began to grow restless. After an hour, the less-involved members of the group began to filter out of the laboratory. After two hours, only Luigi, Courtney, and Jason were left in the room. By now Luigi was sitting at a desk in the corner, doing his personal paperwork.

There would be no history today.

At 4:00 p.m., Courtney finally said, "Come on, Jason. Time to go home."

Jason's eyes had not left the digital readout display for five hours. He had poured every ounce of himself into perfecting the calculations of the potential frequency emissions, and coordinating with the Italian authorities in the modifications necessary to adapt their state-of-the-art enhanced electron microscope for this particular test.

It had all been for nothing.

That evening, Courtney Ellis took a long walk alone, through the calm streets of Naples. She frankly enjoyed the few hours of respite from the emotional intensity of Jason Poe, and indeed from the burning desire for success common to the entire string theory project. Stepping away from that environment, she felt a welcome relief at the lack of tension, finding this outside world to be one where a person was only expected to conform to and obey the sensible rules of society, where personal striving and passion were blessedly absent. As the evening went on, this new world made more and more sense to Courtney Ellis.

At 10 p.m. that evening, there was a knock on the door from the room adjoining Jason's. He opened it. Courtney, returned from her walk, agreeably asked, "You okay?"

It was the opening in the emotional dam that Jason had waited for. He stood up, let forth a sobbing outburst, and wrapped Courtney in a fierce hug, holding her close and letting his frustration come pouring out.

Courtney's body tensed for an awkward moment in Jason's embrace. She pulled herself free and stepped back, waving with her hands for him to stay off her. "What are you doing?" she asked. "It was just a test, for God's sake."

"It's years of my life wasted," he said. "I just need to hold somebody." Jason stepped forward again.

"Sorry, not me," said Courtney, and stepped back again, then turned and went back to her own room, still cringing at the unwelcome intimacy.

<u>April 24, 2010</u>:

"As millions of people watched on television, the National Aerospace and Space Administration allowed the Hubble Space Telescope to crash into the California desert today. The telescope had not been used in the last eight years as scientific and public interest in its images and information waned."

The image of Tom Mayfield, NASA spokesman, appeared on screen, and he said, "You can't argue with public opinion. Sure, we learned some information about other stars and solar systems and galaxies, but really, what does that have to do with us? We had this huge thing, an archaic dinosaur really, orbiting the earth, and when the orbit started to decay, we thought, well, we can control it pretty well, let's allow everyone to watch it crash and get some use out of it. And you have to admit, that crash was really cool."

The camera returned to Kathy Leigh. "And so an era comes to an end. Is this the end of human exploration itself? Since the dawn of man, we have reached out beyond ourselves, and as of today, that effort seems to have ended.

So yes, it seems this is indeed an historic day. This is Kathy Leigh with a CBS News Science Update."

Kathy turned away from the camera, a tear coming to her eye. She tried to recall her father and Cassiopeia and those nights in the backyard, but found the memories fading from her consciousness.

Friday, 7:35 a.m.:

Brother Amos looked at the monitors quizzically. He did not know what to make of these new readings.

Sister Esther, answering Amos' call, came scurrying into the control center. She quickly looked over the indicators and made a few adjustments. The aberrant readings were quickly returning to normal.

"Here, let me replay the readings we got," said Amos. He flicked a few switches, and the monitors played back the strange readings from a moment ago.

"But it's died down now. So everything's okay, right?"

"I don't know," said Esther. "I hope so. What concerns me is that whatever it is, it might have started some time ago, and the monitors are just now picking it up."

"Is it - is it - a - a -?"

"Yes, I think it is. We'll have to report it."

May 25, 2010:

Serena Madison breezed into the conference room, airily dismissing her usual tardiness with a cheery, "Cookies, all!" She swept about the room in a mock ballet, drawing the still-warm tray of aromatic chocolate chip cookies under the nose of each of her fellow committee members, allowing each one just enough time to take one cookie. Except for Bryce Thomas, that is, who deftly snatched three.

"Thank you, Miss Disarray," fumed Sean Masterson, his near-religious fervor for punctuality once again frustrated by the antic Ms. Madison. Did you fill out the annual progress report, Serena?"

"No," chirped Serena, paying only the scantest attention to Sean's entreaties, as she blithely cruised around the table a second time, this time chatting briefly with each person as she made her social rounds, playing her beloved Florence Nightingale role.

Sean Masterson, the self-appointed team taskmaster, did have reason for his compulsiveness. The project would mark its ten-year anniversary on June 6th, only twelve days away, and the team was expected to present a detailed report to the National Science Foundation Theoretical Physics Sub-Committee Director and his staff. With so much progress on the theoretical side, Sean had ordered a separate team meeting to specifically catalog progress in those areas.

"Have you prepared at all?" he asked Serena pointedly.

"Hmm - now that you mention it - uh, no, actually, not a whit." Serena cocked her head to the side and looked up comically, eliciting yet another wave of laughter. She flashed Sean her most ingenuous smile and paraded toward him, holding out her tray and offering him the last cookie as she curtsied before him. This was too much even for Sean Masterson, whose mask of discipline finally cracked, and he took the offered cookie and shook his head, smiling in resignation.

Rose Pupa watched Serena's little production with detached amusement, amazed at Sean's apparently eternal inability to cope with the whirlwind that was Serena Madison. Rose also knew that Serena was fully capable, with no preparation whatsoever, of making a detailed extemporaneous exposition of every aspect of the entire committee's theoretical work, including an almost daily recounting of her own progress during the past year.

Sean continued. "All right, you poster children for dysfunctionality, we actually do have business to conduct. Could we possibly impose on you to act like civilized human beings for just a bit and allow us to proceed?" At last everyone sat quiet. Despite their anti-authoritarian leanings, their scientific curiosity drove each of them to desire the project's success desperately, and they appreciated Sean's acceptance of the thankless job of disciplinarian. "Melina," Sean asked, finally moving past his exasperation, "are there any major items we need to address?"

Melina Valin's eyes darted over the laptop screen in front of her, as she flicked from one spreadsheet to another. Despite three days of constant preparation for the meeting, she still did not believe herself to have adequate control of the project. She frequently told herself that she was in the tenth year of tracking a global research effort headed by the most brilliant (albeit juvenile and undisciplined) minds on the planet, and one could not expect to have every fact on one's fingertips, now could one? But such were her standards. No amount of control could ever really be enough.

"Hey, Miss Library of Congress, could you remind us what Action Item #7 was from March of 2002?" It was Grant Zenkman, asking an absurdly obscure question as his way of sarcastically skewering Melina for her obsession with control.

Melina, quite unaware of Grant's semi-malicious intent (in

fact pleased that someone would ask her for such information), let her fingers fly over the keyboard. Unfortunately for her would-be antagonist, Melina's data retrieval capabilities were easily up to the task. Her eyes danced across the laptop screen, following each sub-folder as it opened. At last, at the twelfth level down in the hierarchy, she found what she was searching for. Fourteen seconds had passed.

"Actually, there were two official meetings in March of 2002," Melina replied, as Grant sighed, knowing the game was up. "Oh yes, I remember this one," she said brightly. "In the March 7 meeting, Action Item 7 was for Darryl to synthesize Lie Algebras, conformal field theory, and hermitian operators into a single mathematical functionality, in the hopes of obtaining an all-encompassing perspective on possible projected properties for the superpartner particles. Let's see, umm, oh yes, here's the follow-on report - on May 9 Darryl stated that he was successful at merging Lie Algebras and conformal field theory, but, yes, here it is -"

"Okay, okay, you made your point," sputtered a crestfallen Grant Zenkman.

Darryl Johnson, hearing one of his concepts discussed, brightened from his usual catatonic state in meetings, and jumped in. "It was possible to reconcile the hermitian operators perfectly well with either of the other two fields, but there were mathematical inconsistencies with the three-way hybrid. Too bad. I really thought it would work. I was sure I completed the analysis correctly, but it was just impossible to combine the three concepts into one grand synthesis."

Melina recalled thinking there were real prospects for the three-way synthesis that would have provided many insights into string theory, and made a note to herself in her database to look at it later.

Melina looked at Grant, still unaware of his true motives. "Don't you want to hear about the other Action Item 7? It was from the March 21st meeting and, coincidentally, it was yours, and, oh - you never completed it. Hm." It was true. She lifted her eyes to meet his, and was confused at his apparent irritation with her.

Grant, who had lately taken to going on long walks alone through the city in the afternoons, excused himself from the meeting, slamming the door behind him on his way out.

Melina's eyes again went down to her computer monitor, but she cautiously glanced just high enough to see the others' faces. Finally they could stand it no more, and Max Cherry burst into laughter, leading the entire group in applause at Melina's upstaging of Grant. "Score one for anal retentives!" crowed Max. Then his eyes opened wide in mock horror. "God, I wonder what she's got on me." Melina wondered what joke she had missed.

After a momentary pause, Melina continued. "Actually, we've had an excellent last couple of years. And since our decision earlier this year to give up separate residences and all move here, into the National Science Institute building, our completed action items are up 23.7 percent." The other team members alternately shook their heads at Melina's predictable level of detail and nodded in agreement with the fact they enjoyed living together very much.

"I've got pretty good documentation on where we are, but if we could just review the major milestones, that would be helpful for me in preparing the presentation on the 6th." Melina did not mind preparing the presentations, but thank God for people like Sean Masterson and even the undisciplined Max Cherry, who were willing to actually make the presentations to the Institute's directors. "Can we start with one I think I have a handle on? The mathematical explanation of why Calabi-Yau structures are stable with three holes, no more nor less, and how that relates to the three families of fundamental particles we find experimentally."

There followed a short, cordial discussion among the group members, describing the possible variations of "Calabi-Yau shapes," the microscopic 6-dimensional structures that, according to string theory, make up the hidden dimensions of the universe beyond the three familiar space dimensions and the "fourth dimension" of time.

There was also considerable amazement at the recent Hubble Telescope crash, and Zena wondered ruefully, "How could they lose interest in our window to the dawn of time? Something's got to be wrong with the human race.....".

Melina understood all the Calabi-Yau concepts perfectly well. Since the 1920's, the most fundamental bits of matter and energy were visualized as tiny particles. This conception allowed a great many accurate predictions about the universe, but many gaps remained in the understanding of quantum physics. When the fundamental particles were described as tiny vibrating string loops instead of single-point particles, however, many of the theoretical problems inherent in the microscopic world of quantum physics were suddenly solved in one fell swoop. In the 1960's it was discovered that the standard equations for vibrating strings, such as from a violin or guitar, were a remarkable match to the properties that had been found for the subatomic particles identified in particle accelerator experiments. This discovery was completely accidental and unanticipated. How could our familiar musical instruments possibly relate to subatomic particles? To make the mathematics work, the theory held that the universe exists in ten dimensions: the three space dimensions, the time dimension, and the six tiny dimensions of the Calabi-Yau structure. Although the Calabi-Yau structure was far too small to be directly observed, its structure defined the interactions between the fundamental subatomic particles which make up the universe, as well as their masses and other properties. Although the hope for the future (and a major goal of the committee's lifelong project) was to find direct evidence of the structure of the Calabi-Yau spaces, at this point the analysis of Calabi-Yau shapes was performed entirely in the realm of mathematics. There were tens of thousands of possible Calabi-Yau shapes - the Holy Grail was to identify the specific structure of the one that makes up the universe, and prove it to be so. The string theory project was the grand task of putting all the pieces of one single unifying theory together to explain the nature of the universe, from the subatomic particle soup at the time of the Big Bang to the grandest galactic structures in the present-day universe. Melina knew the facts, but another run-through with this group of brilliant minds would provide her one last chance to hear the concepts expressed by the people who knew them best, and she would undoubtedly find a clearer way to express a few of the ideas for the less-knowledgeable audience they would be addressing in two weeks.

The concept of supersymmetry, which defined the relations between the known particles and each one's predicted but yet-to-be-discovered "superpartner" particle, was discussed at length. The mathematics of string theory required that each known subatomic particle be paired with a much larger "superpartner." As yet, no experimental data existed to proved the existence of such particles, and this proof would be one of the major milestones of the entire project.

The conversation then turned to string theory's prediction of the graviton particle, a unique feature which made string theory the only field which combined quantum physics and gravity in one theory. The theoretical toolbox was not full yet, but enough tools were in place that the physicists could envision what the final product would look like. They fairly salivated with anticipation at the notion of understanding the universe in its entirety.

Bryce Thomas managed to remain serious just long enough to explain how the observed collection of subatomic matter particles identified in particle accelerator experiments can be divided into three families with similar properties but different masses. Bryce explained that Calabi-Yau structures could have holes, and the number of holes corresponded to the number of families that the string vibrations and their resonant patterns represent. After a great deal of mathematical development, it had been shown that for all numbers of holes other than three, the vibrational patterns of particles and their superpartners would tend to cancel each other out over time, making any particles developed extremely short-lived. Only a three-hole structure produced stable vibrational patterns which reinforce each other continually. Mathematically, therefore, there could be three and only three families of fundamental particles. "Kind of like a pendulum," said Bryce, "sometimes you see one or two or four or five holes, but it always swings back to the only sustainable steady state of three holes and three families. So the mathematics predict that we will see three families of subatomic particles, and that is exactly what we see experimentally. One more domino down in the string theory game," said Bryce with satisfaction. "We're getting there."

Leaning back after his discourse, Bryce pulled a straw from his pocket, ripped a corner off a piece of paper and rolled it up, put it in his mouth for a moment, placed the straw into his mouth, and fired the spitwad at Darryl, who as usual was into his own meditative theoretical world far beyond anyone else.

Melina nodded as she furiously typed away, capturing every word Bryce had said, until she was suddenly startled.

"Damn!" shouted Max Cherry, glancing at his watch, as Serena Madison clapped her hands in glee. "Bryce, you just cost me 20 bucks. I bet Serena you couldn't act like an adult for 20 minutes. And here you made it by *15 seconds,* you twit." Sean Masterson rolled his eyes.

The committee took a break after four hours. Rose Pupa asked Max Cherry, "Where's Jason? I haven't really talked to him for a while."

"I asked him to come today," said Max, "but he didn't want to. Most days he's okay, but he really still hasn't gotten over what happened in Italy, and he pretty much keeps to himself.

"He's still not over it?" Rose asked. "That was over a year ago."

"I know," replied Max. "But you have to understand Jason. He takes things hard. Plus he hasn't really found a niche for himself since then. He's not sure what he should be working on."

Zena, sitting nearby, could not help overhearing. She replied, "I know what he's going through. I'm in pretty much the same situation. I'm on hold in terms of significant particle accelerator experiments until the Large Hadron

Collider comes online, and that's not for at least four more years. With so little going on experimentally, it's hard to feel like part of the team. I thought about not coming today, but I thought I might learn a few things from you theoretical types."

Max replied, "I told him he should get the Enhanced Electron Microscope shipped over here from Europe. The Italians seem to have completely lost interest in any of the explorative sciences. But I think Jason's afraid of another failure, so he hasn't pursued it."

The ever-rational mind of Rose Pupa could not fathom such long-term self-retribution.

The meeting returned to order and turned to the concepts of perturbative analysis and the coupling constant. A "perturbative" analysis is performed by assuming a single factor to be the dominant one and making an approximation of the solution, based on that one factor only. Then other factors are considered and their effects are measured as "corrections" to the estimate produced from the initial approximation. It is a method for working up to a solution for a complex problem when an all-encompassing theory is not available, but there are limitations on when it is useful. The coupling constant determines the tendency of a string to temporarily split into one or more "virtual pairs" of strings, absorbing energy from the surrounding space. These virtual pairs will quickly annihilate each other and return to a single string form, returning their energy, but the mathematics indicates that the number of virtual string pairs produced has a large effect on the energy and properties of the universe as a whole. The trick was to prove how many string pairs would typically be created, and then demonstrate that this number of pairs explained the observable properties of the universe.

It was like examining a television screen pixel by pixel to understand what the overall picture would look like. The problem was that the understanding of string theory was not yet mature enough to provide an exact equation to quantify the coupling constant. One of the great difficulties had been the inability to specify it. If known, the coupling constant would be the key to many of the unanswered problems of string theory. Some facts could be known, however, even if the coupling constant was not exactly specified. In cases where the coupling constant was less than one, perturbative analysis was valid, and had been used to successfully calculate and predict some string properties.

The discussion of the coupling constant prompted Rose to ask a question. "I'm not as up on coupling constant theory as I might be. If you get multiple pairs forming, breaking up, and reforming, how does that translate into energy? What are the mathematics behind it?"

Serena Madison rose and went to the board. Serena was quite buxom, and the eyes of the male committee members followed her involuntarily. She breezily wrote several partial differential equations, stepping through the energy calculations, demonstrating that with each virtual pair created, an exponential increase in energy absorption and subsequent release was created. "That's why we need to understand the physical mechanism behind it," Serena said. "If the distribution shows that a large number of virtual string pairs is created before recombination, the energy structure of the universe is radically different than if the normal pattern is only one or two virtual pairs."

"That concept still escapes me," said Zena, hopeful that she might learn something useful. "I wish I had a better conceptualization of what a virtual pair actually is."

Rose had noticed the men's reaction to Serena's figure, as contrasted to her own decided lack of physical endowments. She innocently intoned, "I think I can explain, Zena." She glanced down at her own flat chest. "I've got a virtual pair right here."

The entire room collapsed into hysterics, Zena and Serena most of all, as Rose smiled slyly to herself.

It took several minutes for the team to return to business, and Sean Masterson just let the mood work itself out.

Finally, Serena spoke up. "We've made so much progress with perturbative analysis, I think our presentation should recommend that we continue to emphasize it. If supersymmetry is considered, along with the Parsons' concept of the five string theories being one, we can keep using perturbative analysis in some areas to develop conclusions in other areas where perturbative methods don't work. Perturbative analysis has been so fertile, I think we need to pursue it as far as it will take us."

Much to the surprise of the entire room, Darryl cleared his throat and prepared to comment. Almost all of his work was done alone, and he seldom interacted with the other team members on technical subjects, or on any subject for that matter. He had always been in his own thought world, even as a little boy. And so everyone's attention riveted on him as he spoke. "You can do what you want, but perturbative analysis will be a dead end at some point. You can't approximate your way to complete solutions. Perturbative analysis is like running through an enormous maze, only being able to see what's directly in front of you. You can't tell where you are really going. The string theory maze is so large you will never find the way out. You have to rise above the maze and see it all at once. Somewhere there has to be a comprehensive, elegant, overarching concept that encompasses all aspects of the string theory problem. Just look at the universe. If it was expanding a billionth of a percent slower, it would be clear that it would eventually collapse back upon itself. If it were expanding a billionth of a percent faster, it would clearly be on its way to runaway expansion. As it is, the universe is *perfectly* balanced on the edge of whether it will expand forever or collapse again. That can't be an accident. And the other end of the size spectrum is perfectly balanced as well. The strong nuclear force could not vary by a billionth of a percent and still perform its job of holding protons and neutrons together in a stable system for billions of years. And it's the same, *or worse,* for all the forces, particles, masses, interactions, everything. The balance is too perfect, too precarious. You will never understand it by using perturbation theory, which is nothing more than a very exotic guessing game. Underneath it all must be a deeper truth, and I do not believe that the shotgun approach of perturbative analysis will ever reveal it."

The team went silent at Darryl's uncharacteristic outburst.

Friday, 11:55 a.m.:

Sister Esther stood before the Underling Oversight Committee, smiling a terrified smile, her eyes darting back and forth throughout the room. She was ninth on the agenda, and throughout the long meeting she had been unable to decide whether she preferred to wait forever, or just to get through it. At last Brother Bartholomew, the Committee Chairman, called her name, and now she hoped she could remember the well-rehearsed words she had prepared.

This time there was no getting out of it. This time no one could address the Committee except her. As the lead technician, this issue was her responsibility, no one else's, and after the way she had failed to back up Matthew when he was on the hot seat, she realized this was just desserts. For his part, Matthew had proven his character by volunteering to help her rehearse as much as she needed to. The problem was, no amount of practice would be enough.

It was time.

"Umm, my name is Sister Esther, from the Underling World Observation Center under the Quality Assurance department. One of our tasks is to monitor the Sonic Vibration Frequencies," she began. She felt a dry spot in her throat, and the second sentence was more difficult than the first. "At 7:35 this morning we detected a, a Sonic Deviation. It is the first one we have ever recorded, and I felt I should bring it to your attention." Esther smiled tentatively, thinking she had gotten through the ordeal, indeed, it seemed she had delivered a major speech. Matthew gave her a thumbs up from the back of the room.

"Is there any significance to this?" thundered a dark voice from the main table. Esther looked up at Brother Bartholomew, whose bulbous nose and narrow eyes framed by great bushy eyebrows created a most disagreeable presence. One of his minor obligations was to serve as Omniscience Committee focal point for Quality Assurance concerns, but he had in fact never given any consideration to these issues. Any concern coming out now from the Quality Assurance group would, of course, reflect negatively on the perception of his capability, and he was thusly motivated to quash this issue as quickly and forcefully as possible.

Esther shook noticeably.

Brother Bartholomew smiled to himself. He thoroughly enjoyed dressing down the Committee's working staff members; it taught them to keep higher standards, and also served as an invaluable lesson in the exercise of leadership for the other Committee members.

"Well, umm, I mean, it was the first Sonic Deviation ever," stammered Esther, wishing she could vanish.

"Haven't we ever had disturbances before?"

"Oh no. Not like this. A Sonic Deviation means the universal vibrational frequencies are disrupted. It could indicate a significant problem.

"So what? One little deviation. Is it still occurring?"

"Uh, uh, no, it subsided," uttered Esther almost inaudibly.

"Well, then, we don't have anything to worry about, now do we, my dear?"

Esther tried to think, as Bartholomew continued. "Do you understand the issues we are facing? We have schedules which must be adhered to. We have deadlines we must meet. There is that little matter of preparation for the Eternal Festival. We who hold highly responsible positions understand much better than a person in your position what the impact would be of a slide in the schedule. So we don't want that, now do we?"

Esther tried not to cry. She managed to say, "It's the first one ever, and we thought we should make sure nothing is wrong."

"The only thing wrong is you're telling us to disrupt our schedule!" bellowed Bartholomew. "What if the Omniscience Committee were to hear of this? Everyone knows the entire system runs by itself and does not require outside maintenance, so let's not go fixing things that don't need to be fixed. Now go away, young lady, disposition this item 'No Action Required,' and do not come back here again, do you understand?"

Bartholomew's job complete, he smiled and calmly continued with the meeting. "Now - moving on….."

Esther ran out of the room in tears.

February 19, 2011:

"And the winner of this year's Grammy Award for Album of the Year is………John Tesh for 'John Tesh Sings the Hits of the 70's!'" The audience applauded thunderously as Mr. Tesh climbed to the dais to accept his award.

July 9, 2011:

In the year after the failed proton breakdown experiment in Italy, Jason Poe was shaken almost as much by Courtney Ellis's emotional distance as much as the experimental failure in Italy. Courtney remained cordial and friendly, but from that day forward he felt any real connection between them slipping away. To him, the experiment represented a three-year emotional flight that had ended in a spectacular crash of utter failure, and his mental wiring was such that an extended period of grief and self-retribution was inevitable. He came to understand that Courtney was incapable of relating to any of this. Many nights he lay awake, wishing for that "roll off your back" attitude that Courtney had come to possess. But he knew this weakness was not his fault, that he could not be Courtney Ellis any more than she could be Jason Poe.

Glenn Glass was the quietest member of the string theory team, with the possible exception of the perpetually dreaming Darryl Johnson. Glenn's initial reluctance to have his life committed to the team was quickly overcome by the supportive team atmosphere and the prospect of a long-term, stable project with real technical merit, a true rarity in the research world. An outcast in the academic world at Cal Tech, Glenn found the string theory team to be the haven he had always wished for. Despite his apparent lack of social skills, Glenn was surprisingly gifted at reading the emotions and temperament of others, and he had willingly taken on the role of restoring Jason Poe's confidence after the electron microscope debacle in Italy. It had taken many nights on the town, and many long alcohol-enhanced discussions of life, death, poetry, beauty, science, survival, and women, but with Glenn's steadfast encouragement Jason finally emerged from his depression and regained his enthusiasm for his work.

In attempting to restore Jason's spirit, Glenn had also spoken at length with Max Cherry. Glenn knew that Max and Jason had been friends since boyhood, and Max in turn appreciated Glenn's support. Glenn agreed with Max that bringing the electron microscope over from Italy was just what Jason needed, for his own well-being as much as for the good of the project, and it was at Glenn's gentle insistence that Jason had finally initiated the shipment of the microscope back to the United States.

Jason quickly learned that Glenn Glass was much more than a shoulder to cry on. Day after day Glenn pored over Jason's calculations, as well as the instrumentation and equipment setup for the hoped-for proton degradation measurement.   Through painstakingly detailed analysis over the course of a year, Glenn and Jason developed several corrections and potential improvements to the original experiment.   Over the last several weeks, they had checked and rechecked all the equations, circuits, and instruments. The night before, Jason, Glenn, and Max conducted the final equipment checks together. Glenn ordered Jason to go home at 11 pm, knowing that the emotional roller-coaster that was Jason Poe would require all the energy he could muster to get through the next day. Max stayed well into the night, partly because he was by nature a night owl, but also because he needed to complete one last task. Glenn remained to help Max, but even after every preparation had been made, he did not feel like going home to bed. And so it was that Glenn Glass found himself alone in the darkened electron microscope laboratory at five o'clock in the morning, looking everything over one last time, drinking in the emotions from the experiences of the past year.

To show its unanimous support of Jason, the entire string theory team showed up at the laboratory at 7:30 am, even Max and Bryce, the notorious late risers. Bryce even looked rested. Noting the look of surprise on Sean's face, Bryce said breezily, "Trust me, Sean, this is not a lifestyle change. But I did skip a party for this, so it better be good." He gave Sean a wink.

Jason was visibly taken aback to see the entire team waiting when he arrived at the laboratory at 7:45. He hadn't slept much, naturally, but he knew he had prepared as well as he could, and the continuing support of Glenn and the others despite the proton degradation failure somehow validated his membership on the team. As he strode to the observation window which provided a view of the laboratory, Jason saw that Max Cherry had, between midnight and two a.m., etched the words "Fourth Grade Science Fair Grand Prize" in large letters on the side of the gleaming titanium electron microscope. Max was fully aware of what that long-ago day had meant to the confidence of the young Jason Poe, and his recollection of it now brought a laugh of recognition. Jason's eyes also found those of Glenn Glass, and the two shared a moment of mutual acknowledgement.

Jason could not help but recall the incredible rush of emotion that he had experienced at the prior trial in Italy three years ago. The point-particle theory of traditional quantum physics had no place for the phenomenon of proton degradation. If the proton signal was altered as predicted by Jason's equations, it would be undeniable proof that string theory was fundamentally correct, and that string vibrations were the fundamental building blocks of the universe. It would not answer all the questions of how string theory worked, but it would eliminate any doubt about its validity. Jason's excitement, however, was tempered by his dread of the sobering reality that a failure would represent. It had taken three years to prepare for this second attempt. Failure this time would return the effort to square one, with success more distant than ever. Jason tried, quite unsuccessfully, not to think about that possibility.

The revised proton degradation experiment had a number of refinements. The hydrogen was stored in liquid form at only a few degrees above absolute zero, as this provided a more stable signature for the emitted signals from any degraded protons. In addition, the entire test apparatus was now housed inside a large glass enclosure in the far corner of the laboratory, eight feet on each side and fifteen feet tall, equipped with state-of-the-art vacuum pumps and seals. The test environment could now be subjected to a near-perfect vacuum environment, to eliminate any signal variation due to atmospheric disturbances or dust. The chamber was also subjected to an anti-static treatment to eliminate any traces of electrical disturbance. These alterations, of course, required substantial equipment modifications to the entire laboratory, but they allowed the electron microscope to take advantage of electronics advances in the sensors and observe signal deviations of one part per ten trillion, or one hundred times smaller than had been possible four years ago.

All eyes were on Jason and Glenn as they stepped through the startup sequence for the microscope. Once that was completed, the twelve teammates pushed up close to the test chamber, resembling a gang of impatient children on a Saturday morning, noses pressed against the outside window of a candy store, waiting for it to open. The liquid hydrogen was drawn through a thick insulated tube into the specimen chamber, and cooling currents circulated around it to keep it at the required temperature. Finally Jason took a deep breath and turned on the final switch, activating the sensors. They warmed up momentarily, and then flashed their first readings:

Signal Type	Frequency	Fraction of Signal (Parts Per Ten Trillion)
Degraded Signal 1	53.219653	0
Degraded Signal 2	57.112947	0
Degraded Signal 3	68.777431	<u>0</u>
Total Degraded Signal		**0**
Standard Proton	74.257985	10,000,000,000,000
Total Signal		10,000,000,000,000

Jason waited a moment, and clenched his teeth. Even with a hundred times greater resolution, no proton degradation was detected. Glenn's arm draped across his shoulder. Thirty seconds passed, then one minute, then two. Everyone on the team looked toward Jason, who was already contemplating how long and difficult his recovery would be from yet another disappointment. Jason's eyes remained fixed straight down. He couldn't look at the signal readout. In his mind, he could see the digits laughing at him in cruelty. Finally his eyes lifted.

The digits flashed, then momentarily read as follows:

Signal Type	Frequency	Fraction of Signal (Parts Per Ten Trillion)
Degraded Signal 1	53.219653	0
Degraded Signal 2	57.112947	0
Degraded Signal 3	68.777431	<u>3</u>
Total Degraded Signal		**3**
Standard Proton	74.257985	9,999,999,999,997
Total Signal		10,000,000,000,000

The numbers quickly switched back to the original figures. No one else had seen it. Jason's eyes became wide as saucers. Had he imagined the change?

The digits flashed again:

Signal Type	Frequency	Fraction of Signal (Parts Per Ten Trillion)
Degraded Signal 1	53.219653	1
Degraded Signal 2	57.112947	2
Degraded Signal 3	68.777431	4
Total Degraded Signal		**7**
Standard Proton	74.257985	9,999,999,999,993
Total Signal		10,000,000,000,000

Jason's eyes saw the numbers, then flashed to his companions to see if their eyes saw the same thing.

A thunderous "YES!! YES!! YES!! YES!! YES!!" roared from the throat of Sean Masterson, his shout a complete betrayal of the normally icy demeanor intended to keep others at a distance. The others roared in concurrence. The numbers flashed back to their original reading for a moment, then reappeared as follows:

Signal Type	Frequency	Fraction of Signal (Parts Per Ten Trillion)
Degraded Signal 1	53.219653	3
Degraded Signal 2	57.112947	4
Degraded Signal 3	68.777431	6
Total Degraded Signal		**13**
Standard Proton	74.257985	9,999,999,999,987
Total Signal		10,000,000,000,000

After a few more back-and-forth flashes, the figures stabilized at this level. It was undeniable that measurable emissions were occurring at the frequencies which indicated proton degradation. Proton degradation was a reality, and therefore string theory was a reality as well. The initial roar was followed by silence as everyone waited until the numbers resolved themselves, and suddenly Jason felt his back pelted by the well-wishing arms and hands of his teammates. His pain at the onslaught had no effect on the glowing pride bursting from within himself. He turned and hugged Glenn Glass fiercely, knowing full well the debt he owed.

As Courtney Ellis took her turn at a hug of congratulations, Jason gently kissed her cheek. He felt her stiffen awkwardly.

The ensuing party did not end until 19 hours later, when they were kicked out of the last bar in town at five a.m. The sight of the normally buttoned down Sean, Melina, and Rose liberated by alcohol into completely uncontrolled exhibitionists was nearly as startling as the morning's physics breakthrough itself, and the entire night was spent in gleeful celebration. The inebriated discussion, despite frequent moments of incoherence, pursued every possible avenue of string theory research available in the coming years, and the team stumbled home in a fog, fantastically energized by the knowledge that string theory was correct, and they were indeed on the pathway to complete understanding of the workings of the universe. The answers were there, failure was no longer a possibility, it was merely a matter of time until all truth was uncovered.

<u>October 18, 2011</u>:

"In our final story this evening, the CBS television network today cancelled CSI-Mars, the last scripted show left on network television. This past season, CSI was the lone holdout against the tide of reality TV shows which now dominate network broadcasts. The trend began with MTV's Real World, then moved to the so-called trash talk shows and personal court cases, and went big-time with the Survivor television series. The success of Survivor spawned dozens of similar series, and now shows such as Cockfight Night, My Kid Can Beat Up Your Kid, Mutilate Yourself, and Get Your Neighbor Convicted have become the most popular series on the air. Said CBS Chairman Michael Kobelski, 'In its day CSI was what the public wanted. They cared about the characters. But we had to face it, the world is becoming more modern every day. There was one last hurrah for scripted television with the popularity of Desperate Housewives and Lost in 2004 and 2005, but looking back, those shows represented a dying gasp, not any sort of comeback. Hey, we tried to spice up the CSI concept as much as we could, taking it to Mars and introducing the storyline with space aliens impregnating the entire staff, including the men, but it just wasn't enough. And really, why should we care about people who aren't real? People just want to see real life, they don't want to think so hard. That's why you never see boring shows like Masterpiece Theater and Shakespeare any more. Even the actors were tired of doing the show, they didn't like having to pretend to feel emotions that aren't real. Sure, there is some regret at having to give up on scripted drama, but you have to go with the times.'

"Well, that's too bad. I still liked that show. Anyway, that's it for us tonight, this is Kathy Leigh, speaking for the entire crew here at the KIRO Evening News, wishing you a pleasant evening."

Friday, 12:12 p.m.:

Matthew and David took a stroll, glad to be on a break. At the end of the hallway, they realized they could no longer hear other voices and stopped, savoring the quiet for a few moments, until they noticed their friend Esther from the Quality Assurance group coming toward them. "Hi, how's the Festival planning coming?" she asked.

"Oh, OK, there's lots to do," said David, "and as long as we don't ask for approvals we're OK. But those Safety Committee hearings - I mean, you don't need to worry about safety unless you are mortal, right? They just don't get that - I can't understand." A momentary silence followed, and they listened to the gentle background music, a slightly dissonant song of unknown origin.

"Didn't you prefer the classical we used to have? It was so calming, always so, so *angelic*," said Matthew, motioning toward the speaker with a sly grin.

"Oh, I sure did," replied Esther, laughing at Matthew's pun. "I'd love to know who's making these choices." Esther wanted to express her sympathy for Matthew's plight with the Efficiency Committee, but her guilt over not coming to his defense before the Committee gnawed at her. "For me," she continued, "I must say my job is a lot more interesting these days. In the beginning, we *never* had any sonic disturbances, now they happen all the time. They don't seem to cause any problems and we can't pinpoint a source, but we're always off to review them, write up a report, and make a disposition. It's a lot better than sitting around looking at screens all day with nothing to do."

David gave a puzzled look and asked, "Well, is that all right? I mean, are these sonic things affecting permeation?"

"Not that we can tell," responded Esther. "We think it's just an instrument problem, because the disturbances are always temporary and localized, and hey - just look around - you see anything different?" She grinned. "Besides, Brother Bartholomew, despite his obnoxious personality, actually made my life easier. We're under orders to always disposition them, 'No action required at this time.' Just makes for a lot of busy work with no real stress. I feel a little guilty just ignoring them, but it does make life a lot easier."

David said, "Yeah, I see what you mean. Why make waves? Oh well, glad you're staying busy."

"OK, see you around," Esther called as she walked away. "Ugh. I do hate that music." David and Matthew nodded in agreement.

January 26, 2013:

In Congressional action today, the National Endowment for the Arts was officially cancelled by a unanimous vote. Five years ago this would have been quite controversial, but public interest in art has dwindled to such a point that no protests have been made. Congressman Rod Munroe stated that there had not even been any requests for funding this year, so it only made sense to cancel the program.

March 25, 2013:

Melina Valin had never been comfortable with it. It had gnawed at her imagination for eleven years. She had made several notes to herself over the years to look at it when she had spare time, and felt guilty every time she thought about it, because she had never acted. There were plenty of other tasks to work on, and it wasn't really her responsibility anyway, so she kept telling herself that someone else on the team would pick up on it. Yesterday, however, she had recalled it once again, and finally decided that enough was enough, and she must scratch this itch once and for all.

"It" was Action Item #7 from March 2002. Melina, whose excellent grasp of string theory's subtler concepts was somewhat obscured by her fanatical attention to detail and her role as group documentarian, had never been comfortable with Darryl Johnson's failure to synthesize Lie Algebras, conformal field theory, and Hermitian operators into a hybrid analysis tool. Significant areas of overlap already existed, and Melina intuitively felt the synthesis was possible. Each of the three mathematical fields provided hints about the predicted properties of the superpartner particles that Zena hoped to find experimentally in a few months when the Large Hadron Collider came on line, and if realized, this powerful new tool would likely cause other conclusions to fall out as well.

Melina awoke at 6:00 a.m., showered for her usual twelve minutes, and dressed in the bathrobe and slippers she had neatly laid out the night before. To be doubly sure she could work uninterrupted, she had decided to devote an entire Sunday to this effort, and taken pains to ensure that she had no other tasks required that day, going so far as to wash her laundry a day early, a traumatic alteration in the standard routine of one Melina Valin. She opened the laptop on her large dining room table, and set out several reference materials. She further placed a number of fruits, vegetables, and bagels in a bowl on the table, as well as a pitcher full of ice water and a large glass. It was 6:37 a.m. She was ready to begin.

Six hours later, she was ready to quit. Melina scoured every one of Darryl's equations, looking for that subtle flaw she was sure she would find in his elegant line of reasoning. She only succeeded, however, in working her brilliant but rigidly disciplined mind into a frazzled state, that level of concentration being impossible to maintain for an indefinite length of time.

She went to the kitchen, removed a large premium-grade Swiss chocolate bar from the pantry, and ate it. She felt much better.

Melina knew that in order to continue, she needed a dose of calm and practical rationality. There was only one person to call. Ten minutes later, Rose Pupa knocked on Melina's door. Five more minutes and a shared bagel later, the two women were sitting together, staring at the first of 23 pages of equations on the laptop screen, written in Darryl's original childlike scrawl, digitized for computer storage. Some years ago Melina had adapted a large number of special keyboard characters specifically to enable herself to duplicate Darryl's notes, which not only employed his brilliant but utterly chaotic writing style, but also his entirely original mathematical symbols and terminology, for which a normal keyboard had no equivalent characters. These notes, however, were the originals from Darryl, they had never been updated.

Page after page of abstract equations rolled up the monitor as Rose and Melina traced the logic of Darryl Johnson's mathematical argument. Darryl not only used English and Greek letters as algebraic variables, he felt it necessary to invent a number of symbols of his own, each with a particular significance. By 4:00 p.m. both women were once again exhausted, still unable to find a pathway to the synthesis Darryl had sought. Finally reaching a point where she could no longer continue, Rose rhetorically asked, "Don't you just love Darrylinian Mathematics?" There was no such official branch of mathematics, of course, but Melina agreed that the sobriquet was well-deserved.

Rose's understated insistence on a dinner break prevailed over Melina's protests to continue, and forty-five minutes of pasta, wine, and discussion of the misadventures of life as a 43-year-old woman left them refreshed and ready to continue their quest.

Melina again returned to the first equation, a simple differential equation that signified little. "Darryl," she said out loud, "I know you're a genius, but somewhere in here there is a conceptual error. I know it. I can feel it. I will find it." She pumped her arms like a bodybuilder, a gesture so out of character that Rose collapsed in laughter and exhaustion.

Rose leaned back for a moment. "Wait. Maybe we're doing this all wrong. We're assuming that Darryl missed something in the logic. Like you said, we've been looking for an oblique conceptual flaw. Now think about it. This is Darryl we're talking about. What kind of error would Darryl Johnson make?"

"You're right," said Melina, the light going on. I've *never* known Darryl to miss something conceptual. Forget his pants to a dinner with the Queen? Yes. But a logical error? I doubt it."

"OK, let's try something different. Instead of looking for relationships between equations, let's just start with a simple proofread," replied Rose.

The women again scanned down through the equations, this time at breakneck speed, looking for something far simpler than they had previously. Melina, whose eye for detail was unmatched, saw it first.

On the eighth page of equations, off in the margin, was a scribbled note:

$$[1/(\beta)^2] \, [4\delta/(x/\beta^3)] = 4\delta/\beta \, x$$

The "$4\delta/\beta x$" term was plugged into the next equation, and Darryl had continued his analysis from there.

"Oh my God!" squealed Melina, her usual obsessively professional veneer shattered by the discovery. "Rose! Do you see what he did? I can't believe it. He screwed it up when he tried to invert and multiply. It should be $4\delta\beta/x$, not $4\delta/\beta x$. It's a *seventh grade algebra mistake*!" She stared blankly at the monitor.

Rose just shook her head, realizing they should have looked for something like this from the beginning.

Melina's fingers now flew over the keyboard, reproducing Darryl's equations, but with the corrected factor. As one equation flowed into another in Darryl's original attempt at the synthesis, the tiny algebraic error had magnified itself, becoming so entwined in the other expressions that its role in the growing mathematical breakdown was impossible to see. In the end, Darryl only knew that the mathematics made no sense, but he had no pathway back to the source of the error.

At 10:00 p.m., sixteen hours after she had started, Melina typed out the last equation of the synthesis between the three mathematical fields. Rose watched attentively, furiously taking notes from time to time. It was clear that with correctly input basic particles, the new equations could predict the properties for the superpartner particles that Zena would be trying to find in a few months. Furthermore, a number of tantalizing hints remained in the new equations, indicating more truths to be discovered. Rose, flush with the adrenalized thrill of discovery and quite outside her usual state of composed thoughtfulness, could not wait one more minute. As soon as Melina got up to stretch, Rose sat down at the computer to indulge a hunch.

Branching off from one point of the synthesis equations, Rose began deriving a new set of integrals. Now it was Melina's turn to watch. After four hours Rose typed out the last equation, and sat back, both women understanding the significance of the scant few characters on the screen in front of them.

"Oh my God, you got it," whispered Melina.

"Lovely, isn't it? That's why it's all in perfect balance."

On the left side of the equation was an eigenvalue function, a mathematical operator which in this case described the parameters affecting the expansion rate of the universe. After many pages of derivation and simplification, the right hand side showed an integral sign ($\int$) followed by a different eigenvalue function. The eigenvalue equation on the right hand side of the equation could be seen to be the derivative of the one on the left hand side.

In simple terms, the equation appeared as follows:

$$\text{(EigenFunction A)} = \int \text{(EigenFunction A's Derivative)}$$

A first-term freshman calculus student is taught that the integral of a function's derivative equals the original function itself plus a constant, usually symbolized by the letter C. The constant C, based on the preceding equations leading to this point, represented the long-sought cosmological constant.

Thus, the equation could be simplified as follows:

$$\text{(EigenFunction A)} = \text{(EigenFunction A)} + C$$

From this equation, the cosmological constant "C" was obviously equal to zero. Proven mathematically. More than a hundred years since Einstein and the earliest cosmologists had first pondered its significance.

The cosmological constant, in loose terms, represented the average energy of the vacuum of space. A cosmological constant less than zero meant the universe's expansion would eventually slow to a stop, and the universe would contract upon itself, ending in a "Big Crunch." A constant greater than zero implied an accelerating force, and the universe would continue its expansion forever. A cosmological constant of exactly zero meant the universe was precariously balanced on the knife edge between eternal expansion and eventual contraction and collapse. There was no obvious reason why the constant had to be zero, but empirical calculations over the last century had shown it to be zero down to the 120th decimal place. Proof of this value had eluded physicists for decades. It now existed on Melina Valin's dining room table.

"Too bad they disbanded the Nobel Prize committee a few years back," a grinning Rose said to Melina. "You would have just earned one in your bathrobe and slippers."

"Well, a shared one with you and Darryl," laughed Melina.

Rose and Melina simply had to share the news with Darryl, and marched off to find him, knowing he would still be awake, as he seemingly always was. His condominium was at the opposite end of the sixth floor living quarters from Melina's, so it was about a two-minute walk. As always, Darryl sat on the floor of his living room, alone, accompanied only by candlelight, pondering equations in silence. His door was cracked open, and the two women peeked in.

"Hi, Darryl," called out Melina. "Can we talk to you?"

"Certainly," said Darryl stiffly, unaccustomed to visitors, especially females, late at night. He was a bachelor and likely to stay that way.

Melina stuttered a bit trying to explain their activities that day, until Rose stepped in, knowing her gift of diplomacy would smooth over the situation, should Darryl take offense at the women reviewing his work.

"Melina and I took a look at the work you did a few years ago to synthesize the Lie Algebras, conformal field theory, and Hermitian operators," said Rose.

Before she could proceed, Darryl nodded and replied, "Did I make a stupid error someplace? I always thought I must have."

"Well, I wouldn't call it stupid, the entire progression is the most elegant construction I've ever seen, but yes, there was an algebra error that was the source of the incongruities you encountered. We found the error, here, let me show you."

Darryl, not put off in the least that someone had discovered his error, looked with interest at the new $4\delta\beta/x$ expression. A slight smile crossed his face, and he nodded imperceptibly. "So you resolved the synthesis?"

Melina and Rose described their adventures of the day, and Darryl listened with bemused interest. When Melina showed him the final expression of the synthesis, Darryl asked matter-of-factly, "So, did you continue on to the cosmological constant value?"

"How did you know?" asked Melina wonderingly, and she and Rose began to describe their nine-page derivation that resulted in the cosmological constant expression. Darryl, however, interrupted her after only a few moments.

"Oh, no, you don't have to do all that, from here you can

complete the derivation in seven equations." Darryl pulled out a stubby pencil and scribbled down the equations on a scrap piece of paper he found on the floor, reaching Rose and Melina's final expression for the cosmological constant in about ninety seconds.

Rose and Melina, egos properly chastened, each gave Darryl a kiss on the cheek, leaving him silent and blushing.

Friday, 12:57 p.m.:

Brother Jacob and Brother Joseph greeted each other ten minutes before the Underling Oversight Committee meeting was to start, as was their custom. They enjoyed these moments together. They had reviewed the Underling World reports from the working level staff, and in these private moments they could be more open with each other than they could in the Committee meetings.

"Jacob, have you reviewed the Creativity Index lately? There's been something of a prolonged decline, and at this point in the permeation process that really shouldn't be happening."

"Yes, Joseph, I had noticed that, and it bothered me as well." I also noticed the Stability Index is way up, almost off the charts. The other Committee members see that as a strong positive, but I'm not so sure. Do you think we ought to request Bartholomew to conduct an investigation?"

"No, no, no. Trust me, we'd just be seen as alarmist. This is detail stuff. Bartholomew not only chairs our Committee, he has to report to the Omniscience Council, and the last thing he wants to hear is an unsubstantiated report that something is wrong with the Underlings. An investigation would never get approved anyway, and he'd never listen to us after that. We're not doing anything unless we get solid evidence that something is really wrong."

<u>June 26, 2014:</u>

There is nothing so beautiful in all the universe as the view from a Swiss meadow as the sun rises behind the Alps in the distance. As the blazing ball of thermonuclear exquisiteness inched its way into view, such was its impression on Zena Dunn at 5:48 a.m., as she lay in the cool grass, awake and feeling more alive than ever before in her life.

After the near-spiritual experience, Zena jogged the half mile across the meadow back to the Large Hadron Collider command center, arriving just as she began to break a sweat. Noting her reflection in the large glass entrance door, Zena flashed herself a smile of recognition and satisfaction. At age forty-four, she was the best she had ever been. The awkward teenager had matured into a passably attractive young woman, but as she had aged, Zena maintained an athletic figure through a disciplined workout regimen and now looked better than ever. In her chosen profession, her technical command of experimental practice had acquired unsurpassed breadth as well as depth over the years, and her ability to interpret particle accelerator tracings was legendary. While others waited for the computer readouts to analyze experimental results, Zena's ability to decipher the residue of muons, neutrinos, quarks, and the rest in the blurred lines of the raw visual pictures was near psychic. With the Hadron Collider ready for testing, and the even larger Superconducting Supercollider only a few years off, Zena knew the next few years would be the most fulfilling of her already notable career. Zena was most proud of the fact that she had completed her evolution from the insecure days of her youth to become a mature, strong woman without losing any of her characteristic thirst for accomplishment. She still woke up every morning with a driving ambition to create something meaningful, but now her need for success had only to do with the work itself, not some self-absorbed need to justify her own existence. She had learned to pour herself completely into her work without having its results dominate her self-image.

Zena Dunn recalled her frustration in the early days of the string theory team. By the 1990's, particle accelerator trials had reached a plateau of progress caused by the energy limitations of the test equipment, and the experimentalists were forced to take a backseat to the theoreticians. The successful proton degradation tests, however, resolved some of that discrepancy, and with the construction of the Swiss Large Hadron Collider, the experimentalists would once again return to the forefront. Zena closely followed the Swiss construction effort. In a manner similar to Jason Poe's experience with the Italians, Zena found the Swiss engineers puzzlingly blasé about the entire project, quite uninterested in the potentially profound implications of the future Collider experiments regarding the nature of the universe. Their lack of scientific curiosity, however, was not any sort of hindrance to the project, as the Swiss were efficient, effective workers who followed instructions to the letter.

At 6:15 a.m., Zena sat at the main control console of the Large Hadron Collider command center. One hundred fifty feet below, buried under the most beautiful landscape on earth, was a 47-mile circular tunnel, through which atomic particles were carried by an electromagnetic field to unimaginable velocities. When top speed was realized, the particles would be allowed to smash into atomic nuclei, the collisions creating enough energy to shatter the particles into their fundamental components. Through such experiments over the past eighty years, the three known families of the subatomic particle zoo had been identified, leading to many of the proofs of quantum physics theories, as well as many of the conclusions regarding string theory itself. What was lacking was an accelerator large enough to produce the energies required to create the superpartner particles, the much larger companions to the known particles, as predicted by string theory. The existence of the superpartners would prove the validity of a "supersymmetrical" universe, a mathematical term implying all sorts of elegant solutions to sticky problems that had plagued theoretical physicists for decades. Supersymmetry had long been believed to be valid, but without proof of superpartners, it could only remain an unsubstantiated theory.

Recalling Jason Poe's disastrous initial foray into the proton disintegration experiments of several years ago, Zena had decided that she would not have any surprises in the first public trial of the Large Hadron Collider. The first run was scheduled for 2:00 p.m. that afternoon, but Zena had come in late last night and turned on the main power and the vacuum required throughout the tunnel, and then awakened at 5:30 a.m., first to gain inspiration from the glorious sunrise, and then to carry out her surreptitious scheme in solitude. As she looked over the control console, everything was in readiness. Zena entered the sequence of commands to start up the Collider operation, each step so familiar as to be part of her very being. Considering the immense size of the Collider, it still amazed Zena how quickly the particles were brought to near light speeds. The particles were now zipping through the entire forty-seven miles of tunnel more than three thousand times per second. Zena closed her eyes and centered her thoughts on her breathing for a few moments. The particles were at peak velocity. She pushed the button moving the target nuclei into the high-speed particles' pathway and looked at the computer monitor in front of her.

Exactly 1.6 seconds later, a knowing smile crossed the face of Zena Dunn. Several streaks were imprinted on the screen at much greater widths than any previously known particle would create. Zena could already estimate the mass and energy of the superpartners, based on the width and pathway of the tracings. She didn't need to see any more prior to the afternoon's display. She would feign surprise and delight at the results of the afternoon experiments along with everyone else, and patiently wait for the computer analysis to verify the conclusions she already knew.

Zena shut down the accelerator and returned to the meadow.

February 17, 2015:

"In our top story tonight, the Education Department reported that nationwide, student scores on standardized tests are up for the tenth straight year. President Schwarzenegger, two years removed from his Electoral College sweep in the Presidential election, hailed this announcement, stating that it proves the effectiveness of his administration's policies and those of the last three Republican administrations. For more on this story, we take to you our newest network correspondent, Kathy Leigh, in Washington, D.C."

"Thank you, Sam. Well, test scores are up all over the world, so I don't see how President Schwarzenegger can claim all the credit for himself. Students in Europe, Asia, South America, and even the Middle East have also dramatically improved their performance the last several years. These changes in behavior have, in fact, been remarkably significant in the Middle East, as a key factor in the decreased threat of terrorism we have seen in recent years. It seems that young people would now rather listen to their math teachers than to the final few religious extremists in existence. Amazing. It now seems clear that the seemingly monumental terrorist threat of the first few years of this century was in fact the last dying gasp of a culture past its time.

"The upward trend in student performance actually traces back to the late 1990's, but the improvements have really stepped up in the last four or five years. And not only are test scores up - attendance is up, truancy is almost non-existent, and discipline problems in our nation's schools are virtually a thing of the past, as is crime among young people. And although we may disagree with giving all the credit to the President, it is hard to argue with his assessment that society seems to be entering a Golden Age.

"So what has happened? We know that the number of university students pursuing liberal arts degrees has decreased dramatically, forcing many colleges which emphasize the liberal arts to close or change their curriculum, as students flock to courses they consider more useful. What about the students themselves? Have they just gotten smarter? Do they work harder? Have teachers gotten better? Do parents participate to a greater extent than in the past? We went straight to the source and interviewed dozens of schoolchildren and teachers all over the country.

Let's hear what they had to say."

The image of a well-scrubbed young boy appeared on screen, with the caption, "Michael Moberly, first grade, Lexington, Kentucky" below him. "My brother is 18, and he told us how school used to be," the boy said in his delightful southern accent. "He said when he was in first grade, they did lots of coloring and songs and stuff like that. I'm glad we don't have to do stuff like that any more. My favorite things are memorizing arithmetic and vocabulary words. I like it when the teacher tells us something and I can repeat it back to her just like she said it."

Next was a black girl in a cream colored blouse and a dark blue skirt. "Detroit School District" was embroidered on the front of the blouse. The caption read, "Alice Tinsley, sixth grade, Detroit, Michigan." She stood in front of her school. Alice said, "My favorite thing is the uniforms. Everyone looks the same, and we all like that. They're very sensible. I just can't understand how they say things used to be. Kids used to skip school, and sometimes even made messes in the neighborhood and didn't clean them up. No one would do that now, see how clean the street is? Our job in school is to do what we're told, so that's what we do."

A teacher appeared on screen with the caption, "Nick Ellis, ninth grade teacher, Stockton, California." "I'm proud to say that our state was the first to implement the new '3R' program. That stands for 'Repetition, Repetition, Repetition,' and I must say, the kids have surely taken to that. First of all, it's a big burden off us as teachers, not having to think up all those time-wasting creative exercises, we can just stick to the Fact Curriculum and teach the kids what they need to know. But there's no doubt there's also a difference in the kids. Guess they're just smarter than we

233

were," he said with a chuckle.

The final student was Tom Lorsbach, a high school senior from Denver, Colorado. He looked confidently into the camera. "Honestly, it's a little hard to explain. My grades have gotten so much better since elementary school. I guess the 3R program has something to do with it, but it's like in grade school my head was always filled with distracting thoughts. I was thinking about a hundred different things, and I couldn't focus on what I was supposed to learn. Now it's like there aren't any other thoughts in my head, and all I want to do is absorb what the teacher is saying. It's just easier, I can't explain it. Oh, and you should see the younger kids. Sure, I stay on topic better than I used to, but they NEVER lose focus. I still have to work at it, but for them it's completely natural to just do what they're told and soak up the information. I mean, I'm sure I'll turn out fine as an adult, but the younger kids are really going to be something. They amaze me."

The camera cut back to Kathy. "Well, there you have it. Student after student had similar responses to those you've seen here. We don't really know the cause, but today's students repeat information better than any previous generation. Does that make it a Golden Age? Or are we losing something precious with the reduction in emphasis on creativity? I suppose history will be the judge. This is Kathy Leigh for CBS News, Washington, D.C."

The president of CBS News personally called Kathy later that evening. After briefly introducing himself and going through the formalities of politeness, he got to the point. "Now look, Miss Leigh, I know you're brand new here at CBS, so I'm cutting you a break. My staff showed me your report this evening. This Department of Education report is purely good news. What is this crap about losing something by not emphasizing creativity, and history judging us? Scores are up, discipline problems are down. That's good news, and we will report it as good news. Get with the times, Miss Leigh. Your fuzzy-headed angst over 'where society is headed' went out a long time ago. Don't make any more comments like that on the air, ever again. Good night."

Kathy Leigh did not sleep that night, puzzling over a nagging feeling that she couldn't put her finger on.

March 3, 2016:

The small desktop computer in the bedroom of twelve-year-old Sally Jennings of Butte, Montana, quietly and obediently performed the repetitive calculation for the 176,926,433rd time. This time was different, however. The endlessly changing stream of numbers and symbols came to a halt. There were no more iterations. A final answer was at hand. The 469 simultaneous equations that Glenn Glass had derived were fully completed to a unique, exact solution.

The tiny computer, one of several thousand networked computers of all sizes which had constantly worked at solving the equations for many months, dutifully uploaded the final version of the solution to the National Research Council's central computer, where it would be seen by a stunned Melina Valin early the next morning. She would wake everyone else on the team with the news that the algorithm had identified the exact form of the Calabi-Yau structure for the six microscopic dimensions, ending the quest that Glenn had begun twenty-five years earlier at Cal Tech University.

<u>May 1, 2016:</u>

As was his habit, Christopher Parson left the Institute just after 2:00 p.m. to stroll the spotless streets of Washington, D.C. With litter a thing of the past and undesirable people and behavior headed the same way, the large cities were pristine and sterile in comparison to previous times. But none of this mattered to Christopher. He loved to take in every nuance of his surroundings, running his fingers over the texture of the old marble columns on the government buildings, looking at the transition from the dark gray asphalt streets to the white concrete curbs, enjoying curvatures in city statues he had not noticed before. To Christopher Parson, nothing was ordinary, nothing was mundane. He gaped in wonderment at every sight his eyes beheld, and to him the world was infinite in its delights. Sometimes his walks covered miles of ground, while on other days he would stop within a single block and study a small insect as it worked for hours until he understood every detail of its movements, and then return home.

On this lovely spring day he approached an older man, who was walking with a young boy and the boy's dog. The dog, upon seeing Christopher, leaped forward, his leash breaking free from the boy's grip.

"Good puppy, good puppy!" laughed Christopher, kneeling down as the dog raced to him and lapped at his face. The boy started to come forward, but held up behind his grandfather, unsure about this stranger for whom his dog showed such affection.

The grandfather strode forward, a stern look on his face. "Explain yourself!" he said, showing no pleasure whatever in the dog's joy. The look of alarm on his face was evident.

"Good puppy, good puppy," repeated Christopher, happily oblivious to the stern feelings of possessiveness from the grandfather and grandson.

"My dog!" shouted the young boy, certain of his rights, and now emboldened by his grandfather's presence.

"Puppy needs to play," whispered Christopher, instinctively understanding a deficiency in the dog's upbringing. The dog rolled over, thrilled at the long-neglected opportunity to have its stomach scratched.

The grandfather and grandson withdrew into silence, uncomfortable at the unseemly display of affection between the dog and this oddly behaving man.

"Why is he doing that?" asked the boy.

Christopher laughed and laughed, his own eyes reflected in those of the rapturous puppy.

The older man took in the situation. Dogs were rarely seen these days. They were something of an anachronism in this modern age of efficiency. For families who did desire pets, cats were generally preferred over dogs, due to the typical emotional detachment of felines. The boy was an only child, however, and his parents had believed that a dog, although not truly a "productive" commodity in terms of child development for future societal economic utility, might serve the function of occupying the boy's time when they were busy, and teach him responsibility, even though children these days hardly needed lessons in responsibility.

And so the old gentleman did not quite know what to make of this grown man rolling around on the grass with the small dog. He vaguely remembered pet dogs from his youth, but recollections of affection such as that presently before him had long since faded.

It was the boy who took control of the situation. "I'm the boss of that dog, not you. Give it back."

Chris rubbed the delirious dog's ears. "Nobody is boss of a dog."

The boy looked again at Christopher, noting the simple words, the slow speech, and the childlike eyes and smile.

"There's something wrong with that man," said the boy, pulling on his grandfather's sleeve. "Grandpa, he's retarded, isn't he?" The boy had never seen anyone with a mental disability, as nowadays they were typically hidden from public society or aborted after screening during pregnancy, but his parents had told him that people used to be this way sometimes.

Now alarmed at the potential threat of this deficient individual, the grandfather stepped forward and forcefully said, "We have to leave now."

Christopher cheerfully said, "Okay, bye-bye," and placed the dog into the boy's arms. The boy awkwardly dropped the dog, uncomfortable at the intimacy.

The grandfather, realizing Christopher was not a physical threat, stepped closer. "What are you doing out in public?" The boy stepped forward, alongside his grandfather. The dog yipped happily at Christopher.

Christopher finally stood up and smiled broadly, having thoroughly enjoyed playing with the dog. Christopher's communicative disabilities precluded any sort of detailed verbal interaction with the people he met, but as a boy he had instinctively learned, much as pretty girls do, that his disarming smile had a way of making people act kindly toward him, and thusly his smile had served as his pass through the outside world to this point in his life. He had not understood the hostile intentions of the grandfather and grandson, and to wish them good day, he beamed his brightest smile. As Christopher's smile glowed, his eyes twinkling, the grandfather felt old sensations flooding back to him, and his demeanor softened.

The boy, however, was untouched by any sentimentality for this defective human being.

"Come on, Grandpa, let's go."

They strode off together, the old man looking back at Christopher several times as he walked away.

Once they were out of sight, Christopher walked slowly home, whistling softly as he went.

May 15, 2016:

As was his habit, Grant Zenkman left the Institute just after 1:00 p.m. to stroll the spotless streets of Washington, D.C. He had begun these walks a few years before, using them to clear his mind and ponder the riddles of string theory, away from the constantly raging storm of genius that was the Institute. He often took his walks in the company of Bryce Thomas, but today he preferred solitude. He had hoped to untwist some of the recently developed Calabi-Yau solutions into simpler forms, but his mind was not on it.

The outside world was, in many ways, everything the Institute was not. Although he had no real artistic sense, Grant loved the esthetics of the modern Washington, D.C. Automobiles were seldom parked on the streets any more, as the population accepted the economic benefits of mass transit, and few tourists entered the city for sightseeing or historical interest purposes. On this spring day, Grant especially appreciated the decision two years ago to cut down all the cherry trees and eliminate the maddening white blossoms that cluttered the streets every spring. The clean look of the streets and buildings stood in stark contrast to the mayhem of his string theory compatriots, who left notes and papers everywhere, filled with equations and partially formed ideas, not to mention the general atmosphere of anarchic thinking. Creativity was one thing, but the repugnant lack of concern for decorum was something else entirely.

As Grant began to have more contact with the outside world, he found he greatly enjoyed the far different ideas that were in vogue outside the insular cocoon of the Institute. He realized that his previous total focus on string theory resulted in a limited, stilted view of the issues facing the world.

A block ahead, Grant's favorite coffee shop came into view. Grant found it a haven for stimulating conversation, and he loved sitting and listening to informed people discussing the important issues of the day. After obediently waiting for the "Walk" signal, despite a total absence of traffic, Grant crossed the street and sat down in a booth directly across from two men, both in gray suits, white shirts, and blue ties. Grant had, in fact, seen these two men here several times before, and he invariably found their conversation riveting as they spoke in hushed and urgent tones. When his coffee arrived, he pretended to read a newspaper while the two men spoke.

"Yes, yes, there are big plans ready to be implemented," said the first man. "We're drafting an omnibus bill to address everything in one fell swoop. Dissolving the Ministry of Welfare, dismantling the federal prison system, and downsizing or even eliminating the Ministry of Justice - they're all on the table. These functions just aren't needed any more, and can you imagine the benefits of freeing up those resources for private use? I know I've told you before, Brett, but isn't this an exciting time to be an American?

"Absolutely, George," said Brett, and the two clinked their coffee cups together with a smile. "At Interstate Communications, we'll be able to benefit right away, by converting the Justice Department's international communications capabilities into our own global network, when we set up a single world system. Nationally, the country is already at 99.6 percent employment, and not only will that figure improve, but at companies like mine, we will be able to transition low-productivity jobs to higher productivity categories as the new work force and capabilities come on line."

George continued, "And comparatively, we're just beginning. The Economic Ministry is already putting out monthly recommendations on purchasing patterns to local consumer test groups. In our first three trial months, the positive responses started at 48.6 percent and increased to 73.9 percent, and the reports are the percentage is still increasing. That's incredible."

"Sorry, I'm not familiar with that one," replied Brett. "What kind of recommendations?"

"Oh right. Sorry. Our analysts study the quarterly data from each economic sector. Let's say, for example, that out of our various categories, the agricultural and energy sectors did not perform as well as expected. We simply publish updated recommendations each month on the percentages of family income that should be spent in each area, and indicate a higher percentage for agriculture and energy. We mail the recommendations to ordinary citizens. Along with the basic recommendation, we list a number of suggestions for specific beneficial purchases that consumers can make, such as purchasing more farm products for food, and taking vacations involving travel to increase gas and oil consumption."

"And the people are accepting it?"

"Yes, and they're enthusiastic about it. Kind of puts the old theories of economics to shame. The old way was, "Satisfy the consumer. Satisfy the consumer," like the entire economic system needed to tailor itself to the ill-defined selfish needs and wants of the populace. It was incredibly inefficient. Those theories showed the economists had *no* understanding of consumers and what they are willing to do."

"But wasn't this idea already tried with Communism?"

"Ah, but they tried to *force* a controlled economy on the population. They never understood that it was so much simpler, that all we had to do was *ask*. These trials prove that we can tell the public what they should buy, and they *will* buy it. When we implement this nationally, we will have total economic control. It's unfathomable to me that earlier economists didn't see this."

"What about the benefits from doing this internationally?" asked Brett.

"Even greater than here in America," replied George enthusiastically. "It's an even bigger opportunity. The increased sense of acceptance of authority, especially among younger people, opens up the idea of single global economic systems, sort of like Europe did with the Euro fifteen years ago, but this time all over the world. I'm sure you've noticed governments all over the world becoming more stable and adopting similar policies, which is huge in terms of eliminating obstacles to economic growth. The political and religious extremists have all been marginalized, and now the whole world can reap the benefits. It's a great time to be alive. And all it took was global realization that conformity to the common will is the highest virtue. So simple, and yet it was seemingly impossible until now."

Grant listened to every word with rapt attention. Yes, his aptitude was science, and yes, he had a certain interest in cosmology and affection for his string theory compatriots, but he found himself unable to dispel the thought that everything in his life was frivolous. In the face of the sweeping societal changes he had just overheard, what was the point of the team's Ahab-like pursuit of arcane equations describing an event which occurred twenty billion years ago? Grant had grown up, he realized, become a different, better person than the one who joined the string theory team so many years ago. He was frustrated with partial conclusions, tentative theories, and unresolved intellectual puzzles. In this world outside, answers could truly be known. Scientific curiosity had its place, but this world, the one outside the Institute, it was so much more - *real*.

Friday, 6:33 p.m.:

The alarm still ringing in the background, the emergency Omniscience Council meeting was called to order. "Will someone *please* shut off that damnable alarm?" shouted Brother Michael. "That thing is driving me crazy." Sister Esther, shaking, finally found the correct button and shut it off. The conference room was jam packed, with representatives from the Omniscience Council, all three major committees, many of the workgroup focal team members, and a large number of interested citizens of the City who had heard something was up.

With such large attendance, the meeting was held in the City's largest conference hall. At one end of the hall, the Omniscience Council was seated on the higher of two stages. The Council members sat at one long table, a microphone and nameplate in front of each person, with Brother Michael in the center position as chairman of the Council.

The senior members of the City's three main Committees, subordinate only to the Omniscience Council, sat in front of the Council on the lower-level stage, facing out toward the hall floor. Each Committee had its own table with chairs and microphones, similarly to the Omniscience Council, but the Committee tables were shorter and the members had to crowd together more closely. In front and to the left of the Council was the Festival Preparation Committee. The Efficiency Committee senior members were located directly in front of the Council, and on the right was the Underling Oversight Committee. The faces of the Council and Committee members on both stages were filled with resentment at the disruption caused by this undoubtedly false alarm. On the hall floor were the working team members and the general public, looking up at the two stages filled with dignitaries.

Brother Michael, chairman of the Omniscience Council, smacked the table on the upper stage with his gavel to quiet the audience. "All right, all right, what's this all about, why are we here, and how can it be fixed so we can get back to business?" The room was silent. "Anyone, anyone at all. This is irritating. I have other things I could be doing. Somebody tell me what's going on. How about someone from the Efficiency Committee?"

All eyes turned toward Joel, the Efficiency Committee Chairman. He stood, turned around to face the Omniscience

Council table, and calmly replied, "Brother Michael, I assure you the Efficiency Committee is taking this issue very seriously and will take all appropriate action to resolve any concerns."

Peter, seated just to the left of Brother Michael, replied, "And what 'appropriate action' might that be?"

"Well, sir, we are certainly not allowing any schedule slides. We are still on track with all our tasks." Joel smiled confidently.

"Of course there will not be any schedule slides," said Michael. "That is a given -"

Brother Peter interjected, "But that doesn't resolve the problem of what happened. Joel, what exactly is your committee doing to determine why the Main Frequency Alarm sounded and what can be done about it?"

Brother Michael gave a stern look to Peter, glad that he was asking hard questions, but not thrilled at Peter's interruption of him.

Joel hesitated, then determinedly said, "I assure you, none of our committee's activities caused this anomaly, and I'm sure everything is fine. Perhaps we could just disable the alarm?"

Sister Deborah, most unimpressed with her fellow Efficiency Committee member's inability to follow standard protocol, and seeing an opportunity to elevate her own image in the eyes of Brother Michael, said with disdain, "That is not a root cause corrective action and must be strictly a fallback position at this point. Timothy, what does the Festival Preparation Committee have to say?"

Brother Timothy rose and said, "I stand together with Joel in our resolve to address these very serious issues. We will not rest until a root cause analysis is completed, as you so ably stated." His attempt at an ingratiating smile was decidedly forced.

Michael, trying to project an image of calm control while in actuality wondering if anything of substance had actually been said, sat down, folding his arms as authoritatively as possible.

Peter leaned toward his microphone. "So just what will you do?"

"We will, of course, follow all appropriate contingency procedures and policies as outlined in our Standard Operating Procedures."

Peter continued. "Timothy, do you have any idea what would make the Main Frequency Alarm go off?"

"We have a staff of people working on that very issue -" began Timothy. "We do too," chimed in Joel.

"That's not the question I asked," said a frowning Peter. "Just how well do you understand these systems? What type of occurrence would be required to do something as fundamental as set off the Main Frequency Alarm?"

Timothy and Joel looked at each other, now speechless. "Comments from anyone else?" requested Peter.

Jacob and Joseph looked at each other and reluctantly stood up together. "Brother Michael, we are on the Underling Oversight Committee, and although we have no information specifically regarding the Main Frequency Alarm, there have been some readings from the Underling World that have us somewhat concerned. The Creativity Index is in serious decline, while the Stability Index is way up, and other indicators also are not at expected levels. We do not know if these events could be related to the current problems, but we thought you should be made aware of them."

"Bartholomew?" asked Michael. "What can you tell me about this?"

Bartholomew, member of the Omniscience Council and chairman of the Underling Oversight Committee, glowered at Jacob and Joseph with indignation and embarrassment at this public display of his lack of awareness of his own Committee members' activities. He slowly stood up, raised his hands plaintively, palms upward, said nothing, and sat back down.

Peter turned back to Jacob and Joseph. "Why have I not read about this in your Committee reports?" asked Peter. The other Omniscience Council members snickered to themselves at the thought that Peter actually read the interminable reports.

"Because we had no proof of the seriousness of our findings, and we felt the Committee would reject our concerns, I'm sorry to say," said Joseph.

Brother Michael resumed control of the meeting. "As we sit here, we run increased risk of schedule slides, and that will not be allowed to happen," he thundered. "The Festival is our only priority. I'm looking for a can-do attitude here, a win-win proposition, and I'm not hearing one. Is there anyone in this room who can say anything that is actually useful?"

Sister Esther slowly rose to her feet out on the main floor. No one really noticed her at first, the room still silent, no one willing to speak. Esther finally cleared her throat nervously, and all eyes slowly turned toward her.

"Yes, young lady? Do you have something to say?"

Esther addressed Michael, her throat parched. She had desperately hoped someone else would understand the situation and speak up, but no, it was left to her. "Sirs and

Madams, I'm Sister Esther from the Underling Observation Center in Quality Assurance. Our group is in charge of Sonic Frequency Monitoring."

She had everyone's attention now.

"I don't know quite how to say this. The Main Frequency Alarm cannot go off unless we have an irreversible Sonic Regression."

"And what does *that* mean?" roared Brother Bartholomew from his seat at the Underling Oversight Committee table. Esther's anxiety level rose exponentially at the sight of Bartholomew, who had so thoroughly intimidated her the only previous time she had ever addressed a major Committee.

"It means the permeation progress has stopped. It means we are no longer progressing toward full 10th-level permeation. The vibrations of the strings are breaking down."

"So? Do your job. You're a technical person. So go hit a switch or something and get them vibrating again," blustered Bartholomew.

"You don't understand," Esther protested. "This is a catastrophic universal sonic failure. It is like punching a hole in the hull of a boat that is out in the middle of the ocean. The boat will fill with water. The boat will sink. It is inevitable. That's what this is. The permeation will regress. The harmonics of the universe are fundamentally flawed as of now, and the fabric of the universe will unravel and come apart."

Michael stood up. "Wait, wait, wait. Young lady, *I'm* in charge here, not *you*, and *I* will tell *you* what is or is not inevitable. What *is* inevitable is that permeation will progress to completion without interruption, and that will instigate the Eternal Festival. The system runs itself. This is something that everyone in the City knows. So just what are you talking about?"

Before Esther could respond, Bartholomew interrupted. "Wait just a moment. You're the same one who brought us that Sonic Deviation nonsense, aren't you?" He chortled loudly with satisfaction.

Esther put her hands on her hips and sneered at him, her temper simmering. She softly said, "Well, I guess it *wasn't* nonsense, now was it? This latest event isn't a simple Sonic Deviation like it was before. This is the Main.... Frequency.... Alarm."

Esther stared at the table full of dignitaries before her. "You don't know what that means, do you?"

Brother Bartholomew folded his arms, distinctly uncomfortable.

Esther continued, her confidence growing. "We don't know what caused it, but something has fundamentally disrupted the universal string vibrations, and permeation is no longer moving forward within the 10th dimension. You are correct, Brother Michael, the system was designed to run by itself, that's why the Architect felt free to move on to other projects, but something has interfered with the intended course of events, and universal sonic failure is what will happen."

Michael smiled patronizingly, not wanting to appear threatening, and said, "All right, young lady, I appreciate your honesty. Now how do we 'patch the boat' without causing any schedule slides?"

Esther lowered her voice. "We don't. We don't know how. We never did. There are some manuals, but nobody's read them since the Great Unfurling, and we don't understand them any more. We've never actually worked on any aspect of the system, and we don't have any control mechanisms. We can only monitor what is happening, we cannot affect it. I think you still don't get it. The strings will literally fly apart as the vibration frequencies become skewed -"

"So stop it! Stop it! Turn it off! Turn it around! Whatever! Do your job!" roared Bartholomew. "Why are you bothering the Omniscience Committee with such details?"

"Shut your fat trap, you ignorant blowhard!" screamed Esther, as she turned the full force of her newfound wrath on Bartholomew, who was visibly taken aback. "You have no concept of what I'm talking about, do you? You *can't* 'turn it around'. You can't reverse entropy. Not with unguided natural processes. We can measure the permeation level as it regresses, but we have no means of controlling it. It's all coming apart and there's nothing anyone can do about it. It's over."

Michael, now soberly reflecting, said softly, "Just what are you saying? Exactly what will happen to the Underling world?"

Esther shook her head ruefully, astonished at the opacity of the Council. "No, no, no. You still don't get it. I'm not just talking about the Underling world. The entire universe is constituted of strings, and not just the physical universe. The City too. These buildings. Us. Me. You. Everything. It's all coming apart. It's all gone. We're all gone." Finally Esther broke down and dissolved into tears. Matthew ran from the back of the room and held her.

Peter sat silently in his chair at the Council table. For so long he had been blithely optimistic, cheering on the troops and crowing about how inevitable the entire process was and how pointless it was to worry over the details. He looked over at Thomas and their eyes met. They both knew Thomas had been right to have his doubts, so long ago in the Omniscience Council meeting chamber.

Joel spoke from his seat in the front row. "Isn't there a form we can submit or something? Can't we create a new subcommittee?" The questions were met with silence.

Michael finally spoke. "There's no point in alarming all citizens of the City. Meeting attendees are instructed to notify no one of the events which occurred this evening. The Omniscience Committee will decide on a course of action at a future meeting."

June 6, 2016:

"And in conclusion, allow me to recap the highlights of our 20-year progress report. The National Research Council String Theory Project appears to be on the brink of finalizing a single Grand Unified Theory of the universe. Most of the components of the final theory are already in place. The proton degradation experiments were the first to demonstrate that string theory is indeed the key to understanding the fundamental processes driving theoretical physics. We have demonstrated why the cosmological constant is indeed zero, ending a quest that lasted almost a hundred years. The Large Hadron Collider experiments identified a number of the predicted superpartner particles and validated the concept of supersymmetry, with its many implications regarding resolution to many of the previously unresolved problems in quantum theory. Some of the newly discovered superpartner particles did have the previously unobserved spin values of $1/5$, $1/13$, and $1/53$, as predicted by the theory. With the Hadron Collider data input into the equations, we were recently able to establish the final solution to the Calabi-Yau structure, which has in fact proven to have predictive capability. In analyzing the structure, we were able to make new predictions about certain superpartner masses and energies. Then we returned to the Large Hadron Collider data and analyzed it further, looking for these particular features, and they were exactly as predicted by the string theory parameters derived from that specific Calabi-Yau structure. When the Superconducting Supercollider comes on line in a few years, we expect to be able to verify the existence of the graviton particle, which is the long-sought connection between quantum mechanics and gravity. We also expect to identify the remaining superpartner particles, and prove the rest of the string theory predictions. At this point the remaining theoretical work consists of synthesizing the equations for all ten vibrational dimensions into a single form that defines all parameters simultaneously, and reconciling all equations so that they apply equally well to the Big Bang conditions as well as the present-day expanded universe. Our current equation forms basically solve one piece of the puzzle at a time, and the final form needs to address all dimensions and times at once. But based on our progress to date, it seems inevitable that the final solution will be accomplished in our lifetimes."

"On behalf of the entire team, I thank you for your time, and on a personal note I would like to add that this team is the most dedicated, tight-knit group with which I have ever been associated, and it has been my pleasure to work with them for the past twenty years." Sean Masterson looked up from the podium, across the large conference hall. The team had expected to be now basking in the glow of a standing ovation from audience. That would obviously not happen, however.

There was exactly one person in attendance.

Arnold Sandwith, the assistant deputy director to the undersecretary of the National Research Council's finance department, had not understood a word of the presentation, and had only attended as a courtesy. "Is that all? Can I go? I have another meeting," he said in a monotone, and without waiting for a response, he stood, turned on his heels, and strode out of the room, far more interested in the next meeting's opportunity to dissolve one of the other research departments.

November 22, 2019:

Grant Zenkman, eating breakfast at the National Science Institute for the first time in a month, smiled in anticipation as Jason entered the dining hall. "Hey Jason, I appreciate you showing me how to work the electron microscope and the proton degradation experiment. Just for fun, I repeated your experiment yesterday. I haven't done experimental work in a long time. I was trying to see if I could get myself interested again."

Jason Poe, surprised to see Grant, idly replied, "Oh, good, hope you matched our results."

"Well, here, you can see for yourself. I put your old results next to my results so you can compare them. Actually, there's been a definite increase in proton degradation since you did your first experiments eight years ago." Grant placed a piece of paper in front of Jason, which read as follows:

Signal Type	Frequency	Jason's 2011 Test Signal Fraction (Parts Per Ten Trillion)	Grant's 2019 Test Signal Fraction (Parts Per Ten Trillion)
Degraded Signal 1	68.777431	6	87
Degraded Signal 2	57.112947	4	55
Degraded Signal 3	53.219653	3	40
Total Degraded Signal		13	182

Standard Proton Signal   74.257985

Jason looked at the numbers for a moment, trying to regain his concentration. Finally he said, "No no no, these are way off, Grant. Look - look at the percentages. According to your data, the total signal degradation increased from 13 parts per ten trillion to 182 in the eight years since we ran the first test. That's impossible. That would mean there has been more than ten times as much proton degradation in the last eight years as there was in the previous 20 billion years of the universe. Sorry - something's got to be wrong."

Grant replied, "Oh no, I'm sure I did it right, I even had one of the lab guys with me, and we did it twice and got the same answer. In fact a couple of the numbers changed by one or two digits between the two runs."

Jason, still looking at the paper with the test results, asked, "You ran a second test?"

"Yeah."

"How long after the first one?"

"Oh, I guess it took a couple of hours to re-calibrate. Maybe three hours total."

"And you saw a *different* result between the two test runs?"

"I already told you, yeah." Grant began to fidget with impatience.

"What were the settings on the receiver?"

"Reading across, left to right, 127.8, 87.2, and 58.6, just like the procedures specify, Jason."

"Okay, what about the proton emission signal?"

Grant sighed, annoyed at Jason's inquisition. He'd just wanted to have some fun in the lab, and he had better things to be doing than listening to Jason give him the third degree.

"I *can* read and I'm not a moron, Jason."

"I didn't mean it that way -."

"Nothing personal. Just do it yourself if you don't trust my work."

"No, no - Grant -."

Look, Jason," said Grant. "I'm a little worried about you. You are way too wrapped up in this project. It's just a job, a way to pay the bills. There are lots of things more important in this world than whether protons decay."

Jason, slipping into internal thoughts, softly said, "Well, if protons really are decaying that fast, then no, there might *not* be too many things that are more important."

Grant, his momentary bubble of revitalized interest in the team completely deflated, placed a concerned arm across Jason's shoulder. Seeing that Jason was now completely absorbed in his own thoughts, Grant finally rose and walked away, realizing it was time to find a meaning to his life.

Jason stared at Grant's test results for a good hour.

November 23, 2019:

Grant Zenkman wanted to present himself as professionally

as possible, and was concerned that the undisciplined environment of the string theory team would adversely affect him, even if only subconsciously. He pulled his blue tie tight and examined himself in the mirror, happy to see that the gray suit and white shirt provided the look he desired.

With that, Grant went downstairs and walked to the exit door of the Institute. He took one look back. Christopher Parson's eyes met his own, and they looked at each other for a moment.

"Don't," said Christopher.

"I have to," replied Grant, more to placate Christopher than anything, for Christopher could not possibly know what he was about to do. "There's nothing left for me here." Grant's eyes took in the entire room, and a wistful look came across his face momentarily.

Probably Chris would not be able to relay the message, but Grant felt compelled to say, "Tell everyone goodbye and good luck, but I have to do this." With that, Grant's resolve returned and he headed out the door. Not wanting to be impolite, he had left a note explaining that he wished everyone the best, but that he no longer found fulfillment in the string theory project, and he needed to contribute more to society than he could working on this quixotic quest.

A tear slowly drifted down Christopher's cheek.

Ten minutes later Grant was at the door of the Full Employment Bureau, a division of the Ministry of Labor. Checking the directory, Grant found that his desired destination was Room 405. He climbed the stairs and entered, meeting a friendly looking young man at the front desk. Grant briefly explained his business, and was ushered into the office of a woman named Sarah Lott.

It took a few minutes for Sarah to understand what a "String Theory Project" was, and why this gentleman would have spent all his time on such a thing for the last twenty-three years. Grant, in fact, had the same question himself. Sarah had to admit, however, that there had to be a place in the economic system for a person with so much scientific training and an IQ of 189.

An hour later, Grant Zenkman left the office, gainfully employed, and now living in a world that made much more sense.

February 27, 2020:

The Democratic Party officially dissolved today, ending a long and historic tradition dating back to Thomas Jefferson. Over the past two decades the American electorate has become a far more homogeneous entity, and when the Republican Party transformed into the Unification Party. Many Democrats joined them, frequently resulting in pluralities of 95 percent or more for Unification Party candidates and many instances of unopposed candidates. This dissolution is really a formality, for the Democrats did not win a single state in the last three Presidential elections, and have not fielded a candidate for this fall's election. There are only seven Democrats remaining in Congress, and none of them is considered a potential winner in this fall's coming elections. Political pollsters have repeatedly found that voters no longer want difficult choices, that standardization is favored over diversity. As Ralph Haynes from the Gallup Poll stated, "It wasn't so much that the electorate was wild about Unification Party policies. It was simply that they just didn't want to choose any more, and they selected the party with the most consistent platform. There was too much debate within the Democratic party over what they wanted to do, and that turned off the public." With the end of the Democratic party, it appears there will be no challenge to the Unification Party in the foreseeable future.

The Unification Party, in fact, is now the ruling party in 47 nations around the world, with more tending in this direction, and this has allowed the establishment of standardized laws and economic policies. With the ongoing global trend toward conformity, the dream of a single world government seems to be a true possibility. As peace and prosperity have spread across the world, one can only be thankful that this is a revolution which did not require military might, merely the willing adoption of a common mindset by billions of individuals all over the world.

<u>May 5, 2020:</u>

Sean Masterson drummed his fingers against the table top impatiently. Thirty minutes was just too much.

"All right, everyone, we have to get the meeting started. It's almost 8:30, we were supposed to start at 8 o'clock, and we all have work to do."

Glenn Glass, ever supportive of his fellow teammates, objected. "Sean, not everyone is here yet. We've always had a pact not to start meetings until everyone is here. Everyone counts. That's what this team is all about."

Sean quickly replied, "We've started lots of meetings with people missing."

"Not if we knew they were in the building. Bryce is here someplace."

Serena Madison, just as impatient as Sean but for a

different reason, countered, "Maybe it's time to break the pact." With an ill-disguised hint of sarcasm, she continued, "Maybe, just maybe, 'the pact' is not Holy Scripture. We're doing okay. We're not making the progress we've hoped for, but we're doing okay, and frankly there are other things to do in this world besides wait for meetings to start. Times have changed. We're not going to achieve any big breakthroughs today or tomorrow or the next day, maybe it's time to drop all this life-and-death thinking. Let's just get through this meeting and move on. Besides, we've certainly lost enough time over the years waiting for Max and Bryce to show up for morning meetings, right? What will it hurt if a couple of people miss a few things?" What Serena was thinking, but dared not say quite yet, was that her motivation was to start the meeting as soon as possible for the express purpose of ending it as soon as possible.

"Hey! Hey! Hey!" laughed Max Cherry, always able to accept a joke at his own expense. "I know Bryce and I used to stay out all night, but I don't anymore, I'm here and ready to go, these days I'm a good little boy." He smiled his most ingenuous smile. "I don't know where Bryce is, I'm sure he'll be in soon - well, maybe. Yeah, he has been out more and more lately."

Glenn spoke again. "I know we lost Grant, and everyone feels bad about that. Maybe part of the reason we lost Grant was we didn't keep him in tight with the rest of us. He went on his walks every day, and we all just let him go. I don't want to start doing the same thing with other people."

"There's only so much each of us can do," said Courtney. "You can't force people into close relationships, it has to just happen."

The room was quiet for a moment at the thought of Grant,

until an uncharacteristically serious Max Cherry broke the silence. "I really do miss that guy. He was so lovably oblivious to everyone else, wasn't he?" He laughed at the recollection in a bittersweet way, and a few of the others smiled tentatively.

"I was so shocked," said Jason. "He was so matter-of-fact about it. No emotion, no turmoil, he just made a decision and left."

A tear drifted down the cheek of Zena Dunn, as she remembered a remarkable 15-year-old boy named Grant Zenkman who had affected her life so profoundly.

After an appropriate moment of reflection, Sean, ever mindful of progress to be made, brought the group back on track. "There's no point in getting upset about it. As Serena said, things change, and we have to accept that."

Serena chimed in, "And I really have other things to do, so let's get on with it."

"Who's got progress to report?" asked Sean.

Rose, in her typically measured tones, said, "We all have issues with Grant leaving, but I think there's more than that. We all know our progress has slowed. We've lost the feeling that big breakthroughs will keep occurring, and that's wearing on all of us. It's completely understandable."

"Working here used to be an adventure every day," said Jason. "Now it's just a job." These were words that Jason had never expected to utter.

Heads nodded throughout the room. The baffling proton degradation results were still not understood, and the lack of interest in the 20-year report-out still gnawed at everyone. A lot of the mathematics was still unresolved. The Large Hadron Collider Experiments were no longer producing new information. The twenty-six years of togetherness seemed intolerable in these times when progress was stymied.

"Does anyone else think we might not ever make it?"

It was Melina, voicing the fears of failure and mortality that plagued all of them at this point. The words ripped at the heart of Sean Masterson, for every leader knows that the battle is lost as soon as the troops begin to doubt victory.

"Come on, come on, it's only temporary," said Glenn Glass, trying to rally everyone. "We have a lot of projects coming to fruition in the next few years, and maybe one of them will crack string theory wide open for us. We have to stay together."

Zena gathered herself and agreed, saying, "Glenn is right. We're going to have the Superconducting Supercollider in five or six years, and that's going to give us a lot of new data to verify the theoretical work. So all we have to do between now and then is resolve the conflicts in the current equations, and I'm sure everyone is willing to dedicate themselves to that. Hey - I've been strictly experimental, but I'll do the theoretical stuff for a while if that will help."

Max couldn't resist a poke at Zena, and said, "Sorry, Zena, but we don't have any math problems that only require addition and subtraction." Zena's specialty was most definitely not abstract mathematics, and everyone laughed, including Zena, in spite of herself. The mood of the room improved measurably.

"All right, so what's everyone working on?" asked Sean, nearly desperate to get the conversation back on track.

Serena, now irritated that even more time had been wasted, jumped in. "Sean, you know perfectly well what we've been working on. We each have an aspect of the equation set, and we're trying to reconcile the differences between them. Zena, not to question your willingness to help with the mathematics, but things have changed since the early days. Even with the proton degradation problem, you experimentalists are ahead of our theoretical work, and we're struggling. Resolving the conflicts isn't some trivial math exercise."

Zena now wondered if her offer to assist with the math hadn't been taken as an insult.

Glenn, realizing that convincing the group to wait for Bryce was a lost cause, said, "Serena is right. When I try to enter all the known parameters for the fifth-dimensional vibrations, for example, the resulting conclusions match our current theory and the Hadron Collider experimental data. So that's all good. The problem is that those same conclusions imply certain things about the phenomena that must be occurring in each of the other dimensions. If I take those fifth dimensional implications for the eighth dimension, or any other dimension, for that matter, they contradict the equations we already know to be correct."

Max Cherry added, "It's that way with all the dimensions. Each dimension's equation set creates implications for the other dimensions, but we can't reconcile the implications with the known information for those other dimensions. It's as though each piece of the puzzle looks correct individually, but when you put the puzzle together, nothing fits. Even if you get two or three perfect fits, the next dimension's equations don't match the others, and you're back to square one. I'm sure there's a solution, but right now we don't have any mathematical way to find it other than trial and error, and there are millions of possibilities. It's not like the Calabi-Yau structure solution, where we can do iterative solutions via computer and solve it, because in this case the equations themselves change from iteration to iteration. It's just painful laborious work."

Melina piped in hopefully, "Then I think we need to go through the equations in detail."

"Oh, join reality, you minutiae-obsessed pinhead!" It was Bryce, finally having arrived, and just slipping into his chair. "Get out of your little notebooks, Melina, and get a clue. I'm sorry, but everyone has gone over all those stupid equations and they just don't work. For someone like you to tell us we haven't reviewed them properly is just arrogant."

"I'm sorry, I'm sorry," said the thoroughly intimidated Melina. She knew Bryce was positively brilliant, and she had no intention of debating with him. But she had never seen him be cruel like this. "I just wanted something to report for progress at this meeting." She intentionally avoided eye contact with Bryce.

Bryce went on. "I think all of us need a reality check. Does it make sense for this many people to study one arcane subject for our entire lives, with almost no chance of accomplishing anything worthwhile? Isn't it time we grew up?"

Jason interjected, "But Bryce, you loved theoretical physics more than any of us - "

"Yeah, well, I was an ignorant kid. As for you, you all are just a bunch of ignorant middle-aged old farts, and that's worse." He laughed. "Maybe I shouldn't have shown up at all today." With that, Bryce stood up and started walking toward the door. "Anybody else want to cut out for a long lunch?"

To everyone's surprise, Courtney rose from her chair and left with him.

Thoroughly deflated, the team sat silent at the table for a few minutes, each one deep in his own thoughts. There would be no more discussion of string theory today. It was Jason who finally spoke.

"Have you guys watched TV lately?"

Most of the heads shook from side to side. In their isolated existence within the Institute, there was little awareness of the outside world.

"I watched all through the night last Saturday. Did you know there's basically no music industry left out there?"

"Is that why we only get old music over the sound system?" asked Melina. "I wondered about that."

Christopher Parson, sitting at the table in silence as usual, suddenly spoke up, much to the surprise of everyone.

"No one listens to music except us."

Christopher's eyes wandered about the room, as if he was speaking to no one in particular. Jason knew Christopher often took long walks through the city, and would know better than the others what was happening outside.

"Do you ever hear music outside the Institute, Chris?"

Christopher shook his head, almost imperceptibly. Then he smiled at some internal thought and started whistling, and was obviously off into his own internal world again.

Zena said, "Yeah, even the other floors of this building have the music shut off these days."

Jason continued. "That's the least of it. I watched the news. They're moving toward a single world government, crime is almost unheard of, and the world's economy is on a level of prosperity we never dreamed of when we were younger. Art is gone, drama is gone, and athletics is gone except for rote calisthenics to maintain fitness. And we all know how little interest there is in science, at least science without a direct profit motive. It's like we're the only ones left with any intellectual curiosity or desire to improve ourselves, and I don't understand that."

"No wonder nobody's interested in string theory," said Rose.

"You're making it sound like these changes are a bad thing," commented Serena scornfully, directing her point toward Jason.

"It's just not the world I grew up in," he replied,

"Well, maybe that's an improvement," continued Serena. "We've all been cloistered in here like nuns for far too long. Maybe we all need to get out more. I've been going out in the evenings lately, and I'm starting to see what Grant found so appealing." With that, Serena unilaterally decided the meeting was over, and left the room.

By the time the meeting broke up, Bryce Thomas and Courtney Ellis had quickly packed a bag of necessities and left the building, never to return.

Sean Masterson, seeing the seeds of disintegration within the team, closed his eyes and tried to block out the realization that he was failing the biggest test of his life.

Saturday, 8:05 a.m.:

Michael called the Omniscience Council meeting to order. There were no attendees other than the Council members themselves. Michael rose to speak. "There has still been no progress on the permeation issue," he said. "The vibrations are continuing to degrade. At this point no viable options have been identified." Michael then proceeded to read the minutes from the previous meeting, and a voice vote was held to approve the minutes. There was no Old Business, which was not surprising considering the current circumstances. No one had even proposed any action items for the last several meetings. Brother John presented the City's safety statistics since the last meeting, which as always were perfect. When Michael asked if there were any items to be brought up as New Business, Brother Timothy spoke up.

"I know this is a crisis, but I still don't like the schedule slides. I have a Festival to plan. And to take the extreme negative view, if the universe does explode or collapse or whatever it is supposed to do, this will reflect very poorly in our performance metrics. This concerns me."

Peter glared at Timothy. "What's the matter with you? Who cares anymore about the schedule or the damned performance metrics? Who cares about appearances? We have blown it. We are sitting here having nice calm meetings per proper procedure when the entire system is coming down before our eyes! The stinking schedule won't be the only thing sliding if something isn't done, you moron! What are you thinking?"

Timothy fired back, "That kind of unprofessionalism is undoubtedly what got us into this mess in the first place! You're always so big on good ideas! Go - go - go…. go think outside the box or something. I'm here to run a professional meeting!"

Peter turned to the entire group. "Gentlemen, we need to report the true status to all City dwellers. People know something is wrong, and we're withholding vital information from them. Number one, the people have a right to know the true situation. And number two, we need everyone in the City to help us find a solution."

Timothy retorted, "Oh, no, no. It's bad enough that *you* know what's going on, you're always causing more trouble for us. No more of that do-gooder bleeding heart stuff. I'm not so sure I believe all these dire reports anyway. Just because every instrument records the same information, they could all be off, couldn't they?" Timothy frowned, obviously not believing his own remarks. "I don't care. I'm not going to cause unnecessary concern, and I am definitely not going to risk the reputation of the Omniscience Council.

"You idiot! You're risking everything! Literally everything!" cried Peter.

The Omniscience Council voted 8-2 not to publicly announce the crisis, Peter and Thomas being the only no votes.

October 18, 2027:

The actual ceremony itself was quite short. A brief introductory speech by the World Religion Council Chairman, the signing of the documents, a few handshakes and poses for the photographers, and it was all done. The evolution of a passive society had allowed the formerly unthinkable - one world religion. The pope's willing, indeed enthusiastic, surrender of his religious authority to the Council two years ago had eliminated the final significant obstacle in the movement, and today's events made global religious unity official. With extremist factions a thing of the past and worshippers the world over happy to follow traditional authority figures, there was no longer any reason to oppress, discriminate, or exclude, and this allowed the great religions of Christianity, Islam, Judaism, Hinduism, Buddhism, and virtually all others to coalesce into one unified global church. It was a great day. The ancient divisions were no more.

February 28, 2029:

All eyes turned toward the face of Zena Dunn. Her blank expression spoke volumes.

There had been no secret trial run this time. Thirty-three years after the morally challenged leader of the free world gave the project go-ahead, Zena Dunn sat at the main control board for the Superconducting Supercollider, the SSC she had dreamed of since her college days. In stark contrast to the pastoral Swiss setting of the Large Hadron Collider fifteen years before, the SSC resided under the surface of the tumbleweed-strewn barrenness outside the tiny town of Perseus in central Texas. The 120-mile tube incorporated a superconducting electromagnetic field capable of accelerating protons much closer to the speed of light than the Hadron Collider. At these speeds, Zena's calculations indicated that all of the physically significant theoretical subatomic particles could be created, providing the answers to the remaining questions in the string theory team's equations.

Sean Masterson searched Zena's eyes for an indication of whether the SSC's tracings held the answers to the team's long journey. Now stooped and gray, Sean was visibly weary from so many years leading the team, playing the thankless role of taskmaster, setting the standards for the others. His iron will fading, Sean knew he could not keep on for many more years. The equations were tantalizingly close to complete resolution when confined to any one of the dimensions, and these close approaches to success maintained the team's focus and motivation. When the equations for multiple dimensions were combined in an attempt to develop a simultaneous solution for the entire system, however, mathematical alignment between the dimensions invariably broke down, causing the entire theoretical construct to collapse like a house of cards. Sean recalled the example of Thomas Edison's painstaking quest for a proper filament for the electric light bulb, where the sure path to success was thousands of failed experiments. Sean's confidence, along with most of the team's, was bolstered by their belief that the long-awaited SSC results would light the pathway to the final resolution.

Darryl Johnson looked at his monitor, then at Zena, and then at the floor. The vague feeling of unease that had gnawed at him for years was running high on this day. He did not share Sean's hopeful comparison of the string theory team to Thomas Edison. In every previous conceptual physics breakthrough, from Galileo to Einstein to Adam and Eve Parson, a new radical vision of reality had preceded the actual breakthroughs. Although early string theory was full of such prescient insights, the recent years had more closely resembled blindly foraging through a mathematical forest, hoping by sheer luck to stumble upon some unknown treasure. Darryl's personal dream, kept entirely to himself, was to be the one to see that new reality before anyone else. His constant dreaming was not without purpose; he believed that truth would come not from solving bewilderingly complex equations, but from seeing a pure and simple truth that had always been in plain sight. He certainly hoped for new insights from Zena's SSC trial today, but even if that were to happen, he would be dissatisfied in not having reached the new understanding through the power of pure thought.

Jason Poe's attention was quite frankly not on the SSC experiment. The death of Glenn Glass six months prior had left a great void in his life. Glenn's heart attack was completely unexpected, and it pained Jason that fate had left him no opportunity for a goodbye. Jason's last twenty years had only been possible because of Glenn's unflagging efforts after the failed proton disintegration experiment; Jason understood this full well. In Jason's entire life, no one had loved him as purely as Glenn Glass, and now there would never be a way to repay the debt.

Melina Valin reached into a pocket and pulled out a piece of folded paper, trying to maintain a professional veneer and hold back the tears welling at the corners of her eyes. As much as Glenn Glass's death hurt Jason Poe, Rose Pupa's matter-of-fact departure left an even larger void in Melina's heart. At this climactic moment for the string theory team, Melina felt she had to make it a point to remember her trusted friend. For all of her 58-plus years, Melina had believed in a world of infinitesimal detail, where control was managed pixel by pixel, and rational thought always determined one's course of action. Melina's predicament was that she herself was very much a captive of her own emotions, even as she approached sexagenarian status. Her relentless yet futile pursuit of every fact, every detail, and total control of her world inevitably led to her own questioning of her competence and worth. Her standards for herself were unattainable, and her resulting situation was characterized by outstanding performance and withering self-doubt. The others were empathetic enough to sense Melina's inner conflicts, but Melina perceived their proclamations of support as emotion-driven and therefore unreliable. Melina could not trust advice unless she was sure it was based on the rationality she craved but did not possess.

And so the blessing that was Rose Pupa had entered Melina's life. In every situation, Rose was the calm voice of reason, supportive yet objective, unerringly guiding Melina to productive activities, while gently urging her to abandon her pursuit of the pointless minutiae which so attracted Melina.

Waiting for the SSC tracings to appear, Melina read Rose's farewell note one more time:

Dear Fellow Teammates,

I cannot deny that I have enjoyed much of the past thirty years with you. For a long time I too believed in the worth of attempting to discover the origin and nature of the universe. However, I can no longer rationalize my own participation in this project. Ultimately, it does not lead to any tangible benefit for society. Accordingly, please accept my resignation from the String Theory Team, effective immediately.

Cordially yours,
Rose Pupa

Much like Grant before her, Rose had simply left the note on her dining room table and slipped out of the Institute one morning before anyone else was awake. Coming from Grant, this was believable, almost typical. The team had even laughed about it after the disappointment had worn off somewhat. But from Rose Pupa, such an unfeeling departure was a real shock.

Jason Poe's hurt was that Glenn Glass had not had a chance to say goodbye. Melina Valin's hurt was that Rose

Pupa had *chosen* not to say goodbye. It was difficult to say whose pain was greater.

Serena Madison desperately wished for the SSC experiment to be a colossal success. She had worked her beloved equations for two-thirds of her life. She wanted to see the end of the project, but her appetite for the adventure had waned long ago. She prayed for Zena's eyes to light up in the recognition of the final breakthrough, so Serena could at last find rest from her lifetime of searching.

Zena stared at the tracings from the particle collisions, not knowing what to make of them. Under normal circumstances, she could instantly perceive particles and energies and physical phenomena, while others could only see something resembling the most wildly abstract of paintings. On the SSC monitor before her, Zena could make out a proton or an electron signal here or there, but many of the tracings were unidentifiable, random coursings across the screen, not representing any real or even theoretically imagined particles. If the long-sought graviton particle or the anticipated superpartners were in there somewhere, they were lost in the maze of nonsensical tracings on her monitor. It was like a new universe, in comparison to what had been learned in nearly a hundred years of particle acceleration tests. Either the instruments were wildly out of calibration, or the subatomic particle zoo had suddenly metamorphosized into something entirely different.

<u>March 26, 2031:</u>

"The Cultural Control Ministry today announced that it has officially given up on its efforts directed toward brainwave modification to restore proper societal attitudes among non-conforming citizens. The original research was conducted fifteen years ago on chimpanzees. Scientists found that exposing chimps to certain discrete extreme high-frequency sonic vibrations, thousands of times higher than the audible range, significantly affected the behavior of the chimps over time. The chimpanzees became more curious about their environment and more considerate of one another. Researchers believed a similar effect might occur with humans, and might provide a method for retraining citizens who resist the uniformity rules governing modern society. The vibrations did, in fact, affect humans in much the same way, but the outward manifestations were increased intellectual questioning, greater concern for the weaker members of society, and desire for self-improvement. Furthermore, an almost psychic understanding of the internal emotions of others appeared in some test subjects. These characteristics have all been identified by sociologists as counterproductive to the efficiency improvements desired by the government, as they tend to propagate instability. Years of effort to obtain different results were ineffective, and researchers have agreed that the quest was fruitless."

Dr. Grant Zenkman regretfully finished the paragraph and emailed it to the Ministry's press group for release. Since taking over as technical director of the Cultural Control Ministry seven years ago, he had spearheaded numerous projects designed to maximize societal efficiency and suppress the few counterproductive individuals still active. Brainwave modification through specific sonic exposures had seemed such a promising therapy, but sadly, only negative effects could be induced, those which induced exactly the behaviors which were undesirable. It had never been determined why these particular frequencies would have such effects, and it was unfortunate that practical benefits to society would not be realized from this work.

Nevertheless, progress was being made on all fronts, and Grant smiled with satisfaction in the knowledge that his work made a positive contribution. There would be further opportunities. He smiled ruefully at the irony of his current life - that a certain level of curiosity and creativity on his part was required to develop the technologies necessary to eliminate those exact qualities among the populace. He looked forward to the day when he too would be able to act as a simple, obedient servant, without the need for thought, analysis and reflection.

March 31, 2033:

Sean Masterson threw down his pencil in disgust. Finally distrusting the computers, he had taken to performing his calculations by hand. After seventeen years of constant effort, the string theory team had still not resolved the disparities between the equation sets of the various dimensions. The problem of obtaining simultaneous synchronized vibrations in all dimensions seemed unsolvable. Furthermore, the global support team had dwindled to nothing over the years, as Sean's worst fears were realized. For the enemy of the research scientist is not active opposition - it is apathy. A good researcher can prevail over even the strongest opponent by providing irrefutable test data and letting the data itself win the day. But apathy is the enemy most to be feared, for how can the researcher succeed if no one cares if he is right or not? The spirit of discovery seemed to have disappeared entirely from the world, and its microscopic remnant was embodied only in the remaining string theory team members. Serena Madison had left the team two months before, disheartened by the failure of the SSC, and so now they were down to six - Sean, Max Cherry, Melina Valin, Jason Poe, Zena Dunn, and Darryl Johnson. These six had always spent the most time inside the Institute, most often working together. Sean, however, could only see the lost unity of the team, and took the missing team members as a sign of his own failed leadership.

The SSC tests had been repeated many times, of course, always with similar results: the apparent presence of a large number of bizarre particles never before seen and not predicted by any cosmological theory. Either a catastrophic error had been made in the construction of the hundred-billion dollar Collider, or somehow an entirely new physics had been discovered, in which case the team was hopelessly far from any final solution.

Sean Masterson walked out the main door of the Institute and headed toward a beautiful park two miles away which held a six-story tower with a vantage point overlooking a good share of the city. As he walked, Sean pondered the choices he had made in his life. He had consciously forsaken personal intimacy for the efficiency of professional relationships, firmly believing that a person should be measured by his actions and accomplishments. Behind this carefully constructed façade, however, he truly cherished every member of the string theory team. They had been his only family, and he was now torn over the choices he had made. He had withheld himself in the name of discipline and progress, and with the team fragmented and its objective seemingly no longer achievable, Sean Masterson counted himself a failure both personally and professionally.

Sean reached the park, climbed to the top of the tower, and

stood at the railing, looking out over the park. He closed his eyes. The image he saw was that of his father, sneering in disdain at the failures of his son.

Sean Masterson climbed the railing and threw himself off.

Saturday, 9:39 a.m.:

To: All City Dwellers
From: Brother Peter, soon-to-be former Omniscience Council
          Member <bigpete@omni.com>
Sent: Saturday, 9:39 a.m. City Time
Subject: Permeation Regression

I, Peter, your fellow Citizen of the City, am taking it upon myself to notify all City Dwellers of a critical situation facing us all. I have been forbidden to do this by the Omniscience Council, but my conviction is so strong that this is just and necessary that I am willing to accept whatever disciplinary measures the Council sees fit to impose upon me.

You have previously been notified that there have been some anomalies in the Permeation readings. The situation is far more severe than that. We have measured a definite rate of vibrational permeation decay, and it is an exponential function, meaning that the regression will accelerate faster and faster until catastrophic universal sonic failure occurs. At the present time this process is irreversible and inevitable. The universe as we know it, including the City and its residents, will cease to exist. At this time we cannot predict when that will be.

We can, however, make back-calculations based on the regression which has occurred to date, and determine that the initial disruption occurred Thursday, between 6:55 and 7:00 p.m. Unfortunately, this information has not provided any useful clues regarding why the sonic regression has occurred, or what can be done to reverse it.

Any City Dweller having useful information in terms of understanding or reversing the permeation regression is requested to contact the undersigned immediately. All City Dwellers have a right to know the facts, and we all must pull together and face this crisis. Good luck.

Brother Peter

<u>August 23, 2035:</u>

Kathy Leigh sat in the make-up chair, thinking about, well, she didn't know what. The network professionals could make her up while she read the newspaper, while she spoke to her producer, even while she talked to several people at once, moving all around. They could do it without a word, without disrupting her in any way. She felt bad that she had not properly appreciated the job they did. She tried to hold still just this once. Kathy wondered what had ever become of Martha, her makeup artist and surrogate mother way back on KMAX in Bend, Oregon. Of course, Martha would never have referred to herself as an artist, that would have been too "hoity-toity." Kathy laughed at the memory. How amateurish it all had seemed, and she shuddered at how bad she must have been on camera in those days. But Kathy had to admit that Martha could make her up as well as any of these experts. Of course, it wasn't fair to compare the make-up job required for a woman of 63 compared to that fresh-faced girl of 17, she said to herself with a wry smile.

In the twelve years she had been network news anchor, so many people had come and gone. The news itself was not as interesting, certainly not as exciting as those old dangerous days with military threats, political scandals, scientific breakthroughs, and controversies of every sort. The Global Societal Standardization programs had brought stability and efficiency, there was no doubt of that. Crime had largely been eradicated, war was unknown, and the global standard of living, while no longer rising substantially, had been leveled worldwide to completely eliminate poverty, except in the few discordant areas where standardization had not been accepted. Yes, humankind's Golden Age had certainly come to pass, just as it had been anticipated 20 years ago. A large part of the benefit came from the elimination of wasteful programs, such as charitable efforts, the arts, and pure scientific research, and thankfully no one was interested in those pursuits anymore anyway. Yes, it was a great era for humanity. Perhaps the greatest advance was the sublimation of the desire to stretch oneself, to push oneself beyond one's limits. The sociologists had found that most of humanity's problems could be traced to this issue. They had proven that society's ills are largely caused by people who push to change and improve themselves and the world. Imagine the tension that could have been avoided had people like Martin Luther King or Thomas Jefferson not lived! That was the great success of Societal Standardization. In the new merit-based society, racism was eliminated, just as King had dreamed, but without all the social upheaval. Anyone who conformed to societal norms, regardless of sex or race or anything else, was welcomed and accepted. It was Thomas Jefferson's dream without Thomas Jefferson's war. And what made it so perfect was that the people themselves had caused it to happen. Societal Standardization was the final evolution of humankind. It was not forced upon society through dramatic upheavals, as women's rights or racial equality had been in the late 1900's. The people themselves willed it to be so. Humanity had finally found a form of government defined by the average citizen. When the desire to improve oneself was sublimated, so was the need for authority figures to oppress or discriminate. All became equal because all were willingly subservient. The divisive issues of the past simply melted away. It was as near to Utopia as humanity had ever imagined. Kathy laughed again to herself as she realized how hard she had worked as a young woman to improve herself. With what she now knew about Standardization, that had certainly been the wrong approach. But there was no denying her silly affection for those long-ago days.

"You're done, Ms. Leigh, " said the makeup artist. Kathy shook herself out of her stupor and rose from the chair. She walked to her anchor's chair and sat down, looking around the studio to orient herself. The routine was so familiar by now that she had to make a conscious effort to get her mind working, otherwise she would just go on autopilot. Not that she couldn't do a perfectly good newscast that way, but she enjoyed it more when she was fully engaged. Another anachronistic quirk, she felt.

"Ten seconds, Ms. Leigh. Five, four, three…" The director silently counted down two and one with his fingers, then pointed to her. "Good evening, ladies and gentlemen, this is Kathy Leigh bringing you the CBS Evening News, August 23, 2035. Our top story tonight is the Congressional passage of the Great Quarantine measure. This bill will set aside the city of Dunsmuir, Texas for those citizens who have failed to adapt to society's needs. The president spoke on this subject today."

The screen cut to an image of the president. "I wholeheartedly support the Congressional action on this bill," he said. "The overwhelming majority of America's population, well over 99 percent, are upstanding, productive citizens and happily fulfill their obligations to society. In every possible way, America is the best it has ever been. Despite our best efforts, however, nearly 18,000 people in our country insist on their own personal independence over the greater good of our nation. They demand to select their own occupations. They speak out in public on controversial topics. They teach their children that independence is better than uniformity. My fellow Americans, our era is the greatest in American history, and you are the ones who deserve the credit for that. In our efforts to become a more efficient society, we must stop wasting resources on those who do not assist in our efforts. Accordingly, with Congressional and Senate support, we have created a bill to require that those citizens identified as Anti-Standardization will be confined to Dunsmuir, Texas. Barriers will be erected around the city with armed guards to prevent the residents from escaping. Let me emphasize that we are not a cruel people. The facilities for normal existence will be provided, with the exception of airplanes or any other mode of transportation that might allow escape from the Quarantine zone. But we as a nation will no longer support the inefficient lifestyle of these people. They will be responsible for their own survival, that is what efficiency demands. Once again, I applaud Congress for its rationality in unanimously passing the bill, and we look forward to an American future of unbridled optimism."

Kathy Leigh reflexively vomited. She no longer understood why.

<u>June 5, 2036</u>:

Zena Dunn, fatigued and feeling ill, reviewed her results one last time, analyzing all the possible hypotheses that might provide rational explanations of the nonsensical SSC results. She questioned whether she had the nerve to bring up an idea as radical as the one she had been considering for the last month. She remembered a quote from Sir Arthur Conan Doyle, her favorite author, and the creator of Sherlock Holmes, a character to whom Zena felt a definite kinship.

"When you have eliminated the impossible, whatever remains, no matter how improbable, must be the truth."

<u>Saturday, 9:44 p.m.</u>:

Dunstan, trying to get his mind off his frustration, sat down at his computer. *Hey, an email,* he thought. *Probably another junk subscription offer, that's all I ever get.* His idle cynicism was torn asunder, of course, by the revelations in Peter's email. *Oh my God,* he finally said to himself after reading it twice. *Is this really happening?* Suddenly the ancient frustration over not being able to play Gabriel's Trumpet seemed trivial. He wondered what he could do to help. Dunstan was merely a musician, he couldn't change universal physics. The only thing of real interest that had ever happened to him (not that he would ever admit it) was the time when he pulled out the Trumpet and played it for a moment. Yeah, that had been a real disaster.

Then it hit him. As Dunstan read through Peter's email a third time, he noted the estimated time of the original sonic disruption. Thursday between 6:55 and 7:00 p.m. He thought back for a minute. When was that? Where was I? His eyes grew wide as saucers. *Oh damn. Oh damn! Oh damn! damn! damn!* It was him! It was Dunstan who had done it! With Gabriel's Trumpet! Right at that moment! Why oh why had he been so insistent on playing that damnable Trumpet? He dropped his head into his hands. *What have I done?*

June 6, 2036:

The remaining five string theory team members punctually reported for the team's 40th anniversary report. "Report" was actually a misnomer, as there had been no outside attendees for several years, and this time no one even bothered to go through the motions of writing up any results. By now, they knew each other so well that no words were needed to express the familiar camaraderie between them. They still enjoyed their work and each other, but the bittersweet tenor of their relationship was palpable, as the odds of ultimate success became more remote with each passing year. To mark the occasion, the team had reserved a conference room at the White House, and the five aging theoreticians sat down at the same ancient table where 40 years ago their lives had been irrevocably altered. No one knew who they were, but they had valid credentials and funding, surreptitiously and permanently established so long ago by Bill Clinton and Elmer Schmidlapp, and nothing else was necessary in a world that never questioned authority.

"Damn, where's the guy with the combover, I've got a

few rubber bands in my pocket," said Max Cherry, eliciting smiles from the others at the familiarity of the old memory.

Jason looked around the table at his oldest friends, his only friends, his smile fading. He felt the lump in his throat growing, the occasion bringing back all the fond memories, as well as profound regret at the lack of progress and outside interest in his lifelong quest. He softly asked, "Do you think this will be the last anniversary?"

Everyone was silent for a moment, eyes making contact. Then Max grinned as impishly as ever. He would not let the proceedings become maudlin. "Jason, haven't I had any impact on your miserable life? Ever? Tell you the truth, I don't care if we get there or not, this has been a beautiful way to spend my life. Why would I quit now? I'm 66 years old, I'm with the only people in the world that I love. What am I going to do besides this? Can't be a fireman anymore. I'm not going anywhere, buddy."

Max's comment brightened the entire room. Melina, still taking notes after all these years, smiled to herself. She too still enjoyed the quest, although she certainly missed the adventure of believing success was just around the corner. In her rational mind she realized that five people could not solve the remaining parts of the string theory puzzle in the few years they had left, but she could still delight in the tiny steps of progress along the way.

Darryl, too, had no intention of leaving. In this group, Darryl the dreamer had found a home and a family. In the "real" world, especially this strange new outside world, where curiosity was a cause for scorn, there would be no place for him anymore; he knew that. Far from thinking about giving up, Darryl experienced a dread fear of a frightful future day when he could no longer explore the universe in his mind.

It was left to Melina to put her finger on it. "So none of us wants to leave. I was thinking about that, about how Grant left first, and then Bryce and Courtney, and so on. Tell me if I'm way off base here. In every case, the people who left were the ones who were spending the most time away from the Institute, away from the team. Grant was the first to leave. He used to spend all his afternoons on long walks away from the Institute, in the outer world. Bryce often walked with Max, and Courtney spent a lot of time outside as well. Then look at the five of us. We were always the ones hanging together, keeping the energy among ourselves. It's almost like being away from the group sapped the motivation of each of the ones who left. Once they started spending time away from the group, they lost interest in string theory, in anything that wasn't a 'practical' activity. I can't explain it, but it's like as long as we're here with the group, we're in a protective cocoon, kept safe from whatever it is that's outside."

Max's eyes lit up in recognition. "You know, you're right, I never hit on that before. I did my share of partying in the early days, but then I got so caught up in the beauty of string theory that I gave it up and I never missed it, and from that point on I did notice I felt much closer to all of you - and to the work."

"That doesn't make any sense," said Jason, "but I guess not everything has to. I agree, though - I've often felt that if I walked away, I'd never want to come back."

Darryl spoke up again. "Maybe we should all stay together. All the time. Maybe there's some strange emotional synergistic effect caused by being together."

"Why not?" said Melina. "What else do we have left here? Let's do it. Together all the time. Twenty-four hours a day.

No going out. Not even sleeping in separate rooms. There are only five of us, we could take one of the larger rooms and all share it. Can all of us make that kind of commitment? God, I want to solve string theory in the time I have left."

Everyone looked at Max, easily the most individualistic of the remaining team members. "Works for me," he said. "Everybody else okay with it?"

Heads nodded all around the room. "Great, we're agreed," said Max. "Hope you don't mind my passing gas in the middle of the night, I don't have such great control over things anymore, if you know what I mean," he said, still able to get a laugh any time he wanted.

"All right, all right, enough from the eternal thirteen-year-old," laughed Melina, as she hit the backspace key repeatedly, deleting Max's last comment from her notes. In Sean's absence, Melina had taken over the leadership role of the team, and in the process developed a newfound confidence in herself, even at this late stage of her life. "I know everyone has been working on reconciling proton degradation data and SSC results with traditional theory and past data. We all know that the tests from the past several years have given different results than the particle accelerator experiments not only conducted by ourselves, but ever since 1930. Has anyone come to any conclusions? Has anyone come up with a theory as to why the tests from recent decades are giving false results?"

A long silence ensued. The five were together almost every day. They all knew that no one understood the false results.

Zena, who uncharacteristically had not said a word yet, took a deep breath. It was time to say what she had to say.

"I'm not so sure they *are* false results, Melina. I've been over it and over it. We repeated the tests endlessly, and the results were always the same, even getting weirder than what we saw in the initial SSC trials. But there is one way that it just might make sense. I can calculate altered string vibrational patterns that would create particle signatures just like what we found in the SSC tests. They match the proton degradation results as well. I know this sounds nutty, but the data is perfectly consistent with a universe in which the basic string vibrational patterns, which define the subatomic particle properties, have actually changed. I swear there's nothing wrong with the tests. Scientific principles don't change, that's one of the fundamental tenets. And if the test is not wrong, then - then -"

"Then something has changed with the physical universe," whispered Jason Poe.

Zena continued. "Yes, crazy as it sounds, that's what I think. I mean, there's nothing you can point to. No tests other than these quantum scale subatomic evaluations are showing any changes at all. But if you rule out a defect in the test, then you're left with only one possible conclusion."

Melina slowly absorbed Zena's words. "What in the world could cause a change like that?"

"I wish I knew," replied Zena.

The team sat silently for a minute or two, until Melina spoke again. "Oh my god."

"What is it?" asked Jason.

"I hope this isn't out of place," said Melina, "but can I tell you about something I read the other day? You know how I'm always looking up historical information or data to try to pick up a clue here or there that might help us. I ran across a news item from five years ago. Did anyone read about the sonic vibration tests the Cultural Control Ministry ran, where they subjected chimpanzees and then people to high-frequency vibrations to try to restore proper attitudes among people considered to be troublemakers?"

Darryl, Zena, and Jason shook their heads uncomprehendingly, but Max replied, "Yeah yeah, that rings a bell, sounded like Big Brother to me."

Melina continued, "The sonic vibrations did have an effect. They increased curiosity, creativity and empathy, to the point where people could sense one another's emotions."

"Why are you telling us about this?" asked Zena.

"I thought the article was interesting and I looked up the actual report. The vibration frequencies they used are in the same range as our fundamental particle string vibration patterns. My god, I noticed that when I read the report, but I didn't think anything of it."

Zena replied, "What? You mean when people were subjected to vibrations at the same frequency as the strings, it changed their behavior?"

"Yes, markedly," said Melina. "And think about it. Increased curiosity? Creativity? Empathy? It's all exactly the opposite of the trends that have swept through global society in the last twenty or thirty years."

"Wait a minute," said Max. "Zena says the experiments show that the string vibration patterns are changing, or breaking down, or something. Then you say that exposing people to the original string vibration frequencies affected their behavior, in exactly the opposite way of what we see happening in society?"

Melina nodded, still thinking it through. "Is this a crazy idea? Could the strings affect more than the physical world? Is there a real string vibration breakdown occurring, and is it actually affecting human behavior?"

Max replied, not a hint of amusement in his voice, "Yeah, it's a crazy idea, all right. The question is whether it's crazy *enough*."

Saturday, 10:30 p.m.:

Peter strode into the Omniscience Council meeting, dragging Dunstan by the wrist behind him. Brother Michael rose to his feet. "So, you've come back? A little late, don't you think? We actually appreciated you not showing up at the last two meetings, we thought if you never showed up again, we'd be spared the task of formally dismissing you. But I guess we can take five minutes and kick you off the Council right now."

"Shut up, you old fool!" Peter was wild-eyed in his intensity. "None of that matters now. This is Dunstan, he's the Minister of Incidental Music, and he knows what happened. Listen to him!"

Brother Abraham slowly stood, his craggy features lending him an undeniable aura of authority which had served him well in his previous term as Council Chairman. "Peter, we've really had enough of you and your tirades and causes. We're all tired. If this crisis is as you say, then it doesn't matter what we do, our fate is determined. And if the crisis is not as you say, which we all suspect, well then, there isn't a crisis at all - now is there?

"Oh for God's sake - listen to him for one minute," implored Peter. "One minute. If you still don't think any of this is worthwhile, I'll leave and never come back. Come on, Dunstan, just like you told me. Come on. Now!"

Dunstan stood before the Omniscience Council,

completely cowed. His embarrassment at what he now had to say was palpable. He haltingly explained his epochs-long frustration over not being able to blow the Consolidating Tones, his jealousy of Gabriel, and his ill-fated attempt to play the Trumpet for himself. He quietly concluded his statement. "When Gabriel blows the Trumpet, it cements the permeation level, and allows the next level to begin. I know that much. I never thought playing it at the wrong time, or with the wrong musical sequence, would make a difference. I just had to play it. I was foolish and stupid. And now look what I've done."

"Well, this is absolutely preposterous!" bellowed Brother Bartholomew from his seat at the Council table. "I never heard anything so foolish -"

"No it's not!!!" came a tiny but resolute voice from the back of the room. Sister Esther had slipped into the hall quietly at Peter's request. "In preparation for this presentation, Peter brought Dunstan to us. Dunstan really is a talented musician, and he was able to tell us the sequence of tones he played. We can't change the course of the permeation, but we can calculate the effect of certain frequency inputs, and everything indicates that his session with the Trumpet was the event that triggered the crisis. I can take you down to our control room and run the simulation for you. It's true. Believe it."

Brother Michael sat down with a thud. It was all too much to bear for any of them. For an eternity the City had run with nary a glitch, and now it was all coming down around them. All from a moment of weakness by a jealous musician? It seemed unfathomable.

Peter tried to gather his wits. Finally he had gotten their attention, but what to do, what to do. He began to muse out loud before the silent assembly. He had spent a lot of time talking to Esther and learning about the entire string system. "All right, what do we know? We know the vibrations of the strings permeate progressively throughout each of the ten dimensions. The strings begin to vibrate in a given dimension, and slowly permeate throughout that entire dimension. When the permeation of one dimension is complete, Gabriel blows the Trumpet, and the frequency generated by the Trumpet consolidates the permeation, locking it in for that dimension. At that point, the vibration of the strings in the next dimension begins, and follows the same gradual process of permeation throughout that dimension, and so on. In the first four dimensions, which comprise time plus the three spatial dimensions, the permeation was almost immediate, resulting in the Great Unfurling, the "Big Bang" of the visible universe, as the Underlings put it. The other six dimensions are "curled up" at a subatomic level, not apparent as something they are aware of, but they are just as important as the first four, if not more so. The fifth dimension corresponded to the first thermonuclear fusion reaction in a forming star, initiating the processes to fire the evolution of the universe, including the formation of new chemical elements during supernova events. The permeation of the sixth dimension was completed at the stage where planets formed around stars. The seventh dimension, oh how I loved announcing that one. Life. Microscopic, unthinking, beautiful life, having no idea what it signified."

Esther's mind reached back to Wednesday morning and Peter's triumphant announcement that the first replication had occurred, and contrasted the victorious feeling she experienced then with the dread she now tried so hard to hold back.

Peter continued. "The conclusion of the eighth dimension corresponded to the first conscious thought of the Underlings. The ninth was the development of the Conscience, of the idea that life meant something beyond survival as an organism, of a belief in something larger than one's own existence. It was such a beautiful system. The strings' vibrations not only drove the physical evolution of the universe, it also drove the spiritual evolution of the Underlings. And the tenth dimension, the tenth, oh my God, what it would have been. To see the physical and the spiritual come together, to see the Underlings discover that it's all the same thing, that to understand the physical universe also means to understand the nature of humanity itself, to see the final breakdown of the barriers that isolate each Underling within his own thoughts and emotions, to see true shared human experience, to usher in the Eternal Era of Understanding….." Peter's voice gave out at his hopelessness.

Esther spoke softly. "Through our observations of the Underling world monitors, we know they are conducting experiments which replicate string-sized interactions. From the specific frequencies being generated, we know their physicists are working on the final stretch of string theory development. Had the crisis not occurred, our assumption is that when they successfully unraveled the threads of the mystery, the physical/spiritual connection would be revealed to them. This would coincide with the physical completion of the permeation of the tenth dimension, and all Underlings would literally comprehend everything - the mental, the physical, the spiritual - all at once. But with the Sonic Regression, none of that can occur. From our position here in the City as spiritual beings only, we have no means to correct the course of events, all we can do is monitor. At this point, if they understood what was happening, I don't doubt that the Underlings would have a better idea of how to reverse the regression than we do. Regardless, they are the only ones who can physically affect the material universe. It's all up to the Underlings."

Brother Bartholomew, chairman of the Underling World Oversight Committee, gruffly broke the silence of the Council members. "Lot of good this is all doing. They're Underlings, on the Underling world. This is all quite unacceptable. We are the Omniscience Council. We are high-level strategists and policy-makers, we should not have to concern ourselves with such details of operation. Our staff members have obviously failed to take their Team Building training to heart. I recommend a cross-disciplinary SWAT team in a lock-up offsite meeting to establish a recovery plan and complete the 10th-dimensional permeation by 12:00 midnight as per our original six-day schedule. That leaves us ninety minutes - I for one look forward to meeting this challenge."

Esther looked at Bartholomew incredulously. "Are you still worried about the *schedule*?"

"Of course," Bartholomew replied. "Performance, cost, schedule. The three pillars of project management. You would do well to listen to those of us in positions of leadership. You have ninety minutes to complete the project. I suggest you get going."

"Have you heard anything we've -" Esther's voice trailed off. She and Peter looked at each other, not knowing what else to say.

There was silence in the room. Finally Brother Michael spoke. "I have a question for our trumpet player here.

Granted, perhaps a mistake has been made, but it seems to me that he is the only person here who has actually taken any form of action. And that is what you were doing, taking action, now isn't it?"

Dunstan looked confused, and answered, "Uh, yes, I guess so," not at all sure where this was leading.

"And in our current crisis, we need men of action, now don't we, people who think outside the box?"

"I - I suppose so."

"And with Peter no longer on the Council, we have an opening, don't we?" Michael looked around at the other Council members, who were now getting the point and beginning to nod their heads.

"Wait a minute!" Peter shouted. "He's the one who got us into this mess!"

"Well, then, perhaps, he is the one who can get us out of this mess." said Brother Michael. "He is appropriately remorseful for his mistake, and what kind of people are we if we don't give someone a second chance? Furthermore, I for one would rather see someone with a take-charge attitude like that on the Council, helping lead the effort. Mr. Dunstan, the City needs more people like you."

With Michael's decree, the deal was done. Dunstan, his visage turning noticeably brighter at this remarkable turn of events, assumed an air of regal superiority as he was escorted to Peter's old seat among the other Council members. Within minutes, he was leading a discussion regarding whether the Council had the authority to arbitrarily declare 10th-dimensional permeation complete, and begin the Eternal Festival on schedule.

May 4, 2037:

Kathy Leigh turned on the television and flipped through the channels. So this is retirement, she thought to herself. She hadn't watched normal TV in years. The party last night had been grand, everyone had congratulated her so cordially, and several of the speakers had made fun of her old independent streak. She had laughed along with them, she didn't know where it came from either. Oh, those bones ached. She looked forward to massages and spas and pampering herself and the end of 12-hour days.

She alighted on Channel 7, the Scottsdale CBS affiliate. It was 8 p.m., family viewing hour, and the show just coming on was "Death in Dunsmuir". She recognized the title as that of CBS's top-rated show. With the screen still dark, the following introduction scrolled down the screen. "The images you are about to see are real. They come from the quarantined city of Dunsmuir, where thousands of remote-controlled CBS cameras monitor all activity. Please note that CBS only uses professional executioners, and only residents of Dunsmuir are killed. No animals or productive citizens were endangered in any way during the filming of this show."

Kathy lay back against the couch and watched in rapt fascination, along with 181 million other Americans.

Sunday, 12:10 a.m.:

With a defiant flourish, Peter pushed open the door to the large conference room and strode in, Esther alongside him and two strangers close behind, looking out of place. Peter knew what to expect, and in fact welcomed it. He was glad of the fact that the large door hinges creaked quite loudly, and before he even entered the room, all eyes were upon him. He could feel anger from all of them except Thomas, who watched in tired resignation.

"You! You!! What in heaven's name are YOU doing here!!" shouted Michael. "Surely you know you are not welcome, you should not be welcome anywhere in the City. Do you have any idea what you have done? It is now *Sunday*. The schedule is irretrievably lost. The permeation through the ten dimensions was intended to be complete in six days. It is now the *seventh* day, the day we were supposed to *rest*, and celebrate with the Eternal Festival. Do you see anything festive going on? Do you? If you and your meddlesome new friends had not brought us all this unwanted news of sonic deviations and disruptions and regressions, everything would be fine. Everything would be just fine.

"What are we to do if the Architect should return for an inspection?"

Peter finally spoke up. "If I may - I have brought two people who might be of interest to you."

"Oh, rest assured, neither you nor anyone you ever met could be of the least interest to us," said Abraham.

Peter was undeterred. "Sister Esther has just returned from the Waiting Area. As it turns out, there were two people there who may be able to help us. I would like to introduce to you Mr. and Mrs. Adam and Eve Parson."

September 2, 2039:

The sixty-nine year old Max Cherry trailed behind his fellow team members as he exited the One-World Airlines Boeing 797 and walked slowly up the exit ramp from the airplane. They were returning from a two-day trip to the Superconducting Supercollider in Texas, where it was hoped that recalibration of the instrumentation would provide new clues as the true nature of the mystifying string vibrational patterns. The trip had been unsuccessful. Reaching the terminal, he reflexively scanned the faces of the passengers waiting at the gate for the next flight. His eyes stopped at a vaguely familiar face.

The eyes. The eyes were still the same. No doubt.

"Kathy? Kathy Leigh?"

"Excuse me? Do I know you?"

After all these years he remembered the voice. "You are Kathy Leigh, correct? The television news anchor? I haven't watched TV in years, but I used to see you."

"Well, I'm retired now…..".

"I'm sure you don't remember me. My name is Max Cherry, and I'm a theoretical physicist. You interviewed me decades ago when you were in Seattle. 1997, I think it was. You interviewed me for three hours, I'll certainly never forget *that*. Maybe you remember my friend Grant Zenkman, who was with me? He was certainly quite taken with you."

Max paused for a moment, wistfully recalling his old partner in crime. There had been no contact in so many years. *I wonder whatever became of Grant…*

Kathy searched Max's face for a hint of a memory. "Tell me again what it is you do?"

"I'm a theoretical physicist. I've worked on the string theory project all these years. I have to admit, it's nice to talk to you again, we don't often find people these days with any scientific curiosity."

Vague recollections returned to Kathy. "String theory -

that has to do with atoms and molecules and that sort of thing, correct?"

Max, a bit disappointed that Kathy did not remember him and had not kept up with the theoretical work, nevertheless was sure her interest would be rekindled once he refreshed her memory. She'd had quite a good grasp of the subject all those years ago, and would doubtless be fascinated with how far the studies had come. He rattled off a basic layman's description of string theory, and waited for Kathy's response.

Kathy paused a moment, and looked down, fingering her purse. "If I may ask, what is the point of your work?"

A smile crossed Max's wrinkled face. "I'll tell you the same thing I told you forty years ago. It was something like, "Someday I might be able to say that I helped figure out how God put the universe together."

Kathy waited for more. "And - ?"

"And what?" replied Max.

"And what's the point? Who benefits?"

"Uh - we all benefit. I mean, this is one of the basic drives of humankind - to understand our origin and our destiny."

Kathy looked at Max blankly, then at her watch.

Max pressed on. "Don't you want to know how the universe began? Why it expands? How the elements formed in these perfect proportions? How we came to be, and where it is all going?"

Kathy calmly asked, "You're saying I interviewed you about all this?"

"Yes, in great detail. I was very impressed with your understanding."

"Then I am quite sure you have me confused with someone else - Mr. Cherry, is it? I assure you that such a pointless discussion would have me bored to tears. Would you please excuse me?" She did not get up, but simply turned away from him.

Max began to mention the recent problems with string theory development, and the team's hypothesis that the strings' vibrational patterns might be physically breaking down. He looked again at the elderly woman so determinedly ignoring him. She obviously wouldn't care, no matter what he said. He looked around the airport. All these people, dutifully going about their daily business like worker ants. None of them would care.

Max considered for a moment that maybe he didn't care so much any more either, a feeling that did not go away until he caught up with the others back at the Institute.

<u>Saturday, 11:47 p.m.:</u>

Exactly twenty-three minutes before Peter barged into the Omniscience Council chambers with Adam and Eve Parson in tow, Sister Esther had happened upon a brilliant idea. It was clear that she needed some expert help, and no one in the City was qualified. The search itself was not difficult. She spoke to the Waiting Area's Gatekeeper and requested a listing of the past 750 million arrivals, using the search criterion "Theoretical Physicist, String Theory, World's Leading Authority." The Gatekeeper complained about the recent balkiness of the equipment, but Esther was quite clever about obtaining specific results from these automated searches, and sure enough, after a couple of system error messages, her request resulted in an output of exactly two names: Adam and Eve Parson. Esther further requested the Gatekeeper to perform a search of the Waiting Area to identify the room in which the Parsons were being housed, waiting for the processing of their paperwork prior to entrance into the City. Esther was aware that the paperwork usually took quite a long time, and that most likely any recent arrivals would not yet have been processed for access to the City itself.

Esther politely knocked on the door, and a genial, studious-looking gentleman opened it. "May I help you?" he said.

Esther, her voice trembling just a bit, asked, "Are you Adam Parson?"

"Why, yes," said the 50-ish gentleman. "And you are?"

"Esther. Sister Esther. Is Eve Parson here as well?"

"Yes, yes, I'm here," came a cheery voice from the back of the room.

"Is there something I can do for you?" asked Adam. "Would you like to come in?"

"Umm, yes," said Esther, as Adam opened the door. Esther beheld a wondrous sight. Huge sheets of paper covered all four walls from floor to ceiling, and three of the four walls were covered with the strangest scribblings Esther had ever seen, characters quite unknown to her, yet totally compelling. There was also a small computer in the center of the room.

"What is all this?" asked Esther.

Eve said, "Oh, we got a bit bored waiting here since we arrived, so we asked if we could borrow some paper and work on developing equations, and a computer to make calculations as we needed them. Well, one thing led to another and soon we found we needed all the wallspace to continue our discussion. So we asked for large sheets of paper, and somehow they found these huge rolls that cover an entire wall. I must commend you, you are wonderful hosts.

The only complaint we have is the piped-in music. It was so lovely when we arrived, but now it is just a screeching, horrible sound. We had to turn it off and sing to each other when we wanted music."

Adam chimed in. "We've gone through a number of sheets on each wall. I am truly amazed at the service we've gotten here. And I've never seen a computer this size that can process the equations we're inputting. The solutions required billions of iterations on a huge scale, and normally that takes weeks on the best computers I've ever seen. I'm actually not sure how long we've been here, but we've been able to make a lot of progress. Eve, doesn't it seem that our thinking has been awfully clear since we arrived here?" Eve nodded, even then her attention being distracted as she looked at one of the equations near the end of their writing to date.

"Is that all you've been doing since you arrived?" asked Esther.

"Yes, pretty much," said Adam, as Eve resumed making notes on the wall. "Funny, it seems we've been here a while, I mean, we've accomplished a tremendous amount, really, but we haven't slept, we haven't eaten, we're not tired, we've just kept ourselves busy working on the string equations." Adam grinned at Esther. "I think we're getting there, too, this is really exciting. By the way, Esther, exactly where are we?"

Esther realized that it would probably be best not to explain anything to the Parsons just yet.

She closed her eyes for a moment, then opened them and said, "Mr. and Mrs. Parson, would you please come with me? There are some people you need to meet."

<u>July 28, 2040:</u>

"No, no, no, invariant cohomology can't be applied to the vector bundles like that," said Darryl Johnson.

"Why not?" asked Max Cherry, as the few wisps of white hair remaining on his otherwise bald head floated gently with the breeze caused by his movement. "This algorithm leads to a simplified untwisting to the trivial bundle, and that's essential for the generalized solution."

"Darryl's right," said Melina Valin, concentrating on the mathematics but also aware of her appreciation of the fact that women do not suffer from baldness. "You're right in that the trivial bundle form must be realized in the final solution, but look here at your line of reasoning." She pointed to several analogous terms in the sequential set of equations. "Your use of the holomorphic function violates the Bott periodicity theorem in this step."

Max let out a long sigh and once again wrapped his aching arthritic fingers around his dull pencil, set to try again, knowing that his once razor-sharp mathematical instincts were fading in his old age.

Such was the theoretical discussion that carried on day after day inside the Institute.

On the other side of the room, Jason Poe and Zena Dunn spent each day, hour after hour, analyzing the computer scans of the proton decay experiments and the Superconducting Supercollider trials, attempting to correlate results between the two. The proton decay percentage was now up to 28 parts per billion, more than a thousand-fold increase from Grant's results in 2019, and the group's sense of urgency was heightened by the uncertainty as to what the eventual result of the decay would be, or the level at which it would begin to affect the macroscopic physical world.

As Jason and Zena systematically identified each superpartner particle and its corresponding mass and energy level, they transferred the information into Melina's theoretical database, where it could be compared to the current version of the string theory equation sets. The task was infinitely complicated by the new vibration patterns, and great effort was needed to distinguish the particles predicted from the original string theory versus the newer particles seemingly initiated by the alterations in the string vibration patterns.

The string theory team no longer separated for any reason. The Science Institute was by now a largely abandoned building, and the team had the run of the place, and there was really no need to go elsewhere, except for the occasional new SSC tests in Texas, when the entire team would go. The work was conducted in a large hall now filled with computers and data storage equipment. Food and other necessities were delivered from the outside as needed. Everyone slept in the same room, and even the bathroom doors were kept open, in the team's superstitious belief that togetherness was vital to maintain the cocoon of vibrational protection necessary to maintain the scientific curiosity required for their intellectual pursuit.

President Clinton had certainly been right so long ago about the funding for the string theory team; even without the slightest public or governmental interest any more in matters of science or the origin and destiny of the universe, the budget sources for the team were still in place. The effort was infinitesimal compared to the early days, of course, because the global support team had evaporated completely. There was never a problem, however, with conducting a multi-million dollar SSC test, because the duty-bound citizenry unquestioningly carried out any funded request from a governmental source. As Zena was fond of saying, "They'd eat all the babies in Texas if we sent out a directive with a valid budget source." Outrage was now an archaic notion.

Chris Parson spent his days building ever more elaborate domino patterns and walking the long empty halls of the Institute whistling his constant aimless tune. Chris's health and vitality remained remarkably high; furthermore, he seemed impervious to the personality changes which so pervaded society. For years Chris had walked the streets of Washington, D.C. daily, spending as much time greeting the birds as he did people, but unlike the other string theory team members who had spent significant time outside the walls of the Institute, his personality remained quite untouched. His smile, his laugh, and his standard bear hug greeting had not changed in his seventy years. It saddened Christopher, however, that those on the outside had long since become uncomfortable with his hugs, and he had to save them for his friends on the team.

By eleven p.m., Max, Zena, Darryl, Melina, Jason, and Chris lay in bed, each one staring at the ceiling. As usual, it was Max Cherry who broke the silence.

"So whattaya think there, Darryl?"

The always contemplative Darryl knew what Max meant. "The equations from each dimension each have mathematical implications for the others, and if the mathematical effects also occur on a physical level, it seems reasonable that a large enough impact on the physical vibration levels in one dimension might propagate outward to the others. Whether that would create a ripple effect throughout the large-scale universe, I don't know."

"Oh, Darryl," said Max in a mock lyrical tone, "it's hard to believe you weren't a real charmer in your day with sweet talk like that. Not to mention that cute ass of yours." He laughed, then paused briefly, and said in a more serious tone, "But really - do you think we could set up some sort of giant collision that could restore the original permeation parameters?"

Zena chimed in, "I think you're right, Darryl, I've had the same idea, but I don't know how to do the mathematics. In some of the SSC trials, we've seen extreme high-energy outputs when we can get simultaneous collisions between large numbers of very high-mass superpartner particles, and in the subsequent fraction of a second we've noted the disappearance of the distorted vibrational frequencies. For a moment after the collision, the vibrational patterns and associated particles will return to the states predicted by basic string theory."

"And by the way, your ass always *was* a lot cuter than Max's."

An awkward moment passed until Zena spoke again. "Come on, guys, stand up. Let's get Melina's opinion." Darryl and Max obediently got out of bed and stood before Melina.

"Turn around. Give her a good look."

Melina, embarrassed at being put on the spot this way, nevertheless played along. She sat up in bed, her eyes tracing the outlines of Max's and Darryl's seventy-year-old backsides, evaluating Zena's opinion for herself. She then looked at Zena, nodded as if in deep thought, and said, "Yep, Darryl's is cuter."

Max laughed harder than any of them at the putdown, and leaned over, putting his arm around Darryl. They climbed back into bed.

Melina finally continued. "So you think there might be a certain specific artificial input from the SSC that could eliminate the vibrational distortions?"

"Yes, exactly," said Darryl and Zena in unison. Zena quickly added, "But we have no data to indicate the restoration could be sustained for any length of time."

"Then that's got to be our focus from now on," mused Jason Poe.

Chris Parson happily but uncomprehendingly listened to his friends and dreamed of new domino patterns.

Sunday, 12:27 a.m.:

Peter's moments before the Omniscience Council had been painful, as he expected. The Council couldn't quite understand what a particle physicist was exactly, and why having two of them in the City might be beneficial in the current crisis. Accordingly, the discussion had been brief and on the curt side, with Dunstan particularly critical, but the Council had grudgingly granted approval for the Parsons to assist in the crisis. (Not that Peter would have obeyed had the Council denied his request). After Peter, Esther, and the Parsons were ushered out of the room, Thomas followed close behind, much to the consternation of the other Council members. Peter led them to a small conference room, and the three City dwellers attempted to convey the situation to the Parsons, who were obviously confused by the furor surrounding them.

Amos was also present, invited by Esther, since she knew that his assistance would be necessary to help teach the Parsons how to operate the controls in the Underling World

Observation Center. For his part, Amos silently groused to himself about being asked to work on the seventh day, and that there better be overtime pay in it for him.

Peter began. "We welcome you to the Eternal City, Mr. and Mrs. Parson. I honestly have no idea where to start. What do you remember from immediately before you arrived here?"

Eve said, "Hmm, it's all fuzzy, we've both commented on that. I know we gave the presentation at the Strings conference, and Christopher went out for the night with Max Cherry, and, and, umm, that's about it. Honey, do you remember any more than that?"

"No, that's about all I remember too," said Adam. "Excuse me, I don't mean to be rude, but can you explain what this is all about?" Adam and Eve together looked wonderingly into the eyes of their hosts.

"This will be hard to accept," said Peter. " I suspect you won't believe me until we have time afterwards to show you the control rooms and prove everything. So please just listen and let us tell you what has happened, and in the end I assure you all your questions will be answered."

Peter attempted to continue. "Well, umm, you're, uh, you've come to, eh, ah, this place is, hmm." Peter baffled by the awkwardness of the situation, couldn't go on. "Thomas, perhaps you can do a better job of explaining all this?"

"Well, to begin with, Mr. and Mrs. Parson -"

"Oh - Adam and Eve, by all means," said Adam. "I never intend to be old enough to be called Mr. Parson," he said, laughing.

"All right. Adam and Eve it is," said Thomas. "I did some checking on how you got here. First of all, our City is, is, well, this is where you come after you, umm, uh, pass away."

"What??" said Eve. "What are you talking about? What do you mean?"

"Eve, if you recall, you left the String Theory conference hall and began to drive home. Unfortunately, on the way home there was a tragic accident, and you were, well, you, ah, instead of going home, you arrived here. This is where you go after you leave the Underling world - I mean, after you pass on."

"Are you saying we're.... we're dead?" asked Adam incredulously.

"Well, ah, well, yes, that's pretty much the gist of it. When Underlings experience what you call death, they come to the Waiting Area until their paperwork is processed, and then they can be admitted into the City."

Adam and Eve looked at each other. They began to cry. Adam softly said, "You know, it does make sense. I mean, we haven't seen anyone we know. We just spent all our time in the waiting room working on the equations, and they brought us anything we wanted. It *was* rather odd. How long have we been here?"

Thomas rolled his eyes, knowing Peter would not like what he was about to hear. "In your time, about forty-six years."

"Forty-six years?" asked Peter. "Isn't that a long time? What time did they arrive here? In our time, I mean?"

Thomas looked at Esther. There was no getting around it now.

"They arrived in the Waiting Room on Thursday at 6:43 p.m.," she said.

"Isn't that - *before* Dunstan played the Trumpet?" asked Peter wonderingly.

"Yes, that's correct," chimed in Esther. "The Parsons' automobile accident occurred Thursday at 6:42 p.m. City Time." She turned to the Parsons, helpfully adding, "After calculating the Liquid Time Correlation, that corresponds to an Underling date of April 15, 1995, at 1:38:26 a.m. Approximately. The vibrational disruption did not occur till 6:66."

Adam and Eve Parson looked at each other, not entirely comfortable with being reminded so precisely of the time of their own deaths.

"So they've been here since before the trouble ever started?" asked Peter. "And we didn't know it? How can this be?"

Esther said, "With the Festival Preparations demanding such high priority, our processing time on new arrivals has been somewhat delayed. Actually, no one has been admitted into the City from the Waiting Area since Thursday at 5:21 a.m., which corresponds, in Underling time, to, umm, your year of 1854."

Peter rolled his eyes, realizing the Parsons had been available since before the Sonic Disruption, but were only now being brought in to help find a solution.

Eve interrupted. "Wait, wait. Can I interrupt? We've been here forty-six *years*? And what is an Underling? What is City Time? What is the Liquid Time Correlation? And who exactly are you all? None of this makes any sense."

Thomas began to slowly explain. "Adam, Eve. We are very pleased to have you here. I'm sure this is all very confusing. This place, our City, is what you would call Heaven, where you Underlings go when you die."

"Unless you are excessively delayed in the Waiting Area," muttered Peter.

Thomas continued his explanation. "The City is also made up of thousands of permanent residents who have been here since the beginning, on Monday, our first day, with what we call the 'Great Unfurling,' when the strings first began vibrating -"

"The strings? What strings?" said Eve. What are you talking about?

"The strings you studied all your life," said Thomas, surprised at the question. The strings that sing, that are the music, the colossal symphony that is the universe. String theory."

"Oh my God," said Eve. "Then we're right? We're on the right track? It *is* the fundamental theory?"

Esther jumped in. "You're closer than you can imagine. The Underlings have almost figured it out, they're dancing all around it." Adam and Eve clasped hands, their attention riveted.

Thomas went on. "You're more involved than you know. Anyway, umm, Underlings. Underlings, that's you. Earthlings -- homo sapiens -- mankind -- humans, I guess you call yourselves. See, we're in heaven, looking down on you all, figuratively at least, so in the beginning it was just natural to call you Underlings, it was our way of expressing how we are here to take care of you." His face went downcast momentarily, knowing the City dwellers had not done such a great job.

"Umm, City Time - that's our time scale here. You Underlings - excuse me, humans - operate in minutes and hours and days and years and centuries and millennia. We have a concept of time as well, but to us, our universe has only been in operation, umm, what time is it?"

"Sunday, 12:29 a.m.," answered Esther.

"Yes, as we measure time, it's all taken just over six full days so far," continued Thomas.

Adam could not resist another incredulous interruption. "Six days? As in a six day creation? Then shouldn't you be *done* by now?" he asked, more than a hint of sarcasm in his voice.

Thomas sighed wearily. "You are quite right. The Master Schedule was to be completed by midnight Saturday, so that Sunday would be the Day of Rest - a great eternal Festival to celebrate your universe reaching its fulfillment. We didn't make that schedule, obviously, and that's why the members of the Omniscience Council were so hostile."

Amos considered taking this opportunity to ask about overtime pay, but thought better of it.

"The passage of time is actually much more complicated than comparing our seven days to your 20 billion years," Thomas explained. "This is where the Liquid Time Correlation comes in. We invented that name ourselves. The City's Architect set up monitors so we can watch the progress of your world, your universe, and as we observed, we noticed that our time flowed faster or slower than yours. In the long epochs of your universe's development when there were no major evolutionary steps forward, our time hardly progressed at all, so that hundreds of millions of your years went by, but it was only minutes to us. At other times your universe slowed to a standstill by our reckoning, so that we could monitor and record billions of events that took place in only a few Underling seconds, such as a complete accounting of the first supernova explosion, which as you know brought into existence the heavier chemical elements, allowing objects other than stars to exist, leading eventually to life itself. The faster and slower flowing of time was called the Liquid Time Correlation. It has its advantages, obviously, but it has a serious disadvantage in that we do not know how much time we have if we are trying to match our schedule to events on the Underling world."

"There's been a definite pattern to it," added Esther. "The timescales are very different now than at the beginning. During most of your history, particularly in the first seven dimensions before there was life, there were few events that required our attention, and so your time could shoot by at incredible rates of speed comparison to ours. Everything up to your last hundred years occurred by Tuesday morning here, about 30 hours of our time. Those last hundred years of Underling time, however, have occupied our entire week since then, because the pace of your significant developmental activities accelerated so dramatically. And it's not just scientific development. Your social changes and spiritual awareness have increased dramatically as well, as the Underlings knock on the door of complete understanding. With so many events happening in your world, we needed your progress to slow down relative to ours, so we could keep track of it all and respond. That's my theory, anyway.

"You people certainly are inventive," Esther added respectfully.

"All right, let me see if I get this," said Eve skeptically. "Your 'Great Unfurling,' what we call the Big Bang, occurred Monday morning, correct?"

"Yes, that's right," said Esther.

"So twenty billion of our years took only a day and a half of your time, but the last hundred years have taken almost five days?" asked Eve.

"Yes, that's it," Esther replied with satisfaction.

Thomas continued. "In the beginning, the Architect,

the Designer, the Creator, the being you would call God, built the City and designed the entire string system. She worked out the equations, set up the equipment to initiate the vibrations, put everything in place. But you see, God is not just the God of this universe, She builds one universe after another, I guess you'd say She has a short attention span. She designs each universe completely differently. This one had odd properties like mass and gravity, and She said it's one of Her favorites. Most other universes, I understand, are entirely ephemeral, just spirit entities, no physical structures, no tangible matter at all. She said She always liked geometry, so She made this universe of solid components."

Adam and Eve just stared, open-mouthed. "So I take it God is a woman?" asked Eve.

"Well, that is just our interpretation," replied Thomas. "It seemed to us that the Architect's characteristically female traits outweighed the masculine ones, so we always referred to her as She."

"Oh yeah, She was a girl all right," interjected Amos. "Kind of a romantic mushball. Said she wanted to invent a new kind of universe this time, one filled with love and passion and tenderness and commitment. She was really excited about that, and She got all choked up explaining it. But then again, She sure did like to build stuff. Maybe She was, you know, sort of an effeminate guy," added Amos, his attempt to help becoming hopelessly convoluted.

"At one point I did put in a suggestion that we develop gender-neutral pronouns," said Esther helpfully. Peter rolled his eyes.

"The Architect doesn't like a static universe," continued Thomas, "one where She just creates the final product and moves on. She wants each universe to have its own story. So this time the Architect designed a truly dynamic universe, its development controlled by the evolving permeation of the strings through the ten dimensions."

"There really are ten? It's a correct representation?" asked Adam. "We always feared there was no physical meaning, that it was just a convenient mathematical model for which the equations happened to work out," added Eve.

Thomas said, "Oh, there are ten real physical dimensions, all right, and every one of them is vital. Here's how it works: At the Great Unfurling, what you would call the Big Bang, the strings began their vibrations in the first four dimensions, time first and then the three space dimensions with which you are familiar."

"Wait, wait, wait," said Eve. "Do you mean the strings initially vibrated only in the first four dimensions, and the others came later?"

Thomas nodded. "Yes. After the first four, the vibrations began in the next dimension and slowly permeated through it until the entire universe was vibrating fully in five dimensions. Then the pattern was repeated for the sixth dimension, then the seventh, and so on."

"Oh Adam," Eve continued. "We never thought of that. We always assumed the strings had vibrated continuously in all ten dimensions ever since the Big Bang. I wonder what that would do to our theoretical predictions." She and Adam looked at each other, their eyes alight with possibilities, their innate scientific curiosity still very much alive, even in this bizarre situation.

Adam replied, "You know what that means, Eve? It means string theory isn't just an explanation of how the universe functions. It actually *controls* the universe. String theory drives evolution itself. Oh my god."

After a few moments of reflection, Adam continued. "So the first four dimensions established the basic physical universe, what we see and touch, right?" asked Adam. "What physical significance do the other six have?"

Thomas went on, describing how the permeation of the strings' vibration into each progressive dimension added another key feature of the universal structure, although on a level not visible in the physical world. At the ninth dimension, the development of the human conscience, Eve stopped him.

"Hold on. You're telling me that when the strings began to vibrate in the ninth dimension, the basic nature of humanity began to change? The strings affect the spiritual as well as the physical universe?"

"Exactly," said Thomas. "At the consolidation of the eighth dimension, people were capable of thought, even intelligent thought, but they operated rather robotically, on instinct, you might say, and they performed their functions in society, but they had no concept of good or bad, right or wrong, individualism, personal creativity, that sort of thing. By the time the ninth dimension was fully permeated, basic human nature as you know it, with all its glorious flaws, was fully formed. Esther, when would that have been?"

Esther replied, "Umm, the ninth dimension completed permeation Thursday at 2:17 a.m.. Oh. In Underling - I mean, Earth - time, that is Wednesday, May 7, in the year 17,876 B.C., at 4:45:01 pm."

Eve couldn't resist a slight smile at Esther's obsession for precise information and sensed a kindred spirit. *A little training and she would have been a nice addition to the string theory team back at Princeton,* Eve thought to herself approvingly. *God knows we needed people who got their facts straight.*

"So, since then, we have been monitoring the permeation through the tenth and last dimension," continued Thomas. "When - and especially if - we get there, it will be the final step, and the universe will evolve into its final, eternal form."

"And what is that?" asked Adam.

"Well, we don't really know," said Thomas. "And that's where we begin to have our problems."

Adam and Eve looked at each other again.

Peter spoke up. "Can I interrupt, Tom?" Brother Thomas nodded. "We don't actually know what your world, or our City, will be like when the strings complete their permeation through the tenth dimension, but we know it will be one great final leap forward to the culmination of human spiritual development, to where you become the species you were meant to be. We do have some clues. We have been monitoring your world very closely, of course, because we're trying to coordinate our Festival schedule with the completion of the permeation. We have seen a number of developments recently that indicate the direction you are headed. Uh, Esther, could you describe this, you know it better than any of us."

"All right," said Esther, thrilled but intimidated at being in the presence of such brilliant scientists. "On a scientific level, you have made tremendous technological strides in all areas, including particle physics and cosmology, and it is our opinion that the permeation cannot be completed until your physicists unravel the final pieces of string theory. We think your intellectual progress and string permeation are inextricably linked. Even stronger clues come from the social progress. In your last few hundred years, progress has been remarkable. Slavery has ended as an accepted institution. Totalitarian governments have been in serious decline. The rights of minority groups were being increasingly recognized and accepted by society at large. Not that the task was complete by any means, or that exceptions did not occur, but each generation was seeing significant improvements in all these areas. Your world was evolving toward democratic forms of government, where the freedom and dignity of each person was respected. We were close enough to the end to see that the final evolution would be to a state where all Underlings recognized the incalculable value of every person, where selfish motives would be a thing of the past. At the time of your accident there were certainly horrible exceptions to these developments from time to time, but the progress was inevitably occurring. Furthermore, we believe that full 10th-dimension permeation would have completely broken down the physical and spiritual barriers that separate people, allowing them to actually share consciousness, to end each person's isolation as a separate being. We believe the tenth-dimension full permeation would have been the realization by humanity of all it can become."

"Would have been….?" said Adam and Eve simultaneously.

Peter resumed speaking. "But we don't know exactly what that will be, you see, because the Architect set up the entire system to be self-sufficient. We don't know what the equations are, we don't know how the system or the equipment works. From the beginning, we didn't have to do anything. The permeation was set up to work its way through each dimension, and that would be that. Our system was equipped with monitors, but nothing that can tell what will happen in the future, and most lamentably, no instruments that can actually affect the progression of the permeation. It was simply assumed that nothing would go wrong."

Adam and Eve again looked at each other, finally realizing that all this was not simply an explanation for their benefit.

"The City's priority has been to organize a magnificent festival to celebrate the completion of the tenth dimension," Peter continued. "That's what we've been working on, the entire City has worked very hard to prepare adequately..."

"So why are we really here?" asked Eve. "Why have you pulled us out of the Waiting Area? What is going on? You haven't told us everything, have you?"

"No," said Peter. "No indeed. It's all gone wrong, and we're not equipped to deal with it. There's one more detail I haven't told you about. When the strings' permeation at each level is completed, Brother Gabriel blows what we call the Great Consolidating Tone on a special Trumpet made specifically for that purpose -"

"Hold on," said Adam. "There's a 'Brother Gabriel' who blows the Trumpet? Brother *Gabriel*? Like the Angel Gabriel they told us about in Sunday School?"

"Oh, right, from the Bible," replied Peter, caught off-guard. "You've heard of Gabriel, I forgot. Yes, yes, that Gabriel, the Angel Gabriel. All of us here, the permanent residents of the City since the beginning, we are what you would call angels. No wings or halos or any of that, however, those were made up by Underling artists trying to boost sales. Actually, aside from being non-physical entities, we're not that different from the Underlings, really, we just work here. Anyway, as for Gabriel, yes, he's real and he really does blow the Trumpet, at the end of each string permeation level. We don't know exactly how it works, even Gabriel doesn't know how it works, he just meditates for a while and blows the Trumpet, and the frequencies he generates are somehow attuned to the permeation of the strings and lock in the dimensional vibrations at the correct frequencies and harmonics, so that the entire system is stabilized at the new level, and at the same time the permeation through the next dimension is initiated."

"And....?" said Eve. She was intuitive enough to know when a story was leading in an unexpected direction.

Peter cleared his throat and attempted to describe Dunstan's disastrous foray with the Trumpet as diplomatically as possible, realizing how ridiculous he must sound, as he told his tale of an angel's petty jealousy resulting in the structural disruption of the universe.

Adam and Eve tried to take it all in. "Do we know for a fact that the universe is affected?" asked Eve.

"Oh yes," answered Esther. "Our monitors all report that the permeation has been disrupted. The 10th level of permeation was 89 percent complete at the time of the disruption, and we are now at 77 percent. That may not sound like a tremendous loss, but we have tracked the rates and the permeation is regressing exponentially. It will continue to erode faster and faster. Further, we are not sure, but we believe that as the harmonics distort, we will not simply move backwards along the line we have followed since the Great Unfurling. The distortions will become catastrophic fairly soon and the universe will literally fly apart."

"Is there any schedule for this?" asked Eve. "Is there some deadline?"

Peter, Thomas, and Esther looked at each other. "Today,

Sunday, the seventh day, the day of the Eternal Festival, wasn't intended to be a 24-hour day like the others. It was intended to be a celebration that would last into eternity," said Peter. "The clocks were supposed to stop once we reached the seventh day, but we see that hasn't happened. There seems to be no provision in the system for an eighth day. So we can't say for sure, but my guess would be that if we can't restore proper vibrational patterns and complete the 10th dimensional permeation by midnight tonight, that will mean - it will….." His voice trailed off.

Adam dropped his chin into his hand and pondered. He was certainly fearful of the possibly tragic consequences of Dunstan's foolish error, but the scientist in him could not resist the intellectual challenge taking shape before him. "So, Dunstan played the wrong frequencies at the wrong time, and that disrupted the strings' vibrations midway through the permeation of the tenth dimension, correct?"

The City dwellers nodded in unison. "So theoretically, there might be some combination of frequencies that could restore the proper harmonics and restore the permeation, correct?" Again everyone nodded.

Adam's eyes now locked onto Eve's, as their thoughts came together symbiotically in the connection they'd always had. He went on, "But you said we can't directly affect anything from here, correct?"

"That's right, that's why we, well, we think it might be hopeless," said Esther, trying to be truthful without panicking.

"Can we - they - the humans - the Underlings - affect the permeation?" asked Adam.

The City dwellers looked again to Esther. "Well, yes, they can, somewhat at least," she said. She had not considered what the Underlings might be able to do. "There are a number of instances where we can relate specific Underling events to significant jumps in the permeation level. In one case, a man named Madison wrote out the first draft of his new form of government, designed so that the governing authority was actually held by the citizens at large, and that caused a sudden permeational increase. The day Mr. Einstein first considered that it was the speed of light that was constant and that time could vary, we marked an instantaneous 1.7 percent jump. And someone named Gandhi also had a notable effect, as did an event described as the Fall of the Berlin Wall. The largest single jump occurred on your date of July 20, 1969, when Underlings first walked on your moon. The ripples from that fundamental breakthrough reverberated throughout the universe, and I expect there were some astonishing consequences. I often wonder what events must have occurred that day. So to answer your question, yes, when significant breakthroughs in understanding or spiritual development occur, there are effects on permeation levels."

Esther continued. "That's an interesting thought. I suppose you are not aware of this, but there is a dedicated team of researchers still working on string theory."

"Well, of course there is," interrupted Eve, "there were hundreds of us, and with string theory having such significance, there must be thousands by now."

"No, I'm sorry, but you have to understand. For quite some time there has been a greatly reduced emphasis on scientific investigation, in curiosity in general, in the Underling world. But one small team has worked on string theory for many of your years, they would certainly be the ones to communicate with."

320

"Who are they?"

"We haven't studied them for some time. I do remember some of the names, if they mean anything. One was Max Cherry, and another was Melina Valin, and there was Jason, Jason something. There are only five of them left."

"Jason Poe. And Melina and Max. My god, the kids are still at it," said Adam, recognizing the names of all three with a mixture of pathos and enormous pride. "They were so gifted."

Adam and Eve had not taken their eyes off each other throughout this entire explanation, their thoughts passing through hundreds of ideas together, their familiarity allowing them to share thoughts without any words passing between them. "Can we communicate with the Underlings?" asked Adam.

Esther once again replied. "Well, a handful of Underlings who've come in from the Waiting Area were able to make subtle suggestions to close relatives, lovers, intimate friends, people with whom they had a deep spiritual connection, but they could never communicate any kind of complex message. I mean, you wouldn't be able to transmit the information from all the equations on the sheets of paper you used on your walls in the waiting room."

Eve quietly said, "That wouldn't do any good anyway. The only person we have that kind of spiritual connection with is our son Christopher, and he is, um, he is mentally impaired. He could not -"

Eve's eyes suddenly filled with tears. "Christopher! Oh my god, Christopher! I hadn't even thought of him! How long did you say we've been in the Waiting Area?"

"Forty-six years, two months, three days, roughly," said Esther.

"What's become of him?" cried Eve. "Oh god, he'd be an old man by now. Is he still alive?"

Esther said, "I assumed you would ask about Christopher at some point. Yes, he is still alive. I conducted a detailed survey, and it appears he was taken in by the string theory team, at least we know he has maintained close association with them. As far as we know, he is fine and has lived a good life."

Eve pushed herself against Adam and tried to compose herself. Adam held his wife, wiping away his own tears.

Taking a deep breath, Eve resumed. "As I said, Christopher is the only one with whom we have that kind of extreme closeness, but he is not capable of understanding any sort of information we could provide about string theory." Tears once again welled in her eyes as she realized how much she missed him. In the Waiting Area those emotions had somehow not come to her.

Adam took Eve's hands into his own. "Come on, sweetie. Let's go see what kind of information Esther can provide us. There's got to be something we can do. After all, we're the best." He gave her a wink, and she couldn't hold back a tiny smile for the man she loved.

April 19, 2042:

"...those files are also broken down into categories. One area you might find particularly useful is the mathematical derivations folder. The complete derivations of all the main string theory conceptual development is there, along with analysis of the mathematical concepts themselves, from asymmetric tensors to Hopf maps to heteromorphic functions, to just about everything else that might be applicable. This way, you don't have to go back and derive any mathematics that is new to you, you can just come here for a concise tutorial. I'd send you to Darryl, he knows the concepts backward and forward, but he couldn't explain them to save his life. Anyway, as for your own work, I've reformatted the database so you can identify every experiment since the program started, either by date, type of test, result obtained, or several other categories. I don't think you'll find it hard to use.

"I thought I would have had more time."

"Shhhhhh….." said Zena Dunn. "You don't need to do this now." She gently laid a hand across Melina Valin's forehead.

Melina gave up trying to lift her head from the pillow. "No, no, this is how I want it to be. My life has been about organizing information, and there's no other way I'd want it to end." This time she couldn't hold back a wince from the pain. "Besides, Zena, you need all the math help you can get."

The two old women, one of them dying, shared a final belly laugh, Melina in spite of the pain. Finally Zena leaned over with a sense of urgency.

"Do you think your life has only been about being *organized*?" asked Zena. "Are you stupid?" She smiled as she leaned over and kissed Melina on the forehead. "Every single person on this team did a better job because of you. Every one of us knows we're a better person because of you. You don't think we understand how much you gave of yourself? Maybe you tried not to show it outwardly, but we knew. We loved you. All of us. *That* is what your life was about."

Melina, even now uncomfortable with the idea of someone

gushing over her, haltingly continued. "Zena, I appreciate that, I really do, but please, just let me do this, it really is what I want." She paused a moment, then whispered, "Tell the others I loved them too."

After a few seconds to collect herself, Melina continued speaking. Zena smiled slightly, realizing with a wry satisfaction that Melina would remain Melina to the end. She sat back and listened closely, knowing that Melina's decades of documenting every aspect of string theory provided her a broader perspective than any of the other remaining team members.

She did need help with the math, after all.

Melina went on, "The key has to be somewhere in the sequence of solutions to the equation sets. I know in some cases the particle traces from the Hadron Collider experiments did not lead to similar interactions in the SSC trials." Zena nodded in agreement. "Shortly after that, Sean and Max worked on that from the theoretical aspect. Go look through my records of their mathematical construct. There are some close similarities in the unsolved portions of those equation sets and the dimensional interaction conflicts that Max and Darryl have worked so hard to solve. Ha - I bet Max doesn't even remember doing those calculations."

Zena noted that even now Melina would not give herself credit for her own very significant contributions to the theoretical work.

"There's also an obscure spatial concept called Kahler potentials that you might want to look into. There might be some correlations between your experimental results that don't match theoretical predictions and the higher-energy vibrational pattern calculations......."

Four hours later Melina Valin passed away quietly, having shared her knowledge almost to her last breath.

<u>November 5, 2043:</u>

Kathy Leigh was having a wonderful Saturday afternoon visiting her newest grandson. Luke had been born six weeks before, and was the most beautiful baby Kathy had ever seen. Luke's mother Lucy was, to be honest, Kathy's favorite, having grown up as the most obedient and docile of her children. Kathy regretted that she had not appreciated Lucy more as a young child. Lucy's twin brothers were born in 1995, and Lucy had followed in 2002. Lucy was always the passive one, and Kathy regretted those early years when she, for reasons she could not fathom now, somehow appreciated the impishness, energy, and juvenile pranks of the two boys more than Lucy's faithfulness and calm. In her later years Kathy came to realize the value Lucy brought to her own life and to society. How wonderful that no extra energy had to be spent in lavishing attention on Lucy, how marvelously efficient she was in terms of the emotional expense of others. A perfect low-maintenance daughter, truly worthy of a mother's affection.

Luke finished eating and closed his eyes to sleep, as mother and grandmother gazed at him lovingly. Lucy sighed with relief, for this gave her a few minutes to dispose of the body of Luke's twin brother Allen, born with deformed legs, who had finally starved to death in the shed behind their house. Kathy went to get a blanket to wrap the body, still glowing from her time with Luke and Lucy.

<u>Sunday, 1:09 p.m.:</u>

"…and this little gauge over here shows you the overall vibration frequency average for the entire universe," stated Brother Amos, reveling in this opportunity to show off his knowledge of the Underling World Observation Center.

"What's this one?" asked Adam Parson, pointing to a large octagonal red button.

"Don't know. Never used it," said Amos, quite unaware that if he had been able to rouse himself from that nap immediately after Dunstan blew the Trumpet, the flashing warnings would have told him that this red button initiated an emergency vibrational stabilization and would have prevented the entire calamity. But it was much too late for that now.

"These instruments are all boring," continued Amos, moving to a new console. "Here, watch this one."

A moment later a picture of a large urban area appeared on the viewer, and as Amos turned the dial on the Isolation Monitor, the image grew larger and larger, revealing a few city blocks, then a series of business establishments on a crowded street, and finally settling on a sign:

"McDonald's Hamburgers - 3,500,000,000,000 Served."

"Ha! Ha! Ha!" roared Adam Parson. "Eve, come look at this! McDonald's is up to three and a half trillion burgers!!"

Eve, too, had to laugh, as much in amazement at the enormous number as at the familiar memory. "How can that be? They were just over a hundred billion when we, well, you know." She looked at Adam, and then asked Amos, "Can you find anything on earth with that?"

"Well, pretty much, yes, ma'am" said Amos, his chest puffing out with self-importance. The opportunity to demonstrate his proficiency with the Underling observation monitors for these obviously important visitors had made him forget his earlier disgruntlement over working on Sunday. Wishing to present an air of professional detachment, he quickly added, "Well, of course there are limitations, ma'am. It's true we can zoom in about as far as we want, but we just get a single snapshot type thing. We can isolate on one object at a time and track it, but it's not like we know everything that goes on."

"Ohhh, Adam, I've just got to see Tony's Bistro again," said Eve, referring to the restaurant where Adam had proposed.

"Ma'am, that might be a bit tough," said Amos condescendingly. I do have to know where to look, I hope you realize that."

"Oh, I know the address," said Eve. "112 Center Street, Princeton, New Jersey."

"Uh, New Jersey?"

"Oh, I forget, you're not from earth. It's in America? You know America?"

"Yes, yes, I know America, I've been looking at these monitors since the beginning of time," grumbled Amos under his breath. He slid away from the viewer and over to the data entry console with the smoothest move he could muster. He entered a few keystrokes and waited a moment. "Okay, got the coordinates. Just a second."

Moments later another image came up on the viewer, and Amos once again zoomed in.

Adam said quizzically, "That's strange. It's the right street corner, I recognize it, but that sign, is, well, look."

The sign read, "McDonald's Hamburgers - 3,500,000,000,000 Served."

"Oh god no," said Eve. "Go to the right a bit. There was another restaurant there."

"McDonald's Hamburgers - 3,500,000,000,000 Served."

Ever mindful of the need for a sufficient statistical basis before reaching a conclusion, Adam and Eve requested Amos to survey a number of metropolitan areas.

It was apparent that all restaurants in the year 2043 were McDonald's.

Putting that aside, Adam pushed forward with the task at hand. "All right, Amos, you showed me the basic monitors for the overall planet indices - Creativity, Empathy, Humor, Stability, and the rest. And the trends have changed for all of them?"

"Oh, right, right. Stability is way up. Violence is way down, barely readable. I do get a reading on Humor, but it's on a low level, very constant, no spikes up and down at all. But to tell you the truth -" he leaned forward to whisper - "if Esther wasn't saying the Sonic Regression was some big crisis, I don't know if I'd think this was so bad. No violence? Very stable? What's so awful about that?"

Esther jumped in and said, "Show them the frequency pattern profiles."

Amos's eyes lit up as he swung around to a smaller console behind him. He typed in a string of characters and a 3-dimensional image of the earth appeared on the viewer. The outline of the oceans could be seen, and the land masses were covered with a dull gray haze, except for a tiny dot of bright pink.

"What are we looking at?" asked Eve.

"Well, the colors used to be a lot more interesting," said Amos. There used to be reds and greens and blues and all sorts of colors, and the patterns would shift around and it was *very* cool to watch."

Esther explained, "It's a visual representation of the general string vibrational patterns over the Underling world - I mean, the earth. As you can see, the earth is covered with the gray pattern, it represents the sameness of thought and emotion that has become the dominant form -"

"Still don't know why that's such a bad thing," interrupted Amos.

"The planet used to contain a far more varied emotional climate. This indicator was one of the first that told us there was a serious disruption to the vibrational permeations in the 10th dimension. Then we looked at the permeation levels themselves on the gauge I showed you before, and that's when we were sure the regression was happening."

"But what's that tiny pink area?" asked Adam.

Esther smiled. "Watch. Amos, zoom in on it."

Amos turned up the signal amplification as before, and the image focused on a smaller and smaller area.

"It's Washington," whispered Adam.

"It's the Institute," whispered back Eve.

"Is it - ?"

"Yes, we're pretty sure it's the string theory team. As far as we can tell, the rest of the planet has pretty much given up on any kind of intellectual pursuit," said Esther. "It really couldn't be anyone else, the picture hasn't changed much for quite a while, except the gray is getting darker."

"How close can you zoom in?" asked Eve.

"Close as you want, ma'am," boasted Amos.

"Can you - ?"

Esther reached around Amos to the controls. Amos, feeling affronted, stepped back with a huff. Esther magnified the images to a view equivalent to a distance of twenty feet, and scanned around the Institute, looking for the brightest pink regions more than any individual object. At last she hit upon a human form, then another a few feet away, neither moving. She continued to scan.

"There! There he is!" exclaimed Eve. "Oh my god, I can't believe I can still recognize him, but that's our son."

Adam and Eve both wept openly and gazed at the seventy-two year old Christopher Parson, fast asleep in the middle of the night, for what seemed like hours. Adam checked the Liquid Time Correlation clock on the wall, however, and noted that only 1.6 seconds of City Time passed while Christopher slept. At last Eve said softly, "Thank you, we really needed to see him. But I guess we have work to do."

Adam shook himself out of his emotional state and said, "All right, let's see what other instrumentation you have. Hey, what is *that*?" He was looking at a large monitor with a picture of a face with a frozen, emotionless smile.

"Oh, that was the Architect's favorite, and most of the time it's the only one I pay attention to," said Amos. "It's kind of a simplified visualization of what's going on with the Underlings. See, the expression on the face changes when the mood of the Underlings does. Like, oh, let's see, on Thursday at 7:00 a.m., that would be, oh, in the 1920's in Underling time, it was a wild partying kind of smile. And a little later, in your, uh, 1940's, it was a nasty scowl, let me tell you. Boy, what was going on then?"

Adam's jaw dropped. "You're telling me that the Architect's idea of an instrument to measure the overall human condition does it with a *smiley face* and a *frowney face*???"

"Oh no, it did a lot more than that," said Amos, not

understanding the consternation in Adam's voice. "It could do all kinds of expressions. There were dumb looks, confident grins, and these funny ones where the nose gets all scrunched up, they were great. You can't say She didn't have a sense of humor. It was hard paying attention to the training sessions with all the jokes She kept telling. Everybody made Her out to be all hoity-toity, but She was as down to earth as they come.

"Heh - heh. 'Down to earth' - get it?" Amos laughed hysterically at his own joke.

Adam stepped back, shaking his head. Apparently there was a God, but not quite what he had imagined. "All right. Do you have any manuals or documentation that tells how everything works and what everything does?"

Amos thought for a moment and said, "Well, you can hit one of the function keys and get to the control documents, yeah, but I've never looked at them."

Esther said, "I've looked at them, but they make no sense to me, there are characters and symbols that mean nothing that I can understand."

Eve replied, "Can you show us?"

"Certainly." Esther turned to the control console and tapped at the F9 key, and an entirely new text appeared on the main viewing screen. Eve scrolled down, she and Adam looking for something recognizable.

Amos quickly lost interest in this unfathomable game being played by the Parsons, and even Esther, despite her burning curiosity at this new world opening before her, found her eyelids getting heavy. But the Parsons, after a lifetime of such study, wordlessly searched every character and every line for a clue to the meaning of what scrolled before them.

"It's the equations," said Adam tentatively. "Look, see that sequence of characters? And then how they are inverted two lines later? They're in exactly the locations they'd be in the invariant topology analysis of the muon superpartner particle."

"Yes, yes," said Eve. "And then the next one repeats the sequence, but those three terms are different. It must be the same analysis for one of the other superpartner particles."

They looked into each others' eyes and smiled the same knowing smile they'd shared since those first wonderful moments together at the chalkboard at Princeton. It was a puzzle, and they had been solving just such puzzles all their lives.

<u>July 24, 2044:</u>

It was five o'clock, and the Ministry of Social Welfare decreed that all citizens were to watch television news at this hour, to promote awareness of governmental policies for the benefit of the populace. For Kathy Leigh, of course, there was no encouragement required, as she enjoyed watching the young people follow in her footsteps as newscasters. The news itself, of course, was usually of minimal interest, as world affairs were well in order, and there were no longer any divisive public issues. Fortunately, the more frequent earthquakes of recent years added some welcome spice to the news. There had been three minor local quakes in the last two months, including one during the broadcast itself, making for an interesting test of the reporters' ability to improvise. They had failed miserably, Kathy chuckled to herself. Kathy particularly enjoyed the young fresh-faced reporters, remembering her own beginnings so long ago. She instinctively watched every vocal inflection and facial nuance, considering how she would have presented the same stories. On this evening a rather vacant young woman delivered the news in the monotone that was now commonly-accepted standard speech.

"The United World Government today presented its highest award, the Stabilization Enhancement Prize, to the proud Viceroy of Rwanda. After decades of hunger problems in that African country, the local authorities have resolved the issue, resulting in economic recovery as well as beneficial technology development."

On screen, thousands of Rwandan natives could be seen marching together into the main square of Kigali, the capital city. The vacant young woman continued with her voiceover, describing the events taking place.

"Twelve thousand Rwandan citizens with incomes below the subsistence level were gathered together, and a modular ten-foot wall was moved into place, surrounding them. A newly-developed variation of sulfuric acid was dropped from helicopters in a fine mist onto the assembled populace. The acid is especially formulated to cling to any surface it touches, and chemically react with increased intensity. The test was entirely successful, as you can see, and all the Rwandans died within minutes. The Government reported that it was pleased at this decisive step to improve Rwanda's economic status. In addition, the Global Industrial Business Council applauded the Rwandan authorities, because the demonstration has commercial applications in terms of outdoor large-scale equipment cleaning applications.

"Rwanda announced that it will proceed immediately with the extermination of its remaining low-income citizens, and expects to complete the operation in two weeks."

Grant Zenkman had also watched the newscast, this time with special interest. Development of the acid extermination process had been his final major project as technical director of the Cultural Control Ministry. He felt that strange old emotion of pride, seeing his research being used so effectively. Grant's career in the Ministry had been long and distinguished, but age had robbed him of much of his energy and skills, and it was time for a younger person to take over. In the name of societal efficiency, Grant had come forward on his own to recommended his own demotion. Any other line of thinking would have been unimaginable. He wondered what would become of him in his remaining days, if there would be a use for him.

Sunday 2:31 p.m.:

"All right. That's enough. You can stop now. Thank you for your efforts. It was a good try." Peter slumped back into his chair, exhaustion overtaking him.

It had been Eve's idea, but Esther felt stupid at not having thought of it herself. After all, she was the one who had brought the Parsons in from the Waiting Area to help in the crisis. The Underling year was now 2044, 48 years since this President Clinton fellow had initiated the string theory team. Some of the original Underling string theory team members were likely have passed away in all those years, and certainly other physicists as well, and they might have an even more advanced understanding of string properties than the Parsons did. If having two string theory experts here was good, how much better would it be to have five or six or ten or a hundred? This idea hit Eve like a ton of bricks just after 2:00 p.m., and all of them sprinted to the Waiting

Area Gatekeeper's office. They found him sitting on the floor playing checkers by himself.

"Sir, we need to retrieve some people from the Waiting Area," Peter said. We have a number of possible names, and we need you to perform a search and find them immediately."

"Nope, not gonna happen," the Gatekeeper had said.

"You don't understand, this is a matter of the utmost importance."

"No, *you* don't understand. My transmission equipment ain't working. Don't have access to the Waitin' Area. You don't just walk in there from the City proper, you gotta align all the string vibrations to transfer us there or them here. Right now you can't get nobody in or out of there. Some kinda interference or somethin'. The strings don't seem to be vibratin' right."

"Can we please try?"

"Be my guest," the Gatekeeper had said amusedly. "If you think you can work them controls better than me, more power to ya."

"Hey, it's Sunday," he added. "Shouldn't I be gettin' paid overtime?"

Adam, Eve, Peter, Thomas, Esther, and even Amos and the Gatekeeper tried every conceivable adjustment of the transmission controls, all to no avail. There would be no more help coming from the Waiting Area.

Esther berated herself, realizing that if she had thought of locating others in the Waiting Area earlier, the effort might have been successful.

Peter, slumped in the chair with a monumental headache, knew what this meant. The strings were breaking down. Access to the Waiting Area had been lost. What would be next? Time was becoming a very precious commodity.

March 5, 2045:

Max Cherry, awake and feverishly working at 4:15 a.m., furiously wrote out one equation after another. He had been through these iterations so many times that he could do the calculations almost as fast as he could write. Three weeks before, Max had achieved correlation of the ninth dimension to the first eight. This was closer than the team had ever been to full synchronization of the equations in all ten dimensions, the Holy Grail they had pursued for nearly fifty years. His entire life, Max had carefully cultivated an outward impression of himself as the insouciant court jester, but within him was a burning competitive desire against string theory itself. Max desperately wanted the victory of understanding universal physics during his lifetime, pure and simple, and would never be satisfied until that day. In these last weeks, Max tried to keep to himself, desiring to spring the complete equation sets on the team as one final surprise, which of course would be delivered with as much comedic effect as possible. Maintaining his privacy was not that difficult. Darryl the Dreamer tended to work by himself in another corner of the room anyway, and Jason and Zena did their experimental analysis together. There had been a snide comment or two about the suddenly sober-minded Max Cherry, but each person was fully involved in their own work, and by now Max could taste the victory that was so close. Sleep was the farthest thing from his mind.

Taking a deep breath, Max put his full attention to the next series of calculations. His was a love/hate relationship with the formulas. He loved them on the days when the calculations produced the desired results, but there was nothing beautiful or elegant about mathematics on the days when the equations resisted his efforts at seducing them into meaningful solutions. Darryl's sense was different, Max knew that. Darryl almost preferred to have the solutions evade him; the futile pursuit of the unfathomable was in fact far more intriguing to him than finding a solution, except for those exquisite occasions when a new vision became the key to resolving a previously intractable mystery. And oddly enough, those moments of revelation most often came from the pursuit of the very enigmas that so fascinated him.

Max blazed through equation after equation, demonstrating the mass, energy, velocity, electric charge, and other properties for each of the many subatomic particles with regard to their tenth-dimensional vibrational patterns. With each new property, his calculations needed to address the implications of the equations from the other dimensions, resulting in hundreds of steps being required for each significant particle property. Every time before, his path had become ensnarled, as the parallel mathematical development from different dimensional relationships reached a point where they would not come together. But Max had finally found the right path. Every line of reasoning was coming neatly together, like an elegant woven fabric, and Max could see the completed product coming alive before his eyes.

At 10:00 a.m., Jason Poe and Zena Dunn, settling into their morning's work together, jumped in agitation at the crash behind them. Max stood in front of his desk, having flipped it over with a ferocity completely unexpected in a man of his advancing years. Darryl Johnson sat at his own desk as usual, staring contemplatively at a blank piece of paper.

"What - ?" was all that Jason could utter before Max burst forth in a tirade.

"This is god damn impossible. Five months of calculations. I was there. I was *there*. Everything fit. Every harmonic of the vibrational patterns synchronized with the other nine dimensions. The vibrational patterns reinforced each other, and all the implied energy translations held true. Then right here at the end, I have maybe two days' work left, I got that damn paradox again. One of the dimensions requires the presence of a top quark vibrational pattern at that specific matrix position, and the other applicable dimensional equation set requires that the particle be a muon. Well, it *can't* be both a top quark and a muon, now can it? I don't believe it. The whole thing comes down right there like a house of cards. I went over it four times. Damn it all to hell. I'm going to die and never see the answer."

Max picked up a computer monitor and hurled it to the floor, crushed by the failure of his lifelong quest. He turned ferociously toward Darryl, who sat, still serene, silent, and implacable. "You listening to any of this? We're done, we're done. I can't go through it again. You ever pay attention, you catatonic slug?"

Darryl blinked twice, his body position and facial expression unchanged.

"Aw hell, what's the point?" cried out Max, and he sat down and put his head in his hands.

Jason walked toward him and put his arm around his oldest friend, but Max shrugged him off, refusing any comfort. He kicked at the table leg and pounded his fist three times.

"We keep trying and trying. We've looked at it every way imaginable. I know I'm doing the math right. I'm accounting for every factor. The vibrations just don't synchronize over all ten dimensions simultaneously. It just doesn't. It's like the dimensions don't vibrate together. That's the end. I give up."

Darryl cocked his head to the side and focused his eyes. The room was silent for several moments, until he uttered a barely audible, "Hunh."

"What's this? The Sphinx speaks?" Max spat out.

<u>Sunday, 4:26 p.m.:</u>

Given the wonderful new instruments with which he could now study the string problem, Adam Parson resembled nothing so much as an eight-year-old boy in the world's greatest toy store. To Eve's alternating delight and exasperation, he chased about the enormous control room from console to console, adjusting scan settings, switching evaluation parameters, and recalculating results. As Eve understood, there was method to his madness, his repeat analyses isolating one variable after another and reaching conclusions regarding the effect of each. For her part, Eve compiled all the results, developed statistical data on experimental variation, and analyzed the overarching concepts revealed in the data.

With historical scans available, Adam and Eve Parson were able to view past vibrational events, observe the outcomes, and thereby conduct "virtual experiments" to assess the accuracy of their theoretical predictions. This, combined with the refinements to the equations they had developed in the Waiting Area, enabled them to make rapid progress in isolating potential solutions to the problem of correcting the vibrational distortions. Eve scoured the equations in the control documents, picking up the missing theoretical components that she and Adam still did not understand.

Giving free rein to his boyish enthusiasm, Adam found it difficult to maintain a sense of the gravity of the situation. Each new gauge or monitor or scanner was a new source of delight, and his wonderment led to constant sidetracking of his attention.

"Adam, quit looking at the global profile scans, we need to get the atomic-scale results. Come on."

"Sorry dear," said Adam in mock shame. He did, however, proceed immediately to setting up the simulation scanner and reviewing the critical equations concerning the mechanism of permeation.

"Can I help with anything?" asked an awed but eager Esther, thrilled beyond belief to see someone making sense of the instruments which had fascinated her for so long.

"Umm, sure, check the monitor over there," said Adam, his focus returning, pointing to a small lighted viewer two rows over. He began to ramble, talking to himself as much as to Esther. "The question is, can the vibrational patterns be modified by an artificial external source? If so, can they be modified in such a way that the distortions are corrected? For that to happen, a localized input would not only have to cause a correction in the immediate vicinity, but the restored vibrations would then have to permeate throughout the universe on a self-propagating basis -"

"What do you mean, permeate on a self-propagating basis?" asked the eager-to-learn Esther.

"Oh," said Adam, resetting several sequential operations. "It has to be like a chain reaction. Once the vibrational restoration starts, it has to feed on itself and spread like a wave across a pond throughout the universe.

Esther nodded, thinking she understood, but not sure.

"What's required is like a seed, an input to the system that reinforces the correct vibrations and cancels out the distortions, a kind of penicillin for the universe."

What Adam did not tell Esther was that one of his two great fears was that even if such a seed existed, it most likely required a cataclysmic blast of energy far beyond the capability of the Underlings to generate.

Eve was quite disturbed by the other obvious fear, the terror of futility, as she realized that even if a solution could be found to restore the proper harmonic vibrations, there was no viable way to communicate the answer to Christopher or the string theory physicists. As Esther had told them, any message they might send could only be delivered to Chris through their strong emotional bond, and even then it could only be a vague general thought, not a complex set of procedures to follow. And even if they could somehow open a clear line of communication into Chris's mind, he did not have the mental capacity to understand the details required to inform the other string team members. Eve was unnerved by the rising panic within her, and she required all her strength to resist it. In all likelihood, she realized, she and Adam would watch the universe unravel before their eyes, knowing how it could be stopped, but powerless to do so.

Again and again Adam created simulated particle collisions, adjusting string tensions, vibrational frequencies, wavelengths, and energies, watched the calculated outcomes, and compared them to his understanding of the theoretical predictions. Some interactions created smooth harmonics, but none initiated a vibration change that penetrated more than a few millionths of a centimeter into the surrounding space.

"Stop! What did you just do?" shouted Esther suddenly, sitting at the Resonance Meter.

Adam and Eve whipped their head around in surprise, wondering why Esther was so excited.

"Just another collision, it didn't progress any farther than the others," said Adam, trying to calm Esther down.

"No, it wasn't just another collision," said Esther. "There was a really big spike in the reverberation value." Having watched so many repetitions of the collisions, Esther was beginning to understand the readings. "The vibrations echoed for almost a millisecond, a hundred times more than for any of the other collisions."

"Bless you!" cried Eve. "Oh my goodness. Adam and I were only looking at the physical distance that the vibrations penetrated into the surrounding space, not how long they lasted. Thank you, thank you."

Esther couldn't resist a small smile of satisfaction, then quickly refocused on the task at hand.

Eve's eyes connected with those of her husband. "What was different that time?"

"I'm not sure. Let me rerun it."

The simulated particles crashed into each other once more.

"Same thing," said Esther, her eyes now darting back and forth between Adam and Eve.

"It's more of a one-on-one collision, not so many other particles around," said Adam. "I didn't really intend it that way, but that's the only difference in this one. The previous trials all had a lot more particles involved in the interaction."

"Try it again," said Eve. "Use even fewer particles."

The collision occurred. Adam and Eve turned toward

Esther.

"Oh my goodness! That was something."

"Umm, could you be a bit more specific, dear?" asked Eve gently.

"Oh, I'm sorry," said Esther, still adjusting to the professionalism of her newfound role as experimental researcher. "The vibrations persisted for nearly a tenth of a second that time."

"That's it!" Dial it way back, Adam. "Do a one-on-one collision with no other particles whatsoever."

Moments later, within the silicon tracings on an integrated circuit chip, two mathematically simulated up-quarks collided in an atmosphere consisting solely of the roiling energy of empty space.

The reverberations from the mock collision lasted fourteen seconds and penetrated 149,751 miles into the surrounding space. The race was on.

"That's the key," said Eve excitedly. "We have a chance. The solution isn't a massively energetic collision. We don't need a thousand supernovas going off at once, thank god. The secret is to find a perfect, pristine non-harmonic vibration, sort of a perfectly pure little tuning fork that becomes the only sound you hear. First we'll refine what we have, Esther and I can do that. Then we just need the right input values to make it self-propagating. Adam, make up a test matrix so we're sure we're addressing all the pertinent variables. We'll need particle type, mass, velocity, string tension, frequency, wavelength....."

March 24, 2045:

Darryl Johnson came bounding down the stairs at 6:00

a.m., exuding a spryness not only remarkable for a man of his age, but greater in fact than the others had seen in decades. Max Cherry, in a worn bathrobe and slippers, still awake from the night before, looked up at Darryl and erratically raised the glass he held in his left hand.

"Hey, what's with you? Want a drink? I special ordered some 1995 Scotch, so I could remember what life was like before we started this damn project."

Darryl strode to Max's table and sat down. "Who says they do?" he asked enigmatically.

"Do what? What are you talking about?"

"Who says all the dimensions have to vibrate together?"

"Make some sense, Darryl, for once, okay? Please?"

"What you said. Three weeks ago. You said the equations don't synchronize over all ten dimensions simultaneously. You said it's like they don't vibrate together. Well, who says they have to?" The glint in Darryl's eye was positively unnerving.

"I don't understand," Max said bitterly. "If they all vibrate harmonically, then they're obviously all synchronized."

Darryl shrugged. "Maybe at the end of the process, but that doesn't mean they had to be that way from the beginning, from the Big Bang. What if one dimension began its vibrations first, then at some point that started the next dimension into its characteristic vibrational patterns, and then on to the third dimension, and so on through all ten? Think about it. The mathematics would actually get a lot simpler if that's how it works."

Darryl's remarkable brainstorm intrigued Max, and his eyes met Darryl's with a laserlike stare.

"Wait, wait, wait. You mean that at the Big Bang only one dimension vibrated at first, and then each dimension's vibrational patterns sort of transferred from one to the next, finally through all ten?"

"I don't know. Maybe. All this time we've assumed that all ten dimensions were fully vibrational from the start. What if that's not the right perception? It does make the whole idea of evolution more coherent."

"Darryl, you have no idea if you're right or not," said Max.

"Max - isn't this the way discoveries have always gone?" Darryl was speaking in complete sentences, a sure sign that something remarkable had occurred within his mind. "We didn't understand the solar system until Galileo gave us a new picture with the Sun at the center instead of the earth, and suddenly it all made sense. We didn't understand atomic theory until Rutherford's alpha particle experiments gave us the concept of a heavy nucleus surrounded by an electron cloud that is almost completely open space. We didn't comprehend the true relationships of time and space until Einstein first entertained the possibility that the rate of time passage can vary, but that the speed of light is always constant. And even Einstein couldn't fathom the idea that the universe is expanding until Edwin Hubble proved it, and once we understood that, it inevitably led to our understanding of the Big Bang and cosmic evolution. Sometimes that's all you need, a new visualization, and then all the details just fall out naturally."

Max looked at Darryl. Darryl's eyes were gleaming in a way Max had never seen. "You've figured it out, haven't you?" Max saw his own wicked grin of satisfaction on Darryl's face for the first time since they had met fifty years ago.

"It's beautiful, Max. It really is."

Darryl walked to his desk and retrieved a notebook. For the next six hours Darryl showed Max the sequential equation sets illustrating the principle of progressive permeation of the strings' vibration patterns throughout the ten dimensions. "It's not that difficult. You start with the time dimension and work out the equations for vibration within it. None of the other dimensions have any vibrations yet. Once the string vibrations have fully permeated the time dimension, you move on to any of the three space dimensions, it doesn't matter which one, they're all symmetric, and the vibrations permeate those dimensions in the same way. Then - once you have those first four dimensions - the implications of the equation sets, those implications that have been so troublesome, all point specifically to just one of the small curled-up dimensions. The strings' vibrations, with all the resonances and harmonics, permeate into that dimension next, and gradually spread throughout that dimension until it is fully vibrating. So that's the fifth dimension. After you work out the equations for the fifth dimension, you are similarly pointed to one of the remaining dimensions, so that's the sixth. And so on. It all leads to one unique pathway through all the dimensions, and all the interactions are perfectly synchronized."

Max pored over the notebook. He saw that Darryl had used the algorithms and equations that Max had developed over the years, repeating Max's conceptual thoughts exactly. "I'll be damned," Max thought to himself. "All those years I thought he was off in his own little fantasy world, but he had memorized every detail of my work."

Max reached the end. Inside Darryl's mathematical construct, all ten dimensions vibrated together in perfect harmony. The equations of string theory, God's instruction manual for the universe itself, lay on the table in front of him, scrawled in an old notebook in the childlike handwriting of Darryl Johnson.

Darryl spoke again. "We're not done yet, not by a longshot. We have the equations, but they don't tell us the implications in terms of physical phenomena. That will take a lot more calculations, but it will be great being here with you to do it."

He could not deliver on that last promise, however. Eight days later Darryl Johnson collapsed from a massive stroke, right in the middle of writing out a new mathematical hypothesis, deep inside the theoretical dreamworld that had been his life. Max would have to carry on the theoretical work alone.

June 9, 2047:

"Mommy, what does 'compassion' mean?"

"What? Where did you hear that word?"

"I was at the library looking for a book, and I found this real old one, and it had a lot of strange words."

"Like what?"

"Like compassion! Do you know what it means?"

"Well, let's go look it up in the dictionary, OK, honey?"

"OK, mommy."

"Hmm, well, I don't see it here. It was c-o-m-p-a-s-s-i-o-n, right?"

"Yep."

"No, it's not here. I'm sorry, honey, I don't know what it means."

"What about courage?"

"Courage? What strange words! Well, let's see..... no,

it's not in the dictionary either. Guess you're really fooling mommy today, aren't you?"

"There was one more. Sympathy."

"Oh, I know that one, sweetheart. A sympathy was a long time ago when they would have lots of people get together and play music in a big auditorium, and other people would come and pay money and listen to them. Do you know what music is?"

"Yes, mommy. They told us about it at school. In the olden days people liked to have these big toys that made funny sounds and they were real loud, and the music people were even on TV, and people liked to listen because they sounded so funny and everyone laughed. People sure were weird in the olden days, huh, mommy?"

"That's right, honey. They liked music and sympathies. Pretty weird."

Sunday, 7:35 p.m.:

Brother Dunstan was not at all satisfied. His well-earned rise to a position of authority had not yielded the expected rewards. The Omniscience Council, since the announcement of the Sonic Disruption, was a hollow shell of its former self, seldom meeting, and even then performing in an entirely listless manner. "The Impotence Council" was a more accurate description, he thought. As Michael said, however, Dunstan was a man of action, and so it was that Dunstan had approached Michael, the Council Chairman, intent on restoring greatness to the City's leadership, as well as status and honor for himself.

Michael loudly rapped his pearl-handled gavel against the podium three times, calling to order the Joint Leadership

Council meeting, which included the Omniscience Council, the Efficiency Committee, the Underling Oversight Committee, and the Festival Preparation Committee.

"Ladies and gentlemen, before we begin, I must acknowledge a debt of gratitude which all of us owe to our newest Council member, the remarkable Brother Dunstan. Through no fault of our own, Festival planning was thrown off schedule, due to these unfortunate announcements regarding the supposed Sonic Regression. We were, I regret to say, not as vigilant as we should have been, and we allowed these distractions to sidetrack our progress toward the fulfillment of our mission. We allowed our subordinates to usurp the authority rightfully belonging to our Council leadership. However, the time has come to reassert our position of authority and guidance. My fellow Council members, greatness in the light of day is an ephemeral thing, not to be trusted. Greatness shines brightest in the darkest hours of the night, when men are challenged to the depths of their souls, when there seems no road to follow. My friends, let us heed the clarion call of these troubled times, let us rise to the challenge before us, let us be giants in this time of small and petty men. We still have a mission, and we shall complete it. Our mission was and is to prepare for the Festival and usher in the Era of Eternal Understanding. I say to you now: I for one do solemnly pledge myself to carry out this mission and fulfill the Architect's vision - no, *our* vision - for the Underling World and the City.

The assembled group stood as one and applauded Brother Michael, who graciously turned to acknowledge Dunstan's inspiration. Dunstan for his part deftly balanced an assumed air of humility with a prideful recognition of his newly exalted status.

Only Thomas was unimpressed, remaining seated at the far left end of the Council dais. When the tumult finally died down, he wearily said, "Excuse me. At last report the 10th-dimension permeation level was down to fifty-two percent, and projections were that the universal unraveling is imminent." Rolling his eyes, Thomas asked sarcastically, "Might I inquire as to whether this august body has discovered a scientific solution to the vibrational distortion problem?"

"Hmmmpphy," sniffed Brother Bartholomew. "Apparently someone was sleeping during Empowerment Training." A gentle rippling chuckle swept through the Council membership. Bartholomew's expression turned fierce. "It is not the vibrational distortion *problem*, dear Thomas. It is the vibrational distortion *opportunity*."

And just how do you propose to take advantage of this *opportunity*?" asked Thomas.

"We shall adopt Supreme Being Management Principles," interjected Dunstan forcefully.

"We shall assess the current situational dynamics," added Deborah, newly promoted to the Omniscience Council for her outstanding performance during this crisis.

"We shall maintain Customer Centricity," said Timothy.

Thomas opened his mouth to question just what Customer Centricity might be, and how it could possibly apply to the current situation, but the discussion was now an unstoppable avalanche of pseudo-profundities. One by one each Committee member added to the torrent of obfuscation.

"We shall build quality into the system, not inspect mistakes after they have occurred."

"We shall implement root-cause corrective actions."

"We shall work smarter, not harder."

"We shall ensure Quality, Cost, Delivery, Safety, and Morale."

"We shall be World-Class in all aspects."

"We shall implement Plan-Do-Check-Act as our process paradigm."

"We shall leverage our synergy to unleash the power of the enterprise."

"We shall plan for success, and develop solidarity through diversity."

By now, every Council member was standing, roaring at full volume with each pronouncement, and punctuating each comment with a fist thrust into the air.

"We shall set aggressive yet achievable targets through impassioned application of our core competencies."

"We shall create a unifying culture of enterprise excellence."

"And with all these intrepreneurial processes in place," said Dunstan, who had found himself to be a quick study in terms of these management principles, "this will really move the needle of our performance metrics."

The Council paused to applaud itself.

Thomas again waited a moment, and then spoke once more. "May I ask one more question?"

"Certainly," said Deborah indulgently. "A good manager is first and foremost a leader, a coach, and a coach understands that failure to listen inevitably leads to goodwill impairment in subordinate resources."

"Could you please explain how any of what you just said will help us restore the proper vibrational permeation?"

The silence was palpable. Finally Dunstan spoke, symbolically taking the Council leadership into his own hands.

"Perhaps Brother Thomas is not a Team Player."

The other Council members gasped audibly - it was perhaps the most damning accusation one Council member could cast upon another.

Brother Bartholomew took his lead from Dunstan's boldness.

"You are failing to process the current situational dynamics, Brother Thomas."

"There is no I in Team," added Deborah.

"The particulars are not what is important. The principles drive the particulars," concluded Brother Michael, glancing at Dunstan for affirmation. Dunstan nodded slowly, closing his eyes momentarily, acknowledging his assent. "Thomas, your obsession with obscure technical details detracts from this Council's ability to focus on its primary high-level mission. Would you say, Brother Dunstan, that a reassignment opportunity is in order?"

"I would indeed," said Dunstan unnecessarily, because Thomas was already walking away. "Not that this is a demotion, of course it should not be taken that way, not at all." The other Council members nodded sagely, understanding that placating subordinates was a prime skill necessity. "We will consider this a cross-functional assignment intended to facilitate realignment to mission-critical objectives."

Deborah, who prided herself on her rapport with animate resources, called after Thomas. "Don't worry, Brother Thomas, we'll be dialoguing on this very soon."

The Council members returned to their seats, once again energized with the dream of a grand and glorious 10th-Dimension Permeation Festival. The issue of Sonic Regression, amazingly enough, was not present on any of the action items generated.

Thomas sat on a bench and tried to think, his meditation disrupted by the constant low rumbling sound that lately filled the City. He wondered what sort of Supreme Being would ever have thought it wise to entrust the universe to such a group as the Council leadership.

July 29, 2049:

Kathy Leigh was disappointed in herself. She fully understood the situation, and enthusiastically agreed that the new governmental policies were desirable and beneficial to society as a whole, but still she was not strong enough to disregard her own selfish motivations. Her own anxiety was proof enough of the government's policy statements that humankind was still not at its optimum state of efficiency. After all, a fully actualized citizen would not carry any negative emotions, they were non-productive. She herself had voted for the individual justification policy, along with 99.94% of all voters, and so she was quite puzzled at her own apprehension. The new Public Exile policies were quite sensible. All individuals were required to demonstrate their economic worth to the state, or the available forms of life support would be cut off. Any attempt to purchase food, shelter, or other survival necessities would be stopped at the bar scan station, and such people would be left unsupported by the state. Decades before, people were sometimes in the same circumstance due to the long-forgotten poverty problem, and they were able to survive by searching for scraps of food available on public streets and in refuse disposal areas. With the wonderful modern ultra-clean environment created by the Sanitation Ministry, however, these sources of food were no longer available, and so these lost souls would typically die of thirst or starvation within a few days, greatly reducing the burden they placed on society.

For aged people such as Kathy, this presented an inconvenience, of course, but it was all for the public good, and everyone understood this. The first version of the new law allowed credit for past societal contributions. Under that law, Kathy was exempt from the Exile policy, because over the course of her life she had obviously provided significant economic benefit, and she was considered to have "earned" the right to be non-productive in her old age. This was blatantly unfair, of course, not to mention detrimental to global economic growth. Under the lifetime earnings provision, if a person such as Kathy Leigh was fortunate enough to generate significant wealth at a young age, she would thereafter not be required to work at all, and allowed to simply enjoy her life. This inefficiency could not be tolerated, and public clamor for change forced the legislators to amend the laws. The new laws were very much preferable, as they required an annual accounting of economic contribution from each citizen in order to maintain societal status.

In its tolerance and wisdom, governmental allowances were made for the aged and the infirm, providing them alternative means of generating economic benefit for society, so long as they were mentally capable of making such choices. Kathy's anxiety over tomorrow's first appointment at the Medical Experimentation Clinic was perhaps understandable, and she appreciated the legislature's kindness in providing this means for her to continue to be a productive citizen.

<u>May 3, 2050:</u>

Zena Dunn was awakened at 8:00 by Christopher Parson, who was the only one who could help her into her wheelchair without assistance. Zena ate a piece of toast for breakfast, and then reviewed her technical notes.

Max Cherry heard Christopher clanking around with Zena's wheelchair, and after that he could not go back to sleep.

Jason Poe finally decided to get out of bed at 9:30 am. His sleep was no longer sound; he typically spent half the night awake, and was only able to get through the day by taking two or three short naps. He hoped last night's sleep would be enough; today would be a long day.

"All right, let's get going, shall we?" asked Jason plaintively. "We haven't had an official meeting for a long time. I agree it's seldom necessary with only three of us left, but before we return to the SSC experiments I think we should hold a documented status meeting."

Zena nodded her assent, but Max coldly said, "So what are you, the reincarnated Melina Valin?"

The truth was that since Melina's passing, her minutely detailed transcription of all team events had been impossible for Jason to maintain, as in fact it would be for any person lacking Melina's meticulously obsessive nature. It was impossible for Jason to record everything, even though the team now consisted of only three members. He could not fathom how Melina was able to keep scrupulously accurate details of the original twelve's every activity. Records of progress were now kept much more loosely, and often not at all.

"It's okay, Max," said Jason. "We'll just do the best we can."

Jason was in fact exhausted from his double duties over the past six years. He tried to support both Zena's experimental analysis efforts and Max's theoretical development, and the dual responsibilities wore down the old man. Furthermore, he did not understand either field as well as the other two, and his relative lack of capability strained his confidence.

Zena began with a review of her recent conclusions from particle collision data. "We know that certain particular collisions do cause a propagation of vibrational energy through space and time," she said. "In the trials we've done up to now, these events were more or less by accident, it wasn't something we were deliberately trying to do, and the permeation lasted only a fraction of a second and penetrated only a few micrometers into space. But I think if we get lucky in a deliberately arranged trial, assuming your equations can get us close to the right energies and velocities, we might have a chance of initiating a self-sustaining vibrational permeation." There was more blind hope than true conviction in Zena's voice.

Max remained silent, so Jason tried to keep the conversation going. "Everything we know so far indicates that there really has been some sort of disruption in the normal vibrations of the strings. We looked at our SSC tracings and the proton degradation experiments from the past few decades, and we see a continual increase in the number of string interactions not predicted by theory. Zena and I did a regression analysis to back-calculate the rate of degradation, and it appears the deviations originated around the year 2000, perhaps a little before that."

Zena replied, "If something accidental happened to cause a breakdown in the strings' vibrational patterns, perhaps a deliberately placed input could restore the permeation to its proper level."

Jason and Zena looked hopefully at Max, who maintained his silence. Nothing they were saying was news, the intent was merely to involve Max in the discussion, because they knew they couldn't make progress without him.

Jason continued on. "The most interesting thing to me is how the 10th-dimensional vibrational frequencies so closely match human brainwave patterns."

"Not all brainwaves," countered Zena. "The only match is from subliminal radiation generated during deeply meditational states, from creative or empathetic situations, where people are stretching their capabilities. This world may have turned into a very strange place, but at least the government's research into mind control helped us find this one little part of the answer."

"And music, don't forget music," replied Jason. "I think we know why music affects people on such a deep level. It reinforces the brainwave resonances that match the string vibrational patterns and literally makes humans more alive. In a very real physical way, music directly touches your soul. The people outside don't listen to music any more because they -- well, they no longer *have* a soul."

Another glance at Max again proved fruitless.

Zena came to the point. "Max, we need you. We all understand what's going on, and that includes you. The universe was created in a systematic fashion and it follows a set of rules. At the Big Bang, the string vibrations initiated in the time dimension, and then permeated through the space dimensions, and then progressively through the six remaining microscopic dimensions of Calabi-Yau space. As of about fifty years ago, just about when we started, the 10th-dimension was apparently close to full permeation. We know all this. The equations predict it, and the experimental evidence from the SSC tracings and the proton degradation data confirms it. Then something went wrong. What or how, we don't know. The world has changed. Not only in our experiments, but in the larger physical world as well. The first changes were societal, which makes sense, because it would be the human-nature characteristics common to the higher 10th-dimensional vibrations that would be affected first, as the degradation works backward. The degradation seems to be exponential, increasing in rate. At some point, the fluctuations in vibration patterns will cause divergent interactions with catastrophic effects. We are already seeing increased global temperatures and higher wind velocities, and earthquakes are up somewhat. It all adds up. No one is working on this problem except us. No one cares about this problem except us. No one can do anything except us. And, Max Cherry, you are the only one who knows enough about the equations to help us restore proper string permeation."

"Do you understand how crazy you sound?" Max Cherry finally broke his silence, and gaped at Zena with a mockingly insane look in his eyes. "Maybe you're right. Maybe the strings have gone haywire, and our Humpty-Dumpty universe will come tumbling down, and all the king's horses and all the king's men won't be able to put it back together again. Oh wait, I forgot. There isn't a king, and there aren't any horses, and there aren't any men. Who is there? Ooh, ahh - Jason Poe, Zena Dunn, and Max Cherry - three octogenarian obsolete former whiz kids who can hardly go to the bathroom by themselves anymore, but think they are God. Get real. If you want to try some nutty Superconducting Supercollider experiment, fine and dandy, you know the equations perfectly well by now, we've been over this a hundred times, but don't ask me to get excited."

"Hey, whatever happened to Max the Irrepressible? You've been my hero my whole life."

Jason's attempt at levity to crack through Max's mood was a dismal failure. "That Max Cherry is long gone," he replied. "I'm here, I'll keep at it, but only because I've been doing this my whole life and I don't know how to do anything different. You have to admit this is all just crazy. Maybe if we had Darryl here, we'd have a chance. But we don't. Give it up. We're fossils."

"Max, maybe it *is* crazy, but we have to try," said Jason plaintively.

"Jason, just don't give me this rah-rah stuff. You've seen the equations. I've been over them and over them. I think they're right, but there's no way to know. The calculations go so slowly. It's taken me five years to get from Darryl's insight about progressive permeation to this point, and I don't think I can go on much longer." Max took a deep breath and tried to continue calmly. Jason and Zena were his lifelong friends, and he loved them more than his own life, but his heart was no longer in the struggle. "I input all the data and yes, our algorithms do calculate a potential solution that would generate a self-propagating vibrational permeation. Well, actually, there were two solutions that were valid mathematically, but only one of them makes sense in the physical world, and might have enough energy to initiate any kind of chain reaction through the strings."

"What was the difference between the two solutions?" asked Zena.

"One is just the reciprocal of the other. The first one makes physical sense, it's an extremely massive collision to start the permeation. The second one, being the reciprocal, means the initial collision energy is so infinitesimal that it doesn't have any significance in terms of what we are trying to do. It - it would be like trying to knock over a brick wall by throwing a marshmallow at it."

"Well, there we are," said Zena. "We have a possibility, don't we?. Let's just go try it. Let's go play the game."

"But that's the whole point, Z. It's not a goddamn game. It's all cold reality now. There's so little time left. The mathematical solution requires a perfectly simultaneous collision of billions of Witten particles. Witten particles are the most massive, most energetic superpartner particles we've ever seen in the SSC experiments. They occur very rarely, and radioactive decay breaks them down in a matter of thousandths of a second. Furthermore, our equations are only approximate, we can't know exactly how many simultaneous collisions we need, or the precise energy they require. So exactly what are the odds of getting billions of them to collide just perfectly? I know you understand what an incredible coincidence you're talking about. It's not like those particles are trained puppies."

Zena spoke very slowly. "Look - the SSC *is* capable of generating Witten particles. We can fire enormous numbers of particles into the SSC tube, and I know the likelihood is small, but maybe a miracle will happen, maybe enough Witten particles will be generated, and maybe that perfect sequence of collisions will happen and start a self-perpetuating fission reaction. If we only have one shot, let's at least take it."

Jason looked Max square in the eye. "I have known you since I was eight years old. No one knows you like I do. Are you willing to just let it all go? Do you just want to give up? Do you want to walk out the front door and become a zombie like the rest of the human race? I don't think so. You are still Max Cherry, for god's sake, don't lose that, it's all you have. It's all *I* have."

"Whatever. Just don't ask me to believe. I can't do that anymore."

November 1, 2054:

Kathy Leigh wheeled herself in front of the television, wanting to leave plenty of time to get settled before Family Viewing Hour began. The genetic modification drugs were not bothering her too much this evening. The Medical Experimentation Clinic had decided to take only one eye, so she could still watch television. She was gratified that at eighty-two years old she was still making a positive contribution to society. She smiled as the television came on. It was her favorite show, naturally on the Springer network, named in honor of the man who had contributed so much to the tradition of the modern entertainment industry.

"My goodness," Kathy thought to herself, "the things they can do nowadays." Fifty years ago, reality shows were either staged at great expense, or were real-life events that depended on the luck of having a camera operating at an unexpected moment when a dangerous event occurred. No more. The most exciting entertainment available, of course, was live action natural disasters. Decades ago these events were rare and unpredictable, and film documentation was incomplete if it existed at all. With the magnificent technology developments of the past twenty years, however, earthquake and volcano prediction was a nearly exact science, and television crews could be dispatched to locales around the globe in time to watch the exciting and frequently humorous carnage. What a fortunate development it was that these types of disasters now occurred on an almost daily basis somewhere on the planet. The satellite seismographs could detect plate shifts or underground temperature gradients at least 48 hours prior to the actual disasters, allowing film crews to be set up in time for the event. Humanity was to be congratulated for turning the apparent negative of increased natural disasters into a hugely lucrative financial enterprise. With luck, Kathy thought, tonight's earthquakes or volcanoes would also be accompanied by floods, making for an entire evening's worth of entertainment.

Kathy laughed out loud as "Survivor-Krakatoa" came back from commercial. The Polynesian natives ran from the flowing lava, comically unaware that another flow was coming toward them from the opposite direction, so there was in fact no escape and their fate was sealed. The camera-work on tonight's show was especially good, as the helicopter shots clearly captured the expressions of terror on the faces of the running victims, even the children. Kathy had to bite her lip to restrain her laughter. At her age, an injury from overstrain was a distinct possibility, so she tried to practice moderation in all things.

November 24, 2054:

As she had for the previous 1,416 mornings, Zena Dunn sat before the main control console of the Superconducting Supercollider in Perseus, Texas, sequentially calibrating each system component, hoping without conviction that today's test would produce the miraculous Witten particle convergence, initiating the chain reaction that would restore the proper 10th-dimension vibrational permeation.

These solitary early morning hours were Zena's favorite time of the day. She was able to lose herself in the dozens of iterative instrumental adjustments and forget the inexorably rising tide of panic within herself as the months went by. It was obvious that the Witten-particle-induced chain reaction was an extreme longshot. Compounding that technical problem was the fact that time was undeniably very short. Her health clearly in decline, Zena knew it was only a matter of months before she would be incapable of running the SSC. She had tried to teach its operation to Max and Jason, but the nuances of the incredibly complex machine were beyond the fading energies and mental capabilities of her two fellow octogenarians. The health of Max and Jason was only marginally better than her own, and prospects for post-Zena experiments were non-existent.

Furthermore, Zena realized, the lifespan of the remaining string theory team members might not even be the most critical element in the dwindling likelihood of vibrational restoration. Despite incessant governmental announcements intended to placate the citizenry, the undeniable planetary changes threatened to bring an even earlier end to the experimental efforts - not to mention humanity itself. Perseus, Texas, the site of the Superconducting Supercollider, had long been an inhospitable place, especially in the summer, when prior to 2040, the record temperature was 117 degrees. Those records, however, reflected a relative oasis in comparison to the more recent climatic upheavals. On the more tumultuous days, as the sun's color shifted from deep orange to white and back again, temperatures could rise or fall by a hundred degrees within a twenty-four hour period. It became necessary to remain close to the buildings to avoid death from exposure, which could occur within minutes at an outdoor temperature of 160 degrees.

Time, therefore, was truly of the essence.

At age eighty-four, however, Zena Dunn could only move at a certain speed; the notion of hurrying was quite beyond her. She could still operate the SSC only because the control panel instruments had been modified so she could reach them from her wheelchair.

Eve Parson, sitting at the main frequency monitor console in the City's Underling World control center, turned to her right, adjusting the signal strength and diffusion coefficient, frustrated at her inability to obtain a clear signal. "What time is it?" she snapped to no one in particular.

"10:14 p.m., Sunday, - " replied Adam.

"Not *our* time, *their* time!"

"That would be November 24th, 2054, 7:13:22.96 a.m.," replied Esther, who now kept very close track of these things.

"How do we even know if they are still alive? They're in their eighties, for goodness' sake."

"Well, if your son is anything like you, ma'am," said Amos, "he's too ornery to have died yet."

"Come on, Eve, you can't think that way," said Adam. "Our last image showed their vibrational cocoon in Texas. They've got to be at the SSC, and they're probably already trying to restore the permeation. They must have figured out at least that much by now."

"Damn these distortions," muttered Eve, the tension causing her, most uncharacteristically, to use profanity. For the last half hour of City Time, and who knows how many years of Underling time, the Sonic Regression had created a sort of encroaching "mist" over the earth, clouding the view of the City's monitors. Even as the Parsons learned to operate the system, the resonant fluctuations increased by the minute, offsetting their increasing skill at the system's operation. Clear views now appeared only sporadically, and it was obviously just a matter of time before the Underling world images were lost for good. Eve reached again to her left to modify the receptor frequency of her monitor.

Adam tried to be supportive. "We have to keep working at it. We'll help them."

"Well, we can't help them if we can't figure out a way to find them," Eve retorted angrily. She was exhausted, even though fatigue was not supposed to happen to City dwellers. Over the last five City hours (corresponding to nine years of Underling time, according to the Liquid Time Correlation), she had made 136,562 unsuccessful attempts to contact Christopher in some way. The Parsons, with the aid of the exquisite instrumentation and computing power of the City's Underling World Observation Center, were reasonably sure they had discovered the proper vibrational inputs that would create the spontaneous permeation necessary to reverse the sonic degradation. But the City dwellers were spiritual entities exclusively; only the humans could physically affect the material universe. The message had to be communicated to the string theory team, or they had to figure it out for themselves. And so Eve strained with every ounce of her being to connect to Christopher across the void between the City and the Underlings. Esther coached her on the methods used in previous successful attempts.

"The first factor," Esther said softly, "is an extremely intimate emotional connection between the individuals involved." Knowing the sacred mother-son bond between Eve and Christopher, all had agreed that this was the best possibility. "Second, the message must be extremely simple, the best connections have been made with only a word or two." But this was the conundrum. How to communicate something as complex as a set of mathematical equations? And how to communicate them through someone with Chris's limited mental capabilities? Eve's emotional strength finally gave out, and everyone agreed to return to the Underling world monitors for the time being.

Zena lovingly tapped at that old balky neutrino meter, its mechanism responding to her light touch with the proper background reading, which she zeroed out.

"Esther, goddammit, get the frequency and intensity parameters in synch!" barked Eve, the strain beginning to break her down.

Esther's eyes rapidly snapped back and forth between the two gauges, and the fluctuations subsided. As Eve returned her concentration to the clouded view of Perseus, Texas, Adam leaned toward Esther and whispered, "She only does that with people she respects. Welcome to the team."

Esther brightened considerably.

Christopher Parson, only now beginning to show the effects of his advancing years, still went about his daily routine, waking Jason Poe and Max Cherry at 8:00 on the dot. Jason was still a strong walker, but Max required assistance to reach the control room. Jason and Max each greeted Zena with a kiss on the cheek, while the ever-childlike Christopher demanded and received enthusiastic hugs from each of the other three. Chris helped Max to his seat at the SSC tube environmental control panel, while

Jason observed the particle energy and velocity values.

His job complete, Christopher left the others and strolled through the cavernous hallways to the enormous conference hall at the back of the SSC complex.

"That's it!" cried Esther. "You got it!"

Eve Parson, up until that moment completely absorbed in the numbers flashing on the signal diffusion screen, whipped her head up and looked into the main viewer. All three pairs of eyes locked onto the image momentarily, then Esther returned her concentration to her own console, determined to maintain the signal as long as possible. On the Image Isolation Monitor, a clear but shaky image of the Superconducting Supercollider building complex appeared.

Adam operated the magnification control, while all three continually adjusted their settings to retain signal clarity. This was the most exciting and important event Esther had experienced since the Great Unfurling, but her immersion in the moment was so total that she took no notice of her own racing heartbeat.

Max Cherry dutifully watched the SSC tube magnetic field sensors, as the atmospheric pressure inside the 120-mile long SSC tube dropped to within thousandths of a percent of a perfect vacuum. Max was no longer hot or cold, positive or negative, for or against the string theory effort; he was just numb. The others knew as well as he that the quest for the titanic Witten particle reaction was as futile as blindly picking a selected grain of sand from the Sahara Desert. Max honestly could not say whether he preferred a conventional death from old age or a cataclysmic demise with the rest of humanity.

The image in Eve's Image Isolation Monitor was now magnified to the point where it centered on one of Zena's monitors. Eve stared, attempting to decipher the picture. "Damn. I've never run an SSC. They hadn't started to build the thing until after our accident. I don't know what the monitors are telling them."

"We'll have to look at the particles themselves," said Adam. He turned toward Esther. "Can we go that far?" Esther nodded. He continued to increase the magnification.

A low hum filled the entire Superconducting Supercollider complex as the 120-mile long magnetic fields synchronized to the immaculately timed sequence that would impel the subatomic particles to near light speed. Jason Poe checked and rechecked the field, waiting for the pulses to align into perfect strength and rhythm. Jason, like Max, could no longer be described as particularly motivated to carry out his work, but he maintained his appreciation for the beauty, symmetry, and elegance of the mathematics which governed the physical universe. The SSC magnetic field was yet another example that so enthralled him. The field strength itself was almost immeasurably small, not enough to lift a single metallic dust speck. Controlled by the equations embedded into the computer code, however, the unfathomably small subatomic particles would at first be moved almost imperceptibly, quietly drawn along by the miniscule yet gently insistent magnetic field. In microscopic increments the magnetic field would speed up, incrementally pulling the particles to faster and faster speeds, through all the velocities familiar to humans, and finally into the realms of speed reserved for relativity effects, seamlessly transitioning the particles' velocities and energies into an unimaginable state where time, space, and matter all turned inside out, conditions not seen since the origin of the universe. All of it controlled by mathematical equations, the same equations today as at that seminal event twenty billion years ago. Despite everything, Jason Poe never tired of these contemplations.

Having the equivalent of twenty billion Underling years of experience operating these controls, it was Esther's role to follow the viewing area and find the target image. As Adam's increasing magnification reduced the field of view from meters to centimeters to millimeters to nanometers and beyond, Esther tracked the viewer to locate and lock onto the particles inside the SSC's magnetic field. All three constantly modified their gauge settings, tuning and re-tuning the incoming signal, to allow Esther a clear image to follow.

The Monitor's image locked onto the streaking particles with perfect clarity.

As the particles accelerated to impact speeds, Zena, Jason, and Max followed their procedures in a rote mechanical routine, their sense of anticipation dulled by 1,416 consecutive failures.

The placid scene in the Underling world contrasted wildly with that of the City's control center, where Adam, Eve, and Esther frantically moved from one control adjustment to another, desperate to catch a clear glimpse of the particle collision while keeping the universal harmonic distortions at bay, knowing with the encroaching obscurity that they might never get another opportunity to peer into the

Underling world.

"NO! NO! NO! NO! NO!" screamed Eve Parson. "They've got it wrong! Oh no, oh god no. They'll never get it now...."

Silence was never broken in the SSC center as the 1,417th consecutive unsuccessful particle collision came and went. A relative handful of Witten particles were generated and the vibrational fields restored on a nano-scale level, but the effects were limited to no more than a billionth of a second and a billionth of a centimeter away from the point of impact.

In an instant, Adam Parson was next to his beloved wife, his eyes poring over the readouts along with hers. Eve's face crumbled as she broke down in tears.

"What? What is it?" Esther asked plaintively, desperate to understand whatever tragedy had just taken place.

After a moment of study, Adam realized the cause of Eve's collapse. "Oh, I see," he explained. "They've done something wrong in their calculations. They're trying to initiate the chain reaction with some kind of incredibly massive super-collision. I suppose that theoretically something like that might work, but with their present SSC technology, it's a trillion-to-one shot." He sighed. "It's over. They got the wrong answer." Tears filled Adam's eyes as he looked back at Eve. The unknown fate of Monday awaited them, less than two hours away.

Zena, Jason, and Max matter-of-factly stepped through the SSC shutdown sequence as they had so many times before. Chris Parson helped Zena into her wheelchair and then assisted Max in getting to his feet. Chris was saddened that his old friends no longer felt the great sense of adventure that had brought so much fun in their younger days, and he tried to keep their spirits up as best he could. Jason and Max again gave Zena a perfunctory kiss on the cheek, and they returned to their living quarters.

The grim resignation of the humans was a celebration of ecstatic joy in comparison to the funereal atmosphere in the City's Underling World Observation Center. Adam, Eve, and Esther sat on the floor, heads together, arms around each other, sobbing audibly, unable to control their grief. Until this very moment there had been a bit of fun in all of it, a denial of the possibility of the disastrous outcome that was now inevitable. That hope was now gone. They sat this way for twenty-two City minutes, which corresponded to three more years of Underling time due to another slip in the Liquid Time Correlation.

Conversation finally returned to the three, as Adam and Eve again quizzed Esther regarding previous communications between people in the City and their loved ones back on the Underling world. Esther could only repeat her admonitions about the need for an intimate personal connection and a simple message to communicate, advice which provided no solace, considering the complexity of the mathematical message and Chris's impairments. Tears flowed anew as the three pondered their impossible situation. Eve closed her eyes and tried once again to make the mother-son connection, talking to herself to work up to the task.

"They're trying to use a sledgehammer when all they need is a perfect tiny little touch, that's all it takes," she whispered softly. "God, how do I communicate the physics of that to

Christopher? Just a tiny little touch. How can we show them that they miscalculated?"

Adam, his mind going a mile a minute trying to think of some alternative, snapped to attention at a familiar memory and gaped at Eve. "What did you say?"

Eve looked at Adam wonderingly. "I said," she stammered, "how do I communicate the physics to Chris?"

"No, before that."

"Umm, I don't know what you mean."

"I know what he means," said Esther. "You said they're using a sledgehammer, when all they need is a little touch." Eve and Esther looked at Adam, having no idea what his point might be.

"No, that's not quite what she said. Eve, you said, 'All they need is a perfect tiny little touch, that's all it takes.' That's what you said."

"Yes….?" replied Eve and Esther in unison, still not understanding.

Adam, now deep in thought, softly said, "A perfect tiny little touch, that's all it takes."

"I've got an idea."

<u>July 6, 2057:</u>

With great difficulty, Kathy Leigh pulled on her nightgown for the last time. Her routine was to pull it from the dresser drawer, wheel herself over next to her bed, and lay it out across the bed. With one hand on the nightstand and the other against the arm of her wheelchair, she could still get to a standing position, and usually hold it long enough to pull her nightgown over her head, before collapsing back into the wheelchair. There was, in fact, an odd sense of

372

relief in knowing that this nightly effort would no longer be required.

The difficult task accomplished, Kathy repaired to the bathroom. As she brushed her teeth, she was oblivious to the irony of diligently attending to her dental health even though she would be terminated in eight hours. It was her routine, and there was no sense in changing it now. Watching her own ancient face in the dimly lit bathroom mirror, Kathy wondered how a modern day news reporter would present the current global situation. The thought was moot, of course, but Kathy entertained it anyway. The worldwide natural disasters had destroyed society's economic infrastructure. Most roads were no longer passable, at least over long distances, rendering scheduled transportation of goods impossible. Power systems were no longer reliable, and electricity and heating were reserved for those with portable generators, which were no longer widely available. Shipping across the oceans was risky because of frequent tsunamis, due to the constant earthquakes, especially around the Pacific Rim. Seismic upheavals destroyed airport runways faster than they could be repaired, bringing commercial airline service to a halt. Yes, it would be a grand time to be reporting the news, Kathy chuckled to herself, if there was still a communications industry left. The nearly constant electrical storms, however, disrupted the earth's magnetic field, rendering mass communications such as telephones, television, and the Internet non-functional. Governmental instructions were now communicated by dropping leaflets from helicopters, which is how Kathy, along with the majority of her fellow San Franciscans, had been served with the termination notices the previous morning.

The economic consequences, of course, were staggering.

Michael Thompson

A government designed for the sole purpose of maximizing free market economy forces had no means of coping with a breakdown of fundamental resources. For forty years the streamlining of wealth accumulation processes, along with Citizen Standardization Initiatives, had allowed major corporations to drive economic growth at unprecedented rates and generate wealth for all compliant citizens. With disruptive forces from low-efficiency human activities dropping to near-zero levels, there was no impediment to focused development, and society had enjoyed a pinnacle previously unimagined in human history. Initially the seismic and climatic disasters were seen as a healthy means of pruning the few remaining unproductive elements from society, and even provided new substantial economic opportunities from the inherent entertainment potential of mass destruction. But the nightmarish developments of recent years were completely unanticipated and the Golden Age came crashing down. In a desperate attempt to restore global economic activity, the government even asked the populace to take it upon themselves to perform individual acts of ingenuity, courage, and self-sacrifice, but these concepts were completely foreign to modern-day society. Not having a proposal for increasing the economic base, the government took the only action available to it: drastic reduction of human inventory. The world government accelerated the termination process as much as possible, seeing the only solution to be an extreme concentration of wealth into as few hands as possible. Thus it was that Kathy Leigh, no matter her character or past contributions, was deemed "excess inventory" as part of the societal imperative to maintain the world economy.

Her preparations for bed finally concluded, Kathy felt an

odd urge to go outside for one last look at the world she had inhabited for so many years. These sensations were normal, she told herself. Millions of years of evolutionary development of the survival instinct would not be completely undone by fifty years of even the most brilliant societal re-engineering. Kathy could indulge these emotional whims while fully cognizant of, and in wholehearted agreement with, the wise guidance of her global government, whose only concern was the continuous betterment of humankind.

Kathy Leigh wheeled herself through her bedroom sliding glass door and onto her back deck, which looked out over San Francisco. The only significant lights came from various uncontrolled fires across the city. Kathy's eyes involuntarily tilted upward to take in the night sky. As she gazed skyward, three new supernovas exploded into existence, one being Betelgeuse, the giant red star that represented the left shoulder in the constellation Orion. She smiled in surprise at the vague recollection from her childhood Arizona nights with her father, but found herself utterly unable to comprehend why anyone would find the stars to be of any interest, especially in those old days when supernovas were not a nightly occurrence.

<u>July 7, 2057 (Sunday, 11:58 p.m.):</u>

An horrific crash from the adjoining laboratory shocked Jason Poe awake at 5:24 a.m. His well-conditioned reflex upon awakening was to look over at Max and make sure he was still breathing. Each kept a five-dollar bill in his shirt pocket at all times as payment preparation for their macabre bet: Whoever died first lost. Noting Max's chest still rising and falling rhythmically, Jason went out to identify the source of the cacophony. No longer able to move with anything other than a trudging gait, by the time he reached the doorway all he saw was Christopher Parson hastily exiting the room and heading down the hallway, dropping a small black object on the way out. Jason saw a spectrophotometry calibration unit on the floor of the lab, knocked off its table but fortunately unbroken, apparently a victim of Christopher's enthusiasm. Jason went back to the sleeping area to rouse Max.

Without Christopher's help, Jason had difficulty getting Max out of bed and dressed. Although not confined to a wheelchair like the now-departed Zena, Max had surrendered to age and required assistance for the simplest physical tasks. Jason helped Max out to the kitchen and prepared two bowls of cold oatmeal, as usual putting extra brown sugar onto Max's. Finally the two ancient friends sat down together to eat, nearly eighty years of comradeship making speech quite unnecessary.

These last days were a bittersweet mix for the two final string theory team members. On a remarkable Texas day two years ago when the modern tumultuous weather patterns had given way to a gloriously beautiful interlude of sunshine, Zena Dunn had completed one final Superconducting Supercollider particle experiment, and then gently sat back, closed her eyes, and died without so much as a word, her last act being to view a particle tracing on her console monitor, a skill she possessed to a greater degree than any other human being. Jason hoped that his passing could somehow be as blissful, doing something he loved. As Zena breathed her last, so too did the last breath of life in the string theory effort give out. Jason and Max returned from the SSC site in Texas, and moved back to their old home in the Science Institute in Washington, D.C., to live out their last days.

Slowly and sloppily lapping up the last of his oatmeal, Max Cherry broke the silence. "Missed July 4th, didn't we?"

"Max, they don't celebrate July 4th any more," said Jason. "It's all a one-world government now, there aren't any individual nations."

"Yeah, yeah, I was just remembering the fireworks when I was a kid."

Jason replied, "Max, we don't have it so bad. We've got governmental budget, so the accounting people still see us as productive citizens. If they knew we were just a couple of old men living out our old age, we'd be getting termination notices. It's a strange world."

"You really think it's the breakdown in the strings?"

At that moment another slight tremble was felt throughout the building.

"You have a better explanation?" asked Jason rhetorically. "It's all changed, first the social, then the physical, and it all traces back to when we first noticed the proton degradation and everything that followed. Heck, I don't know. I guess we never will."

Max smiled wryly. "Damn. I wanted to save the universe. Just once."

Max's spirits were actually higher now than in the last days of the SSC experiments. Yielding to the inevitable failure of the tests relieved him of the burden of hope, and his days now were comfortably spent reading or talking with Jason, often reminiscing about what they had learned along the way. It was easier to deal with an accepted fate than fight against it.

Jason laughed at Max's remark, at the jarring juxtaposition of such a statement of hubris coming from this shriveled-up shell of a man. He patted his old friend on the shoulder. "Max, we really did do pretty well, all considered. When we started, nobody knew if strings really existed. Nobody knew how to resolve the conflict between general relativity in the large-scale universe and quantum mechanics in the subatomic world. Nobody had a rigorous theory of gravity. That was us, all us. We determined the characteristics of every particle that makes up the universe. We showed that the universe is made up of an unimaginable number of identical strings that vibrate in a vast symphonic range of frequencies and harmonics that control time, space, matter, energy, gravity, and motion. We identified the Calabi-Yau structures of the six small dimensions that determine the exact nature of the vibrations of the infinitesimal strings that fill the universe. We demonstrated why the universal expansion is exactly on the knife edge of eternal expansion and eventual collapse. We learned that the strings' vibrations are reflected in the subliminal brainwave emanations, that human nature itself reflects the harmonics of the strings. Maybe it sounds arrogant, but more than anyone else, we were the ones who came to understand the mind of God and his creation."

Max took this all in. "Well, you're right about one thing. It does sound arrogant. And what's left at the end of your precious universe is exactly two people who know or care, and neither one can do a damn thing about it."

Jason softly asked, "What do you think it will be like at the end?"

"Well, there are ten dimensions," said Max. The first one is time, the next three are the spatial dimensions of length, width, and height, and the rest, as you said, are the small curled-up dimensions defined by the Calabi-Yau structure. When the distortions become severe enough, I imagine that time will stop and start and become discontinuous, and the large dimensions will shrink while the small ones enlarge. The simplest description I can think of is that the universe will turn inside out."

Adam Parson put his right fist through one of the instruments on his control board in his frustration at the totally obscured images on the Underling World monitors.

Jason rose and picked up the empty oatmeal bowls, and went to the kitchen to wash them.

Christopher Parson burst through the outer door, a gleaming smile on his face as his eyes alighted on the seated figure of Max Cherry, his best friend.

"Come on! Come on! You have to come with me!" shouted Chris gleefully, having lost none of his childish enthusiasm or purity of spirit in eighty-seven years of living. He grasped Max's wrists and dragged him to his feet.

"Ow! What the hell are you doing?"

Christopher, quite oblivious to Max's discomfort, pulled him across the room and down the hallway, Max's feet quite involuntarily keeping him upright. After an interminable two minutes of scurrying through the maze of hallways, Chris turned into the massive double doors leading to the main convention hall of the Institute.

"Close your eyes! Close your eyes!" shouted Christopher, even more animated than usual. At last he wrapped a strong arm around Max to support him, and escorted him about forty feet by Max's estimation, turning enough so that Max had no idea which way he was facing.

Christopher finally paused, and was silent for a moment. "Okay, open your eyes!"

Max's failing eyes slowly opened and required a moment to readjust to the light. His eyes flashed around the room, taking in the dazzling view before him. The hall spanned approximately 150 feet by 200 feet in area, covered in a beautiful wood parquet floor surface, and Max and Chris stood at one end, a few feet from the wall. Across the entire room, covering almost every square inch, were hundreds of thousands of black dominoes, arrayed in hundreds of exquisitely interconnected patterns, from tiny intricately detailed floral simulations to giant sweeping arcs to geometrically perfect examples ranging from simple triangles to three-dimensional visualizations of incredible complexity. Max stood motionless, jaw open, his breath faltering, taking it all in. It was the most beautiful thing he had ever seen.

Jason Poe rushed into the room at that moment, entirely out of breath from his frail attempt to catch up. He stopped short in the entryway, also taken aback. He slowly made his way over to Max, never taking his eyes off the magnificent display before him. "When did you do this?" he was finally able to ask.

"Every day for one hundred and fifty-four days. I counted," said a beaming Christopher with entirely justified pride in himself. "I got an idea to do lots and lots of dominoes. Lots and lots and *lots* of dominoes," he laughed.

Jason's eyes locked onto a small pattern composed of a few hundred dominoes about forty feet out onto the floor. He stared for quite some time, then turned Max's attention to the same area.

"Do you see what I see?" Jason asked, his voice catching in his throat. "Is that what I think it is?"

It took Max a few moments to see the pattern. Once seen, however, there was no doubting it. "Jason, my god, that's it, you're right. It's - it's the Calabi-Yau structure." It was a perfect two-dimensional representation of the Calabi-Yau structure that defined the six microscopic curled-up dimensions as defined by string theory. Something entirely beyond the mental capabilities of Christopher Parson.

Jason turned to Chris. "You see that little pattern out there, Chris? Who showed that to you?"

Christopher happily replied, "I don't know, I just got the idea. Good idea, huh? It's real pretty. Hey, wanna knock 'em down? You want to start it?"

Max and Jason looked at each other and smiled in happy befuddlement. It was the most refreshing moment they'd shared in years. "You go ahead, I'll watch," said Max, and he hugged Jason.

"You sure?" asked Jason, already moving toward the first domino excitedly. He slowly crouched down, and started to reach a hand clumsy with age toward the first domino in the colossal sequence. Max watched his old friend with great fondness.

"No! No! No!" interrupted Chris. "Not like that. If you don't hit the first one right, that will mess it all up. Here, like this."

Chris helped Jason get down on all fours in a comfortably balanced position, and took Jason's right hand, gently extending Jason's forefinger. Jason, amused and touched, allowed Chris to direct his actions. His finger moved to within centimeters of the first domino.

"Okay, here we go," whispered Christopher Parson

in anticipation. As he had thousands of times before, Christopher repeated the words from his childhood. "When you want to start the dominoes falling, it's not a big bang. It's a perfect tiny little touch. Just a perfect tiny little touch, that's all it takes, and all of them will tip right over."

Guided by the gentle hand of Adam and Eve Parson's son, Jason's finger delicately tapped the first of more than half a million dominoes and started the most beautiful chain reaction Jason had ever seen. Chris clapped with delight.

Max Cherry's eyes widened in shock at the significance of the words he had just heard, and he slumped against the wall, sliding down into a sitting position on the floor.

Kathy Leigh's alarm clock went off, and she realized she needed to get moving to be outside in time for the helicopter at 7:00 a.m. San Francisco time.

Seconds turned into minutes as Jason Poe watched seven hundred thousand dominoes fall in perfect sequence. The patterns of the falling dominoes were even more beautiful than had been the stationary layout, and a tear gently formed on Jason's cheek.

Max Cherry was not paying the slightest bit of attention to the dominoes.

Adam and Eve Parson hugged each other in their grief, motioning Esther to join them.

"Is it midnight yet?" Esther asked.

"I don't know," Eve said. "The chronometers have all gone down."

With about four hundred thousand dominoes down, Jason Poe turned toward his oldest friend to share this wonderful moment. He was shocked to see Max on the floor, a glazed look in his eyes, and feared the worst. He rushed over and took Max in his arms.

"What is it? What is it?"

Max tried to speak, but was unable. Jason put his ear to Max's mouth to check for breath, and reached his hand into Max's shirt to feel for a heartbeat.

Max caught himself. "I got it wrong. I got it wrong."

Jason took Max's head between his two hands and stared into Max's eyes from not more than six inches away. "Got *what* wrong?"

"The Witten collision. *That's* the answer that doesn't make physical sense. The reciprocal solution, that was the one to restore the permeation."

"What are you talking about?"

Max recovered his voice somewhat. "I had it. I had the answer right in front of me. There were two mathematically correct answers, and I picked the wrong one. It was just like Chris said. All we needed was a perfect tiny little touch. We didn't need some colossal Witten particle collision to start the chain reaction. We were using a wrecking ball when all we needed was a gentle kiss. And I had the answer. Right in my lap."

"I still don't have a clue what you're talking about," said Jason, his concern over Max's health not yet assuaged.

Max's wits slowly returned to him, and he explained. "Remember? Remember when I calculated the potential particle collisions that could start the chain reaction to restore proper vibrational permeation through the universe? That would stop the degradation?"

Jason nodded, listening carefully now.

"When I did the calculations, there were two

mathematically valid answers. The first was the massive Witten particle collision that we tried to initiate in the SSC all those years. I was a damned idiot. I assumed the only collision that could work was a huge titanic blast, but I knew from the start that we'd never get enough energy into the SSC to accomplish it. The other solution was the inverse, the reciprocal of the Witten energy, such a tiny amount that I never even considered it. Why didn't I open my eyes? Why didn't I let my imagination consider the possibility? You saw the dominoes. One tiny little touch from your finger, and hundreds of thousands of dominoes fell down. When I saw that, it just hit me. That's how the strings are. They're already in place, just like the dominoes, the physical phenomena are already happening, all we needed was one pure tiny vibration with no harmonics to start it, and it would self-propagate at an exponentially increasing rate throughout the universe. It would be like dropping a pebble into a still pond, and watching the waves spread over the entire pond. I mean, I can see the equations in my head right now. It was right in front of me."

Max Cherry dropped his head into his hands. *Darryl would have seen it,* he said to himself.

"Maybe it's not too late to start *your* dominoes," said Chris, his own dominoes having finally all fallen, exactly as he had planned.

Jason's mind raced. "Maybe Chris is right. Maybe it's not too late."

Max sighed derisively. "Jason, come on. We can't go back to the SSC, the earthquakes and weather patterns have destroyed it, you know that."

"Tell me about the conditions that would have to be present to create the pure collision you need."

"I need to see the calculations again."

The three rushed back to the laboratory with all the speed they could muster.

Forty minutes later, staring at his notes from seven years before, Max Cherry let out a sigh. "Well, it looks like a collision between two neutrinos. But it wouldn't propagate unless the surrounding space were completely free of other matter particles. We'd need essentially pure vacuum, and a really weak magnetic field that would be unable to hold the more massive particles and would allow them to leave the accelerator, leaving a high concentration of neutrinos. The temperature wouldn't matter in a vacuum. Then we'd just need to get lucky and have a well-timed collision at low speed. But where are we going to get an accelerator like that?"

"Will you listen to yourself? Come on, Max. We spent all our lives trying to get more and more power and speed to create all the massive, complex particles. Now you're telling us that this time we need the cheapest, crappiest, leakiest little cyclotron we can find, as long as we can get the vacuum. We've got Zena's old tabletop cyclotron back in the lab. We never threw it out, it should be perfect! We can get the vacuum by putting it in the proton degradation chamber, it's still perfectly functional."

"What about power? We don't need much, but the electricity's out again." Then, answering his own question, Max said, "The lab generator should be fine. Let's go."

Kathy Leigh straightened her scarf and pulled the brush through her hair a final few times. She wished her termination to occur while she looked her professional best. She turned and wheeled herself toward the door. She wanted to leave plenty of time, because some days she was only capable of moving the wheelchair very slowly.

"Chris, do you know what the cyclotron looks like?" asked Jason. Although it was not large, Jason knew that he and Max would have great difficulty lifting it. Chris nodded.

"Then bring it here, and be very careful with it. We need you to help us in the laboratory."

Chris's eyes lit up at the opportunity to be a real scientist at last, and he ran to find the cyclotron.

Max struggled to walk the few steps to the vacuum chamber. "Can we hook up both the cyclotron and the proton degradation chamber to the generator?" he asked Jason.

"Sure, we've got all the power cables," said Jason, scurrying off to check the various lab cabinets.

Max, his mind finding itself focused again for the first time in years, opened the old proton degradation chamber, which was still installed in one corner of the main laboratory, but had not been used in years. The giant electron microscope had long since been put into storage. The chamber was essentially a small room, eight feet square and fifteen feet high, with thick glass walls and numerous gauges to monitor the air pressure, temperature, and other parameters. There were also power outlets inside the chamber. With great effort, he grasped a small desk and pulled it over to the chamber, pushing it inside to the center. Jason brought the cables, and Chris carried the cyclotron with a gentleness normally reserved only for his beloved dominoes.

"Chris, set the cyclotron on the table inside the chamber," said Max. Chris enthusiastically did so, still moving with suppleness and grace. Zena's cyclotron was, in essence, a simple circular hollow glass tube about four feet in diameter and one inch thick, with tiny electromagnets wired in sequence to generate particle flow through the tube. At one point of the circumference there was a tiny slot into which the magnets could divert particles to the target area for collision. Zena had especially enjoyed the glass tubing, because she could literally see into the very space where the collisions were occurring, and this warmed her spirit. The collisions were far too small to see, of course, but just the idea of knowing they were happening in front of her always brought a wistful smile to her face.

Jason, moving as quickly as he was able, connected the generator to both the main and secondary proton degradation chamber power inputs, and then connected the secondary power outlet inside the chamber to the cyclotron.

Kathy Leigh heard the helicopter in the distance, working its way through the San Francisco hills. She primped her hair one last time.

The old man stared intently forward out the helicopter's cockpit window, determined to complete his duty. Even at his advanced age, he was proud to still be capable of supporting the needs of society, even though he was no longer working in his real field of expertise. He was obviously distressed at the calamities befalling Earth, but there was a job to do now and he had to do it. He looked over at the young pilot, so energetic and talented, with such a future before him, if only he would get to see it. The old man checked the gauges and the list of names and correlated it to their flight path and schedule. "Bear left 22 degrees, just over that hill there, that's where the next one will be, name of Jensen, not that it matters."

"Yes, Dr. Zenkman," came the reply from the respectful young pilot, lowering the gunsight headgear over his face as he approached the target.

Max was closest to the generator. He reached up to the main power switch. He flipped it on. The generator slowly warmed up to its gentle whine, and settled into its smooth function.

Nothing happened.

Dunstan covered his ears at the screeching sounds emanating from every portion of the City. There was no longer any pretense of governing Committees, or for that matter, any productive activity whatsoever. The City dwellers had lived in utter peace and safety in the seven days since the Great Unfurling, and were completely incapable of emotionally coping with danger of any sort. Panic swept over the City.

"How long should it take?" Jason asked.

"Only a few seconds," replied Max. The vacuum is on, the particles are certainly up to speed by now, and all the larger ones should have slipped out of the magnetic field by now. We should have an environment of almost pure neutrinos in there, and they should be colliding."

"Then why isn't anything happening?"

"Could other particles get in?" asked Jason. They looked at each other.

"Light!" They shouted in unison. The proton degradation chamber and the cyclotron tube were both made of glass. The photons from ordinary light particles would be streaming into the cyclotron tube, corrupting the pristine environment required to start the chain reaction.

"Chris, turn off the lights!"

The room plunged into darkness. The two old men slumped to the floor together in the darkness, arms around each other, waiting for the end, whatever it would be.

Kathy Leigh looked down at a caterpillar crawling just to the side of her wheelchair, and reached down to pick it up. The tiny legs thrashed at the air, and the reddish brown fur tickled her fingers. She couldn't remember being interested in insects before, and found this new sensation quite intriguing.

Across the valley, she saw the laser beam from the helicopter streak across the sky and sear through the body of Samuel Jensen, an acquaintance for many years. Surprised to feel herself recoil in horror, Kathy placed the caterpillar back on the ground, taking care to be sure he was a safe distance from her wheelchair. The helicopter now turned toward her, and she saw it grow larger and larger against the background sky. She knew her civic duty. She would do her part to assist in economic recovery by participating in the human resource termination program, designed to efficiently leave the remaining world economic wealth with the fewest number of people possible, to facilitate prosperity among whatever remnant of the population was left. A nagging doubt arose within her, however, about the wisdom of this course of action, even as the helicopter bore down upon her. As the pilot aligned his sights, Kathy Leigh suddenly turned in her wheelchair and moved quickly to the left, making sure not to hit the caterpillar. The laser blast bore a two-foot deep hole in the ground where she had been. "Fuck you!" cried the old woman, suddenly finding these new emotions strangely energizing.

Grant Zenkman watched in amazement as the old woman in the wheelchair dodged the laser blast. He considered giving the pilot advice on handling this unique situation, but decided to let the young man determine the best way to dispatch the target himself. He leaned back in his co-pilot seat, and suddenly felt a violent buzzing in his brain, a vibration that was at first intensely painful, then slowly dissipated into a sensation of calm that seemed to seep into his very being. He shook his head to clear it, and looked over at the young pilot, who was blinking his eyes furiously.

The next blast was just ahead of Kathy Leigh as she rolled down her driveway. She quickly realized she needed to keep moving downhill, it was the only way to maintain the speed necessary to be evasive. As she rolled near her house, she again turned quickly left, as a blast removed half of the garage door. She reached the side of the house and turned right, temporarily out of the line of fire, but everything was uphill from where she was, and she was so exhausted by now that she could barely move. The black helicopter moved around to her side of the house, and came in lower, settling about fifty feet above the ground, the pilot now having a clear shot.

The helicopter hesitated for several seconds, then began to descend again, coming to twenty feet, then ten, then alighting on the ground, only about twenty-five feet from the exhausted and terrified Kathy Leigh. Two men in military fatigues, one wearing gunsight headgear, sat in the helicopter, appearing to have a very intense discussion. Kathy cowered before the helicopter, now shivering uncontrollably in her wheelchair.

One of the men slowly clambered out of the helicopter.

He turned back to the one with the headgear and put his hand on his shoulder as though consoling him, then walked toward Kathy.

"Are you all right?" asked the old man in a wavering voice. He looked down at her, his eyes softening. Kathy trembled, not understanding.

Grant Zenkman didn't understand either. He stared at the ancient woman before him, then back at the young pilot in the helicopter, still in the prime of youth. The pilot stared forward blankly. Grant turned back to Kathy, as eight decades of sensations returned to him. He remembered. He remembered what his life had been, and what it had become. He looked down at his own trembling hands, and softly said, "What have I done?"

Kathy Leigh took Grant's hands into her own as tears began to roll down his cheeks.

"It's all right, it's all right," she offered. She looked at the nametag on his uniform. *Dr. G. Zenkman.* An unexpected glimmer of recognition came to her. "Do I know you?"

Grant dropped to his knees. He knew who she was. He remembered the team and Max Cherry and the interview so long ago with that cute television news reporter.

And then, in a sudden blinding flash, Grant Zenkman could see all of string theory before him. He could see the equations, the vibrations, the harmonics, the progression through the ten dimensions. He could see everything, and it was beautiful.

A giant light pierced across the sky above them. Grant Zenkman and Kathy Leigh held each other, looking up in wonder and awe, as a glorious brilliance unfurled from horizon to horizon.

Sunday, 11:59:59 (and holding):

The Omniscience Council stood before the entire City population in the Hall of the Eternal Festival, the members' hands linked together across the stage in a victory celebration. Great cheering filled the Hall, as the City Dwellers and billions of former Underlings mingled together. In between joyous hugs with his former String Theory teammates, Jason Poe was quite thrilled to catch a glimpse of Benjamin Franklin. The reunion between Christopher Parson and his parents was wonderfully emotional, of course, Adam and Eve telling Chris over and over again how proud they were of him for his part in the string restoration. Max Cherry also shared a poignant reunion with the Parsons, and was fascinated to learn of the remarkable events in the City which had paralleled the Underlings' efforts on Earth. Once past the emotion of the moment, however, Max quickly recovered his natural verve, regaling all who would listen with hysterical tales of the adventures that last day in the laboratory. All the team members particularly wished to reunite with Sean Masterson, who had literally given his life for them, but Sean was locked in a tearful embrace with his father, the effects of the now-completed string vibrations finally allowing the two former antagonists to see past their differences and make peace. Melina Valin, ever the rationalist, carefully watched the swirling crowds of people, especially looking for Zena, and noticed that few if any words were being exchanged in the Hall. As the evening went on, she realized a new sensation coursing through her, a connection to everyone else in the room, a breakdown of the separation of being between people. She found herself able to look into the hearts and minds

392

of people she had never met, to bond in a way heretofore impossible, to literally feel what others experienced. The room was no longer full of isolated beings - they were still individuals, but completely interconnected spiritually. The emotional connection was thousands of times deeper than any previous human experience. At last she saw Zena, to whom she felt so much gratitude, and the two women held each other. Melina looked into Zena's eyes and saw that Zena also realized the new fundamental changes in human interaction. Finally Zena grinned and spoke the first words between them. "Hey, the tenth dimension *rocks*, doesn't it?"

Finally the banging of a gavel at the front of the room quieted the throng. Brother Dunstan, the recently appointed Chairman of the City Omniscience Council, stepped up to the podium.

Gabriel and the Architect sat together just to Dunstan's left, enjoying their angel food cake and chatting amiably.

Dunstan spoke. "Ladies and gentlemen, allow me to welcome you to the Eternal Festival in celebration of the completion of 10th-dimensional permeation!"

The entire room roared its approval.

Dunstan continued. "For seven days of City Time - that's 20 billion years to you Underlings - the City Leadership has used foresight and wisdom to control the evolution of the universe. Through no fault of your Council Leadership, of course, we did encounter trials along the way, but we maintained our poise and character, we turned these problems into opportunities, and we are proud to stand here before you this evening as the leaders of this great enterprise. Thanks to the diligent efforts and management skills of your Council members, we have completed 10th-dimensional permeation, and we can now celebrate this final level of spiritual attainment. In honor of this great achievement, I hereby declare the Eternal Festival open!"

Max leaned over to Bryce Thomas and Grant Zenkman and whispered, "I guess now we party for a trillion years or so. This might be our kind of place!" The three raised a toast to the eternity of trouble-making ahead of them.

Another roar arose from the crowd, and Dunstan had more trouble quieting them this time. "To commemorate this awe-inspiring occasion, I can think of only one suitable gesture." He reached underneath the podium and pulled out a small white case, with the outline of a dove embossed on its outer surface.

"Umm, Dunstan, are you sure about this?" asked Brother Michael from a few feet away.

Dunstan bent over, opened the case out of view of the audience, and pulled something out.

"I - I think it might be better if, if I did that," said Brother Gabriel tentatively.

Dunstan lifted the gleaming golden Trumpet high above his head so that all could see it.

"*NOOOOOOOOOO!!!!!!!!!!*" screamed Sister Esther.

Dunstan inhaled as deeply as he could, pursed his lips, brought the Trumpet up to meet them, and blew for all he was worth.

THE END

207805

Made in the USA